IT'S SEXY. AND IT'S SIMPLE.

They talk. You listen. And every great talker loves a great listener. Now, in new letters that leave a scorched trail through the U.S. postal system, *Penthouse* readers have a lot more to tell about their latest, sexiest escapades. And their intimate encounters and orgiastic revels are more sizzling than ever. Believe your ears. 'Cause you ain't heard nothin' yet. Party with teasers and peepers, lovers into heterosex and multisex, the dominated and the dominators—taking you all the way from the first shiver of foreplay to the fireworks finale.

LETTERS TO PENTHOUSE VI

Other Books in the Series:

Erotica from Penthouse
More Erotica from Penthouse
Erotica from Penthouse III
Letters to Penthouse I
Letters to Penthouse II
Letters to Penthouse III
Letters to Penthouse IV
Letters to Penthouse V
Letters to Penthouse VI
Letters to Penthouse VII
Letters to Penthouse VIII
Letters to Penthouse IX
Letters to Penthouse X
Letters to Penthouse XI
Letters to Penthouse XII
Letters to Penthouse XIII
Letters to Penthouse XIV
Letters to Penthouse XV
Letters to Penthouse XVI
Letters to Penthouse XVII
Letters to Penthouse XVIII
Letters to Penthouse XIX
Letters to Penthouse XX
Letters to Penthouse XXI
Letters to Penthouse XXII
Letters to Penthouse XXIII
Letters to Penthouse XXIV
Letters to Penthouse XXV
Letters to Penthouse XXVI
Letters to Penthouse XXVII
Letters to Penthouse XXVIII
Letters to Penthouse XXIX
Letters to Penthouse XXX
Letters to Penthouse XXXI
Letters to Penthouse XXXII
Letters to Penthouse XXXIII
Penthouse Uncensored I
Penthouse Uncensored II
Penthouse Uncensored III
Penthouse Uncensored IV
Penthouse Uncensored V
Penthouse Variations
26 Nights: A Sexual Adventure
Penthouse: Naughty by Nature
Penthouse: Between the Sheets
Penthouse Erotic Video Guide

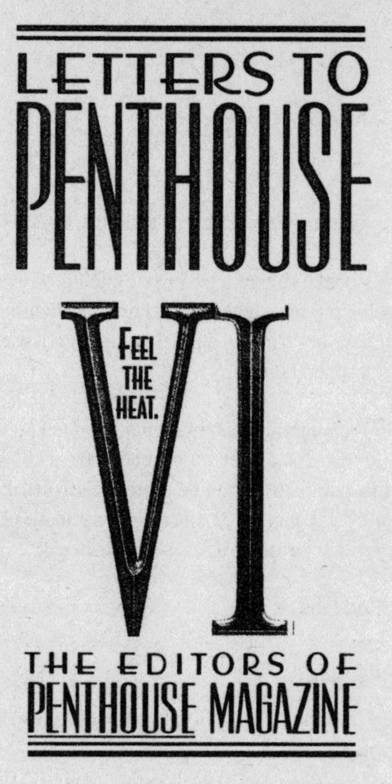

GRAND CENTRAL
PUBLISHING

NEW YORK BOSTON

Cover design by Don Puckey

Grand Central Publishing
Hachette Book Group
237 Park Avenue
New York, NY 10017
Visit our Web site at www.HachetteBookGroup.com

Grand Central Publishing is a division of Hachette Book Group, Inc. The Grand Central Publishing name and logo is a trademark of Hachette Book Group, Inc.

Printed in the United States of America

First Paperback Printing: January 1996

25 24 23 22 21 20 19 18 17

CONTENTS

Penthouse Letters will captivate you with its latest collection of erotic letters. They're romantic, sensual and provocative. Have you been naughty and in need of some chastisement? Try a dose of "Domination & Discipline." If you're into voyeurism, then turn the page to "Someone's Watching" and get an eyeful. Are you fantasizing about making love to someone of the same gender? Then "Girls & Girls/Boys & Boys" is what you'll need to fulfill your desires. Feel the need to make a confession? So did this gentleman in "True Confessions: The Wife Watcher." Whatever your preference in sexuality is, we at *Penthouse Letters* are sure you will enjoy our newest accumulation of carnal letters.

Kate Kraig
Penthouse Letters

True Romance

MORNING MINGLING PROVES SWEETER THAN THE MIDNIGHT LOVING MISSED

It was a cold, cold day, and the bed was so warm. I pulled the covers more tightly under my chin as I rolled over to snuggle into Margie's back. Her long, strawberry-blonde hair gently covered my face and tickled my nose. It smelled of springtime and sunshine. Her skin was soft and hot, like a hug in the shower. A little sigh escaped from Margie's lips as I pressed my morning hard-on into the crack of her ass. She wiggled her hips and arched her backside against me slightly. She always did enjoy a little appreciation for her ass, even in her sleep.

We slept nude. It was a Saturday morning. The previous night had been one of our rare party nights. Hours of drinking with good friends and dancing to good music had given us both a healthy desire for the opposite sex. The plan was to crawl into bed for a night of screaming, barking, shake-the-headboard, scare-the-cats, call-the-fire-department, knock-the-lamps-over sex.

Two friends offered to drive us home in their van. The ride had been full of sweaty teasing. Margie had slipped her panties off earlier, to tease me while we danced a long, groping slow dance. In the darkened back of the van I had employed two fingers to explore her pussy's most sensitive spots while she stroked my cock through my jeans. In time, Margie even put her head in my lap, telling our friends she was sleepy. She pulled my zipper down, ever so quietly, and licked my swollen dickhead as a kitten licks cream.

We sat on a blanket and kept quiet so as not to arouse anyone's suspicion. The thrill of sneaking around was reminiscent of making out on her parents' couch after a late date. When my fingers quickened their rhythmic pumping in and out of her pussy, Margie muffled her little whimpers by taking as much of my prick down her throat as she could. She pulled it out to grin at me and lick her lips when I bucked my hips.

"You little wench!" I hissed into her ear.

"I like to tease," Margie giggled. She laughed out loud when I humped my hips up toward her mouth. When she turned her head, my cockhead only managed to touch her ear. My fingers were tangled in her hair as we kissed passionately. All this movement finally drew the notice of our friends, who joked and teased and generally put a stop to our fun.

At the house our two friends, another couple, stayed to talk and drink some more. After an hour Margie disappeared, only to return in a short, red satin robe that did nothing to hide the fact that she was naked underneath. For some reason, no one got the hint until I suggested that our friends stay the night in the spare room.

I took them up to get them settled. The door had barely closed before the bed began its telltale squeaking. When I returned to the kitchen, it was clear the night had finally taken its toll. Margie was asleep, her head on the table. I carried her into bed and settled beside her for a long night of frustrated dreams.

Apparently her dreams were just as hot as mine. As I lazily floated back toward consciousness in the morning, the strong scent of Margie's pussy juice filled my senses. My hand slid along the curve of her waist and across her belly. Hugging her tightly, I slid my hard-on up and down her ass-cheeks in fast thrusts. My cock jerked and throbbed with every brush against her sweet crack. If it hadn't been morning, I would have come right then and there.

Margie moaned quietly, and her legs reflexively spread apart a little bit. My hand went gliding over the rise of her hips and down to her wet, slippery cunt. It was smooth and hot, soft, quivering and very wet. Two of my fingers drove deeply into her with one smooth thrust. Once they were in as far as I could reach, they ran in little circles around and around that little rough spot in her pussy just behind the clit. Margie's moans turned to whimpers as I rotated my wrist and circled my fingers around the smooth walls of her vagina.

"Yes, yes, yes," was all she said when I replaced those probing fingers with my cock. Lying on my side, entering her from behind, my chest against her back, my pole only reached about halfway in. Margie responded after a few thrusts by wiggling her ass and pressing it hard against me. Then she rolled over onto her belly. I stayed with her, ramming my cock as deeply inside her as I could. She grabbed the headboard with both hands, raised herself onto her knees and pushed against every thrust with her whole body.

I grabbed her hip with my right hand, tangled my left hand in her hair and eased her onto my prick. Her back arched like a panther's. She growled deeply in her throat to complete the image of a cat in ecstasy. I pumped and pumped, deeper and harder with every move. She matched me stroke for stroke. We were sweating profusely. The sun had become noticeably brighter and higher in the sky while we fucked. I had never lasted so long in this position, and began snorting and bellowing like an animal myself. Just as the pressure in my balls built too high to hold back, Margie lay flat on her belly, then rolled over onto her back.

I lay on her belly and reached underneath to grab both ass-cheeks while I licked her right nipple. Margie screamed and bucked like a woman gone mad when she came. I kept my cock buried as deeply in her pussy as I could, and held on. Margie's pussy grabbed and sucked on my cock. The feeling drove me wild. I leaned back and grabbed her legs. She spread them as wide as they would go, and I rammed and slammed until I couldn't hold back. I bellowed and hollered.

"I love to feel you come," Margie cooed as I lay on the bed panting and trying to come back to reality. "Want to join me in the shower?" she added.

I was still breathing hard and gasping weakly, but was not about to give up a chance to shower with this beauty. "Sure," I said, trying to sound recovered.

In the shower, we soaped each other up. Margie paid close attention to my balls, which I keep clean-shaven for her. She says it's sexy to lick and suck them that way. This time she wasted no time getting down on her knees to enjoy them.

It took maybe two licks, combined with the sight of her kneeling in front of me, to get my prick back up to its full size. Margie swallowed the whole shaft in one move. I fell back against the wall as she bobbed up and down on my staff. She moaned almost as much as I, showing how much she was enjoying this. Just as she felt my balls tighten up to blow a load down her throat, Margie stood up and giggled. Turning around, she asked me to wash her hair.

Naturally I was frustrated, but comforted myself with the idea that I could once more rub my turgid cock along her ass and at the same time have both hands full of Margie's glorious hair. I washed and rinsed and rubbed and bucked, and whispered into her ear how hot she made me. Margie pushed back against my cock, arched her back, wiggled and giggled. Finally, when we were both clean and I expected her to turn off the water, she looked over her shoulder and asked if I could come for her again. "Oh, yes!" I replied.

She braced one hand on the wall, bent well over and reached between her legs to grab my cock and rub it against her pussy. "Do it, baby!" she yelled. I grabbed both hips and thrust. Under the hot spray we humped and pumped, until I exploded deep inside her. Margie held still and gripped my cock with her pussy until it softened and popped out. She turned to kiss me good morning, adding, "Let's spend the day in bed."

How could I say no?—*L.A., Memphis, Tennessee*

TWO WOMEN, A MAN, A BEAUTIFUL HOUSE, A WORK OF ART

It was one of those rare days in Southern California. Rather than bright sunlight and cool ocean breezes, cold winds raised white, gauzy draperies of mist. Rain gently pattered down on the waxy leaves outside the window.

Lying next to me was my wife Marlene, whom I'd married just twelve months earlier. Ever amazed by her glossy black hair, and its tendency to relax into a flowing pattern that mimicked the smooth, soft contours of her slender body, I sat staring at her great, dark curls. From time to time I glanced into her jet-black eyes. Entranced by the soft shadows the dim light was pushing across the ceiling, Marlene languidly followed them with her glance as they shifted shape.

She didn't notice that I had awakened, which gave me time to gaze downward, enjoying the complete picture. The blue satin sheet clung to her naked body as though it were a second skin. Those magnificent breasts, which I had spent countless hours appreciating in my mind as well as with my lips and hands, could never be copied by a sculptor. Her thin, high waist seemed to point like an arrow toward the flare of her hips and the treasure that lay between them. From that juncture sprang two of the most beautiful legs ever seen. It was those legs that made me give up trying to paint the human figure, for no brush could ever capture her smooth, flawless skin. Thighs like a bowl of cream, calves with curves that should shame the designers of exotic cars, and sexy, thin ankles, completed the picture.

Then she turned that goddess's face, and with the softest smile on her lush lips, said, "Do you want eggs for breakfast?"

"Any other options?" I asked. Her hands, pressing lightly on my shoulders, suggested an alternative, and she met little resistance from me. So began a memorable day of unhurried pleasures.

I lay for several minutes just nuzzling her pubic hair with my lips and chin. My hands roamed over the silk of Marlene's thighs. The scent that rose from between them grew ever stronger, beckoning me to explore her mysterious depths. Finally placing my hands behind her knees and raising them, I watched her legs fall open and reveal her lovely secret. Her outer lips were already pink and swollen with impetuous desire.

Perhaps a stronger man would have sat back and observed this miracle of beauty a little longer, but I dove forward with a little cry and buried my tongue in her nectar. Her rich, thick honey coated my tongue and drove me into a frenzy. I began lapping at both her inner and outer lips, wanting to touch her everywhere with my mouth.

The pretty rosebud of her clitoris peeked shyly at me from under its hood. I rained soft kisses all over and around it. Then I closed my lips over the swollen morsel and slowly rocked my head left and right. The pace at which Marlene thrust her hips up, pressing herself against my chin, told me how fast she wanted me to move. The tempo increased steadily. So did the urgency of her surging hips. Soon I let her clit slide free, but continued shaking my head as fast as I could, my lips running smoothly over her swollen button.

When her orgasm arrived, her hips remained in the air, still vibrating but no longer banging against the bed. My mouth was plastered against her slippery opening, and Marlene twined her fingers through my hair, pressing my face even more firmly against her. She gasped and moaned for a good two minutes, then collapsed.

By noon we were both thoroughly relaxed and glowing, but the idea of rising from our bed held no charm at all. Nonetheless, there were things to do. Marlene insisted that we pull ourselves together and spend the afternoon looking at houses, something we talk about endlessly but never seem to get to. My paintings were selling well, after years of hard work, but the commitment to years of debt still scared me. Marlene melted me with a look and said, "I've made an appointment with a realtor for one hour from now. Please, lover, be nice." How could I resist?

The house was perfect, which of course translated as out of our price range, but Marlene said it would cost nothing to look. She mentioned that the owner was the realtor, and had just lost her husband.

Lilly made an immediate impression. She was perhaps fifteen years our senior, but her face and figure gave no clue to the fact. As she walked us through the spacious rooms, her heels clicked almost musically on the marble floors. Furnished with style and taste, the house also displayed some of the finest art we had seen in some time. Nearly all the works were by the same artist. Many were nudes, and many of the nudes were of Lilly, well-painted pictures of her flowing red hair and graceful body. She explained that her late husband was the painter, and the next stop on our tour would be his studio.

I was, of course, instantly engrossed in a close study of the studio. Lilly told us that she had an appointment, and we offered to leave, but she suggested that we make ourselves comfortable. Saying she would return in about an hour, she left us in her husband's beautifully appointed workroom. It had huge northern windows, a twenty-foot ceiling, and room for monumental canvases. We were both aghast at its sheer size.

Marlene walked over to the daybed in the center of the room. A sly smile told me what was on her mind. "Maybe we can't own it, but we could make love here just this once," she said. As she slipped out of her dress, she spun like a ballerina, letting the sun play on her porcelain skin. Marlene has never been one to appreciate underwear, so as soon as her dress slid to the floor, she reclined naked on the bed. Her head on the pillow, one leg raised at the knee, she instructed, "Off with those clothes, lover."

Leaving a trail of my clothes, I advanced toward the bed, but stopped short when, from behind me, I heard a gasp.

Turning, I saw Lilly in the studio door with a bottle of champagne in one hand and three glasses in the other. Staring and short of breath, she walked quickly to the table by the bed and set everything down. Marlene had not moved. She sat on the bed wide-eyed with embarrassment.

Lilly turned and smiled at me, then turned to Marlene. She

bent over the bed and firmly planted a quick kiss on Marlene's lips. Then she stood up, slipped off her dress and knelt, spread-legged, over Marlene. She again kissed Marlene, then turned her head to me and said, "I am sure you can afford this house."

Marlene looked at Lilly, but spoke to me: "Lick her real good, lover, because I want this real bad."

Always one to face a challenge head-on, I moved to the foot of the bed and caressed the soft, white cheeks of Lilly's bottom. It was perhaps a little wider than when her husband had painted her, but no less firm. Bending forward, I placed a kiss on either cheek. At the same time, Lilly was laying kiss after kiss on Marlene's lips, eyes and cheeks. The breasts of the two women were pressed together, flattened by the pressure of their rapidly increasing passion. When Lilly lifted herself for a moment to look at Marlene's face, I could see that both women's nipples were swollen, wrinkled and as dark as cherries.

Using both hands, I parted Lilly's thighs to make way for my exploring tongue. Her scent was different from Marlene's, but no less pungent or compelling. The groans that greeted my first licks let me know that it had been some time since she had been caressed by anyone but herself.

At the first touch of my mouth, she trembled and collapsed forward. The two women continued to explore each other with their lips, their bodies molded one against the other. I separated Marlene's legs as well, and now had access to two lovely treasures at once. Immediately taking advantage of the fact, I ran my tongue from the bottom of Marlene's opening to the top of Lilly's, then plunged back down again. Soon both women were writhing in ecstasy, their copious fluids mixing in a delightful carnal cocktail, which I lapped up as fast as I could.

Marlene was the first to reach her release. She threw her arms around her newfound friend and held her tightly. Lilly held both of Marlene's nipples between the tips of her long fingers, as Marlene thrashed beneath the attentions of my tongue.

When Marlene's climax had begun to subside, I turned my attention to Lilly. Burying my tongue deep inside her vagina, I stroked in and out while circling her clitoris with my thumb. As she came closer and closer to orgasm, I moved more and more slowly, until at last her climax rolled out of her in a long, strong, steady flow, accompanied by a moan that came from the depths of her soul.

The two women lay side by side on their backs in luxurious relaxation, holding hands and feeling the sun on their skin. Lilly stirred lazily and, looking at me, said, "Don't you want your release, too?"

"Oh yes," I replied. "But sometimes I get it in a different way." And I returned to my task of setting up an easel and mixing paints, then added to my explanation: "I'll be fine, as long as the light holds out."—*S.C., San Diego, California*

COMING TOGETHER AGAIN, AFTER BEING APART FOR MUCH TOO LONG

Over the hiss of the shower she heard the front door slam. Her husband yelled, "I'm home, honey!"

She kept quiet, knowing he would find her sooner or later, and anticipating his reaction when he did. She heard him wandering around the house until he finally reached the luxurious bathroom that graced the master bedroom of their large, ranch style house in the Canadian Rockies.

Through the rippled glass of the shower door, she could just make out his form.

"You okay in there?"

"Yes, honey, I'm fine. Thanks."

"Can I get you a towel?"

"No thanks, I can get one!"

"Well, I guess I've just about run out of excuses to come in there."

"Since when did you ever need an excuse?"

While saying this, she seductively swung open the glass shower door. The steam and filtered light silhouetted her form just so, her curves seeming to glow in the dimness, her nipples crinkling in the cold air, her hair wet and slicked back from her face.

She had one arm high on the shower door, the other hidden behind her, and her full, ripe breasts had never looked so enticing. Tiny, crystalline drops of water dangled from their watermelon-colored tips. Her body shimmered with dampness and steam, her legs smooth and her place of pleasure smoothly shaved. He could clearly see the precious cleft that enclosed her sweet pleasure-button, and the rosy petals, already moist from the shower's heat, growing moister from within.

She beckoned to him with a finger, and he slipped off his tie and shirt, not wanting to remove his pants just yet, not wanting to return to the torrid pace of the workaday world. He wanted their time together to last, needed it to, and if he allowed himself to be too close to her right now, he wouldn't be able to control the desire that burned like white fire in his loins.

He stepped toward the shower, his chest, slightly tanned and sporting a tattoo of a large dragon, already sweaty from the excitement of seeing her like this. He let his hands roam over her for a moment, feeling the wetness of her body, the heat, the wonderful curves that had made him so happy for so long. He reached up to cup a breast, and marveled at its heavy fullness in his hand. He kissed the tightly knotted nipple, gently at first, but with ever-increasing passion, as his need for her grew until he could control it no longer.

His trousers seemed to fall away, freeing his manhood from its confines. It forced itself out into the steamy air, fragrant with the aroma of her womanhood. He slipped his hand between her firm thighs as she whispered his name and bent her knees slightly, opening herself to him. He felt her slick juices on his fingertips and brought them to her mouth. She sucked his fingers furiously, tasting herself, tasting her need for his love, his embrace.

He sensed her readiness and, removing the rest of his clothing, stepped into the shower with her. Closing the door behind him, he shut out the world, giving them time and space to relish each other's company. Here and now they could enjoy each other's body in a way that had lately been rare and, therefore, treasured.

Their bodies, wet and heated, slid together in a passionate embrace. He took her head in his hands and parted her quivering lips with his thrusting tongue, searching and exploring her. She returned his caresses, kneading his ass with her small, gentle hands. He felt his loins tighten at her touch, and his erection throbbed between her legs. He pivoted his hips back and forth a few times, the water creating a wonderful friction when it was mixed with her sweet, musky juices.

She cried out for him and placed one leg around his hips, begging him to carry her to the heights of ecstasy, but he refused, groaning that it was too soon. He wanted to give her pleasure in a way she'd never forget.

He lifted her ass onto the low shelf of the shower wall, knelt between her glistening thighs and moaned at the way her petals opened up to him, revealing her dark, moist passageway. As she began to shudder, he teased her swollen clit with the very tip of his tongue, making her cry out and grasp his hair, pulling him closer. He drank the sweet honey from her special place, swallowing it in great gulps as the water cascaded down her breasts and belly. He sucked hungrily at her, licking and nibbling her until she felt faint. Ass perched on the edge of the shelf, back arched and head thrown back, hair matted in wet tangles over her burning brow and well-toned shoulders, she began to heave and buck. Her legs were raised high and her ankles rested on his shoulders, tightening in pleasure as he teased her.

Finally he stood, and let his large erection bump against her open lips, slightly parted now to welcome him. She stuck out her rosy pink tongue and touched him there, tasting his salt, letting it ride over her tongue, letting him wait.

Suddenly she took him deep in her mouth, swirling her tongue around his knob, making him stiffen with shock and pleasure. She heard him groan, and felt him place his hands lightly on her head, guiding her, encouraging her. She drew back and, using her tongue quickly and ticklingly, she moved down his shaft again, clasping her lips tightly around the base of his cock and sucking as hard as she dared, making him cry out. She sucked harder, enjoying his reaction to her caresses. She released his cock and held it gently, lifting it slightly so she could get at his firm balls, taking one in her mouth and kissing it with her tongue. She hummed, and the sweet vibration sent incredible shock waves through him.

She loved him this way for a little longer. Then they both stood and she kissed his lips. Staring into her eyes, he hoisted her so that her legs were wrapped around his waist. When she felt the soft tip of his manhood bump against her place of pleasure, she angled herself so that he slid slowly in, making her spurt with wetness and push herself to him in her need. He drew back and rammed into her, needing her urgently. His balls slapped her ass as he pounded into her, their wet bodies making squishing sounds as they moved, the odor of their coupling wafting to them through the steam, the friction bringing them to absolute ecstasy.

Their motions slowed, and he lowered her to the shower floor, still straddling him. They shared their long-held passion until she felt him shudder, as his life spilled into her. She rested her head against his strong shoulder and sighed.

He remained in her until the water turned cold. Then they dried each other with massive towels and went to their bed, where they lost no time in making up for the weeks they had been apart.—*B.B., Augusta, Maine*

LIGHTNING STRIKES TWICE—OUTSIDE THE WINDOW AND IN THE BEDROOM

As the rain poured and the thunder cracked outside, my lover's eyes sparkled in the candlelight. I live for that fire in Robin's eyes and the way it lights her face when she sees me. Robin is so beautiful. Her tan skin is so soft and responsive to the touch of my hands. Her desire for our love radiates with an intensity unlike anything I've ever felt before.

We kissed, and I closed my eyes and felt her breasts press against me. With my fingertips I gently caressed her face and stroked her beautiful hair. Barely touching her skin with my hands, lightly brushing her lips with mine, I started to drive her wild. Knowing how much she desired me gave me a deep surge of fulfillment. Neither of us wanted our embrace to end.

I could have kissed Robin for hours, my lips pressed against hers, slightly parted, our tongues tangled. Instead I opened my eyes and broke the kiss so that I could look at the rest of my darling. I moved my hands along Robin's neck, her shoulders, arms and breasts. I couldn't get enough of Robin's body. My fingers wandered underneath the straps of her red negligee and slid it down her shoulders, exposing her perfect, round breasts. Teasing her breasts with my mouth and hands, I avoided her nipples as long as I could will myself to resist. Robin's nipples were hard, and so was I, as her hands began to roam over my body. Our breathing was heavy, our bodies hot—it was heaven for both of us.

We continued exploring each other's body, yearning for each other. I moved my kisses lower, moving around Robin's love-nest but avoiding direct contact, kissing and touching everywhere except the center of her desires. Her body was begging for release. Breathing lightly on the lips of her pussy, I extended my tongue and moved it along the outside of her labia, from bottom to top, then down the other side. Next my tongue ran along the insides of her lips, lightly at first, then harder.

Finally I approached Robin's musky entrance, and began pushing my tongue as far inside her as I could. Her pussy is so soft, and it tastes sweeter than a dream. When at last I focused my attention on her clit, it grew inside my mouth as I sucked on it. Robin climaxed again and again, spreading her juices all over my face. The waves started low, rose to a furious intensity and then subsided.

I moved up to kiss her again, and our lips met with as much passion as before. Kissing me, she used her tongue and mouth to taste her own sweet juices. Robin couldn't get enough of her slick essence, and the sight of her tongue darting here and there, seeking the feminine flavor, deeply excited me.

She was on fire as she grabbed my hardness. Robin wanted to take it in her mouth. With her tongue she teased me for the longest time, finally engulfing my cock. Oh, what a feeling it was, having her warm mouth all over me. Her breasts rubbed against my legs, my balls, my shaft. I was breathing so heavily that my face started to tingle. Then slowly the warm, prickling sensation spread through the rest of my body. I felt her hair and her skin with my hands. I wanted to explode in her mouth, to see my come dripping from the corners.

But not this time—I wanted more to be inside her. Robin gasped that she longed to feel my hardness inside her. Straddling my cock, Robin slowly swallowed my cock with her velvet sheath. My penis seemed to swell until it filled her up inside. The feeling is difficult to describe, but I know I'll never forget it. I rolled on top of her and surrounded her body totally with mine, slowly moving in and out of her. At first I went in and out just an inch at a time, then another inch, until we could no longer bear the pleasure and I buried my cock inside my beloved. I pulled out the entire length, then slid in again repeatedly, stimulating her clit by moving my cock back and forth as I reached the deepest part on each stroke. Intense pleasure built inside our bodies. Our climaxes couldn't be stopped, and we writhed in each other's arms as our bodies exploded from an overdose of lovemaking.

I will remember this always as the most sensuous and passionate experience in my life.—*A.M., Chicago, Illinois*

THE BEST LOVERS ALWAYS START OUT AS FRIENDS FIRST

I've been friends with a wonderful man for years. His name is Eric. He is very handsome with a beautiful, warm smile and a great personality. We've always been close and have often had conversations about sex but we never actually made love together until one night last month when I decided to seduce him.

After thinking about it for a while I concocted a scheme. Eric has his own business so I arranged for a friend of mine to call him and make an appointment to discuss a business venture with him. This person asked Eric to meet him at his hotel since he would only be in town for one night. Of course I was the one who had something to discuss with him.

When Eric got to the door on the prearranged night he found a note telling him to come in and make himself at home. He walked in to find the room filled with candles and roses. There was a bottle of chilled champagne with two glasses sitting on the coffee table next to a tray of caviar and a bowl of fruit. He called out, "Hello," thinking he must have the wrong room.

I walked out wearing a black lace bustier with garters, black nylons and high-heeled pumps. His jaw dropped in shock as I walked slowly toward him. He couldn't take his eyes off my full breasts, which were peeking over the top of the low-cut bustier just enough to give a hint of my pink nipples. I closed the door behind him and poured us both a glass of champagne.

I took one look into his passion-filled eyes and knew I couldn't wait any longer. I pressed myself against him, pushing him against the wall. The full force of his masculinity so close to me was overwhelming. I looked into his eyes and hungrily gave him a deep, probing kiss. I could feel the tip of his growing cock pressing into the small space between my legs.

Pulling myself away from him I lay back on the sofa. After slowly taking off my panties I wet my finger and started massaging my juicy cunt. He looked at me with a devilish smile and the bulge in his pants grew larger.

I took a banana from the fruit bowl, peeled it and started to mold a penis out of it with my teeth and fingernails. I pulled him over and unzipped his pants, freeing his cock so I would have a model for my sculpture. I ran my fingernail down the length of the banana to make the underside ridge and then I used my teeth to carve the tip. At the same time I fondled Eric's rock-hard cock to make sure I got it right.

When my sculpture was perfect I began to lick the banana, my long tongue caressing the soft, curved flesh. Eric's breathing got heavier. I pulled him toward me and closed my lips around the tip of his cock, sucking it deep into my mouth.

His hands pulled the straps of my bustier off my shoulders and he slowly searched my breasts until he zeroed in on my hard nipples. I moaned with pleasure from the combination of his rock-hard cock in my mouth and the feel of his fingers slowly moving across my sensitive nipples. I let the shaft of his penis slowly slide out of my mouth and then pressed it between my large breasts, never releasing the head of his long cock. He moaned with pleasure as I slowly licked up the pre-come that dripped out of his cock.

Suddenly he pulled me up to him, pressing my breasts against his broad chest. He began kissing me deeply and passionately. I ran my fingers across his nipples as he worked his way down to my wet pussy. He separated my labia with his fingers and placed his tongue on my clit. The pleasure was so intense I couldn't stop moaning. Every flick of his tongue brought me closer and closer to orgasm. Finally I couldn't stand it any longer. I had to have him inside me.

I turned around and bent over, pressing my ass against his cock. I could feel the head of his huge cock nestled at the entrance of my vagina, probing gently. I guided him into my moistness. He slid in inch by inch until our bodies touched.

The sensation of his large cock moving slowly inside me drove me to a frenzy. His lips began to wander down my neck and my nipples hardened in readiness as his fingers played over them. As I ran my fingers up his thigh and around his balls he moaned loudly.

"Fuck me," was all I could utter as his hands gripped my hips. In perfect unison we thrust against each other. His fingers rubbed my clit and I screamed as the sensation took me over the edge. The spasms of my climax made him come and I could feel his prick convulsing inside me as his warm come filled me. We collapsed, sighing in pleasure, totally spent.

As we lay there I murmured, "I've wanted this for so long!" He took me in his arms and gently kissed me. "Me too!" he said.—*L.S., Austin, Texas*

DARING DUO RISK EXTRAMARITAL EXPOSURE WITH PUBLIC PLAY

Sara and I have enjoyed a loving relationship for more than six years. We are both married to other people and accept that it has to stay that way. Therefore we are very careful about keeping our relationship a secret because we do not want to lose either what we have together or separately. Fortunately from time to time we get the opportunity to enjoy each other's company and to express our pent-up feelings and passions.

On one of the rare occasions that both of our spouses were out of town I suggested we go out for a romantic dinner. Sara had a better idea. We live very close to the ocean and she wanted to have a sunset picnic of sushi on the beach.

As soon as I left work I went to her favorite Japanese restaurant, ordered an assortment of sushi and a carafe of sake. Sushi is such a sensual food. It was a perfect choice for the evening we had planned.

We met at a previously agreed upon spot: a sand dune that is topped by wooden walkways and benches so people can just sit and look out at the ocean and enjoy the balmy breezes. The walkways start about ten feet from a very busy street that runs parallel to the beach. We laid out a blanket at the base of the dune within fifty feet of the ramp that comes down from the top. It was still light out when we sat down.

Sara is a beautiful blonde with sexy blue eyes and a smile and body that make both older and younger men lust after her. She's a flirt and loves male attention. She takes pride in herself and dresses in a way that makes most of her contemporaries jealous.

I poured the sake and we toasted our evening together. I spread out the sushi and we began to eat.

Although we need to keep our relationship a secret, Sara and I can't help being exhibitionists when we're together as far as showing our passion for one another is concerned. Although we are over thirty we sometimes act more like teenagers. I guess we like shocking people.

Well, we ate most of the food and drank through about half of the sake before we began caressing one another and engaging in our typical deep-throat kissing. The remaining wine got kicked over and the food pushed aside but by this time we were too turned on to care.

We were both dressed briefly. Sara wore a low-cut top tied below her full breasts and a pair of shorts. I had on shorts and a tank top. While we kissed we began pulling off each other's clothes and it was only moments before we were completely nude. People were walking by in the sand but we just didn't care.

As we knelt back and looked at each other, Sara commented that she loves the sight of a naked man.

I lay Sara down and began slowly kissing her body all over, hesitating only slightly at her soft and sensually aromatic bush on my way to her toes. This really turns her on, especially when I stop and visit those gorgeous tits on the return trip. Her nipples are large and dark, and the velvety texture of her skin and the firmness of her flesh are enough to keep me happily kissing and sucking for a long time. I began to finger her moist, swollen clit while I alternated between kissing her mouth and her tits.

But there was more to indulge in and I soon proceeded back down the center of her torso. I probed her belly button with the tip of my tongue. Then I teased my way down to that golden bush, which rivaled the beauty of the moon just visible above the horizon.

We both had fleeting fears that the police, who patrol regularly, would either happen by or be called to the scene by someone who was offended by our antics. But we were too far gone to even consider stopping.

I was lost in the wonderful taste and smell of her pussy and I wasn't about to relinquish her until she had been satisfied. I've been told I have a talented mouth and I proceeded to apply what I had learned would give her the most pleasure. I nibbled lightly on her swollen clit and then slid my tongue into her. She raised her hips to meet my tongue. Then it was back to teasing and licking her clit. Sara held off as long as she could but was soon gushing oceans of love juice and writhing all over the blanket.

As soon as Sara calmed down a bit I kissed her while I held her close. After all it's love that keeps us together, and the sex is so much more pleasurable because of our feelings for one another.

Sara said, "Now it's my turn." She turned us over and let her mouth dance lovingly over my chest and stomach. My pole was throbbing by the time she teased her way down to it. She knelt between my legs and began to suck on my cockhead, drawing out the pre-come and relishing its taste. She slid her hands under my buttocks and pulled me up into her waiting mouth. She would alternate between encircling the tip of my prick with her tongue and driving her head down to the base of my tool. I enjoyed the sweet sensation as long as I could but my cock was soon exploding down her throat. She swallowed every drop, which always pleases me. She stayed there sucking me until I was totally dry.

We had not been conscious of our surroundings for a long time so we nervously looked around to see if we had drawn an audience. Luckily we hadn't. We caught our breath as we stood and held each other close.

It was getting dark and Sara was expecting a call from her husband shortly so we put on our clothes, picked up our belongings and climbed back to where our cars were parked. We really had no idea if the looks we received were in appreciation, envy or disdain. Looking into each other's eyes, we knew that we had just enjoyed something that would stay with us for the rest of our lives. We kissed deeply and proceeded to our cars.

When I got home I found that Sara had left her panties around the base of my passenger mirror. I've kept them as a keepsake and she has kept the sake glasses and carafe as a reminder of one of our most glorious and passionate evenings.

The public exposure enhanced the passion far beyond what we would have normally experienced. We don't know if we will ever top this fantasy fulfillment but we will certainly keep striving to do so.—*J.K., Tampa, Florida*

COWORKERS WHO RUB EACH OTHER THE RIGHT WAY FIND THEY MAKE A GREAT TEAM

The company I work for has an important client in England and it was my turn to fly to London to take care of some business. Accompanying me on this trip was my coworker Mae, who incidentally is one of the sexiest women I have ever known. Mae and I often travel together and we get along very well.

One of the biggest drawbacks of traveling to Europe is the jet lag you experience while adjusting to a new time zone. My usual method of combating jet lag is to try to stay awake until what is considered to be a normal bedtime for the local time zone. Since I knew my coworker would be accompanying me on this trip, I decided we should try something a little different to keep us awake until then.

When we arrived at our hotel near Hyde Park I suggested that she take a nice warm bath to wash away the grime of the trip and the stiffness of her muscles. Then I told her to wrap herself in a big towel and give me a call when she was through. She said that sounded intriguing and went off to carry out my suggestions. Meanwhile I took a shower, shaved, changed into a pair of running shorts and a tank top and waited for the phone to ring.

About twenty minutes later she called and said that she was ready for me. Grabbing some massage oil, I headed across the hall to her room.

Upon arrival I told her to lie down on the bed on her stomach so I could give her a back rub. After she lay facedown on the bed I rearranged the towel to give me easier access to her back and other parts of her anatomy.

I slowly began to rub her shoulders and neck, applying some of the oil to make my hands slide more easily across her lovely skin. After a while I began to massage her arms and back, continuing down her body until I came to the towel, which draped over her lovely, tight ass. I then began to massage her legs, starting at her toes and slowly working my way back up her body, getting closer and closer to her inner thighs. I removed the towel and, using more oil, massaged her ass. Though she had been purring earlier she now moaned softly.

I continued this for another twenty minutes or so, massaging her ass, back and neck. Then I replaced the towel on her ass and asked her to turn over so that I could massage the front of her body. Without hesitation she turned over and readjusted the towel to cover her pubic area but to my surprise left her breasts bare. Starting at her neck and using the oil liberally, I massaged her chest, just touching her breasts but not her nipples—at least not yet! I continued to work my way down her stomach until I once again reached the towel. At this point just like before I moved to her feet and started to massage my way back up her body. But this time I occasionally let my hand graze her pubic mound. Each time my hand passed over her pussy she let out a slight moan. After about fifteen minutes of this I poured some more oil onto her chest and slowly began to massage her breasts, this time teasing her nipples to hardness.

As I rubbed her breasts and stomach she pulled off the towel, put one of my hands on her clit and moaned loudly. Taking the hint I slowly massaged her clit and her nipples, and she continued to moan and squirm around on the bed. About twenty minutes later she clamped her legs together and had her first orgasm of the evening.

After she recovered she said it was my turn for a full-body

massage. I took off my tank top and running shorts, exposing my hard-on. She reached over, gave my cock a squeeze and a quick kiss, and said, "This is just a little sample of what you're going to get later."

I climbed onto the bed and she switched positions with me. She started to rub the oil onto my neck and shoulders, mimicking my movements. Since she is such a petite person she was able to sit on me while she was performing the massage.

The real fun began when she asked me to turn over onto my back so that she could massage my front. At this point my cock was so hard it ached. Starting at my neck she worked her way down my chest, her dainty fingers just brushing against my skin. When she got too close to my cock she moved down and started massaging my feet. As she slowly worked her way back up my legs I could see that she was looking at my cock with hunger in her eyes.

When she reached my crotch she poured some oil onto my balls and slowly worked it into my skin, which drove me crazy. Finally she poured some over my cock and started giving me a hand-job like I've never had before.

After what seemed like days but in reality was about fifteen minutes I warned her I was going to come. She increased the pace and aimed my cock at her tits. I exploded, covering her nipples with my come.

After I caught my breath I massaged my come into her chest. I then poured some oil on her and rubbed it in, paying special attention to her soaking wet pussy. I kept massaging her clit and pussy until she had another orgasm.

By this time I was once again hard as a rock. She had me lie down on the bed, then she poured some oil on my cock and began to massage it again. After about ten minutes she crawled up my body, positioned her dripping wet pussy over my hard cock and slowly lowered herself onto it until it was in her all the way.

She started to fuck my cock using just her pussy muscles. As she massaged my cock I began to rub her tits using some more oil. The sensation of having her pussy massage my cock while the rest of her body stayed still is hard to describe. I had never felt anything like that before! After thirty minutes of rubbing her breasts while she massaged my cock, we both came together in what has to be the most intense orgasm I have ever had in my life.

Afterward we realized that it was almost nine o'clock and we were glad to see that we had been able to stay awake (it was three in the morning according to my internal clock). We hopped off the bed and took a shower together to clean off some of the oil. I started to get dressed to return to my room but Mae said, "Please spend the night with me."

How could I say no? I pulled off my clothes and climbed in bed with her. After a good night's sleep we awoke early, refreshed and ready to start a new day. The rest of our time in London was also terrific but that's another story.—*T.A., Stowe, Vermont*

WEEKEND GETAWAY TURNS INTO A THREE-DAY FESTIVAL OF SUN, FUN AND SEX

My lover Ted and I live in different cities so most of our meetings have been on the run—an afternoon here, an evening there. But last week for the first time we were able to spend three incredible days and four glorious nights together.

I flew in to his city and he picked me up at the airport on Thursday evening. We hadn't been together in seven weeks and the passion was running at an all-time high. I'm sure the people in the airport knew it! The moment I saw him standing there waiting my pussy got wet.

Ted gave me a big bear hug and there was no mistaking the large bulge in his tight jeans. We could hardly contain ourselves in the car, feeling and groping each other and exchanging long, deep kisses at red lights. Our destination was a beautiful beachfront hotel and we couldn't wait to get there. We looked forward to caressing each other's body and enjoying more hot kisses. He is a terrific lover with incredible staying power. Our bodies fit together perfectly and he always brings me exquisite pleasure.

We finally arrived and unpacked. We had a dinner reservation so we just lay down on the bed and rubbed against each other like two teenagers afraid to go any further. I wrapped my legs around his, and we rocked and rubbed. It felt great. When he changed his clothes I got a chance to kiss and lick his magnificent cock as an appetizer (my favorite first course). Then off we went to the restaurant. I'm sure the food was good but I hardly tasted it. I was saving my appetite for more of that great cock for dessert.

Back in the room we undressed each other slowly and reacquainted ourselves with each other's body. Ted has the most incredible body I have ever lusted after. He is all man—hard, lean and very strong. His muscles are beautifully defined and he has the greatest ass I have ever had my hands on. Do men object to having their cocks called beautiful? Well, his is. It seems to always be erect and very hard, like marble. Its size is perfect for me—about nine inches and just the right thickness. Ted shaves his balls and that really turns me on! He tells me he loves my body too. I'm a small woman, only five feet two (36-24-36), and I do have to admit I have great boobs and a fantastic ass. My breasts are very round with small brown nipples that beg to be sucked. My ass is high and firm and my shaved pussy is very tight.

We got into a hot shower and rubbed soap all over each other. His slippery body felt wonderful. My hand kept going back to his dick as I jacked him off and caressed his soapy balls. He rubbed his hands around and around my breasts and teased my nipples, then caressed my hot pussy and my ass-cheeks. We toweled each other off, licking the excess water from each other's body.

He led me into the bedroom, laid me down on the bed and spread my legs wide. His tongue was in me so quickly that it startled me. My fingers entwined in his long, curly hair and I pulled his face into my love-box. Oh, that man knew what to do with his tongue! He didn't miss one single erogenous zone. He licked and sucked my clit and then pushed his tongue deep into my hole. I was in ecstasy and begged him to fuck me. He licked and sucked my pussy until I was completely lost in passion, engulfed by waves of orgasm.

Suddenly he was on me and in me. His hard tool drove into me faster and deeper. He touched places inside me no one's ever touched before. We were both moaning and grinding into each other. After what seemed like hours we exploded together in our first massive orgasm of the weekend. That one was just the beginning of many more to come.

Afterward we lay there catching our breath. The time had finally come for me to savor the dessert I'd been dreaming of all evening. I love to suck on Ted's dick and he is always ready for me to go down on him. He was hard again almost immediately but I made him wait while I licked and kissed his body. He tasted of salt mixed with his cologne and my perfume.

Starting at his lips I worked my way down his neck and across his chest, stopping to suck on his hard nipples. I continued down his taut, flat stomach, encircling his navel with my tongue. I temporarily bypassed his throbbing cock and went directly for his balls. They were musky with the scent of our sex and tasted delicious. I sucked them into my mouth and gently rolled them around on my tongue. They kept slipping out so I'd catch them with my tongue and pull them back in. I pulled his knees up so I could have better access to his scrotum. After circling his balls one last time I worked back up to the tip of his cock. I could taste my own juices on his shaft. He rewarded me with a few drops of pre-come, which I savored on the tip of my tongue.

My pussy was throbbing and I knew it wouldn't be long before I was coming myself but I held back. I circled his cock with my tongue, kissing it and teasing it. His cock was completely engulfed in my mouth and I slid my mouth up, down and around, sucking every inch of him and sliding the head of his cock to the back of my throat. Ted was moaning and bucking and I knew that he was ready to explode. I sucked harder and he shot his come down my throat.

He quickly pulled me on top of him and sat me on his cock, which was still hard. Rocking and moaning, I came in an incredible orgasm that left me weak and exhausted.

After a short nap nestled together like spoons I awoke to feel his hard dick probing me from behind. I raised my left leg and put it over his so that he could slide his cock into me. We lay there for a while, staying perfectly still, just enjoying the sensations. We were both still half asleep and the closeness felt exquisite. We made small, slow, almost dreamlike movements, gently making love in this fashion for almost an hour. We came simultaneously without ever changing positions. I'm not sure if we even fully woke up until our mutual orgasm. Then we drifted off to sleep again.

The next day we left for a fabulous resort in the desert. We had our own little cabin with a private pool and spa. After we settled in we went straight to the pool, stripped off our clothes and jumped in. It was very hot out and it seemed as if our bodies sizzled as we hit the cool water.

We kissed and caressed passionately, our naked bodies pressing up against each other in the water. Ted lifted me up and I wrapped my legs around his waist as his cock slid into my pussy. He moved in and out of me slowly at first, then propped me against the side of the pool and fucked me long and hard. He brought me to a rather intense orgasm before lifting me off his cock.

Ted, who hadn't come yet, sat on the steps of the pool. His dick was sticking up halfway out of the water. I licked the tip, then wrapped my lips around the shaft and slid down it. My face was underwater when I reached the base of his cock. I was enjoying blowing him so much that I didn't want him to come right away. When he did I pulled back so that his hot come spurted into the water, and we watched it float away.

Ted pulled me out of the pool, led me inside and laid me down on the bed. With two fingers he spread my pussy lips. My body was still wet from the pool and my cunt was dripping with excitement. He sucked up my juices and teased my clit with his tongue and fingers. He left me for a moment and returned with a very lifelike vibrator. He turned it on and slid it into me. I reached down and stroked his cock at the same time, bringing it to full erection.

Ted worked the vibrator in and out of me. It was an exhilarating feeling to have the vibrator buzzing in my pussy while he licked my clit. My orgasms were coming in long, steady waves. When one would end another would start.

I wanted him to enjoy it too, so he pulled the vibrator out of my pussy and replaced it with his throbbing cock. We rocked and rolled all over the bed, having fun with our new toy.

Afterward we were both exhausted. He fell asleep and I got up and put on the very tiny thong bikini he had bought me. It barely covered my nipples and pussy. I got a cold beer from the fridge and sat outside on the deck. I decided I'd read for a while. I got the copy of *Penthouse Letters* Ted had brought. While I was reading I got so hot from the sun and the letters that I spent the rest of the afternoon playing with my nipples and clit. When I got to the point of no return I climbed into the Jacuzzi. I positioned my twat in front of one of the jets and treated myself to a very private and sensuous orgasm.

That night we had dinner at a Greek restaurant where we were entertained by a belly dancer. The woman had a very voluptuous body and every move was extremely sensual. We ate our meal while watching her and touching each other under the table. I felt very sexy in the new dress Ted had brought me. It molds to my body and really shows it off, especially since my breasts were spilling out of the top. I had fun watching the waiters check me out.

When we left we were both thinking that we'd like to take the dancer home with us. I knew we both wanted to play with those large breasts, which she had been enticing us with all evening. We were so excited driving home that I wasn't sure if we were going to make it in one piece. When we finally arrived safely, he began undressing me as we walked to our cabin. There was only a small hedge separating us from a busy street. He pulled my dress off, exposing my bare ass to anybody passing by.

Once inside, I excused myself to put on a very sexy nightgown, which I had bought for this very occasion. It was floor-length satin with slits all the way up the front of both legs. My breasts spilled out of the top with my nipples just visible. Ted loved it, especially when I told him I'd bought it just for him.

As he lay on the bed I pulled up the gown and straddled his naked body. Reaching up, he ran his hands all over me. The combination of the soft satin and his hands on my body felt wonderful. We probed each other's mouth with our tongues. Did I mention that his kisses are the best I've ever experienced? He can bring me to orgasm just by kissing me, and he did. We had another fantastic night of lovemaking. Somewhere along the way I lost that sexy nightgown but I don't even remember how.

We spent Saturday morning making lazy love, playing in the pool, laughing and just enjoying each other's company. Early in the afternoon my lover called the front desk and ordered a VCR for the room. We both watched the delivery boy install the machine and I know we were both considering the possibility of a threesome. But somehow we both knew that this wasn't the right person or time.

Ted had made a little love-nest on the floor in front of the TV with pillows from the sofa and blankets from the bed. We settled in to watch a movie. It was a shock to discover that the lead character was a hermaphrodite. The star had a beautiful face, full breasts and a functioning set of male and female organs with which she/he fucked everybody in the room! It was wild and kinky—a real turn-on. We got sidetracked with some kinky play of our own and never saw the lead character reach her climax because we were so busy with our own. I brought Ted to a ball-splitting climax with the vibrator buzzing against his balls while I rode him for all I was worth.

That night after dinner and numerous glasses of wine we smoked a joint. I wanted to make his evening memorable so I asked him to sit down on the sofa while I put on a cassette of Joe Cocker (just the name makes me hot!). I did a slow, sexy striptease, first removing my tight black skirt and then my black lace blouse. I unhooked my garters and sensuously slid my stockings down my legs one at a time. All that was left was a black-lace bustier and a G-string. I got close enough for him to reach out and touch me but didn't permit him to do so until I said so. I danced around some more before stripping naked.

Once I was totally bare I danced over to him and pressed my pussy into his face. After slowly undressing him I finally allowed him to touch me. I played with his stiff dick, rubbing it between my full breasts. Finally we went on to bigger, better things.

Sunday was our day of rest—after we had spent the morning making sweet, sensual love. Fortunately our trip back to the city was relaxing, because we were both exhausted. He left me at the hotel to run some errands and I spent the afternoon reflecting back on our wonderful weekend and writing this letter.

That evening we had a romantic dinner together. I don't quite know why but our lovemaking that night was beyond anything we'd ever experienced together. I screamed in ecstasy as each wave of orgasm ripped through me. I knew that with this man I had found my true sexual identity.—*T.O., Los Angeles, California*

HE'S GOT THE WEDDING BELLE BLUES UNTIL BRIDESMAID COLORS HIS WORLD

My best friend Nick got married last September and I was one of the ushers. I had just broken off a relationship and was looking for female companionship to relieve my sexual tension. But when Nick informed me that all the bridesmaids were married or going steady I figured I was out of luck.

At the rehearsal dinner Sharon, the bride, told me that the bridesmaid who was to be my partner had just broken up with her boyfriend and would be attending the wedding alone. Sharon asked me if I would dance with Miriam and entertain her because she was very depressed. Being a good friend, I assured Sharon that I would do my best.

While eating dinner that night I tried to make small talk with Miriam but she was abrupt with me and not very pleasant. I focused my attention on the other people and had fun anyway.

The next day was the wedding. Afterward I escorted Miriam down the aisle. She was still somewhat cold to me but she wasn't as unfriendly as she had been. She really was quite an attractive girl. She stood about five feet eight inches tall with reddish brown hair and a forty-two-inch chest. She was wearing a low-cut dress, and since I am six feet three a bountiful expanse of snowy white cleavage was spread out before me. I immediately became rock-hard but resigned myself to the fact that she was not interested in me.

After the ceremony we went to the reception at a catering hall. The wedding party all danced the first dance and since Miriam and I were partners we danced together. When it was over I asked her if she'd like to keep dancing, and she smiled and said yes. That was the first time I saw her smile and it was beautiful. While dancing she told me that her boyfriend was screwing anything that moved and she was totally fed up with his behavior.

I remarked that he must be a jerk because if she were my girlfriend the only thing on my mind would be how to keep her happy. After I said that Miriam reached up and gave me a French kiss. I was stunned. She then took my hand and led me out to the lobby and into the coat room where we embraced and kissed.

I pulled away to tell her to slow down because I was getting a rise in my pants. She smiled and dropped to her knees. Miriam pulled down my pants and underwear and took my cock into her mouth. My dick is six inches long and it was as hard as steel. She started sucking and massaging my balls like an expert. Reaching down, I caressed her tits and rolled her nipples between my fingers. Her breathing became labored and I too was losing control. A few more strokes of her tongue and I exploded a month's worth of sperm into her mouth. She gobbled down every drop and came up smiling.

Not able to resist any longer I pulled her dress down and took off her bra, exposing her creamy tits. I feasted on those beauties as I fingered her snatch. After a short while we both realized that we would have to get back to the reception or our absence would be noticed. I stuffed her bra in my pocket and we got dressed.

All during the reception I was fondling her tits and running my hands under her dress. When the reception was over at around eleven we got into my car and headed for my apartment.

As soon as I unlocked the door I picked her up, carried her across the threshold and straight to my bedroom. As she shed her clothes I stripped off my tux. When she turned around, I saw her beautiful furry red bush. I gently laid her on my bed and feasted on that red pussy. I drank down every drop of nectar she produced.

I kissed my way up her body, stopping for about ten minutes at each breast. I then entered her for the first time. Her pussy was so hot and tight that once I was completely in I knew I was in heaven. I pumped her for about fifteen minutes, bringing her to two orgasms, and then blasted a fresh load of cream into her pussy. She was exhausted. I rolled onto my side and we kissed and caressed each other for about an hour. Miriam revealed that Sharon had told her I was a great guy.

We stayed in bed all weekend as Sharon didn't have any other clothes to change into. Being naked was more fun anyway. I can't remember how many times we made love but she has since moved in and we are now engaged. We decided a September wedding would be most fitting.—*D.R., Indianapolis, Indiana*

Different Strokes

SHE GETS GOOD VIBRATIONS WHEN SHE EXPERIMENTS WITH SEX TOYS

For years my husband tried to convince me to use vibrators and dildos. I had always refused, telling him that I was completely satisfied with his big, hard cock.

Then one day Charlie pulled a muscle in his back at work. He was in a lot of pain, and a friend suggested he get one of those cordless massagers with the big, round ends to help work the cramps out. When Charlie got home he showed me his new toy. He charged it up, and I held it to the sore muscle in his back. I could feel the vibrations reverberate in my hands, and it was quite soothing.

After about half an hour, Charlie said his back felt much better. He looked at me, grinned and announced that it was my turn. Charlie took the massager and began pressing it against my calves. At the time I was wearing only a bra and panties. The massager felt great on my legs as Charlie slowly worked it up to my thighs. When he ran it along the insides of my thighs, I could feel it vibrate against my pussy, and I let out a moan.

I spread my legs wide as Charlie began running the massager all around the insides of my thighs and over my pussy. I was getting quite aroused, and soon my panties were soaked from all the stimulation. When Charlie finally placed the vibrator on my pussy mound, I came instantly. He worked it all over my pussy as I had one orgasm after another.

Before the night was over I had three more sessions with the vibrator. During one of the sessions I masturbated, using the vibrator, while Charlie watched. In the past he had often asked me to masturbate for him, but I had always refused. This time, however, I was so turned on that I couldn't refuse his request.

The next morning, after Charlie went to work, I charged up the vibrator and spent the entire day masturbating with it. I never even got out of bed that day. I fantasized about being fucked by different men while I used the vibrator on my cunt. I had no idea that anything could make my pussy feel so good.

When Charlie came home that evening, I was lying spread-eagle on the bed, with the vibrator resting on my now very tired but well-satisfied cunt. Charlie told me he had a surprise for me and handed me a paper bag. When I looked in the bag, I saw four more vibrators of varying shapes and sizes.

We spent the entire evening trying out each different one on my pussy. The one he had originally bought for his back was still the best and most powerful. Over the next few days I barely got out of bed.

As I masturbated in bed, sometimes I fantasized that I was being fucked by two guys at once. To help this fantasy along, I'd put a vibrator in my pussy and a dildo in my mouth. I also pretended that groups of men took turns fucking me. I was completely hooked, and most of my free time was spent masturbating with my vibrators. Charlie didn't mind, because every night when he got home, I let him fuck me and come in my mouth. Prior to this, Charlie and I had had sex twice a week at most.

One night it was Charlie's turn to have his friends over for their weekly poker game. I figured I would take a night off from my vibrators and just watch TV, because I didn't want Charlie's friends to wonder what the incessant buzzing noise coming from the bedroom was. Charlie and five of his buddies were engrossed with their game while I watched TV in the bedroom.

When Charlie came up to the bedroom to check on me, he was surprised that I wasn't masturbating. He grabbed the massager from the drawer and pressed it against my clit. I immediately spread my legs open wide. While he was working me up to an orgasm, he told me that he was preparing my pussy to be fucked by all his friends. Now, getting gang-banged had been my number-one fantasy, but I'd never thought I'd have the opportunity to live it out. I admitted that it would be a real turn-on to get fucked by all his poker buddies. He said that first he wanted to get my pussy wet and ready with the massager. At this point, I could only groan in agreement.

By the time he called out to his friends to join us upstairs, I was having multiple orgasms. When they walked in, I moaned that I wanted everybody to fuck my wet cunt hole. Charlie told me that by the end of the night my pussy would be well-fucked and overflowing with come. I was still in the throes of a very intense orgasm when I moaned that my pussy and mouth were wide open and ready for fucking.

Each of Charlie's friends took a turn fucking my cunt while I held the massager against my clit. The more I came, the more I wanted to be fucked. Afterward, all the guys told me that they could feel the vibrations from the massager on their cocks while they were fucking me. They also agreed that I had the wettest pussy of any woman they had ever fucked.

After they left, Charlie told me that he always suspected he could turn me into a nymphomaniac. Charlie held the vibrator to my clit again and told me that he'd enjoyed watching me service so many men, because that had always been his fantasy. While stimulating me, he asked me if I wanted to do it again sometime. I moaned that he could use my cunt any way he wanted and that I loved having all that cock.

Now the poker game is held at our house every week, but the guys rarely play cards. First I masturbate for the guys and, after I explode in my first orgasm, I tell them that I'm their whore for the night. While I'm working on my pussy, they play a hand of poker, and the winner gets to fuck me first. Eventually each guy takes a turn fucking me. By the end of the night I am well-fucked.

Recently Charlie confessed he often fantasizes that I am a lesbian, and he intends to invite some women over to use vibrators on my pussy while I eat them out. This has become one of my fantasies too, and I look forward to living it out. Charlie also told me that I could have sex with anyone I want as long as I never refuse him. While I haven't yet had sex without Charlie, I have often fantasized about having sex with a few black men and intend to do so at my first opportunity. Charlie knows that I'll agree to perform any sex act for him and his friends when he has the massager on my pussy. I never knew that I could love having sex all day and I'm just sorry that I didn't try vibrators and massagers earlier.—*J.M., Danbury, Connecticut*

WILD, WANTON WOMAN SHARES HER SEXPERTISE WITH OUR READERS

I am a thirty-nine-year-old woman who wants to share the details of my fucking, sucking and exhibitionism with my fellow

Penthouse Letters readers. I live with a man who shares my philosophy on sex and love. Not only do we agree on everything, but he actively promotes situations that allow me to fulfill all of my sexual desires.

It is very difficult for me to describe the pure animal pleasure I get when I am with my lover and have the opportunity to fuck other men and women. I love the sex and the physical release, but I also get off on having my man watch me perform. I love feeling a good, hard cock fucking me while I flirt with my lover or hold his hand. Reaching orgasm is normally a very special moment for me, and being able to share this moment with my lover makes me so hot that I would gladly do it every night.

I have participated in almost every sexual situation that I can think of. Although I enjoy them all, my favorite is when a man or a woman spends the night with us in bed. If we're with a man, of course I sleep between him and my lover and just revel in the glory of being the center of attention. If it is a woman who's spending the night, I put her in the middle and, after my guy fucks her, I eat that come-filled pussy with such relish that most of the women ask me if I'm a lesbian.

My exhibitionism is geared toward attracting attention to myself when we're out in public. My lover and I always go out of our way to come up with different methods of showing me off. It's really a very exciting game!

Naturally, I usually wear short skirts, and I love it when people check out my long legs. I also enjoy going braless, and always walk in such a way that ensures my tits bounce as much as possible. When we're drinking in a bar, I'll use the men's room rather than the ladies' room. You should see the looks on some men's faces when I walk in! At home, when I'm expecting company, I've been known to answer the door wearing only my bra and panties. I love to see how a married man reacts in front of his wife!

Even though I have many tricks, my absolute favorite exhibitionistic game is to flash my hot pussy in public. For example, when we go out drinking, I always sit on a bar stool rather than in a booth so that I can expose my pussy. My skirts, which are short to begin with, usually ride up a little above mid-thigh when I sit. I make sure it rides up high enough on my legs so that anyone sitting near me has a direct view of my panties or my naked cunt. My lover and I have this game down to a science. We are most amused when guys come over to talk to me and are unable to take their eyes away from my crotch. More than once I've reached orgasm like this, and let me tell you, it's a trip to be sitting on a bar stool while a guy stares at your crotch and you know that you're about to come. Occasionally, when I do wear panties, I've been known to pull off my panties and toss them to the guy who was staring at my pussy. As I leave, I smile and say, "Thanks for watching. Keep the panties as my present to you." That always leaves them slack-jawed.

I'm sure I could go on and on about my sexual antics, but writing this letter has made me so horny that I just have to fuck my man. I'm so glad that my lover and I are totally in tune when it comes to sex!—*T.V., San Diego, California*

EXHIBITIONISTIC BACKYARD BALLERS DISCOVER SPLENDOR IN THE GRASS

My lover Toni and I decided to watch an X-rated movie one night recently. We sat close beside each other on the sofa and soon were getting hot as we kissed passionately and watched the writhing bodies.

When I noticed Toni's hard nipples standing up under her shirt, I couldn't resist gently tweaking them. In response, she slid her hand across my thigh and massaged the growing bulge in my jeans. It wasn't long before she had slid off the sofa and onto the floor in front of me. With a deft motion she unzipped my pants and freed my cock, which was aching for relief by this time. She slowly ran her tongue up and down the shaft before sucking the tip into her mouth. I was transfixed by the sight of her full, red lips wrapped around my cock, making it rock hard.

Once she had me good and wet, Toni stroked me with her hand and fondled my balls until a drop of clear, sticky pre-come oozed from the tip. Toni licked it up and told me she loved the taste.

I asked her to turn the TV off so we could concentrate on our own pleasure. Toni switched it off and stripped off her jeans and panties, exposing her partially shaved mound. Then she climbed back onto the sofa and straddled me. She slowly lowered her hot, wet pussy down onto my cock. We both watched as her beautiful pussy engulfed every inch of my cock. I groaned with pleasure as she slid all the way down to my balls. Toni began riding my cock while I kneaded her large breasts. The feeling was incredible.

I suddenly got the urge to make love to Toni while standing up, so I reached under her legs and grabbed hold of her ass-cheeks. At first she was surprised as I stood up, holding her in my arms, and began pumping into her, because we had never fucked in this position before. But always quick to adapt to any situation, she merely held on to my shoulders and wrapped her legs around my waist as she bounced up and down on my cock. Toni got very excited and, after a few minutes, asked me to fuck her from behind, which is probably our favorite position.

We went into the dining room and Toni leaned over the table. She reached back to spread her pussy lips wide open while I rubbed the head of my cock along her slit. The pink folds glistened with her sweet juices. Holding her by the hips, I slowly drove the full length of my cock deep into her. She moaned with pleasure, and so did I. I started to fuck her faster, and she responded with cries of "Fuck me harder!" Toni came two times in quick succession, and I was getting close to orgasm myself.

I asked her if she would suck my cock some more. Toni loves to suck me until I come in her mouth, so she eagerly agreed. I suggested we try something a little different and go out onto the screened-in porch. I told her I thought that the added stimulation of semi-public sex might be fun. Toni just grinned her sex-hungry grin at me, and out we went. It was a clear, warm summer night on the Massachusetts coast, so the temperature outside was just delightful.

She sat in a lounge chair and began once again to drive me wild with her mouth while I stood in front of her. Her sucking soon made my knees get weak, and I suddenly felt as if I couldn't stand up much longer. I asked Toni if she wanted to try something really daring. She nodded her head, her lips still wrapped around my cock. I asked her if she wanted to fuck out in the backyard, under the stars.

She was hesitant at first, but with a few passionate kisses and strokes of her pussy, I persuaded her to try it. I took her by the hand and led her out the screen door and down the steps into the moist night air. Toni quickly got down on her hands and knees in the soft, dew-covered grass. Kneeling behind her, I gripped her firmly by the hips. Neither of us could believe we were about to screw outdoors, where we might be seen by neighbors or passersby. But we were so hot to fuck each other by this time that I don't think we could've stopped even if we'd wanted to.

I teasingly slid my cock between Toni's thighs, and she reached back to guide me into her dripping snatch. We wasted no time and immediately began pounding into one another. Toni and I both came quickly in hot, sweaty, mutual orgasms, shuddering with pleasure, certain that someone would hear our moans in the dark. It seemed like a long time before we were able to regain our senses and move again. Finally we helped each other up into the house, laughing. Toni is a wonderful lover, and that was one midsummer night I'm glad wasn't a dream!—*R.L., Provincetown, Massachusetts*

OPEN-MINDED BOYFRIEND REALLY GETS OFF WHEN SHE KISSES AND TELLS

This letter is primarily about my fiancée Mallory, who is twenty-four years old. I am thirty-six. We have known each other for several years and we live in the San Francisco Bay area. Mallory stands five foot two and weighs one hundred eight pounds. She has dark hair, green eyes and a creamy complexion. She has nicely shaped, medium-size breasts capped with a large, pink areola and tipped with inverted nipples. For years I have trimmed her pubic hair so that her love-tunnel is unobstructed when exposed.

Mallory has an effervescent personality and is basically an all-American girl. She is a senior at a prestigious university and works part-time for a small but well-established real estate firm.

Only a small, very select group of men know that, under the right circumstances, she can be an uninhibited exhibitionist and sexual libertine. I am the voyeur and occasional participant with whom she shares her adventures. Her most recent escapade is encapsulated below.

Over the last several months, Mallory has made several trips to the Los Angeles area, where she befriended a young man named Rick. Like her, he is a college student, but unlike her, he is really painfully shy. Their relationship has been warm and affectionate but, until recently, platonic.

A few weeks ago she had to return to Los Angeles on business, and they made plans to meet for dinner.

Mallory returned home about midnight. When she came into the bedroom, she turned on a light, which woke me up. Before she went into the bathroom to prepare for bed, I gave her a groggy greeting and we exchanged a little small talk. She came out of the bathroom wearing her bra, which was somewhat unusual because we always sleep in the nude. She sat on the edge of the bed, and I asked her how her day had gone. She gave me a hug and a kiss and replied coyly, "Oh, it was interesting." I placed my hand between her legs and rubbed her pussy lips, causing them to spread apart a little. Then I licked the nape of her neck, inserted my finger into her moist tunnel and playfully said, "We seem to be unusually sticky tonight."

She giggled awkwardly and, after a long pause, replied, "Well, he came all right, but he didn't come in my pussy."

Bolts of electricity surged through me. It always turned me on to hear her talk like that. Though I was still half asleep, my cock instantly became tumescent and I could barely mumble, "What? What do you mean?"

Hesitantly she admitted, as if she had done something really naughty, "He . . . uh . . . came in my mouth."

My excitement mounting, I interjected, chuckling, "You little cocksucker! How many times? And where were you?"

She continued, "Well, three times. We were in his car. He came in buckets. I've never had a load that big."

I was overwhelmed—literally trembling—from a combination of intense arousal and curiosity. I didn't know which emotion to explore first. I could barely speak. In a dry voice I said, "Take off your bra, you sweet little cocksucker."

We exchanged an electric kiss. She then pulled away and looking directly, almost tauntingly, at me, brought both hands up to the front clasp and slowly unhooked and removed her bra. As her tits swung into view, the reason for her modesty became clear: her breasts were covered with hickeys. Still looking directly at me, she cupped each breast, lifted them slightly and arched her back. In a brazen voice, she said, "He really liked my tits."

I laid her on the bed, inserted my finger into her warm lovetunnel and said, "You little slut. Did you show him your pussy? Did you ask him if you could suck his dick? Did you come? I want to hear every single detail."

By this time, she was giggling. We had gone through this routine too many times to count, and it never failed to inflame us with passion. She grabbed my pole and began stroking it up and down as she asked in a solicitous voice, "Do you want me to tell you or show you?"

"Both," I answered. She bent down, rubbed the tip of my dick against her lips and said, "At seven o'clock last evening, this is exactly what I was doing to Rick." She licked my oozing cock several times in a circular motion, then gently engulfed each testicle in her mouth, caressing it with her tongue. Turning her attention back to my cock, she ran her tongue up and down the underside of my shaft several times. Next she placed her lips around the tip and gently, yet firmly, slid her mouth up and down the full length of my shaft twice. With that she stopped and calmly said, "On the third downstroke he came like a broken fire hydrant," before continuing to suck my cock.

Though I wanted her to tell me more, I could not bear to interrupt the exquisite pleasure I was experiencing. As I watched my dick slide in and out of her mouth, I noticed small droplets of saliva form on her lips. I knew that Rick must have been treated to this same, sexy sight, and that thought really got me hot. I also knew that he must have felt the same exquisite pleasure. The combination of the thoughts and the physical pleasure was overwhelming. I came in an explosive orgasm that left me completely drained.

After a silent recovery period, she kissed me passionately and asked me to lick her pussy. When getting licked, Mallory loves to lie on her back, open her legs as wide as possible and spread apart her pussy lips to position her clit for maximum stimulation. As she did this, I said, as caustically as possible, "Didn't Rick lick your pussy good enough? Didn't he bring you off like that?"

Crankily she replied, "No, he didn't. So I want you to lick my pussy."

I smiled and said, "Say please."

Mallory responded to this by groaning loudly and saying, "*Please* lick my pussy now." I did and she thrashed around in ecstasy. She came two or three times in quick succession before collapsing on the bed in a satiated stupor like a boneless Barbie doll.

I, on the other hand, still had a raging hard-on and wanted to hear more. After a few minutes, she went on with her story.

After dinner she and Rick had walked back to their cars, which were parked in a dark corner of the parking lot. When they arrived at her car, he leaned back against her car door while they chatted some more. When she went to give him a good-bye hug and kiss, she stood between his legs and pressed against him. In "one nanosecond," as she put it, she decided to give him a tongue kiss. He responded in kind, and soon they were kissing with passion and grinding their groins together.

Mallory was wearing a knee-length pleated skirt and a silk blouse. As the passion mounted, she decided to increase the level of intensity by raising her right leg, wrapping it around his left leg, and slowly and deliberately humping his thigh. After several minutes, he reached under her blouse, pulled up her bra and began massaging her breasts. She, in turn, rubbed his crotch and squeezed his hard cock through his jeans. When he placed his hand between her legs, she knew that she just had to have him.

Even though they were in a somewhat secluded spot, things were getting a bit too wild for public view, so she told him to get into the car. Once inside, they continued to explore their passion. After several minutes, Mallory pulled away and removed her shoes, stockings, panties and bra. She told Rick, "Unzip your pants and drop 'em to the floor." He complied immediately.

Freed from her restrictive clothing, she soon had her legs spread as wide as possible. He began finger-fucking her as she caressed his cock and balls. She sensed that he was so excited he was going to come imminently, so she slowed the pace, wanting to tease him a little more. When she coyly asked him, "Can I suck your dick?" at first he seemed taken aback, but he quickly responded with a meek yes. But Mallory the Vamp was still not done. She pressed on, "Do you promise to come in my mouth?" Again he meekly replied yes. She then blew him and, as she'd told me earlier, he came on only the third stroke.

After he orgasmed, he still had a full erection. She asked him if he always came so much. He was apparently embarrassed and apologized for it. She then asked him if that meant he liked fucking her mouth? Naturally, he replied, "Yes."

Knowing that he was still in heat, Mallory asked him, while blowing in his ear, "Do you want me to suck your dick again?" He nodded in the affirmative. She then said, "Well, I want to hear it. Tell me to suck your dick again."

With some difficulty, he pleadingly asked, "Will you suck my dick again?"

Well, of course that wouldn't do. Mallory replied, "Don't *ask* me to suck your dick, *tell* me to suck your dick." This, as she well knew, was very difficult for him to do. After several tries, he finally said, "Suck my dick," in a tone that Mallory found acceptable. She said that he took a little longer to come the second time, but when he did his load was almost as large as the first.

Mallory was now very aroused herself, but wasn't in the mood to screw. Instead she leaned against the door, pulled her skirt up, opened her legs as wide as possible and began rubbing her clit and tits. She asked Rick if he had ever seen a girl play with herself, and he said he hadn't. She then instructed him to play with himself but not to come.

She told me that she got herself off rather quickly, and he was transfixed the entire time. Afterward they again began to passionately kiss and caress. She finally asked him if he had any special requests. She knew he craved another blowjob, but was too shy to say so. She probed his ear with her tongue, and he really began to writhe around. Finally it was just too much for him and he managed to stutter out, "Sssuck my cock . . . Sssuck it!" She then gave him his third and final blowjob.

It was now almost nine o'clock and she still had to catch her flight home. They promised to see each other again soon and said their good-byes. Then she left for the airport.

When she finished her narrative, every fiber of my body was inflamed with desire, but I still had some unanswered questions. I positioned her on top of me and, as I slid my tool into her warm, wet tunnel, I asked, "When are you going to stick his pecker into your pussy?"

While gently rotating her hips, she replied in a low, raspy voice, "Soon." I sank my cock in to the hilt.

A moment later we were gyrating in a pre-orgasmic rhythm, and I added "I want to watch him stick it in. I also want to watch his pecker slide in and out of your mouth. I even want to see his come dripping down your chin."

Her last comment before we consummated our passion was a whispered, "I hope you get to see those things soon." You know, I hope so too.—*J.S., San Francisco, California*

GOING DOWN IN AN ELEVATOR LEADS TO LUST IN THE OFFICE

I want to tell you about an experience I recently shared with my lover Tanya. Tanya had to work one Sunday when no one else would be in the office. We had often fantasized about making love at our respective offices, and realized this would be a golden opportunity to turn our fantasy into reality. We agreed that I would join her after she had worked for a couple of hours. The idea of making love on top of her desk, in the employee lounge or in the elevator was extremely exciting to us. The prospect of doing something forbidden really fueled our lust.

When I arrived at her office at the appointed time that summer afternoon, Tanya was waiting for me. She unlocked the door and let me in with a wicked smile on her face. She pulled me close and gave me a deep kiss with her warm, full lips. I threw my arms around her and kissed her back passionately. I closed my eyes and breathed in the familiar scent of my favorite perfume on her neck. We ran our hands all over each other's body while we embraced tightly. It was getting very hot in that entryway so, without saying a word, we finally released each other and, hand in hand, raced up the stairs to her office.

"Have you ever made love in an elevator?" I asked her as I pulled her to me and began gently nibbling on her neck.

"No, but I'd sure like to try it," she answered with a grin.

I led her down the hall and into the elevator. The doors closed behind us, and as the elevator began to ascend, I pressed the Stop button. Tanya kissed me again, her tongue sliding into my mouth. I caressed the back of her neck with one hand and caressed her ass-cheeks with the other before slipping it under her pretty yellow sundress. She had certainly dressed for the occasion—she wasn't wearing any panties. I ran a finger along her slit, feeling a warm wetness between her thighs.

"You're so wet, lover," I said. "I've just got to taste your sweet pussy." In reply, Tanya stepped back and lifted her dress up to her waist, exposing her long legs and firm thighs. I knelt down on the floor in front of her. Her dark bush was now at eye level and I could see the moisture building on her plump cunt lips. It was a beautiful sight! She stepped forward to straddle my shoulders, one hand still holding up her dress, and braced herself against the elevator wall with her other hand. I kissed and sucked her delicious snatch until her knees began to tremble, and I knew she was close to orgasm. Suddenly she grunted with pleasure and came with a gush. Her juices flowed into my mouth, and I savored each drop of her nectar. I just love the taste of her juices, and Tanya comes more copiously than any woman I have ever known—the juices actually run down her thighs.

I slid my jeans off and lay down on the floor as she sank down and positioned herself over my cock. She slowly, teasingly, took the full length of my shaft into her. I kissed Tanya hard as she engulfed the final inch of my cock. Once she had me balls-deep in her pussy, she began thrusting her hips back and forth in a wonderful rocking motion. Pretty soon I could feel the elevator car rocking along with us! This was all too much for me, and I soon came explosively. Feeling me spurt inside her sent Tanya over the edge. I can always tell when she has an orgasm because her cunt releases a flood of juice and a burst of heat—it feels like there's a fire deep inside her when she comes!

We rested in each other's arms for a while, then I restarted the elevator and pressed the button for her floor. We exited the elevator and headed down the hall to Tanya's office, teasing and laughing with an after-sex playfulness. Inside her office we finished undressing each other next to the gray metal file cabinets and computer terminals. Completely naked, we flopped down into swivel chairs and talked. As we did, she fondled my limp cock with her foot and got me hard again.

Soon it was pointless trying to carry on a conversation, so I flashed Tanya an I-want-you-again grin and knelt down in front of her. She sank back in her chair and slowly spread her legs apart. I leaned forward, holding her sexy calves, and began to kiss and lick my way up her firm thighs. I sucked her pussy again, tasting our tangy-sweet combined juices. I slid two fingers deep into her beautiful cunt and began to pump them in and out. After a few minutes of stroking, Tanya got up, lay down on her desk and pulled me between her knees.

I eased the tip of my cock between her very wet pussy lips, took a firm grip of her breasts and sank deep into her. Soon we were fucking so hard that Tanya had to grip the edge of her desk to keep from sliding off. She came again with a loud grunt, leaving a big, wet spot on the desk blotter. I chuckled to myself, picturing Tanya trying to explain the stain on her desk and the smell of sex in the office to her coworkers the next day!

I asked her to lay facedown across her desk so I could kiss and lick the back of her neck—her number-one erogenous zone—which I knew would drive her wild. Looking down at Tanya, I suddenly got the urge to fuck her from behind. My kisses had fired her up again, and I could see she was more than ready to do it doggie-style.

I held her by the hips while she reached back and guided me into her again. The only thing we were aware of was our thrusting and grinding. "Oh, yes, that feels good!" she moaned. "It feels like you're deeper than ever!" I could feel my cock bottoming out in her pussy on each stroke, and I knew I wouldn't last much longer.

After a few more strokes my come surged into her, and she came again as well. All in all, it was an unforgettable afternoon—and she even got paid overtime! We're already planning to do it in my office next month! I can't wait!—*K.R., Atlanta, Georgia*

WOMAN ADMITS THAT SHE PREFERS THE SWINGING SIDE OF LIFE

I am a twenty-three-year-old woman, and I've been married for almost four years. I've also been seeing another man on the sly for about six months. My lover dared me to share one of our recent experiences with the readers of *Penthouse Letters.*

I am married to a very nice, very handsome man. Unfortunately he's also very straitlaced, especially when it comes to making love. You see, he is very religious and even studied for the ministry for two years. He would never read a magazine like *Penthouse Letters* and would never believe that his wife would fuck another man. My husband has a six-and-a-half-inch cock that has always made me come and basically has kept me satisfied. I never dreamed there would be another man besides my husband until I met Evan and Debra.

Debra and I work side by side at the cosmetics counter at a local department store. She and I have often been mistaken for sisters. Like me, she has auburn hair and dark brown eyes. She has a nice pair of tits that are just a little larger than mine, and a firm, round ass. As we became closer friends, Debra began describing her swinging sexual affairs with her boyfriend Evan in explicit detail, leaving me quite horny every day after work. I guess she knew I was envious, because she always asked me if I wanted to join her and Evan for a threesome, or if I wanted her to fix me up with somebody. I always said no. Debra was really surprised when I told her that I had never been fucked by any man other than my husband. She told me that I didn't know what I was missing out on.

I guess Debra could tell that I was feeling a little jealous and getting more than a little curious, so one evening when my husband was away for the weekend on a business trip, Debra invited me over for a drink. When we got to her house, Evan was taking a shower. Debra mixed us each a drink, and we sat and talked about swinging. Debra showed me some home videos she'd taken at one of their parties. I was getting a little horny as I watched all the fucking and sucking. The drinks were beginning to loosen me up, and I admitted to Debra that I'd never had my pussy sucked.

Just then Evan walked in, stark naked, his seven-inch cock hard and sticking straight out. He said he'd love to have the honor of introducing me to cunnilingus. I didn't protest when Evan took me by the hand and led the way to the bedroom. I let Evan undress me. He removed my dress and panties, and I lay back on the bed. Debra also undressed and lay down on the bed. Evan remarked how identical our cunts looked—both had the same shade of red pubic hair. Evan spread my legs and lowered his head between them. Soon his tongue was massaging my clit and probing inside my cunt, sending wave after wave of excitement throughout my body. He sucked my throbbing clit until I experienced one of the most intense climaxes I've ever had.

After my body stopped spasming, Evan mounted me. He fucked me fast and furious as Debra cheered us on. Then we rested and talked about how good it had been for us. We had a few more drinks before Debra announced that she was ready for a good gang bang. Evan voiced his agreement.

I joined Evan and Debra in the shower. Evan had fun washing my tits and pussy. I, in turn, washed his cock and balls. Evan's cock got hard again and he asked me to suck it. Now, I had never sucked a cock before either, but with Debra coaching me I soon had Evan shooting a thick, hot load of come down my throat.

We decided to go out for dinner and drinks, then planned to rendezvous with some of their swinging friends at a local club. Afterward we were all planning to return to Debra and Evan's house to party some more.

Debra lent me a miniskirt, sheer white panties and a see-through blouse that revealed my large nipples. When I asked to borrow a bra, she just laughed and told me not to be ridiculous.

At the club we met Bob and Todd. Bob and I hit it off right off the bat. Evan and Todd were busy taking care of Debra. After a while we decided to go to Bob's apartment, which was nearby. Evan and Todd sat on the couch with Debra between them, and they both began feeling her up. Bob went into the kitchen to fix us all drinks. When Bob returned with the drinks, Debra was sucking Evan's cock while Todd was fucking her from behind.

Bob looked at Debra, then took me by the hand and led me to the bedroom. We set our drinks on the vanity, then we lay on the bed and kissed and fondled for a while. I was completely aroused. Soon Bob unfastened my blouse and started sucking on my sensitive nipples, which never fails to send me into orbit. He unzipped my skirt and slipped it off, his tongue licking a trail from my tits to my navel. He pulled my panties down, then his tongue trailed its way through my pubic hairs to my stiff clit.

I begged him to fuck me. He began stripping his clothes off, revealing the largest cock I had ever seen. It was over ten inches long, and twice as thick as my husband's. He teased me for quite a while before he finally mounted me. My cunt was sopping wet as I guided that huge cock into place. Bob gave me the most outrageous fucking I have ever experienced. We fucked several times that night. Each time we fucked, it got better and better. In fact, we spent the entire weekend fucking and sucking.

The following week I met Bob at Debra's house several times, and each time we had sex. Then I went home to my unsuspecting husband, my pussy still wet and throbbing from my lover's fabulous fucking. Bob has since moved into the apartment next door, and now we're able to get in some fantastic fucking every day. Even though I still love my husband very much, if he ever found out, I would leave him rather than give up my wonderful newfound lover. I know no other man will be able to give me the kind of fucking that my pussy craves.—*R.O., Richmond, Virginia*

COCKY BOXER GOES ONE ON ONE WITH A TOTAL KNOCKOUT

I was an overconfident young boxer, full of energy and arrogance. I knew I was destined to be the next boxing champ in my weight class.

When I moved to a new town, I joined a gym that had a reputation for producing champions. My first day at the gym consisted of sparring, shadow boxing and working out with the other fighters on the various bags.

A week later I was introduced to Simone, one of the boxing groupies, who was a real cute blonde fox. I would've loved to take her on! The other guys told me that she has a thing for boxers, and that any fighter who wanted this babe was welcome in her twat. But when I tried to seduce her, she just rejected my advances! I later found out that I'd have to prove my mettle in the ring before she'd go one on one with me!

I may not have been as handsome or as hunky as some of the other guys at the gym, but I did have one unique asset that the other boxers didn't have: an incredible ten-inch cock. I knew that Simone would have her hands, mouth and pussy full of cock if she ever relented and tried me out.

Not long after that, some practice matches were held in the gym. I did quite well, winning all of my bouts. After the matches were over that day, Simone boldly strode into the men's locker room. Most of the boxers were showering or standing around naked. She had lust in her eyes as she looked us up and down. I was shocked.

So was she when she saw my boner. She quickly disrobed and lay down on the massage table. "Give me a workout, boys. I need a big dick and I need it now," she proclaimed.

"Who do you want, Simone?" asked one of the boxers.

"That big dick!" she shouted, pointing directly at me. The boxers led me over to her as she spread her legs wide open for me. She screamed with joy as I entered her pussy. She was able to take me almost all the way in, which was something no other chick had ever done before! I was amazed at her athletic sexual ability.

I blew my wad in a very short time, but she seemed insatiable. She fucked several more boxers as the others stood around her, watching the show while they jerked off. Even covered in sweat she looked ravishing, energized and eager for more.

Finally she sat up and spoke directly to me. "I still haven't come yet. Will you eat me to orgasm?" Her gaping cunt was dripping with juices. The other boxers encouraged me, and soon I was on my knees in front of her.

I gave her clit a few tender licks, then I began sucking on her labia. Soon I was eating her pussy with gusto. I was drinking the orgasmic mixture out of her and loving every drop. She came in shrieks and moans as I finished her off. The other guys all cheered me on.

Later I learned that this whole orgy had been a setup. It was my initiation into the boxing club. The guys all had a good laugh that I had been so eager to eat their come out of her pussy, and there was some good-natured ribbing all around. I was eager to set up the next cocky kid who joined the club.

Meanwhile Simone and I became lovers. She loved the way I took care of her orally whenever she wanted some action.—*E.V., Detroit, Michigan*

A CLOSE SHAVE FINDS THIS COUPLE ALL IN A LATHER

A few months ago I hurt my arm while I was working in a warehouse. The injury was bad enough for my right arm to end up in a cast that covered most of my forearm and part of my hand.

Because I am right-handed, I was virtually incapacitated. Besides having to take time off from work, I could hardly take care of myself. I needed help washing, dressing and doing all the little things two-handed people take for granted. Let me tell you, having to depend on someone else to do things for you really sucked. My wife agreed, because she was the one who had to do everything for me. Besides having to help me out with everything, she had to do all the driving, as well as her own job and the housecleaning.

For the first week I couldn't even feed or dress myself. I was sort of a baby about the whole thing. I was bored and moody; my wife was overworked and annoyed. But sometimes good things come out of bad situations.

"Helen!" I called out one Saturday morning.

I could hear her in the bedroom muttering to herself. She had just gone to bed a little while earlier. She was a nurse and she worked the night shift.

"Helen! I need your help!"

"Be right there," she yelled back.

She crawled out of bed, no doubt already dreading the day. I was in the bathroom, standing in front of the mirror, wearing nothing but a pair of pinstriped boxer shorts and my famous Cheshire cat grin.

"I know this is stupid, but I can't shave with my left hand. Could you help me out?" I cajoled.

"Grow a beard," she answered with a smirk.

"Come on, please." I knew that my smile was going to get me my way, at least with her.

"All right," she finally relented.

She perched herself on the bathroom counter, turned on the water and grabbed the shaving cream and razor. I stood in front of her, and as she lathered up my face I could tell that she was getting a little flushed. She took a deep breath, and her tits slightly brushed against my bare chest. As she spread the shaving cream around, I noticed that her nipples had suddenly hardened. I could see them standing at full attention under her flimsy cotton nightie. The water was rushing into the basin and starting to steam. She just kept lathering up my face, looking straight into my eyes. I had no idea that this was going to be such a turn-on for her.

"Is something wrong, honey?" I asked.

"No, babe," she answered with a smile.

As she raised the razor to my face, she took in another deep breath, thrusting her tits out at me. My smile widened. I knew her cotton panties were getting damp, because I could smell them.

"Come on," I teased. "Do it."

With her hand slightly shaking, she began to shave my face. All things considered, she was doing a fine job—nice, smooth strokes, no cuts or nicks. Her eyes were dancing with delight, inviting me to make a move. I slid my still-functioning left hand up her nightgown and began to tweak her right nipple. Then I took her whole tit in my hand and began massaging it softly.

"You're enjoying this, aren't you?" I whispered in her ear. She dropped the razor in the sink and wrapped her legs around my waist. She pressed her mouth to mine, and our tongues began to perform for one another. Then suddenly she pulled back. I think she was hotter than I had ever seen her. She tossed her head back and took a deep breath. I began to kiss her neck, all the while continuing to stimulate her nipple between my left thumb and forefinger. She began breathing deeper and heavier. I had her in my clutches now, and I was enjoying every minute. Helen pushed herself off the countertop and dropped to her knees. She raised her big blue eyes to me and just grinned. Half of my face was still lathered with shaving cream.

We stared into each other's eyes for a minute. I put my hand on her face and began tracing my thumb along her profile, running it down her cheek and around her mouth. Instantly she took my thumb into her mouth and began sucking it as though it were a miniature prick. She sucked with great joy, swinging her tongue around my thumb. Then she pushed my hand away and tugged my boxers to the floor.

She began licking the head of my stiff cock and lightly nibbling at the tip. Slowly she took it all into her mouth. Her head bobbed back and forth as she slid it in and out. I moaned as she ran her hands up to caress my clenched ass-cheeks. Helen then brought her fingertips under my ass and began tickling my balls. She knew I was about to get off. I was more than ready for her to drink my salty juices. I could feel I was on the verge of exploding when she stopped. Just as suddenly as she had begun, the little minx stopped. She looked up at me with her own devilish grin.

I took her soft face in my hands and brought her to her feet. "You think that's funny?" I asked. She just smiled. "Well, turnabout is fair play, you know."

"Then turn me about," she answered impishly.

I turned her around and began caressing her ass-cheeks. Dropping her panties to the floor, I put my hand on the small of her back and leaned her over the bathroom sink. I reached between her legs with my hand, letting my fingers dance in and around her cunt and onto her clit. I nestled my cock between her buns like a hot dog, and began grinding back and forth. She was clutching the sides of the sink and moaning passionately, so I knew that she was enjoying this. Soon her pussy lips and clit began to swell up, just begging for my long, talented tongue. Her legs began to tremble, and our moans grew louder.

"Do you like this?" I asked.

"Oh yeah, baby, you're great. Give me your tongue. Lick me. Suck me."

I brought my hand up and wrapped my arm around her waist, holding her close to me. "Oh, I'm going to give it to you, babe," I said. "I'm going to give it good and give it long. You're going to come all over me. Just as soon as you . . . as you . . ."

"As I what?" she gasped.

"Finish shaving me," I said with a grin as I took two steps back.

All that teasing had gotten her so wet, and me so hard, that shaving wasn't really on my list of things to do. Nevertheless, I turned the faucet back on and handed her the razor. After all, teasing is a two-way street. She needed to learn that if you're going to give it, you have to be able to take it.

She settled back on the counter and finished shaving my face as I teased her clit a little more. When she was finally finished, she said, "Well, this job is done. Let's go finish the other one."

"You know, you did a good job, honey," I said while caressing my face, inspecting the fine shaving job that she had done. "When this cast comes off, I'll return the favor."

"You want to shave me?" she asked incredulously.

I ran my hand over her cunt and through her small patch of coarse blonde hair. "Yes, I would love to shave you," I answered. "I'd spread your legs, lather you up and shave you smooth and clean."

Her smile was huge. "I'm going to hold you to that when your arm is better."

"I hope so. But right now I'm going to take you into that bedroom and thank you for all the nursing you've done for me."

"I don't want to go to bed. Just lay down right here on the floor," she replied with a grin. I had never seen such a lustful look in her eyes. I remember thinking that the smell of menthol shaving cream must really do something for her.

So I lay there, clean shaven, nude, my manhood waiting to be gobbled. She straddled me, allowing my cock to slowly enter her soft, tight pussy. I ran my hand over her breasts as she jackhammered up and down.

"Tell me what to do," she groaned.

"Turn around," I instructed her.

She did just that, swaying her smooth, milky ass back and forth in front of me. It was more than I could resist. While my wife was holding onto my knees, I once again caressed her finely developed butt, pausing to kiss it slowly and passionately. She swayed back and forth slowly, then moved faster and faster.

"Pace yourself, babe. Make it last," I warned.

At that she turned herself back around, running her own hands up and down her huge tits. She brought one of her nipples up to her mouth so that she could taste it.

Then she turned around again, still playing with her tits. When she leaned back a little, I ran my hand down her flattened stomach, across her hips and to her blonde thatch. I traced her clit with my finger as I kissed the back of her neck with my willing mouth. Once again she twirled back around. Still fondling her own bosom, she looked at me coolly. "Do you want one?" she cooed.

I reached up at them. "Yes. Oh yes," I said.

"Well, let's hear you ask."

"Please let me have one. Please."

"Are you sorry for teasing me?" she asked coyly.

"You teased me first," I shot back.

"That's not the question," she said as she licked her nipple.

"Yes, I'm sorry I teased you," I answered.

She leaned over, letting her tits fall near my face. My freshly shaved face rubbed against one as my mouth explored the other.

Helen sat on top of me for a few minutes, just rocking back and forth. Then, as things seemed to be cooling off, she began muscle-fucking me while running her hands over my chest. She would squeeze her vaginal muscles every five seconds or so, then she'd raise up, tighten her pussy around the head of my cock, and slide back down again.

I was furiously tugging on her nipples, groaning with pleasure. Eventually she began jackhammering again, and before we knew it we had reached our goal of orgasmic ecstasy together.

She climbed off me and looked in the mirror. I sat up and watched her as she brushed her hair. "Help me up," I asked.

"No," she replied.

"Why not?" I said.

She got down on all fours, once again with her ass toward me. Helen propped up on her elbows and stuck her ass higher in the air. "Because I want you to fuck me doggie-style," she said. "I want it hard."

Bringing myself to my knees, I spread her legs apart. My hands ran up the full length of her torso, then my fingers raced down her spine, making her arch her back like a cat. Her cunt was dripping from our first love bout, as was my dick.

I slid my cock into her damp, sticky cunt and began pumping her. Helen's tits jiggled, her nipples rubbing across the bath mat. She began to moan at the top of her lungs, screaming out, "Harder! Deeper!" I pumped her until she finally released her tasty fluids, then I shot my load deep into her pussy.

When we were done, she turned around and lay on her back. "You know," she said, "this is the first time we've screwed on the bathroom floor."

"You know, you're right," I said. "Hey, let's go the laundry room. We can set the washer on the spin cycle and fuck on top of it. I bet the vibrations will be great!"

"Sounds good," she agreed. "I'll grab the razor and shaving cream."—*Name and address withheld*

MAN WHO MISSES HIS WIFE FINDS A WAY TO GET CLOSER TO HER

I had been married for twenty years when my wife was killed in a car crash. We'd had a very good sex life and had loved each other very much. Living without her was almost more than I could handle. Many nights I just sat around, holding something of hers in my hand and wishing she was still here.

A few months later I still felt a deep loss. I felt something was missing in my life, and I didn't know quite what to do about it. At the time of the crash I weighed one hundred sixty pounds, but I'd dropped down to one hundred twenty pounds. I looked trim, and didn't have an ounce of fat on my body.

After taking a bath one night, I was sitting in my bedroom, reading an issue of *Penthouse Letters.* I came across a few letters about crossdressing.

The letters gave me an idea. After thinking for a little longer, I pulled out some of my wife's lingerie. Then I went into the bathroom and shaved off all my body hair, leaving my skin very smooth and silky. Next I gave myself a manicure and a pedicure, painting my fingernails and toenails bright red. I even put on some makeup and styled my hair.

After all these preliminaries I was ready for the final touch. I tried on a black garter belt and stockings, then added a black bra and a black slip. To top it off I put on a slinky dress and high heels. Then I sat down and relaxed.

As I sat in my room I looked at myself in the mirror. I could hardly believe it was me. In less than two and a half hours I had changed from George to Georgette.

All of a sudden I heard a knock on the front door. Not stopping to think, I answered it. It was my wife's best friend Terri, who was just stopping by to pay me a visit. At first she didn't believe it was me, but she finally recognized my voice. I was afraid she would think that I'd flipped, but she was surprisingly understanding and supportive.

Since then, Terri has helped me out with my crossdressing and with other things. We share a lot together and try to cheer each other up when we're feeling blue.

I'm definitely not gay. I just enjoy dressing like a woman. Somehow it makes me feel closer to my wife. I dress up quite often now. Since I don't have to work for a living, I have plenty of spare time, and I use it to work on my body. This year I have added breasts.

I have gone out with Terri many times while I'm dressed in drag. I love it when men or women hit on me. In fact, one night this week Terri and I were out on the town, dressed to kill. We really looked hot. Up until then, I had never really thought about the sex aspect of crossdressing. But on this particular night, two guys were buying us drinks. The next thing I knew, one of the guys had his hand up my dress. I looked at him in shock, and he said, "I want to suck your meat, honey."

I looked him right in the eye and said, "You know, I'm a crossdresser."

He said, "I know," and proceeded to pump my cock under the table.

Well, now I have men friends and lady friends. My body is looking great. My doctor, God bless her, gives me hormone shots. These days I crossdress all the time, and I simply love it.—*G.T., Topeka, Kansas*

COUPLE FINDS THAT SHARING FANTASIES LIVENS UP THEIR SEX

My boyfriend Roger and I started seeing each other a little over a year ago. From the very beginning our sex life was good, and neither of us had any real complaints. But I had no idea how great our sex would get over time.

We started sharing a few fantasies with each other during sex, and found that it turned us both on. Then we really let loose and began to reveal all kinds of kinky fantasies that we'd had. Eventually we got even braver and decided to act out one of our fantasies.

Roger bought me a beautiful lingerie outfit: a matching bra-and-panty set, along with a garter belt and stockings. He asked me to go into the bathroom and change into it. While I did so, he changed into a sexy pair of underwear and a muscle shirt. His hairy chest and broad shoulders, together with that huge bulge between his legs, turned me on instantly. I felt my nipples harden and my pussy get wet.

He had hung a full-length mirror up on the wall and placed a chair across the room from the mirror. He instructed me to stand in front of the mirror while he sat in the chair to watch me.

I was a little nervous, but very excited. My juices were flowing. He told me to touch my breasts. I slowly caressed my small, round mounds, shivering as I felt my nipples harden.

Next he told me to touch my pussy. I slowly ran my fingers down my stomach until I reached my swollen clit. I could smell my fragrant love juices as I slid my finger down my hot, wet crease. Looking in the mirror, I could see him sitting behind me. I noticed he was caressing that huge bulge in his sexy briefs.

He stood up and came up behind me, pressing his hard cock against my buttocks. He told me to look in the mirror and see how sexy I was as he reached down and stroked my pussy. Moistening his fingers with my juices, he let them dance over my clit until I couldn't hold back. I came like never before.

Then he turned me around and asked me to kneel down as he unleashed his raging tool. He grabbed hold of it and stroked it as I waited in anticipation, watching his cock grow harder and harder. Finally I couldn't wait a minute longer. I slid the head of his cock into my mouth, and as I did he let loose a tremendous load of sweet, warm come.

I'm happy to say that day was just the beginning of a new phase of our relationship. We have acted out many other fantasies since then, and will continue to do so in the future.—*S.M., Melbourne, Florida*

COLLEGE GIRL DISCOVERS THAT FIRST LOVE ISN'T ALWAYS BEST LOVE

Poor Brad. He's my childhood sweetheart and best bud. But now that we're in college together—coming from a small town in Utah to a big eastern campus—Brad is learning the dangers of staying attached to your first love. I wish I could sympathize with him, but I'm having so much fun meeting and fucking gorgeous new men that I don't really have time to hold his hand. In his own puppy dog way, though, Brad is getting off on my adventures. It's like I'm having enough sex for both of us. Maybe I should explain.

Brad has adored me since we were both about nine. Our friendship is deep, but our romance peaked on the night I let him take down the top of my dress and fondle my breasts. (Yeah, guys, you'd love them. They're full and soft and honey-sweet.) That was a mistake—Brad came in his pants almost at once, and vowed he'd love me forever.

Look, I care for him too, but as a lover he doesn't do much for me. Besides, I'd long since lost my virginity to my tennis coach, although I didn't tell him that. Brad, you see, grew up tall and skinny and really serious. He's kind of an environmental nerd. I'm more the fun-seeker type—your classic blonde, curvy, vivacious knockout. The thing is, I didn't know how beautiful I was until we got to college and I had some experienced men come on to me. Poor Brad was left in the dust.

I think he saw it coming—he was really good about agreeing that we should not be "committed," that we should "see other people," and all. But still, the first time I hooked up with a really hot lover, the news of it hit Brad like a ton of bricks.

Maybe I handled it wrong. It was at a party during freshman year at the jock fraternity house—I was dragged along, in my short new miniskirt, by some of my dorm friends. The place was packed, the music was throbbing and the beer flowed. As the night went on, some of the football guys started stripping down and parading around in full view of the girls, bumping and grinding even in front of the ones with dates. It's a famous ritual at this house. Most of them stopped with their jockstraps, but a few went all the way.

I was shocked, but fascinated, too—I had never seen so many beautiful male bodies. Ogling their cocks was a guilty pleasure I never thought I'd let myself indulge. I couldn't help but wish I could reach out and touch one.

Marvin solved that wish for me. Marvin is one of the best-known football players on the team, a truly sexy specimen, with a thin, sensitive face, golden shoulder-length hair and a reputation for merciless tackling on the field. Women on this campus pray for the opportunity to worship him and suck his legendary cock. Suddenly he was standing in front of me, stark naked, looking down at me like a god.

Without speaking, he put a big hand softly on my cheek, under my hair, and by reflex I turned to kiss it—I was a little drunk and already in love with him. Couples in our vicinity turned to watch the scene, and my dorm friends could hardly contain themselves—"God, Nina, you're it for tonight," Terry breathed. I couldn't believe what happened next. Marvin turned and walked away—my eyes were riveted on his muscular, flexing ass—and as he did, my girlfriends dropped to their knees and started tugging at my shoes and dark panty hose.

"You have to hurry," Tara explained as she slid my hose down to my ankles, exposing my luscious bare thighs to all and sundry. "He wants his women ready when they get to his room. He won't wait."

I felt exposed and whorish and exhilarated. Bare-legged, bare-pussied, flushed, drunk on beer and love, I saw the anguished stares of several ordinary guys as I left, but just tossed my head back and strode off in pursuit of Marvin.

It's not that I think a woman should run slavishly off whenever a man desires her. What was so compelling was that Marvin had cut through the bullshit and buildup that always seems to stand between us and sex. Everyone, I think, would like, at least once in their lives, just to have the impulse and go. Believe me, I learned from that night, and I've reversed the roles more than once since then.

I don't know if I could ever find words to describe the fucking that followed. This handsome athlete took me into his private room, on the bed that I know had seen a hundred of his other conquests—women students and women professors alike. Marvin's beautiful dick was engorged and ready when I walked in. I would gladly have knelt and received it on the spot, but he was considerate enough to remove the rest of my clothing, then gently kiss me and caress my shuddering bare body thoroughly, possessing me with his hands and mouth until I sobbed for his cock.

Marvin guided me onto my hands and knees and entered me from the rear. As I screamed my pleasure I thought his shaft would reach my throat. I wanted everyone at the party to hear me; I wanted to take this beautiful man back downstairs with me and share his sexual magic with everyone. I wanted to share my ecstasy with the world.

As it was, I shared it with Brad. When it was over, and we had both come in gushing waves; when my thighs were gleaming with a thick coat of Marvin's pearly semen; when I had finished weeping and praising his fabulous body and handsome face and heavenly technique—when all this was over and I was still splayed naked on his sheets, I asked Marvin in a shy, groggy voice if I could use his phone. He smiled, as if he understood, wrapped a towel around his loins and walked out—back down to the party and another seduction, I suppose.

Maybe it was the beer buzzing in my head and the aftershocks of Marvin still buzzing in my vagina making my judgment falter. Anyway, I had an overpowering impulse to describe this most memorable experience of my young life to my best bud.

Brad picked up on the fourth ring. He'd been deep in his books. "Try to guess what just happened to me," I told him in a kittenish purr, stroking my slick thigh. When I did tell him, there was a long silence at the other end of the line. Then the sobs started, and I knew I'd done something terribly cruel to my dearest friend in the world.

I felt horrible for the first few minutes of Brad's weeping, but then I started to figure a few things out. If this had been Marvin on the other end of the line, he'd have cursed me out and hung up. Brad was a wimp. I decided to find out how much of a wimp.

When he'd stopped to catch his breath, I asked him: "Do you still love me?"

There was a pause, then: "Yes. Oh, god yes, Nina."

Now I felt a rush of something new—a kind of divine wickedness. I took it another step: "Do you understand that this is the kind of girl I am? That I'm not going back to how you knew me, no matter how much it hurts you?"

Another pause, then a small, ashamed voice: "Yes." I knew then that he was mine. I pressed on. "Are you excited now? Are you hard?"

"Oh, God, Nina, yes. I'm so hard it hurts."

"Well, don't do anything rash, Brad. Your Nina is coming over to see you. If you're willing to lick your way through Marvin, you can have my pussy tonight. It's still a very hot pussy. Are you willing?"

This time I thought he was not going to answer at all. Finally, a tiny, almost inaudible voice said, "Yes, Nina."

And that's how I helped poor Brad make the transition from childhood sweetheart to college friend. We're seniors now, and I've had a collegiate sex life like no other, keeping none of it from Brad. He's long since learned to take his own voyeuristic pleasure in my exploits. Sometimes I help him jerk off when I come to his dorm too sated to let him fuck me. I've told him I might consider marrying him after we graduate. I still value his friendship very deeply, and no other man

I've met would come close to letting me have the freedom that I can expect from my sweet little nerdy childhood bud.—*Name and address withheld*

WIFE MASTERS THE ACHY BREAKY, THE TUSH PUSH AND THE HORIZONTAL BOP

My wife of ten years and I have always had an open, honest relationship. Though I'm not interested in getting involved with other women, I've always been aroused at the thought of my wife being fucked by other men.

I am forty-five years old. Maritza is thirty-seven and in her prime, and she needs more sex than I can provide for her. Maritza was hesitant at first about giving her shapely body to a total stranger, but after seeing how much it excited me and realizing how much she enjoyed it, she had no more qualms about it.

Maritza began taking country dance lessons at a local bar a couple of months ago. I don't drink and have never been much of a dancer, so she went by herself and was paired with a single man. Needless to say, she's learned more than a few new moves.

She's developed an insatiable appetite for other men's cocks. Besides making love with her dance partner, she's also made it with all the other guys in the class. She loves to have her mouth and pussy full of stiff dick at the same time. She says she especially loves when I go down on her after another guy has planted his seed in her hot box. I love the taste of a load of come mixed with her sweet pussy juices!

After hearing about Maritza's latest fling (she took on four men at once), it drove me wild to see her hickey-covered tits and stringy gobs of come dripping from her pussy. I asked Maritza if she'd allow me to witness her next gang bang, and she told me she'd not only let me watch it, but she'd even let me videotape it.

She had plans to go out dancing the next night, and we decided that over the course of the evening she would invite several men to an after-hours party at our house. Maritza left the house at eight, dressed in skintight Levi's and a low-cut halter top. At midnight she called and asked if I was ready for the party to start.

I assured her I was more than ready, and she said she was too. To get me excited, she told me that she had already given five guys blowjobs in the back of our van and was more than ready to have her pussy stuffed full of hard cock all night long. I asked how many guys would be coming, and she said she hadn't gotten a final count, but there were nine of them riding in the van with her and a few others following in their own cars.

Ten minutes later I heard the garage door open. As I watched out the window, Maritza pulled the van into the garage while seven other vehicles parked in our driveway and along the street. Anywhere from one to five guys piled out of the other cars and trucks. I stood in disbelief at the number of cocks Maritza was about to take on.

As they entered the house, I was introduced as her voyeuristic husband. I counted heads and came up with twenty-nine. Maritza let everyone know there was beer and mixers in the fridge, and I had put out booze, glasses and a bucket of ice on the counter.

As the guys made themselves drinks, Maritza said she was going to freshen up. Taking my hand, she led me to the bedroom. As she peeled off her Levi's and top, I asked if she was going to be able to handle all of them. She just giggled and said, "Watch and see." Then she told me to fix her a drink and bring the guys up after they all stripped down to their birthday suits.

Returning to the kitchen, I relayed Maritza's instructions. The men all began to strip as I fixed Maritza and myself stiff drinks. The guys who were naked first headed straight for the master bedroom.

When I reentered the bedroom, my lovely wife was wearing a red garter belt, black stockings and red spike heels. The guys had formed a circle around her, and she was sucking each cock in turn. She went all around the circle, keeping a dick in her mouth and one in each hand the whole time.

Soon one of the men, who had an enormous erection, lay on his back on the floor. He asked Maritza to slide her pussy down on his dick. Maritza straddled him, and her already dripping pussy began its descent upon his monster cock, slowly sinking down until his entire tool was buried deep inside her hungry pussy. Maritza worked her hot box up and down his cock while three guys in front of her took turns making their dicks vanish into the depths of her throat.

For the next six and a half hours I videotaped these twenty-nine cowboys ride my wife's sleek body in every position imaginable. When it was all over, Maritza had taken thirty-eight loads of come in her pussy and thirteen in her mouth, and she still had me to contend with. The crowd left almost as quickly as they had arrived, and as soon as they were gone, Maritza said, "Eat me!"

I dove facefirst into her crotch and licked up the stream of hot sperm flowing from her pussy. My God, what a feast! I probed into her snatch as far as my tongue could reach. I scooped up several delicious mouthfuls of the cowboys' cream. I then slid my dick into her luscious cunt, and even as stretched and goo-filled as she was, it felt sensational. As I fucked her, more sperm oozed out of her, so I alternated between fucking her and eating her out. I'm sure I swallowed at least a quart of sperm before I blasted my own load into my wife's beautiful pussy.

In the last two months, Maritza has fucked one hundred thirty-seven different guys a total of two hundred eight times and has given eighty-two blowjobs. Fucking has become an obsession for Maritza and me, but I know I'm loving every tasty drop of it!—*R.C., Waco, Texas*

HE LOVES THE SILKY FEEL OF NYLONS ON HIS THIGHS

I've always been a secret crossdresser. and as I got older, I got bolder! I love to get in my car, put on a pair of nylons and cruise around town. It is quite a thrill to see my nylon-covered legs glistening in the glow from the streetlights as I jack off to the rhythmic beat of rock music! I usually reach a mind-blowing climax.

My dress-up wardrobe now consists of four dozen pairs of stockings or panty hose, five pairs of tights, twenty pairs of panties, five slips, one denim miniskirt, one black wool skirt and one pair of open-toe, three-inch heels. My favorite nylons are Hanes Silk Reflections and No Nonsense control-tops. I've collected these items from thirty-two different women, all with slender bodies and all between the ages of nineteen and forty.

When I visit a friend's house or go to a party, I love to root through the clothes hamper and pick out a new color or style of panty hose or underwear. When I run into the owner of the lingerie, it always gives me a secret thrill to know that I've worn their nylons or panties and jacked off in their honor!

My favorite routine is to put on a condom filled with baby oil, then slip on a snug pair of panty hose. The panty hose holds my six-and-a-half-inch hard-on close to my body. All I have to do is move my hips back and forth, and it feels like I'm enjoying a nice fuck.

My wife Donna also likes to see me dress up. Donna often asks me to put on a pair of nylons that she's specially altered for me. They have a hole in the crotch big enough for my cock to slip through. Then she'll blow me, or we'll fuck, while I wear my nylons!

One year I even dressed up as a woman for a costume party. That night was one of the best I've ever had! So, guys, don't be shy about your crossdressing proclivities. Based on my experience, many women are rather turned on by the sight. I'd recommend that any man who's ever had the desire to crossdress give it a try. I'm sure you'll really like it.—*B.J., Philadelphia, Pennsylvania*

Someone's Watching

IF IT TAKES TWO TO TANGO, THEN WHAT DANCE IS THIS?

I met my wife Lena, a tall blonde with a beautiful face and a body to match, one evening in a bar. She'd been talking with an African-American man, and I watched as she gave him her telephone number and kissed him good night. When he'd left, I went over to her, introduced myself and asked her out.

A few weeks later, after several dates, we were together relaxing on a secluded beach in Maine. We spread a blanket and began to kiss and fondle each other. I asked her if she often fantasized about black men, and she said she did. As we undressed and slowly began our lovemaking, I told her how I'd watched her in the bar that first night and wondered if she and her black friend had ever gotten together.

Lena didn't react too much at first, but I noticed that she was becoming more and more excited by my interest in what she'd done with that man. She gradually told me about her evening with him. She said he'd called her and invited her to his apartment. As she told me of their evening together, she got more excited, and so did I. I slid my head between her legs as she told me how she sat on his couch and rather quickly found herself in his arms.

He undressed her as they kissed on the couch, and soon she was kneeling between his legs, taking his hard cock into her mouth. Their evening progressed quickly, to where she was on her hands and knees on the living room floor, taking her friend's long cock deep inside her from behind. As Lena's description intensified, I ran my tongue over her body, eventually concentrating all my attention on her cunt. She described everything they did that night, knowing full well that with every word, my excitement increased.

My relationship with Lena, not to mention our incredible lovemaking, escalated intensely after that afternoon. Lena would regularly describe her favorite sexual memories as I pleasured her with my cock and tongue. She told me how she once sucked one man's cock while another man entered her savagely from behind, grunting as he plumbed her, doggie-style, with his big dick.

She left little to my imagination, letting me know every detail of each liaison. The best was the time, during a cross-country drive, that she fucked her best friend's husband with her mouth while her friend slept peacefully in the backseat.

I asked her if she ever still had the urge to be with someone else. She told me that if it would excite me for her to be with someone, she would love to do it.

One evening while meeting with a business associate in our home, I found myself fantasizing about him getting it on with my wife. Charles is a tall black man, and after he left, I asked Lena if she found him attractive. Her response left little doubt that she did. Without a word, she quickly removed my clothes, then her own, and made love to me on the living room floor.

I set up another appointment with Charles at my home. This time I arranged to arrive late. When I walked into the house, I found Lena in my bathrobe on the couch, sipping a drink. Charles was nowhere to be seen. Her face was flushed, her hair tossed and her lipstick smeared. As I kissed her, I noticed the smell and taste of sex all over her body.

I sat down beside her and asked, "How did it go with Charles?"

I slid my hand beneath her robe and wiggled my fingers between her warm legs. As Lena parted her thighs, her pussy lips did the talking for her. They were hot and very wet. I finger-fucked her for a few moments, and then Lena told me all about her evening with Charles.

While they waited for me on the couch, their conversation quickly turned from small talk to sex. Charles asked her what she liked to do, and then took her in his arms, kissing her deeply and rubbing her breasts until she was excited. He unbuttoned her blouse and bra, then took her hand and placed it on his granite-hard cock. Naked to the waist and very excited, Lena stroked Charles's cock through his pants, then undid his zipper and his slacks. He took her head in his strong hands and pulled her gently toward his crotch.

"Once I took that long, dark hose into my mouth, I knew I was hooked," Lena said to me. "I'd forgotten how good black dick tasted."

Lena sucked on his meat for a long time, drinking a few drops of his pre-come but making sure he saved his big explosion for a little later on. Finally he carried her into our bedroom. She undressed while he lay on the bed, watching. Charles quickly got between Lena's legs, slid down and plunged his tongue into her. It wasn't long before she responded with an intense climax.

As she lay back, still catching her breath, Charles lifted her legs onto his shoulders and gently slid his cock deep into her. Lena said he was able to stay hard for a long time, and varied the pace of his thrusts so that he could make her orgasm several times. She told me that Charles came twice. The first time was while they were fucking in bed. The second time was right on our screened-in front porch, where Lena sucked his cock once more before he left.

The story complete, Lena and I were soon rocking in the bedroom, my prick buried all the way in her pussy. We made heated love all that night, and the next day made plans to bring her and Charles back together. But this time I would be around to watch.

He arrived eagerly a few nights later. I walked into the living room and said hello, then told him to make himself at home while I got everyone a drink. From the doorway I could see them embrace passionately, kissing and running their hands all over each other. I stepped back, more than excited, and took my time before returning with the drinks. I wanted them to be close to the point of no return by the time I got back.

When I joined them, Lena had Charles's cock out of his pants and was excitedly licking its length. Neither of them seemed to notice, or care, that I'd returned. I calmly sat across the room and began to watch. My wife slid Charles's pants down to his ankles and continued sucking his cock and balls. They both seemed lost in the pleasure of what they were doing.

He stopped her for a minute to undo her blouse and bra. As he did so, I slid behind her and ran my fingers and tongue between her legs. Lena pushed her pussy toward me, then returned to sucking off Charles. As she pumped her mouth up and down his long cock, I slid my cock into her from behind. Before I could get much of a rhythm going, Charles was shooting off into her mouth, holding her head down so she wouldn't miss a drop. I thrust into her and watched with delight as my wife drank his dick dry, then quickly sucked him to another erection!

We all scampered into the bedroom to continue our fun. I stopped off at the bathroom first. By the time I got to the bedroom, Charles had Lena's legs in the air and was plunging his black cock into her with long, slow strokes. She moaned as she slid her tongue into his mouth and urged him to fuck her harder. The sight of his brown shank disappearing into her pink gash was the most erotic thing I'd ever witnessed. Charles finally came again, shooting off inside Lena, then pumping his last few drops of spunk onto her tongue.

Lena kept Charles's soft cock in her hot mouth, and motioned me over to her side of the bed. She took hold of my hard-on and slid it into her wet pussy. She quickly brought me to a long-awaited climax. Then she looked up and asked me to eat her out from behind. As my tongue ran between her legs and touched her pussy, I could see that Charles's cock was back to its full size. He pulled Lena toward him and began fucking her again, this time from behind, until she climaxed, very satisfied. A river of come ran down her sweaty legs.

Lena, Charles and I have continued to meet often to indulge our erotic fantasies. Lena tells me she comes more now than she ever did in her life. Charles and I are also both happy, as she never fails to satisfy us both every time.—*C.F., Philadelphia, Pennsylvania*

FOR PETE'S SAKE! PROUD SPOUSE LOVES TO SHARE HER HOT HUBBY

My husband Pete and I have read *Penthouse Letters* for a number of years, and find your magazine most interesting and stimulating. I have noticed that the letters concerning spouses watching their mates getting it on with others usually involve other men fucking some guy's wife. I guess our marriage is a little unusual, since I very much enjoy watching Pete fuck other women.

It all started about a year ago when I was having lunch with a few of the girls from my office. One of them, Kelly, a real yuppie, was always extolling the prowess of her lover, who, she boasted, sometimes did it to her twice in one evening. My Lord,

I thought, if she only knew what Pete does to me in an evening. Twice is just an appetizer. Kelly kept yapping about her sex life until we were all bored to tears.

Later that night I told Pete about the conversation. He didn't seem too interested, but I kept thinking about it as we watched TV. At about two in the morning, after we had fucked our brains out, I asked my husband if he would do me a favor. I told him I wanted him to give Kelly a royal fucking. I told Pete that she was definitely pretty, and after much cajoling, finally convinced Pete to let me try to arrange a get-together.

The next opportunity I had to be alone with Kelly, I brought up the subject of sex again, and again she started bragging about her boyfriend. Finally I blurted out, "If you think he's so great, you should see what my husband does to me." Kelly was shocked at my outburst, but I continued. "I don't think you're woman enough to take what he can give." Before Kelly could say anything, I hauled a photo out of my wallet of Pete and me at the beach. Her eyes widened because, believe me, Pete is a hunk. He has a very muscular build, dark, curly hair and a smile that lights up like a neon sign.

"I think I would like to try it," said Kelly. "Where will you be while we fuck?" I told her that I wanted to watch, but that I wouldn't interfere. The next thing I knew, we'd set it up for Friday night.

That Friday, Pete and I sat waiting for Kelly's arrival. He seemed relatively relaxed, but I knew that he was horny as hell, anticipating the encounter. For one thing, I had cut off our sex for the previous two nights, just to make sure that Pete was more than ready for Kelly.

We were both into our second martini when the doorbell rang. Kelly looked extremely good as she stepped into our apartment. Her skirt and blouse showed off the tits and ass that were never very apparent in her office outfits. All of a sudden I was apprehensive. Maybe she looked too good. Maybe Pete would never want to fuck me again after slipping inside her sexy cunt. But I put my doubts aside, and we all started conversing like old friends.

After drinks and conversation, I put some slow music on the CD player and asked, "Does anyone here like to dance?" Pete led Kelly to the middle of the room and began to work his magic. I must say that Pete uses his hands like a virtuoso. He moved them slowly and gently up and down Kelly's back, and then began to explore elsewhere. Kelly enjoyed it and let her body blend with his. It didn't take long before he was cupping her tits lightly in his hands. Although I was feeling a bit jealous, I was also becoming very aroused.

Pete, his timing perfect as usual, led Kelly into our bedroom, with me following. He took a long time undressing her, as he does with me. He finished the task by kneeling behind her and slowly slipping her panties down to her ankles. As he did so, he kissed the backs of her legs and the insides of her thighs. Kelly was quivering with excitement. Finally he led her to our bed and positioned her on her back.

His lovemaking was a joy to behold as he caressed, massaged, pinched and kissed every erogenous zone imaginable. He had her so primed for pleasure that Kelly came with the first contact of his fingers against her clit. Pete sucked and fucked this girl every which way, and made a feast of the juices from her cunt.

"Would you like it again?" he crooned to her after he'd already fucked her three times—each time ejaculating profusely into her cunt.

"Oh, God, I don't think I could take much more," Kelly said. But her itchy cunt quickly got the best of her and she said, "Well, once more won't hurt." With that, she spread her legs and let Pete slide his inexhaustible hard-on into her. She was so wet he could've probably gotten a whole arm in there if he'd wanted to.

By the time the evening ended, Kelly must've had a dozen orgasms. For my part, I got so worked up watching that I finally had no choice but to finger-fuck myself. When I tired of that, I finished off the job with my favorite vibrator.

When Pete was ready to come for the fourth time, he was fucking Kelly from the rear. "Turn around, baby," he said to her. She turned to face him, and he put his cock between her fleshy breasts and gave her a long, superb titty-fuck. She watched the tip of his cock as it slid back and forth between her creamy-white tits. His nine-incher was only a short distance from her lips on each upward thrust. When his jism shot out, Kelly eagerly caught it on her lips and tongue. I must say that, while watching adult films is great, watching it all happen live was incredible!

As it turned out, Kelly and I became good friends. She must've mentioned Pete to other women, because in the following weeks I was constantly being asked by my coworkers if my husband was "available." More often than not, I let him fuck them, as long as I could watch them do it. Pete was happy about the whole thing, and our sex life did not suffer. In fact, I found myself hornier than ever, especially when I began to participate with Pete and his new lovers. I found it extremely arousing to play with his partners' pussy lips as he fucked them. Sometimes I would even fondle the girls' nipples and lick their soft tits while Pete did his thing.

Pete just got a promotion at his company, and we were forced to move to another city. I haven't found a new set of women to share Pete with, but that might still happen once we get settled. I have noticed one thing, however. Pete seems to be getting more and more turned on when reading your letters about husbands watching their wives get fucked by other men. He even suggested that I consider trying it. Who knows, maybe I will!—*G.C., Marietta, Georgia*

POOLSIDE PLAYTHING REMEMBERS TO USE THE BUDDY SYSTEM

Like a lot of other people, my girlfriend Edie and I like to spend our summers by the pool, getting tan and staying cool in the water. A wealthy couple who are friends of my parents let us use their pool whenever I want to, so we go there quite a bit. Edie is eighteen and just out of high school, and I'm a sophomore in college.

On one ninety-degree Wednesday last summer, Edie and I decided to go swimming. It's a big pool, in a very secluded yard in a rich neighborhood, so I was hoping for a little action with Edie while we were there. She is incredibly sexy, with long brown hair, a nice trim figure, long legs and full red lips. A lot of people tell her she should be a model. Her best feature is her hot ass. She has extra-wide hips and a creamy-white, fleshy bum that drives me insane. She's definitely not the smartest girl in the world, but that's all right by me because she's so damn fuckable.

Edie knows and loves the effect she has on men, but does a little too much cockteasing, if you want my opinion. She never had a bikini until last year, when a formerly wild friend of hers who'd gained weight gave one to her. But when she got it, that's practically all she wore for the rest of the summer. It was bright pink with black leopard stripes and string ties on the bottom and top.

This suit barely covered anything at all, so when she wore it you could just about see all of her ample tits and chubby ass.

We had been lying out in the sun for a while that day, when she said she was thirsty and asked if I'd get a soda for her. I was reading a book and was very relaxed, so I was a little annoyed at having to get in my car and go find her a soda somewhere. But I'm a nice guy, so I agreed. As I was leaving, I joked to her that if another man came by to fuck her, to tell him to wait for me. "I'll take the front and he can have you from behind."

She laughed and asked, "Why do you want the front?"

One reason is that I love the feeling of her lips wrapped around my dick. Another is that I like the way her face looks with my big cock moving in and out of her pretty mouth. But I didn't give her either of these answers. Instead I said, "It's because I love you so much." That seemed to satisfy her, so I closed the gate, got in my car and rode off in search of a Diet Coke for my princess.

After about fifteen minutes I returned to the house with a six-pack of Diet Coke, only to find a Cadillac pulling into the driveway ahead of me. I was surprised, because the couple that lives there is never home during the day. I parked my car on the street and stood back to see what was going on. Apparently the man of the house had gone golfing with a friend, and had come home for lunch. Both of these guys were obviously in their late forties. They went into the house, and through the picture window out front I could see them gawking at the bikini-clad babe in the backyard. With her Walkman and headphones on, she must not have heard their car pull up. She was lying on her back in the lounge chair, wearing her sunglasses, wiggling her sexy ass to the beat of the music.

The two men walked out to the pool, rubbing their hard-ons through goofy, plaid golf pants. They removed Edie's headphones. When she saw these two older men, she jumped in surprise. The owner said, "What are you doing here, young lady?"

Edie stammered, "I'm really sorry. I thought it was okay to be here. My boyfriend just went to get us something to drink."

"Your boyfriend?" the owner asked.

"Yes. Dave. He says he knows you and your wife."

The owner smiled. "Well, why didn't you say so?" He turned to his friend and said, "Dave is Jerry's kid. Nice boy. And from the looks of it, he knows how to pick women."

Edie sat up straight and smiled at the flattery. I was about to go into the backyard and join them when, to my surprise, I saw Edie reach for the owner's zipper. That's one thing about Edie. All you have to do is toss her a compliment and she's ready to jump your bones. But two old guys like this? In plaid pants?

The owner, obviously delighted that a nubile eighteen-year-old was fiddling with his pants, said to his friend, "Like I said, that Dave certainly does know how to pick women."

As Edie has told me herself, the things she likes to do most of all are fucking and sucking. And now it looked as though she was hungry for her fill of both. While she was unzipping the guy's pants, his friend was at the foot of the lounge chair, staring at her bikini-covered ass. Before the owner could say anything else, Edie had freed his dick from his pants. Boy, was I surprised. This guy had about the thickest penis I'd ever seen. It looked like one of the cans of soda I was carrying, and was covered with purple veins. Edie was practically salivating, and her eyes had grown wide. She whispered, "Please, may I?" looking sweetly up at him, then gently kissed the bloated head of his dick.

The guy was tongue-tied; Edie was anything but. He pulled her pretty little head down slowly onto his cock, stuffing his log into her mouth until his balls brushed against her chin. She started sucking him for all she was worth, drooling and slurping all over his humongous dick. He slipped her bikini top down a little to free her big tits and hard, brown nipples. He gently massaged her breasts, eliciting hums of pleasure from my horny young girlfriend. The old man was really loving it, and Edie was into it too.

As she did this, she wiggled her ass at the other guy. He was staring and grinning like a fool. He dropped his pants and undid the strings on either side of Edie's bikini bottom, allowing it to fall to the ground. Like I said, her big white ass is enough to make a priest forget his vows, and when she's on her hands and knees it's completely irresistible. Her pussy was so wet that, even from where I was standing on the other side of the fence, I could see it dripping.

The owner's friend gave my girlfriend's ass a playful squeeze as he mounted her from behind. She gave a little muffled yelp as his dick slipped inside her, but didn't take the fat prick out of her busy mouth. Her head just kept bobbing happily up and down on that monster cock.

Both the men were smiling from ear to ear now, porking away at this young marvel from both ends. Every time the guy behind her thrust into her hot pussy, her ass would ripple, her tits would shake back and forth and she'd let out a little moan. And with every one of those thrusts, her head plunged down on that flesh lollipop she was sucking, pushing the cockhead deep in her throat.

The men shook hands across her back, and the owner of the place winked at his buddy. "Honey," he said to Edie, "you can trespass here anytime you like." She moaned, but was too absorbed with his dick to say much of anything.

"Cat got your tongue?" the owner asked.

"Nope. Dick got her mouth," his friend chuckled.

Edie swirled her tongue around and around the puffy head of one dick, and backed up hard against the one that was pumping her from behind. "God, you guys are so hard!" she managed to say. "I just hope my boyfriend doesn't see us." She continued slobbering on the owner's thick dick, her saliva dripping down her chin and onto his balls. I'd always thought that Edie was especially pretty with a pair of nuts slapping against her chin. But until now, they'd always been my nuts. I had to admit, I was really turned on by this show.

She lazily scratched the guy's heavy balls while she gobbled his stick, and that was about all the poor sucker could stand. He pulled his dick away from her sweet lips with a little pop, and started groaning loudly. With a few brisk pulls, he began to shoot his load, blowing it straight into Edie's wide-open mouth. I couldn't believe how much come was firing out of that golfer's middle-aged prick. He must've been holding it in for a year! Edie was mesmerized by the size of his load as well, and had to keep her pouty mouth open for a full minute to catch it all.

Meanwhile, the owner's buddy was still sticking her nonstop, doggie-style. He was pumping faster than ever. My girlfriend held on to the owner's dick with her left hand while supporting herself on a chair with her right. Now she started screaming in orgasm. The man behind her started squeezing her plump ass and watching it jiggle, really getting off on her squealing. He wasn't quite ready to come though, and he reached forward to hold her swaying tits while he pumped her. He was pulling on her long, hard nipples as she gasped and panted for breath.

Edie's panting soon turned to more hot moans, as the friction in her cunt and the man's hands on her swollen nipples brought her over the edge again. He straightened up, fucking her fast and jiggling her clit with his fingers. Her shaking body and exclamations of rapture finally gave the man what he was after. He let out a low groan and pulled out of her exhausted pussy, shooting his load all over her upraised ass. His come seemed to keep flying in big spurts for a long time. These guys were terrible dressers, but they could really pump out their share of sperm!

He then pulled away from her, and both men slowly put their pants back on. Edie looked like some sort of sex goddess, propped up on that lounge chair on her hands and knees. With her bikini panties lying on the floor beneath her, and her breasts swaying outside her pulled-down top, her body was just crying out, "Fuck me! Fuck me!" I practically came on the spot. I don't think I'll ever forget that view!

The men said they were glad they'd come home when they did, and each of them gave her soft bottom a little pat. They scooped some of the come off her ass-cheeks and held their hands up to her mouth. She lapped at the gooey stuff stringing between their fingers, purring the whole time, until she'd licked their hands clean. Still on her hands and knees, she smiled wantonly at them, licked the come off her lips and cooed, "Thank you, gentlemen," as they swaggered off to their car and drove away.

I went down to my car, shaking my head in disbelief. I drove once around the neighborhood, then back up the driveway. I carried the sodas to the pool with me. By the time I got there, Edie was swimming. She shouted to me, "What took you so long?"

I asked her if she'd been keeping herself busy, and she said, "Doing what? No, I've been waiting for you to come back. I'm so horny!"

I picked up her sunglasses from the ground. There was come dripping off one of the lenses. "What happened to these?" I asked Edie.

"Ummm . . . I just spilled a little lotion on them," she said.

I just laughed.

Many people don't believe the letters you publish are real, and they'll probably doubt this one too. I'm sure I would if I didn't know better. Edie just seems to be a sex magnet. She's a sucker, if you'll excuse the pun, for a big dick. So now I know your letters are true. Still, I think there are only a handful of women out there who are as wild as Edie. They are a rare treasure!—*Name and address withheld*

BIRD-WATCHER DISCOVERS HIS PARTNER'S LITTLE LOVE-NEST

The minute I met Tina, I knew she was someone special. We have now been married for seven years, and I still feel the same way. She is just over five and a half feet tall, with beautiful brown hair and the best, most suckable tits I have ever seen. Tina and I love each other very much, and we like to try different things when it comes to sex. One thing that turns us both on is the idea of Tina fucking someone else. I've often told her that if the opportunity to get fucked ever presented itself, she should go for it.

Tina works in a nature preserve and has to do a lot of research in the woods. Recently a visiting naturalist named Mark came to study bird life at the preserve for a month. Tina was instructed to assist him while he was there. During his stay they became good friends, and Tina even confessed to me that she found him very attractive and had fantasized about fucking him while they were alone in the woods. I told her to give it a go.

Tina began going to work wearing tight shorts and T-shirts with no bra, and each night when she returned, she would tell me that she could see the effect it was having on Mark. The bulge growing in his pants seemed to get bigger and bigger every day. She would tease him all day long by bending over in front of him, giving him a great view of her tight ass. She told me she also gave him plenty of opportunities to look down her shirt at those wonderful tits.

Near the end of his stay, Mark thanked her for her help by giving her a kiss on the cheek. My wife turned it into a very passionate kiss, but that was as far as it went. Tina was determined to see what was in those pants before he left, so the next day she wore the tightest pair of shorts she owns and a button-down shirt that revealed a lot of tit. Of course, she wore neither bra nor panties. I knew Mark wouldn't be able to resist her this time. It was all I could do to let her get out the front door without laying her down and fucking her myself.

Knowing the area they were working in pretty well, I decided to go see the action for myself. When I found them, I was not disappointed. Through the trees I could see them locked in a passionate kiss, and this time it didn't stop there. I watched as Mark unbuttoned Tina's shirt, revealing those perfect tits. They moved up against a tree, and he started to suck on Tina's growing nipples. I could see how hard the tips were and how excited my wife was. Tina removed her shirt and then stepped back and took off her shorts, revealing to Mark her wet and hairy pussy.

Seeing my wife standing naked in front of another man was more of a turn-on than I'd expected. I pulled out my cock and started to stroke it while I watched her pull out Mark's already hard cock and lick its length. I watched as she licked his big, hairy balls and then took his cock all the way down her throat.

Sensing Mark was about to come after ten minutes of sucking him, my wife stopped what she was doing and found a patch of soft grass nearby. She lay down with her legs spread wide, and finger-fucked her pussy. Mark had by now removed all of his clothes. He walked over to Tina and replaced her fingers with his tongue. My wife loves being eaten out, and Mark was doing a great job there in the great outdoors. Tina was rolling her nipples between her fingers like she always does when I eat her pussy.

By the way she was moaning and pinching her hard nipples, I knew she was close to coming. I heard her beg Mark to stick his shaft into her, and he was happy to oblige. He slowly sank his prick into her wet cave. At that very moment, Tina exploded with orgasm!

Mark pumped his cock into her a few more times, then stiffened and shot a huge load into her snatch. Seeing this, I shot my own load all over the forest floor. When my cock had emptied and softened, I quietly sneaked out of the woods.

That night Tina told me about her little adventure. Was she ever surprised to find out that I'd watched the whole thing!—*Name and address withheld*

SOUNDS LIKE THIS LOVE BOAT RAN AGROUND ON FANTASY ISLAND

My wife Louise and I recently returned from a cruise on one of those "Love Boats"—although "Lust Boat" would better describe the time we had. We are probably among your older readers, both sixty-four years young. We have an active life and have stayed in shape all these years. Louise has kept her nice, shapely legs, tight buns and flat tummy, and I'm very proud of my solid, well-toned build. Over the years, I have often told her of my fantasy of sharing her with another man, and she has usually responded by saying it might be nice, but that he would have to be a "young stud" for her to even consider it.

We boarded the ship in Florida on a Saturday afternoon. At dinner that evening, two of the people at our table were a young man named Keith and his father Ralph. Keith, twenty-two years old, had just completed his pre-med studies at a Canadian university. Ralph, who was recovering from an accident and needed much rest, was giving this cruise to Keith as a present. They were nice people, and we hoped to see more of them before the cruise was over.

The next evening there was a formal dinner on board. Louise looked fantastic in a dress that was extremely low-cut and displayed much of her cleavage. Ralph and Keith joined us at our table. After dinner, Ralph retired for the evening, so I asked Keith if he would join us in the lounge for a drink. At one point Louise excused herself to go to the powder room. While she was gone, Keith said, "She's certainly a ravishing lady."

I suggested that he ask her to dance, and when she returned, that's just what he did. It was obvious that this sixty-four-year-old woman and twenty-two-year-old man were enjoying each other very much. They were dancing extremely close, and appeared to be groping and whispering to each other on the dance floor. Louise even gave him a few quick kisses on his neck.

When my wife and I were going to bed later that night, she remarked about Keith, "Now that's what I call a young stud!" I knew then that our vacation wouldn't be complete until my wife had been fucked by our young new friend.

The following day we relaxed on the upper deck. Around four in the afternoon, Louise headed for the cabin and asked me to bring her a drink. I went to one of the poolside bars and ordered her a whiskey. As I signed the tab, Keith, in a bathing suit and shirt, walked up to me and asked where Louise was. I replied that she was resting, but that she'd probably be thrilled if he showed up with her drink. I took him to our cabin and unlocked the door. I told him I was going for a walk to the casino, and that I'd be back in about an hour. "Enjoy," I said as I nudged him into the cabin.

Rather than going to the casino, I quietly stepped into the darkened dressing area that was separated from our main cabin by a wall of closets. A large mirror on the opposite wall gave me a full view of our bed. Louise was dozing in a pair of panties. Keith stood for a moment, eyeing her body, before saying in a wavering voice, "Louise, I have your drink."

Louise bolted upright, pulled the sheet over her shoulders and asked what he was doing there. When he told her that I had suggested she might like him to bring the drink, she said, "My husband must be a mind reader." She took the drink from Keith, and the sheet dropped from one shoulder, exposing part of her upper body. As she took a sip, Keith reached over and slowly pulled the sheet away, leaving her half nude.

She handed him the drink and suggested that he take a sip. He did, then put it on the table. Then he took her into his arms and kissed her. She wrapped her arms tightly around him. Seeing this encounter develop less than ten feet away from where I was hiding gave me a tremendously hard cock.

Emboldened by her passionate response, Keith cupped one of her breasts and lay down beside her. She told him he had on too many clothes. There was heavy breathing and an electric atmosphere as he removed his clothes. Although Louise quickly grabbed his cock, Keith was in complete control. He kissed his way from her mouth to her neck, and then to her breasts. He kissed her nipples, removed her panties and reached for her pussy as she stroked his erect penis.

This erotic foreplay continued for some fifteen minutes before she asked Keith, bluntly, to fuck her. She turned over on her back, spread her legs and anxiously guided his hardness into her waiting pussy. From her moans and muffled yells, it was obvious that she experienced the first of many orgasms during his initial deep thrusts. He continued plunging his member in and out of her cunt for several minutes before they both stiffened and jerked together in a highly energized, simultaneous orgasm. It must have been the greatest orgasm of Keith's young life. As for Louise, I'd never seen her look so satisfied.

It took a minute for them to catch their breath. "What's it feel like to fuck a senior citizen?" she asked him.

He replied, "You're the sexiest woman of any age that I've ever been with." He went on to say that he hoped they could continue making mad, passionate love during the remainder of the cruise. They returned to groping each other, oblivious to everything but their bodies.

They were fucking wildly when I stepped from the closet, loudly closed the door and stood by the bed. My hard dick was fighting to get out of my pants. Louise opened her eyes and saw me. Noting my expression of approval, she continued to respond to the long strokes of Keith's cock until they both came to another earthshaking orgasm. I was thankful that the cabins were virtually soundproof, as these two were making a hell of a lot of noise.

As soon as Keith realized I was there, he started to apologize. I told him to relax, as I was the one who'd set the whole thing up. I thanked him for getting Louise warmed up for me, and told them that I'd been in the dressing area the whole time and had seen everything that had happened between them. I added that I needed some relief myself, if they did not object.

They didn't, so I quickly removed my clothes, got between Louise's spread legs and, as Keith watched, enjoyed the best fuck I'd had in many years. I had become so aroused by watching them that I blasted off after about three minutes of plunging my cock into my wife's tight cunt.

By the time I rolled off her, Louise noticed that Keith was once more at full staff. "Would you like to fuck me?" she asked him. He readily accepted and plunged his meat into her one more time. Seeing a cock going in and out of my loving wife's slit gave me another powerful hard-on.

As soon as they were done fucking, I asked Louise if I could do her doggie-style while she held her breasts over Keith's face. She replied, "The more the merrier!" So while Keith was taking care of her gorgeous melons, I slid my cock into her dripping pussy and pumped powerfully for twenty minutes before filling her with more jism than I'd ever shot before. I think Louise could've fucked all night long, but by then Keith and I were spent. He left to prepare for dinner, but not until Louise arranged for him to come by again later on.

Louise enjoyed threesomes with Keith and I several times a day for the remainder of the cruise. The time went by so quickly. It was the shortest week of my life, but by far the best.—*Name and address withheld*

THE VIEW FROM THE SHADOWS AT THE END OF THE HALL STAYS IN HIS MIND

Adam, a close friend of my wife's family, came for a visit last week and helped me live out a fantasy, although he didn't know it. He arrived midweek, and was unpacked and relaxed when I arrived home from work. Dinner was ready and excellent, as Mary is a great cook. After a few drinks, we were all taking in the living room, half asleep and ready for bed. Mary was straightening up the room a little, and Adam's eyes followed every move she made as she bent and straightened. She wasn't wearing much, and I know he got a good shot of her tits a couple of times.

When my wife excused herself to go to bed, I sat up a few minutes with Adam to see what he had planned for the next couple of days. I was soon ready to turn in, and Adam said he would lock up and turn off all the lights. Mary was fast asleep when I got into bed, so I kissed her good night, rolled over and fell asleep myself.

Hours must have passed. Half awake and having to pee, I got up to go to the bathroom. It was only when I headed back to bed that I noticed Mary was gone. She gets up a lot at night, so I went to see if she was all right. I didn't see her in the living room or kitchen, but saw a light on in the guest bedroom. I walked over to see what was up, and looked around the corner into the partially open guest room door

Mary was sitting on the bed in a short nightgown, which she wears all the time, talking to Adam. I turned to go back to bed, but was struck by a thought. I was suddenly thinking about what it would be like to see Mary having sex with another man. One of my fantasies is to be a Peeping Tom and to watch two people fucking. This idea in mind, I looked back into the bedroom again. They were still just talking, and I figured that my fantasy wasn't going to be realized that night. Then I heard Mary laugh, and saw Adam turn slightly in bed, revealing a full hard-on. It rose under the covers like a tent pole, just inches from where Mary was sitting. I don't know what they were talking about, but it must have been good.

I was intrigued, and crept quietly closer to the door. I saw that Mary, although covered from his direct sight, was at an angle to the mirror so that Adam could clearly see her shaved pussy—hence the hard-on. When Mary noticed where his gaze was directed, and realized the view she'd been giving him, the laugh followed. She shifted her legs, and I figured that was that.

Then, to my surprise, Mary leaned forward and kissed Adam on the forehead. Adam leaned to meet her and kissed her lips instead. He moved, and the covers fell off to one side, revealing his naked body and rampant erection.

Mary got off the bed. I thought she was leaving, so I backpedaled away from the door. She didn't appear. Slowly I inched back to where I could see the action. The lights were now out, but the glow of a full moon filled the room. Mary was on top of Adam with his penis deep inside her as she pumped up and down, fucking him so fast that he couldn't keep up!

My dick sprang to attention instantly, and I jerked off while watching them. I was mesmerized by the sight of two people fucking just a few feet away, especially since one of them was my wife!

Mary is usually very vocal when we make love, but she wasn't making any noise as she rode Adam. It may be because she didn't want to wake me up, but I think it was more because she was so intent. It all happened so suddenly. I had only stepped away from the door for a few seconds, and when I got back they were fucking furiously. They went from zero to sixty in no time at all, and then just kept accelerating.

Adam didn't make any noise either. Mary sat on his pelvis, her hips sliding up and down his waist so fast they were a blur. Their hands were clutched together next to his shoulders, and she was leaning over him, her tits bouncing up and down like crazy. Their eyes were locked together. The only change as they came close to orgasm was that their eyes got tense and started to close as they struggled to hold back just a little longer. Then that became impossible.

I came at the same time Adam did. That's the only time I heard a sound come from his mouth—a long, soft sigh. Mary soon followed. She closed her eyes and threw her head back, her hair hanging down between her shoulder blades. She slammed her hips down really hard, and I knew from the way her mouth was moving that she was coming, even though she didn't make any noise. She stayed really still for over a minute, then collapsed against his chest.

I haven't said anything to Mary about that night, and I don't know if I ever will. I do know I'm looking forward to watching again when my wife's friend comes to see us. We've had really great sex since that night. I just hope it will continue until Adam's next visit.—*E.O., Tampa, Florida*

SAME OLD PARTY, SAME OLD GUESTS, BUT WAIT A MINUTE! WHAT'S GOING ON OVER BY THE SWIMMING POOL?

Working full-time and going to school doesn't leave me much time for a social life. However, a couple of weeks ago a girlfriend of mine talked me into going to a big party with her. It was the same old scene, with the same old faces, so I decided to go for a walk outside.

After walking around for a while, I was almost ready to go back inside when I heard a woman moaning. I looked around, and there at the side of the pool was a woman masturbating. I moved behind a tree where I could watch without being seen. It was then that I noticed a man directly across the pool from her. He was talking dirty to her. I could feel my nipples grow hard as I listened to him tell her how much he would love to slide his hard cock into her mouth.

He walked around the pool to her, took her and raised her to her feet. I could see that she had been swimming. Her perfect body glistened in the moonlight as he lowered his head to suck one of her breasts into his mouth. I was wearing a miniskirt with no underwear, and couldn't resist reaching down between my legs to feel the wetness there. My pussy went wild at the first touch, and I began to finger myself.

The mysterious man bent his lover over a chair and thrust his manhood between her plump ass-cheeks and into her cunt. At first he went slowly, but the louder she moaned, the more frantic he became. My love juice was running down my leg as I finger-fucked myself harder and harder. He had hold of her tits, and she begged for his load. He pulled his dick out and exploded all over her back. By this point I had two fingers in my twat. As I watched her wipe his come from her back and lick it, I couldn't help but yell out as I came too, twitching and thrusting. By the time I stopped coming, I was sitting on the ground because I had orgasmed so hard that my knees refused to hold me up.

I got out of there as fast as I could, hoping no one saw me. But I'm going to make a point of going to those parties from now on, so I can get my turn by the pool!—*P.M., Seattle, Washington*

A LITTLE SOMETHING ON THE SIDE HAS KEPT THIS COUPLE'S MAIN COURSE APPETIZING

Dora and I have been married for ten years, have seven children, and are a perfectly matched couple. Not only do we agree on everything from politics to the food we like, we are also ideally suited to each other in our unorthodox attitudes about sex. Dora is a hot-blooded woman who loves sex. She's had numerous lovers and several very passionate long-term affairs during our years together. I must in honesty admit that Dora's love affairs do make me jealous, but I don't find that they make me angry. The jealousy is secondary to the sexual arousal her trysts cause me. Our relationship is an ideal match between a sensuous, sexually liberated woman and a natural voyeur.

When Dora returns home from one of her dates, she likes me to lick her juicy, sperm-filled cunt while she softly tells me how her lover fucked her. Because her stories turn me on so much, she jacks off my hard, aching prick. I always come almost immediately. Other times she'll give me a deep, wet kiss, asking whether I can taste her lover's come on her breath from the blowjob she gave him. I'll finger her juicy pussy, and ejaculate almost at the touch of her hand on my prick.

Our sexy lifestyle began when Dora accompanied me on a business trip only three months after we were married. She stayed at the hotel while I attended my first meeting, and had quite a tale to tell me when I got back. A man had started talking to her at the hotel pool, and they had spent the afternoon chatting away. She told me that the guy, Quentin, had really been coming on to her, and had asked her to meet him for drinks and dancing at the lounge that evening. Dora said he was well-built and quite good-looking.

Noticing her obvious interest, I asked her if she'd agreed to see him. Dora's eyes lit up. She was pleased that I'd seen what she was getting at. She looked at my trousers, where an erection had already started growing, and replied, "I said I'd call him and let him know. I told him that if my husband had a meeting, I would meet him."

By now my young bride's tale had given me an incredible hard-on. Dora looked at my bulging trousers and said, "I see it turns you on as much as it does me. Why don't I call Quentin and tell him I'm free, that my husband's tied up. That way you can come to the lounge and watch what happens." Still unsure, but incredibly aroused, I could only nod.

I went to the lounge, and took a seat at the bar, wondering if Quentin was already there and, if so, which of the patrons he was. Dora entered a few minutes later. Every head in the place turned when she walked in wearing a tight black dress that revealed plenty of cleavage and leg. Dora is exceptionally pretty, with medium-length dark brown hair, blue eyes and a sensational body.

A man at the opposite side of the bar got up and walked her way. Dora greeted him with a warm smile and led the way to a table near where I was sitting. I would be able to hear their every word. Dora told him that her husband was at a meeting and wouldn't be back until well after midnight.

As the evening progressed they had drinks, danced, talked intimately and sat close together, with lots of touching. Every so often Dora would secretly glance over at me. This was usually followed by a deep, passionate kiss. A little after ten, Dora asked Quentin, loudly enough to be sure I could hear, "Do you want to come back to my room with me for a while? My husband won't be back for another two hours, at least."

Quentin wasted no time accepting Dora's invitation. He escorted her out of the lounge, his hand on her lovely butt as they walked. My cock was almost tearing a hole in my trousers, so I finished the beer I was sipping on and left the lounge also.

The room we were staying in faced the swimming pool, so I went to a poolside seat in order to watch our window. I couldn't see them inside, only that the light was on behind the closed curtain. There I sat, jealous and horny, my mind full of erotic fantasies about what was going on behind our locked hotel room door. Finally the door opened, a little before midnight, and Quentin left. I waited until he was gone and entered the room.

Dora's dress, bra and panties were on the floor, and she lay naked on the bed, covered to her waist by a sheet. She had a contented glow about her, and she smiled at me dreamily. I undressed and crawled in bed beside my wife, asking her to fill me in on the details. Dora grinned mischievously, kissed me, and asked, "Can you taste Quentin's come? I swallowed a lot of it." I almost came myself when she said that.

Next, one of Dora's dainty hands cupped my cock, while the other pushed down the sheet and put one of my hands on her pussy. It was soaking wet and greasy, and I looked down to see her pubic hair lathered in milky-white semen. I was amazed. Not only had she gone to bed with Quentin, whom she'd met only that afternoon, she'd not even made him wear one of the rubbers in the nightstand. "Did you let him come in you?" I asked Dora incredulously.

She looked at me seductively and replied, "I didn't let him. I begged him to shoot his sperm in me." Dora gave my cock a tug with her hand as she said that, and I filled her palm with my come.

Dora giggled as she snuggled up tight against me and whispered, "Now that you're married to an adulteress, how do you like it? Make you jealous?" I nodded. Then she continued, "But it really turned you on, didn't it?" I couldn't help but nod yes again, because it really did. "Good," she replied nuzzling up to me, "because I've been fantasizing about being a naughty wife ever since our honeymoon. Tonight was the most exciting night of my life." Dora then finished with, "That's what I want to be, a naughty wife. You'll let me be your naughty wife, won't you? You'll still love me, won't you honey, you'll still love your naughty wife?" I did love her, I still do, and I held her tight as we fell asleep, assuring her that I'd always love my naughty wife.—*J.K., Dearborn, Michigan*

HUSBAND WATCHES CLOSELY TO MAKE SURE THE SHOE SALESMAN GIVES WIFE A GOOD FIT

After reading in *Penthouse Letters* about husbands watching their wives have sex with strangers, I wondered what it would be like to see my wife with someone else. When I first brought it up, Monica was adamantly against it. However, with patience and persistence I convinced her to experiment with the idea by flashing a shoe salesman. She agreed, but said that was as far as she would go.

I had her put on a pair of sheer white panties under a dress with a short, full skirt, then drove her to a shoe store in another town, right around closing time. Monica waited until the store was empty, then nervously entered, quickly picked out three styles and took a seat near the back. The salesman, a good-looking guy about thirty years old, sat down on a fitting stool, facing her. I quietly entered the store and crept up behind him. When Monica raised her foot onto the stool, her panties came into view, and her skirt rode up her thigh a little. None of this was lost on the salesman, who boldly looked into Monica's eyes and smiled. She returned his smile, but didn't adjust her skirt.

As the clerk changed her shoe, he commented on how nice her legs were, and started lightly rubbing her calf. Monica smiled and thanked him, then made everything easier to see by slightly parting her legs and lowering her foot to the side of the stool. When she raised the other leg, her skirt slid even higher, revealing some of her sheer panties. The thin material did very little to hide the thick black pubic hair framing my wife's pretty pink pussy.

Monica didn't get up to try the shoes. She found some fault with them and went straight to the next pair. Gaining confidence as the process was repeated, she spread her legs wider, making it possible to clearly see her swollen pussy lips through the sheer panties.

As they started on the third pair Monica was breathing hard, and a wet spot was becoming very evident on the crotch of her panties. The salesman was rubbing her thighs and openly staring between her legs. When Monica lowered her foot this time he moved his leg between hers and moved the stool forward, keeping Monica's thighs wide open. What she did then went way beyond anything I had hoped for. Monica reached down and bunched her skirt up above her waist, completely displaying her most private parts to this man she had never seen before.

My wife's eyes were glassy and her breathing strained, as the salesman's hands slid up her spread-eagle thighs toward her wet panties. She held her breath as he slipped the fingers of both hands inside the leg openings of her underwear, then threw her head back and gasped as he immediately began massaging her clit. Two fingers of his other hand slid into her vagina.

The young man strode over to the door of the shop and locked it. Luckily, just as he got up I had managed to step into the doorway leading to the back of the shop, where he couldn't see me. I listened to their groping for several minutes before inching my way back out of my hiding place.

By that time, they had begun pulling at each other's clothes, fumbling with belts, buttons, zippers and hooks. Soon they were both naked. Quickly moving to a display table, the salesman pushed the shoes aside, then boosted Monica up onto it. She wrapped her legs around his hips and guided his erection inside her glistening pussy.

It was as exciting as the letters said it would be. My lovely Monica humped her pelvis forward to meet every thrust as the stranger plunged his cock into her smoldering pussy again and again. There was something fascinating about the way his butt muscles clenched and unclenched as he drove his dick into her. Even from a distance I could hear the squish every time the thick base of his dick reached her lips and his pubic hair nestled into hers. He lasted a long time too, giving Monica two good orgasms before he came himself. In fact, she slipped into another long, strong series of contractions when he blasted his load of hot, sticky semen deep inside her. Monica clutched him with her legs, wanting him to stay all the way in her cunt. She didn't relax until his dick went completely soft. They talked softly to each other while she held onto his softening prick, and he stroked her breasts and belly.

I thought I'd be cute so, after they had rested for a minute, I came out of hiding and yelled, "Honey, if you're finished, let's go home." The salesman ran to the back room and stayed there, until Monica dressed and we left. I'll bet he still can't figure out how I got in with the door locked.

On the way home I asked Monica how she'd liked her adventure. She told me she couldn't believe she had actually screwed a complete stranger. She added, though, that it had felt so good, she couldn't have stopped if she'd wanted to.—*K.W., Saint Augustine, Florida*

HE DECIDES TO MEET THE WIFE WITHOUT CALLING FIRST, BUT HE'S THE ONE WHO GETS A SURPRISE

My wife Hae Sue works in a big law office. One chilly spring day I decided to surprise her and take her to lunch. I drove downtown, and had just jockeyed into a tight curbside parking space when I saw Hae Sue come out of the building. Before I could signal her, she hopped into a Volvo with a guy I'd never seen before and drove off. I got back in my car, made a U-turn and started to follow them.

Hae Sue is extremely attractive. She's twenty-eight years old and Korean, with shoulder-length black hair and gorgeous brown eyes. She also loves to fuck and, although she has never given me cause to doubt her fidelity, I admit to being instantly jealous when I began to pursue her through the lunchtime traffic.

The Volvo wound its way across town. After a while, it turned off the drive we were on, entering a small park. The Volvo rolled to a stop at the far end of the parking area. I pulled up and waited for them to get out of the car. From that distance I couldn't observe them too well so, when they made no move to get out of the car after a couple of minutes, I left my car to get a closer look.

Circling around through the woods, I was able to get very close to the Volvo. What I saw blew me away. Hae Sue and this guy were making out. He was on her side of the car and was all over her. His hands were busy pawing her tits, and I watched as he thrust his tongue down her throat and into her ear. For her part, it seemed that Hae Sue couldn't get enough of his attention.

After a few minutes the guy started to undo Hae Sue's dress, which buttoned completely down the front. When he had opened it to her waist, he pulled Hae Sue forward, sliding the dress from her shoulders and removing her bra. For several minutes I watched in total disbelief as this guy sucked my wife's sweet little tits to hard points.

After a while he stopped, and Hae Sue pressed her shoulders into the seat back, arching her lower body up slightly. I couldn't actually see what was going on, but it was apparent that the guy was sliding her dress and panties off. When they settled back down, Hae Sue's head disappeared in the direction of his lap.

I couldn't believe it. Here was my wife, practically naked, in a car in a public park, sucking some guy's cock like a whore. I wondered how long this had been going on and whether this guy was her first or one of many extramarital lovers. Every once in a while the back of her head would bob into view, then disappear again. At one point she took her head off his dick and sat there smiling at him. He continued to breathe hard and moan, so I knew that she was working his dick with her hand. He put his hand on the back of her head and begged, and she went back down on him, doing what I knew from experience would be a first-class job of coaxing his cream.

After a few minutes the guy opened his door and got out. He went around to Hae Sue's side and helped her out. She was wearing her raincoat, and still had on her stockings and heels. They walked hand-in-hand to a place slightly away from the picnic area but within sight of it. He led her to a large tree and leaned her against it, facing him. In this position, standing up on the roots, she was almost as tall as he was.

I watched as he pulled Hae Sue's coat open. Beneath it she was wearing only her thigh-high stockings and heels. The scene was incredibly arousing, in spite of my distress at catching my wife in flagrante with a stranger. Her friend had his cock out, and moved forward to impale her with it. Apparently he was having trouble getting it in, because Hae Sue lifted her right leg to allow him better access. Holding her leg with his left hand, he used his right to position his cock at the entrance to Hae Sue's pussy. Hae Sue gasped and her eyes widened as the guy thrust his hips forward, sliding his meat deep into her tight little box.

He started a slow rocking motion as he fucked in and out of Hae Sue, pressing her back against the rough bark of the tree. She kept looking over toward the picnic area, concerned that someone might see them. His response was to take hold of her chin and turn her head so that her eyes looked directly into his. He reached up and pulled the raincoat off her shoulders, fully exposing Hae Sue to anyone who might look their way. She started to look around again, but he planted his lips on hers in order to keep her head from turning. She returned his kiss with passion.

When she's excited, she starts to really writhe around. It's very compelling when you hold her in your arms, but I was even more fascinated seeing it from a distance. Her arms were flailing, and she kept lifting her other leg so that he was supporting her entire weight. She finally wrapped both legs around his waist and started riding up and down as hard and as fast as she could go.

She had both her arms and legs wrapped tightly around him now, and she was squeezing with all her might. Hae Sue gets foulmouthed when she's excited, and from where I was I could see her saying, "Fuck me, fuck me harder." I could tell she was about to come, because she closed her eyes and opened her mouth in a perfect O. Then an orgasm swept over her. She held him as tightly as she could and stopped moving, except for a slight, uncontrollable humping action of her hips. Soon he had his own orgasm, not pulling out but shooting his load deep inside my wife's neatly trimmed pussy.

After they had regained their composure, he withdrew, and Hae Sue closed her coat. He held her hand as she came down from the tree roots, and they walked back to the car and left. I sat there for about thirty minutes and jacked off to the erotic images roaring through my brain.

There's only one problem. I've been unable to confront her about the episode, because I've developed a burning desire to catch them at it again.—*L.B., Baltimore, Maryland*

UNEXPECTED MOTEL MENAGE PASSES THE WEARY NIGHT

Recently I was staying at a motel for several days while attending a series of business meetings. After a late dinner one evening I was returning to my room, and noticed that the drapes were partly open on a room near mine. Like anyone else, I glanced inside. A guy was lying naked on the bed, watching TV and idly fingering his dong. I stopped and did a double take, then leaned on the rail and lit a cigarette, not wanting anyone to think I was peeping.

When I looked into the room again, a beautiful girl had come out of the bathroom wearing only a short nightgown. She had a figure that would make a pecker hard enough to play Chopin. She lay beside the young man and grasped his penis. He smiled at her, then looked toward the window.

Afraid that he would notice me looking, I walked on down the balcony to my room. But I couldn't help noticing that he hadn't made any move to close the curtains. These people were either exhibitionists or they wanted company. Eager to volunteer my services, I dialed their room number. The man answered the phone on the first ring.

"I'm Mike," I said. "My room is just a few doors away from yours. I thought you and your girl might want some company."

"Are you the guy who smoked a cigarette outside a few minutes ago?"

"Yeah, that's me."

"Then come on over. And bring a bucket of ice, if you don't mind. I have some vodka."

I changed from my suit into shirt and slacks, got the ice and knocked on their door. The drapes were now completely closed.

"Hello, Mike, I'm Cal, and this is Annette. Come on in." He was wearing boxer shorts, which didn't hide the fact that he had most of a hard-on. Annette lay propped on the bed. Her short gown barely covered her crotch.

Cal took the ice and mixed three drinks. I picked up one for myself and handed one to Annette. She patted the side of the bed, indicating that I should sit beside her. She took my hand in hers and scrutinized the palm.

In a moment she smiled at me and said, "If I'm not badly mistaken, you're a Virgo, twenty-nine or thirty years old, not married, but you were once engaged. You like sports and all kinds of sex. You are very virile and have a larger-than-average cock." I grinned and nodded my head. I couldn't keep my eyes off her breasts, which were barely covered. Her nipples were darkly visible through the fabric, looking like a pair of cherry gumdrops. She placed my hand over one of her tits.

"Do you like them?" she asked, and I murmured that I did. I squeezed the handful of soft flesh gently, and turned to look at Cal. He was sitting in a chair with his cock standing at attention through the fly of his shorts.

"Do you want to fuck her?" he asked.

"Sure," I replied, gulping my drink.

"Okay, but first Annette is going to give me a blowjob. Do you like to watch?"

"I've never done it, but it sounds good," I answered. Annette got up and went over to Cal. She pulled off his underwear and knelt between his spread legs. She pumped his dick with her hand several times, then licked the length of his shaft while fondling his balls. She leaned back, pulled her gown over her head and shook out her blonde hair. Looking at me through the frame of her tousled hair, she said, "Get naked!"

I stripped, as she held Cal's long dick and eased it into her mouth. He let out a long sigh, like someone taking his first sip of beer after a long, hot day. Turning to me, he said, "Mike, I think you'll agree that Annette is a great cocksucker when she goes to work on you." I sat on the bed and watched Annette's head bob up and down on Cal's rigid pole. Between the sight of her lips squeezing pleasure from him, and that unique sound of wet suction, my own cock was hard as a brick.

"Slow down, sugar lips, I don't want to come yet. Why don't you work on Mike for a while?"

Annette came to me and caressed my cock. "I was right, you are bigger than most men." She rubbed my rubbery dick over her face and twirled her tongue around the head before sucking it into her mouth. I reached down and fondled her tits.

Annette had the one quality that is essential in a cocksucker. She really loved sucking cock. Because she was so into it, I could just sit back and relax, not worrying about whether her jaw was getting tired or she was resenting the whole thing. Usually it takes me forever to come from a blowjob, because I'm concerned about the woman being bored. This time I was ready to come in no time at all. But I didn't want to come so soon.

I stood up, and pulled Annette to her feet. First I nibbled her ears, then lifted her face and kissed her. Our tongues probed each other's mouth. My hands went to her glorious little, round tits, then down to her waist and over her ass. I pulled her crotch tightly against me, so my prick was between her legs. She rubbed her clit on the base of my cock.

"Fuck me, fuck me!" she moaned, then lay on the bed. I crouched between her spread legs, putting one hand on her slightly rounded belly and the other over her cunt. She was dripping wet. I experimented with slipping a finger inside. Her pussy was loose, warm and liquid. "Go ahead and give it to her, Mike. Stick it in. Fill her with that big cock of yours. She loves it," urged Cal.

After withdrawing my probing finger, I teased her for a moment with the knob of my cock before plunging my shaft in. It was like entering a Jacuzzi. She was that wet, that warm, and once I was all the way inside her she started moving like crazy all over the place. She arched her body and put her arms around my neck, gasped for breath, trembled, bit my shoulder and scratched my back as she came, suddenly and violently. In all my years of experience I'd never known a woman to reach climax so quickly.

For over a minute after the first waves of orgasm, Annette was still trembling and moaning softly. I held still until she relaxed a little, then started fucking again, slowly at first, then gradually faster and harder. Her legs squeezed my waist as she bucked against me. Her cunt went from being wide and loose to squeezing me tight as a vise, and back again. "I'm coming," I cried. Her cunt muscles contracted, and we exploded at the same time.

Exhausted, I rolled off to one side. Cal had been standing beside the bed stroking his meat and closely observing our every move. Now he crawled between her legs and began to lick and suck our juices as they oozed from her pussy.

"Turn over," he told Annette. Placing a pillow under her, Cal mounted her from behind. He held her hips and drove his cock into her steaming snatch. I sat up and watched his dick move in and out. Cal shuddered and shot off. Annette slipped her finger down to her clit and brought herself to another small, but apparently satisfying, orgasm.

The three of us lay together on the bed. Annette held a wilted wand in each hand. I played with her boobs, and Cal had a hand over her pussy, stroking her mound gently.

"You liked that, didn't you?" I asked Cal. "You get off seeing another man screw your wife, and you want another man to watch you fuck her. Also, of course, Annette is so sensual that it takes more than one man to satisfy her. I'm really glad you chose me to share in the fun."

"You're right, Mike. We both get off on having another guy in bed. Hey, Annette, what do you think? Can you get Mike hard again? Let me see you suck on his cock."

Annette slid down and nuzzled my crotch. She juggled my balls and nibbled on my cock, licking the insides of my thighs and running her fingers through my pubic hair. I began to twitch and swell once more in response. Cal ran his hands over my belly, probed my navel and tickled my erect nipples. My dick grew thicker and longer. Annette held it straight up.

"It's beautiful, Mike, so full and hard. Feel it Cal," said Annette. He squeezed and stroked my penis several times, then lowered his head and sucked on the knob. I watched as they took turns blowing me. After a while Annette sat back and let Cal take over. She finger-fucked herself and jerked Cal's dick while he went down on me.

Cal was almost as good with his mouth as Annette, and in a much shorter time than I expected, having come once already, I convulsed and shot my come into Cal's mouth. He took it all, then turned to Annette and fed her some of my juice.

I was drained. Cal lay back, and Annette lowered her cunt onto his prick. I cleaned up and dressed as she rode him frantically. After watching them reach a climax I slipped quickly out of the room.

Cal and Annette had left when I passed their room in the morning. The drapes were open.—*M.A., Greensboro, North Carolina*

FRIENDLIER SKIES WERE NEVER FLOWN, AS PILOTS BOFF PASSENGER

My buddy Bob and I own a small plane together, a four-seater prop job. We use it for outings and short weekend trips. Just as some people own fishing boats, we have a plane. Sometimes one of us enjoys simply taking a solo ride through the clouds. Occasionally we taxi people to nearby destinations. We always run an ad in the paper looking for potential travelers.

On one particular Saturday we had a passenger to transport. Her name was Louise and she said she just wanted to go for a ride in a small plane. Louise was in her mid-twenties, had long dark hair and an hourglass body. When she arrived at our small local airport, Bob and I were both taken by her. She was pretty, charming and intelligent, and we both liked her immediately. It could have been a problem that we both found her so attractive, but that turned out not to be the case.

We brought a few soft drinks for our afternoon in the clouds, and Louise brought along a camera bag. The skies were clear, and the three of us were all smiles as we left terra firma. Soon we were coasting at about five thousand feet and enjoying the view. The conversation had mostly been about how Bob and I had gotten interested in owning a plane. It was a little bit of a deviation, then, when Louise brought up the subject of the infamous "mile high club." We all admitted that we had yet to become members.

"That's just ideal," Louise gleefully commented. "I was kind of hoping . . . I mean, I really was looking forward to an afternoon off the ground. But when I saw the two of you, I thought, well, why shouldn't we have some fun in the cockpit?" Well, she had two cocks in that cockpit that were ready to help her achieve her ambition.

Before we could say much more, Louise was undressing. She had the back two seats to herself, and plenty of room to spread out. The body she revealed was gorgeous and, judging from the way her nipples stood proudly up, aching for some attention.

Louise lay back on the seat and hiked her legs up so that one was on my shoulder and one on Bob's. Her secret center was totally exposed and glistening in the afternoon sun. My, my, how delicious!

Louise's next trick came from her camera bag. It turned out

not to contain a camera, or even a roll of film, just a long, studded vibrator. With her cunt wide open and very moist, Louise turned on her toy. She dipped it into her opening as her two pilots took turns gazing. I looked at Bob and made a signal to him to go for it.

He turned in his chair and began running his fingers down Louise's legs. She enjoyed the stroking to accompany her electric friend. The purring of the dildo matched her own. Bob kept petting, and eventually made it to her breasts. Her nipples were standing up like runway beacons, and Bob was soon busy tweaking them between his fingers.

Louise was getting hotter and hotter by the minute. She would slip the vibrator in as far as it would go, then slowly remove it and rub her clit. Her eyes were glazed when she removed her toy and tugged Bob's head into her lap. Bob wasted no time licking his way from her knees to her musky slit.

Bob discovered that he could hold his head practically still, his tongue spread over her juicy opening, and the movement of the plane turned him into a vibrator. After a little of this they were both longing to fly united.

It took Bob a few minutes to slip out of his clothes and into the rear with Louise. She positioned herself on her knees and leaned up over Bob's front seat. Bob was sitting in Louise's seat, setting his sights on one very wet pussy. I don't know if he was moving into her or vice versa, but they melted together rapidly.

The whole time this was going on I was doing my best to steer the plane while watching the whole operation in the mirror. It was a constant battle to remind myself to look out the windscreen from time to time instead of at the sexy action behind me. My voyeuristic adventure had my dick screaming to get out of my pants.

Louise realized my difficulty and asked if I would like some attention. I carefully dropped my shorts, and she eagerly dropped her head down into my lap. That meant she had to squeeze herself between the two front seats, an impressive feat. Louise had her pussy churning away on Bob's stiff shaft, and her mouth full of my cock. That's when I learned about the special added effect the engine vibration had on any physical contact. We were all ready to blow in no time. First came Bob. He gushed his burning incense into Louise. That set her off and resulted in her sucking harder on my dick. The increased suction, combined with a little light turbulence, finished me off, and she had soon drained my member of every drop.

Despite the multiple orgasms, none of us stopped our motions. Bob kept dipping and Louise kept sucking. She had gotten what she wanted, and yet she wanted more. It was my turn in back. Bob and I changed places, and he took up my practice of spending four-fifths of his time staring in the mirror, with only occasional glances out the front for safety.

Louise used her luscious lips to return my dick to its rampant state. Looking me directly in the eyes, she said, "One fuck is fine, but two is my type of screw." We leaned both the rear seats back flat, and I leaned her horizontal onto her back. With a mighty thrust, I grabbed both her legs and slid in. Bob and Louise had produced a lot of juice, and I was ready to add to the mixture. As we glided together and apart, Louise alternated between screaming and gasping for breath.

Seeking to improve the action he was witnessing, Bob tapped me on the shoulder and handed me Louise's vibrator. I smiled, turned that hummer on and applied the tip directly to the point where our bodies joined. She clapped in enjoyment, saying, "That's it, that's it!" That certainly was it, and I let go a voluminous rush of juice. Spray after spray poured into her. She hollered, "Oh, my!" which I thought was pretty funny. I wasn't laughing, though, when her pussy tightened around my dick, pulling more squirts from me and causing her to have a massive O of her own.

Our flight was nearly two hours old. We had traveled a little over a hundred miles. A hundred miles of nonstop fucking. Sometime during my time with Louise, Bob had gotten us turned around and headed for home. We never did get our clothes back on before we approached our home airport.

As we came in for a landing, Louise was busy pumping our dicks with her hands. Bob and I have made better landings, but we got the plane on the ground. As we coasted toward the hangar we realized that Louise was determined to draw one last load from each of us. I wonder what the view was like from the air controller's tower. Anyway, Louise got her wish and swallowed her souvenirs.

Louise appreciated the chance to fly in a small plane. She said, "A jet will never be the same." Bob and I told her that no flying would ever be the same.—*A.J., Atlanta, Georgia*

Pursuit & Capture

EX-CON'S ATTENTIONS TURN LONELY GAL INTO A PRISONER OF LOVE

When my best friend Amanda invited me to visit her at her home in sunny Florida, I decided to take a much-needed vacation. I had broken up with my boyfriend at the beginning of the year. Without anyone to take care of my sexual needs, I was so horny all the time that I couldn't concentrate on anything for very long. I needed a change of pace.

I called Amanda to make arrangements for my visit. She mentioned that her brother-in-law Evan, who had just been released from prison after a seven-year stint, was staying with them until he got back on his feet. I had met Evan some years earlier, and I flashed on a mental picture of him. As I recalled, he was quite a stud. Although I played it cool on the phone, the thought of scratching my ever-present itch with a guy who'd been starving for pussy for the last seven years really sparked my interest.

When I arrived at her home in my rented convertible, Amanda was real glad to see me. We spent some time gossiping and catching up on the latest news. She told me that her husband had been unexpectedly called away on business and wouldn't be back for a few days.

Then Evan came home. He was looking hotter than ever. He had evidently worked out a lot while in prison, as he was in excellent shape. I flirted with Evan for a while and teased him about prison life, asking him whose bitch he'd been. He responded good-naturedly, assuring me he was still all man.

Amanda and I decided to go out and paint the town red. We proceeded to barhop until the wee hours. When we got home, Amanda realized she had forgotten her house keys, so we were locked out. We had to wake up Evan, who was sleeping on the sofa bed in the living room, to let us in.

I was feeling as horny as ever, so I figured there wasn't any point in wasting any more time. I changed into a sheer black robe and went back out to the living room. Evan, who was still awake, seemed pleased to see me.

Trying to be quiet and discreet, I simply pointed at Evan, rubbed my wet box and tilted my head toward the guest room where I was staying. He didn't need any more encouragement to bring his rock-hard, sex-starved cock into my room so he could prove to me he hadn't been anyone's bitch in prison.

My pussy was eager to provide the tightness and wetness he'd missed all those years. I must have needed a truly wild lover too, because after one night with Evan I couldn't get enough of him. The next day I talked him into joining me on a road trip to New Orleans.

Speeding down the highway, we could hardly keep our hands off each other. Evan wanted to hear my most intimate sexual fantasy, so I told him the one about being sent to an all-male prison due to some legal error, and having my fill of all those desperate, tattooed inmates. I thought he might cream his skintight jeans when he heard it! He told me to stick my fingers into my wet pussy and let him taste my sweet juice. He pronounced it delicious.

Things were getting frantic as we cruised along at ninety. Evan wanted me to come so badly, he jammed his right hand down my spandex shorts while he drove with his left. I did a bump and grind on Evan's fingers as we tore down the highway. No doubt the truck drivers we passed got an eyeful. Evan worked me into a frenzy, rubbing my swollen clit with his thumb and sliding his strong fingers deep into my dripping pussy. I exploded before we crossed the state line.

As Evan licked my juice off his fingers, I leaned over and freed his throbbing cock. I licked and sucked and nibbled on his beautiful shaft. He kept saying that we had to get a hotel room so he could fuck me properly.

We finally pulled into a rest area so we could give free rein to our passions without worrying that we'd cause an accident. A busload of retirees milled around the rest area, but neither of us cared. Evan pulled up alongside the most isolated picnic table and gave me his boyish, yet hardened, grin. I simply couldn't resist. Although several people could see what was going on, I kneeled down and sucked Evan off. He moaned and shuddered as he exploded in orgasm. As we got back into the car, he swore he wouldn't make it to the state line if he didn't get a chance to fuck me.

My anticipation had been growing by the mile, so we didn't go too far before we stopped at a hotel. We decided that we needed to sustain ourselves for the bedroom festivities, so we dressed for dinner. Wanting to keep Evan on his toes, I wore a skintight denim dress and panties.

After we were seated at a cozy corner table in the hotel's dining room, I gently picked up his right hand and started to kiss his palms and suck on his fingers while staring passionately into his eyes. When the waiter came to take our order, I pulled Evan's hand under the table and onto my bare thigh. While Evan did his best to place our order, I slowly slid his hand up my silky inner thigh and placed it on my steaming box. The mixture of surprise and delight on his face was one I'll never forget. After a dinner of rather obvious, frantic groping, Evan suggested his own special recipe for dessert. He didn't have to ask twice.

My most incredible memory of that trip is lying spread-eagle on the bed while Evan straddled me, his throbbing harpoon aimed toward my frantic pussy. But instead of the incredible fucking I desperately wanted, he decided to tease me for a while. He gently licked every inch of my body until I thought I would die. It was the most erotic sense of frustration I'd ever experienced.

When Evan stiffened his tongue and buried his face between my legs, I felt as if a volcano was erupting inside me. As my lava flowed, Evan had an eruption of his own. His hot come spurted high into the air. I begged him to give me a taste, but he just laughed and rammed his pulsating, still-hard cock between my legs. He fucked me so thoroughly and completely, I knew I would never be the same. Sex with Evan was so much better than the mediocre sex I'd been having with guys back home.

When you visit New Orleans, you're supposed to remember jazz bands, Cajun food and Bourbon Street, but my memories of the city only include the most incredible sex of my life. Evan, though, has a more permanent reminder of that road trip. Now my sexy face and curvaceous body are immortalized in living color on his right shoulder. That's one tattoo I'll make sure he never regrets.—*P.N., Mobile, Alabama*

AFTER SEVEN YEARS, MELODY FINDS A MAN WHO'S SINGING HER TUNE

I live in a small town in Arizona, and although I have dated a variety of women during my life, I have never met a woman like the one I'm about to describe. Her name is Melody.

I work for a telecommunications company as a telephone repairman, and during the course of a day I visit many private residences and business offices. The view is great when you're making a house call and the lady of the house isn't wearing much, or when you're under a desk fixing a phone line while tan, shapely legs are passing by.

On one particularly slow day, I was in the office looking over some work orders and trying to decide which one I would fulfill that day. Suddenly this goddess walked in. She strode up to the service counter and leaned over, resting her arms on the counter, which caused her T-shirt to dip down and reveal a glimpse of her tits. I couldn't tell if she did this intentionally to get my attention, or if it was purely accidental. From where I was standing, though, the view was terrific.

I headed toward the service counter and asked this vision of beauty if I could help her. When she opened her mouth to reply, out came a voice that was softer than a bird's call. Her frizzy, shoulder-length, light brown hair was tied back. Her brown eyes were inquisitive, as if she were searching for something. Her skin was smooth, and her lips were full. She had large hands, with long fingers and red-painted nails.

She asked me how she could arrange to have her home, which was located in a somewhat remote area, wired for phone service. I told her she needed to fill out an application for telephone service, and that I would personally take care of her request. What a way to get her name and address!

A few days later I went out to Melody's house and proceeded to hook up the telephone service she'd requested. After the installation was complete, I asked her if I could see her again sometime. She replied that it was a possibility.

After letting a few days pass, I called her at her new number. She invited me to her house for dinner that evening. When I arrived at six, she was still busy at the stove making the final dinner preparations. After we ate, we talked for a while about ourselves. We soon realized we had a lot in common. It seemed as if we were meant for each other.

During our conversation, Melody mentioned that she had been divorced for almost seven years and had not been involved with anyone during that time. I thought it would be fun to fuck someone who hadn't made love for so long.

At long last I leaned over to kiss her good night. At first her response was hesitant. We kissed again, and this time I took her in a full embrace. She slid her tongue into my mouth, then sucked on my tongue.

As we continued kissing and tonguing each other, I reached up and placed my right hand on her left breast. She let out a sigh and pressed her lips harder against mine. I caressed her breast gently. It fit right into my hand. I reached around and grabbed her ass-cheek, giving it a firm squeeze. When I did this, she ground her pussy against my cock. Reaching down, she massaged my cock through my pants with an up-and-down motion. No doubt she could feel how hard I was. Then she led me to her bedroom.

She sat me on her four-poster bed. I watched as she took off her shoes and socks. She pulled off her T-shirt in one quick motion, and her dark areolas were visible through her lacy, low-cut bra. I removed my shirt and pulled down my pants, exposing my hard cock.

Lying on the bed, I watched as she unbuckled her belt, unsnapped the snap, unzipped the zipper and pulled her pants down. Her breasts looked like they were trying to pop out of her bra. Reaching behind her back, she unsnapped her bra and removed it. Her breasts were beautiful. She then bent over to remove her panties. Her dark pussy hair was neatly trimmed. She was slim and her tits were full and firm. They stood up proudly, protruding forward. She climbed onto the bed and lay on top of me. We continued kissing as I massaged her tits. Finally I reached down between her legs to see if her pussy was wet and ready.

I rubbed her cunt with my fingers, moving them back and forth until she began to breathe more heavily. Repositioning herself, she put her hand on my cock and very slowly began to lick the head of it. Then she took it into her mouth and began to suck gently. She kept a firm grip on the base of my cock, holding it in place so that she could continue licking and sucking it. She slid her fingers down to my balls and played with them as if they were marbles.

I lay supine, watching her suck my cock as if she were sucking a lollipop. I reached over to massage her tits as I slowly thrust my hips up and down. She moved up to kiss me, and we rolled over, leaving me on top. I began to squeeze her mounds and suck her nipples, which were now about the size of the tip of my little finger.

I slid down her breasts to her stomach, licking and kissing her all the way, until I reached her love-mound. Her cunt hair was soft, and as I spread her legs I ran my tongue along her cunt lips and rubbed my nose in her pubic hair. I spread apart her cunt lips, slid my tongue into her groove and slowly licked upward. When I reached her clit, I began to suck on it while working my tongue over it in a circular motion. With her eyes closed she moaned, placed her hands on her breasts and licked her lips. I reached up to move her hands from her chest. I began to massage and squeeze her tits while simultaneously licking her pussy.

Soon my face was as wet as her cunt. I slid up her body and guided my love-rod toward her mound of damp pubic hair. Her pussy was soaked. She grabbed my cock and guided me into her tunnel of love. As I entered her cunt, she let out a gasp and moaned loud enough for the neighbors to hear.

I slowly began to fuck her with in-and-out thrusts until she was fully lubricated and the sliding action was rhythmically smooth. I looked down so I could watch my rod slide in and out of her. She spread her legs wide apart so that I could watch all the action. Her breasts would jiggle whenever I began to thrust harder.

When I looked up at Melody again, I saw that the color of her eyes had turned from brown to green. I guessed this meant, "Go!" so I began to thrust even harder. She grabbed my ass and pulled me toward her on every downstroke. We kissed and squeezed each other tightly while we continued to hump and pump with everything we had.

I was close to orgasm, and I guess Melody could sense that. She pressed her legs tightly together and began to writhe and pump her hips upward until she came. As I exploded inside her, she let out a cry that I thought the whole neighborhood would hear.

We were both sweating profusely and clinging to one another, so we didn't cool down quickly. While we were both panting and gasping for air, Melody kept her pussy gripped tightly around my cock. She would gently contract her muscles every now and then to get the remaining drops of semen out of my cock. This was the first time I had ever been milked for everything I had. As we lay on the bed next to each other, I told her she was the best I'd ever had.

I asked her if I could take a shower, and she said she'd join me. I turned on the water and adjusted the temperature. We both got into the shower. After I washed myself off, I helped her wash her back. I lathered her up with soap and ran my hands over her breasts and between her legs. We both got steamed up again, and soon were ready for round two.

I raised her left leg up, slid my cock into her wet cunt and fucked her against the shower wall. We both came again, and then finished our shower. We dried ourselves off with big, fluffy towels. I got dressed, but she stayed wrapped in her towel. She climbed into bed naked, and I decided to call it a night and head home. I drove about five miles toward my house, then made a U-turn and returned to Melody's place for the night. I just couldn't stay away.

This affair continued until we went our separate ways. But I'll always be grateful for the opportunity to experience seven years of stored-up sexuality in one absolutely fabulous night.—*N.A., Tucson, Arizona*

COMELY COED COMES ON TO TEACHER—AND SOON THEY'RE PETTING

I am a graduate student at a midwestern university. I am considered average-looking and have never had a problem getting a pretty coed in my bed. Last semester I was assigned to teach an entry-level psychology class that most freshmen are required to take. The class was scheduled for late afternoon, and the campus was very quiet at that time.

On the first day of class, an attractive girl sat in the first row, right in front of my desk. Her eyes followed me all around the classroom. After the class ended, I stayed at my desk to finish up some paperwork. When I looked up, the girl from the first row was standing in front of me. She introduced herself as Mikki. She was petite, standing only about five feet tall. At six foot five, I towered over her. Even though she was wearing a bulky sweater because of the cold weather, I could tell that her chest was huge.

Mikki told me that she had just transferred here from another college and didn't know anyone yet. She said that she had really enjoyed her first class at her new school and wanted to thank me. We sat in the classroom for at least an hour and just talked. Then she asked if I would help her move some furniture in her house. I said sure.

We both got into our cars, and I followed her to an old farmhouse about twenty miles away. She told me that friends of her parents who lived in Florida owned the place. They had offered to let her live there if she kept an eye on things.

The house had a beautiful stone fireplace in the family room. I offered to start a fire, and she said that she would make me dinner if I helped her move some stuff upstairs.

Mikki led me to her bedroom. There was a big trunk in the middle of the floor. She asked if I could move it into the spare bedroom next door. After I moved it, Mikki called me back into her room. She was standing on her bed, wearing a long robe. Extending her arms, Mikki said that I deserved a big hug for being so nice. I walked over to her. As I was about to hug her, she opened her robe. In front of me were the largest, whitest breasts I have even seen.

She pulled me close and smothered my face in those mammoth melons. I started to suck them like a man who was dying of thirst. Her nipples, which were at least a half inch in diameter, stuck out like pencil erasers.

I feasted on Mikki's tits for some time, then slid both of my hands down the front of her jeans. Her skin was so soft that I didn't want to lose contact with it. I unsnapped and unzipped her jeans, and let them fall to her knees. Mikki had an orgasm as I pulled her panties off. I laid her down on the bed and started licking up the succulent juices that were flowing from her pussy like a mountain stream. She was screaming in ecstasy and thrashing her head from side to side. My eight-inch dick was so hard it almost hurt. It yearned to be released.

After her third orgasm, I unleased my love-stick from my pants. Mikki started sucking on it while massaging my balls. I knew I was close to orgasm, so I warned her I was about to come. She continued to suck, and my cock erupted, sending spurt after spurt of love-nectar into her mouth. She didn't let up until every drop was milked from my body.

I collapsed on the bed next to her, and she started to massage my cock to get me hard again. Once erect, I rolled her over and entered her furry love-canal. The warmth and tightness was unbelievable. I kept pumping while she had orgasm after orgasm. As her body shuddered and quaked, I filled her up with my cream. Afterward I lay down next to her. While I caressed her breasts, Mikki told me that she was madly in love with me, even though we had just met that day. I felt the same way toward her. At that moment, my only goal was to give her as much pleasure as I could. We embraced and kissed deeply. I removed the rest of her clothes as well as my own. I wrapped her in a blanket and carried her down to the family room. I laid her in front of the fireplace and unwrapped her from her cocoon. As we lay side by side, I entered her and we proceeded to make love again. We stayed in this position for the remainder of the night, waking up to make love several times.

All this happened two months ago, and we have been living together ever since.—*R.B., Indianapolis, Indiana*

STUDLY HOUSEPAINTER SHOWS WANTON WIFE A FEW NEW STROKES

My husband Jerome and I have had a good sex life ever since we married seven years ago. I had been married before, but my first marriage didn't work out. In the year between marriages I'd had several lovers, and Jerome had been the best one. Since I don't climax easily, we often use a vibrator during intercourse to bring me to orgasm.

Jerome is a salesman, and he spends a lot of time on the road. When he's away, my vibrator and my fantasies keep me satisfied. I'm about five feet eight inches tall and have a rather large build. Though I'm not fat by any means, I have been described as voluptuous. My bust measures 42DD, and I have well-rounded hips and shapely legs. I work out regularly to keep my shape, and I'm proud of the way I look.

Not too long ago, Jerome's best friend Wayne unexpectedly showed up at our house. He and his wife had been having problems and had temporarily split up. To make matters worse, he'd been laid off his job. He told us he really needed to get away from it all and asked if he could stay with us for a few days. Of course, we said he could.

A few days later he heard us talking about having the house painted. He offered to do the job himself. We agreed that he would stay with us until the painting job was completed. The next morning he went into town to buy the supplies he needed. He started work on the house that afternoon.

I couldn't help but notice how his sweaty, muscular body glistened in the hot summer sun as he worked in just a pair of shorts and no shirt. I can't deny that I spent a bit of time looking out the window, watching him work and wondering what it would be like to fuck him.

When he got ready to paint the highest point on the house, he asked me to come out and hold the ladder steady for him. While he was up on the ladder, I looked up and couldn't believe my eyes. He wasn't wearing anything under his shorts, and they were so loose I could clearly see his penis! Unlike any other guy I'd ever made love with, he was uncircumcised. The sight made me so excited that I could feel my crotch getting damp. I decided right then and there that I had to have him.

When he finished painting the high part, I went into the house to fix us some lunch. I'd been dressing pretty conservatively since he arrived, usually wearing jeans and a loose-fitting top. That day, however, I changed into a pair of shorts and a halter top. Then I carried the lunch tray out to the patio, and called to him to come and eat. You should have seen the look on his face as he came around the house and caught sight of me! It seemed as if he couldn't believe his eyes! I just smiled as if nothing were out of the ordinary.

He sat down across the table from me. As we ate, his eyes were glued to my chest. Each time I reached for my glass, I intentionally bent over enough to show him some cleavage. I was getting more and more turned on watching his reactions. He appeared to be very nervous, yet it was obvious by the bulge in his shorts that he was turned on too.

When we finished eating, he picked up the tray loaded with the dirty dishes to carry it back into the house. He unsuccessfully tried to hide his erection with the tray. Back in the kitchen, he put the tray on the counter next to the sink, and I started washing the dishes. What happened next not only surprised but thrilled me. He stepped up behind me and put his arms around me, cupping both my breasts in his hands. He said, "You're so damn sexy. I just can't keep my hands off you!"

With that, I untied my halter top, giving him access to my tits, and leaned back against him. My hands soon found their way between our bodies and I squeezed Wayne's full, firm manhood. Never before had I felt such a big, hard dick. I knew it would be several hours before Jerome got home, and I didn't think I could wait that long to be satisfied. I moaned with pleasure as Wayne gently fondled my tits and tenderly squeezed my erect nipples.

Making a split-second decision, I said, "I want you to fuck me right here and now!" I spun around, pulled his shorts down and got my first good look at his enormous, uncircumcised rod. Standing at full attention, it had to be at least ten inches long and two inches wide. Even though I'd seen studs like this in X-rated movies, I'd never encountered one in real life. I wrapped both my hands around the shaft and still had a couple of inches left to suck. This was almost too good to be true.

Standing up, I pulled down my shorts and kicked them off. Wayne lifted me up on the kitchen table and slid his big dick right into me. I was so wet that it slid in easily. He began pumping wildly into my ready and willing snatch. Never before had I felt so completely filled. I climaxed twice while he continued to pump in and out. I'd never before done that with anyone. Suddenly he yelled out, "Come with me, baby!" and he shot a load into me that triggered yet another orgasm. As I lay there on the table, totally exhausted and totally satisfied, he pulled out, lowered his mouth to my love-box and began to work me over with his tongue.

Wayne stayed with us for another week, and each day we made love after lunch. Then he and his wife reconciled, and he moved back home. Since then we haven't had another opportunity to get together.—*Name and address withheld*

SLY OLD DOG FINDS THAT HE STILL HAS A FEW NEW TRICKS UP HIS SLEEVE

I'd always been somewhat dubious when I read letters in your magazine that discussed men reaching multiple orgasms. I'm sixty-five, and until recently, when I had the good fortune to meet one of the hottest women I have known in my fifty years of sexual activity, I had never experienced one myself.

My life changed one afternoon when I was pushing a shopping cart through the produce section of a local supermarket. I was daydreaming and generally feeling sorry for myself because my wife was out of town visiting relatives and would be away all week. But, to be honest, I was more concerned about what I was going to have for dinner and the fact that I would be eating alone than the fact that I wouldn't be having sex for a week.

Not watching where I was going, I bumped into a cart being pushed by a very attractive, well-dressed lady. Blue eyes smiled at me from a well-tanned face that was surrounded by the whitest hair I had ever seen. I said, "I'm sorry. I guess I was daydreaming."

Looking into my cart she said, "I can see why. A nice red wine, a bottle of 7UP, chips and dips spells only one thing: a wine-cooler party. The only thing I see missing is some good guacamole and an X-rated video."

Although I was taken aback by her remarks, I managed a quick comeback. "Well, the most important thing missing is the little woman. My wife's away visiting relatives."

The woman smiled and said, "Now that is cause for a long face and daydreaming. I was going to offer you my prizewinning recipe for guacamole, but I reserve that for party occasions only."

Not wanting to pass up the opportunity that seemed to be unfolding before me, I blurted out, "Well, I feel a party mood coming on. How about showing me what to buy to make that guacamole. I know a place where I can rent an X-rated flick. Why don't we have a party?" Then I thought, My God, what have I done? This woman isn't some cheap pickup. I'll deserve it if she slaps my face and keeps right on walking.

To my surprise and everlasting thanks, the smile never left those beautiful blue eyes. She said, "Sounds crazy, but why not? I live alone now. My husband passed away six months ago, and it's been a long time since I enjoyed a good party."

I selected avocados, limes, tomatoes and onions to her specifications, and went through the checkout line feeling like a teenager on his first date. Boy, was I high. Even my manhood was beginning to stand tall. In the parking lot I asked for her address, explaining that I wanted to run home and clean up a bit. She said, "Well, please don't get dressed up. Let's make this a relaxed, casual evening."

"Suits me fine," I answered. "But I'm not sure about the relaxed part."

"I know what you mean," she purred. "It's been a long time for me too."

I almost tore off my car door as I got in. At home in the shower I found myself with a hard-on, the likes of which I hadn't seen since I was a much younger man. I was fortunate to find a pair of old BVDs in my dresser drawer. I normally wear boxer shorts, but there was no way in hell a pair of boxer shorts was going to hide that raging boner. I selected a full red rose from the garden, tied it to a piece of fern, and off I went.

I didn't realize how excited I was until I got to her door. When she answered, she jokingly said, "What kept you? It's been fifteen minutes since we left the supermarket."

I laughed and replied, "I guess I'm a little excited about learning how to make guacamole."

She had changed into a sheer negligee that, with a little backlighting, revealed the firmest body I had seen in a long time. I was obviously staring, because she said, "I'm glad you like what you see. It takes a lot of time and energy to keep a sixty-year-old body in this kind of shape."

I apologized for staring and told her that there weren't many thirty-year-olds who could compare with her. She did a little pirouette and bowed with her arms outstretched, giving me a good, long look at a beautiful pair of tits. I was sure glad I had on the BVDs. The old pecker was about to burst a seam.

When I gave her the rose, she leaned forward and gave me a very soft kiss that lasted just long enough for us to make body contact. She smiled and said, "I thought you agreed to dress comfortable. You seem all bound up." But before I could respond, she grabbed my hand and said, "Come on, it's recipe time. Time to cool down with a cool one and learn the secrets of guacamole making."

While we drank wine coolers, munched chips and dip and made guacamole, she told me that her husband's illness had been one that slowly took away his virility. At first they'd tried X-rated videos, which was why she'd made the crack in the supermarket. At the mention of the video, I slapped myself on the forehead and apologized for forgetting to pick one up. "I guess I was just too excited," I confessed.

She said, "Not to worry. I have a collection of X-rated videos categorized by subject." She told me that it had been almost two years since she'd last had sex, that she'd been married twice and that she had only slept with three men in her life. Her first husband had restricted sex to the missionary position twice a week. Her sex life had improved with her second marriage, but then her husband took sick. The X-rated flicks had helped for a while, but had really only served to open her eyes to just how enjoyable sex could be. With her husband's debilitating illness, sex became frustrating, to say the least.

As she refilled my glass, she said, "I really don't know what turned me on to you in the market. I don't normally come on to strangers that way. But the rose you brought—not to mention the bulge in your pants—makes me think that tonight will be a good thing."

By the time the avocado dip was nearly gone, we were working on our third wine cooler and I was beginning to feel very mellow. As many of you probably know, a perfect guacamole requires a lot of tasting to get the right balance between the lime juice and salt. Babette turned simple tasting into an art form. She'd dip her fingers into the mixing bowl and then slide them into my mouth or hers. When it was my turn to taste, she dipped in with two fingers, thus giving me a chance to lick the avocado from between her fingers. When she tasted, she used only one finger and ever so slowly slid it into her mouth, closing her lips around it before pulling it out, all the while holding my attention with her twinkling baby blues. To say the least, our tasting rapidly turned into one hell of an erotic episode.

Realizing that this couldn't go on forever without me shooting a load into my jeans, I reached over, cupped her chin in my hand and brought her lips to mine. As before, the kiss was soft and our lips barely touched, but it was enough to send tremors clear to my toes. I slowly ran my tongue across her lips, hoping to entice her to open them so we could enjoy a little French-kissing. Although they remained closed to my probing tongue.

When the kiss ended, she held me with her eyes and ever so slowly traced the outline of my lips with her finger. My God, I thought, another wave of sensation like that and I'll come for sure. As it was, my shorts were soaking wet. Sensing my agitation, she said, "Let's call the dip done and move to the comfort of the TV room."

When we had arranged fresh wine coolers on the table in the TV room, I took both of Babette's hands in mine and slowly pulled her toward me. We kissed, and once again it was soft but extremely sensuous. This time my tongue found an opening and was welcomed by the tip of her tongue inscribing little circles around mine.

Without breaking contact, I sat her down and slowly eased her to a reclining position on the couch, with me kneeling next to her on the floor. I began kissing her cheek and slowly tracing the outline of her ear with my tongue. As I darted my tongue into her ear once or twice, I felt her body tremble. I tenderly kissed each eyelid as I moved to the other ear. By now her body was moving in slow, sensuous gyrations, and I began to hear soft moans of pleasure. I moved down to the cleft between her lovely breasts, letting my tongue explore until I located the nipple. Now her body was moving uncontrollably, and her moans were quite audible.

She pressed her breasts together so I could suck both nipples at the same time. After bringing both nipples to their maximum firmness, I moved slowly down her stomach, flicking my tongue from side to side. When I reached her pubic hair, her legs were spread wide and the musky odor of her juicy pussy almost drove me mad with desire. I raised one of her legs over my shoulder, thinking I'd slowly work my way down to her clit. She couldn't wait, though. She arched her back and shoved her pussy into my face, moaning, "Suck my pussy. I'm coming!" Of course, I obliged.

I don't know how long I ate her pussy, alternating between sucking her clit and tongue-fucking her tunnel, but it seemed like she came forever. Wave after wave swept through her body until I thought she would pass out. I couldn't believe a pussy could get so hot and wet.

When she finally returned from her trip to nirvana, she said, "Oh, God, that was good. I've never had an orgasm that strong. Now give me your cock. I want to suck you till your balls are drained dry."

I was so charged up that my hands could hardly get my pants and underwear down. My cock was so excited that it was throbbing. As Babette took my cock in her hand, she began moaning and seemed to be trembling all over. I was sure she had come again. Controlling herself as much as possible, she ran her tongue around my ready-to-burst cockhead, slowly taking in more and more of my pulsing cock until I was fully down her throat. She closed her lips, pressed my cock against the roof of her mouth with her tongue and contracted her throat muscles. As she pulled back, she worked her tongue back and forth, paying particular attention to the sensitive underside. As she started down again, I knew that I couldn't take any more, so I pulled free, spread her legs and entered her pussy. Once I was in, she spread her labia, arched her back so her clitoris would be stimulated by my cock and screamed, "Fuck me fast and hard." Unfortunately the fast and hard lasted for about four strokes, and then I started to come like gangbusters. Never had I experienced so strong and long-lasting an orgasm.

When I sat up and accepted the wine cooler that Babette offered, I must have looked sad because she asked me, "Is something wrong?"

I explained, "I didn't want to come yet, because I knew that would mean the end of the evening. I always want to just roll over and go to sleep after sex."

In a low voice just above a whisper, she answered, "Tonight you are going to break all kinds of old habits. Tonight you are going to come and come until you are bone dry. And speaking of bone dry, let's break for a shower. I could use a good scrub-down. I didn't know my pussy could get so juicy, and you must have shot a gallon of come."

She took a sip of wine cooler, swirled it around in her mouth and, without swallowing, pushed my half-hard cock in and began tonguing my cockhead. The cool bubbly drink tickled the tender skin under the head, and, to my surprise and great pleasure, the old boy started to grow again. This was going to be a night to remember.

When I was fully hard, she led me by the cock to the bathroom and turned on the shower. As the water flowed over our bodies, we again shared a soft, tender, passionate kiss. Then she said, "Let's see if the stall is big enough to accommodate the 69 position." She spread out a couple of towels, lay down and spread her legs. I dove in.

The feel of the cool water splashing on my back and the scent of her hot, wet pussy drove me wild. We switched positions, putting her on top, and I found that licking the water cascading off her bushy pussy was a lot of fun. We decided the shower was getting a little cramped, so we jumped into bed without even bothering to towel off.

Taking the top position, I began to slowly lick her pussy, going down one side of her crotch, across the bottom and up the other side, each time getting closer to the center of action. As I would dart across the top, just brushing her clitoris, she would thrust her pelvis up in the air, trying to maximize the contact with her clit. At the same time she would take all of my cock into her mouth. When I finally began working down the side of her labia, she would match my actions with in-and-out motions on my cock. As I crossed over at the bottom, I darted my tongue into her snatch, and she swiveled her tongue around my swollen cockhead, flicking her tongue against the tender underside. When my tongue was between her labia, moving up toward her clit, she was taking more and more cock down her throat. When I reached the clit, I began sucking on it. She again pressed my cock against the roof of her mouth with her tongue and contracted her throat muscles.

We came together in long waves of pleasure. We were both sweaty again, so we went back to the shower, which was still running. We showered slowly, letting the cool water rejuvenate our still-excited bodies. I found myself getting aroused again. Although it wasn't a young man's hard-on anymore, it was still harder than normal.

We dried one another with soft, fluffy towels. Our kisses were now a little more forceful and our tongues moved a little faster. When I was as hard I was going to get, she took me by the rod and led me back to the TV room. She looked through a stack of videos, chose one and said, "Let's watch a movie and relax a little." My God, I thought, how can an X-rated movie be relaxing?

The video she had chosen was a series of bloopers made during the filming of various adult videos. Some of them were really pretty funny. You might say it was just what the doctor ordered to relieve our tensions. After the movie, we fucked in as many different positions as we could think of. Babette came many more times, but I must admit that one more good one turned out to be my last.

Although I am very happily married, Babette and I have a standing golf date every Saturday morning. And although my scores aren't what they were that first night, I am shooting way over par on a regular basis. For a sixty-five-year-old man, I am still hanging in there pretty good, thanks to that blue-eyed bombshell Babette.—M.T., Naples, Florida

ROCK 'N' ROLL DRUMMER GETS A FEW HOT LICKS FROM A LUSTFUL TEENAGE FAN

I've been playing the drums in local bands ever since I turned eighteen. It's not a bad way to make a living, although it ain't exactly the big time! I'm forty-two years old now, married and a little bit thicker around the middle, but much to my surprise I still get an occasional nibble from sweet young things who have an urge to rock and roll.

I went shopping last fall for some new threads to wear on stage, and of course I fell right into The Gap. Most of their stuff is for the younger set, but I finally snagged a pair of blue jeans and a nifty hooded sweatshirt. A salesclerk opened up a fitting room for me so I could try them on. The clerk recognized me from our regular Friday night gig at a nearby club, and as soon as he mentioned the name of my band, the two female voices in the adjoining cubicle, who'd been chattering away like a couple of silly little squirrels, stopped.

"Shhh!" one of them whispered. "He's in that band we saw at Joe's last week."

Teeny-boppers. You gotta love 'em. I smiled indulgently, enjoying all the mysterious rustling and unzipping going on next door, and wondering what the two of them looked like. The one who'd done the shushing had a slightly breathless voice that turned me on sight-unseen—especially when she made an obvious effort to be clearly heard through the thin wall between us.

"Mmmm, I just love this little top!" she gushed. "Look how it matches the flowers on my bra!"

I made a mental note of that and gathered up my gear. When I left the dressing room, the girls cracked open their door to give me the once-over as I passed. I heard a muffled round of girl-giggles and another shushing sound. Then I heard the footsteps of somebody following right behind me.

"You're the drummer, right?" asked a breathless voice just as I reached the cash register. I turned around to see the cutest teenager gazing up at me soulfully from underneath an adorable bob of tousled black hair. "Gosh, you guys are just so great!"

She told me her name was Karen, and she attended the local college. She was a deliciously ripe eighteen-year-old sophomore, with a trim teenage tummy and a saucy, round rump. She pushed the sleeves of her soft gray sweater above her elbows as we chatted, twitched her hips around bewitchingly inside her tight white chinos and seemed just as pleased as a playful puppy when she caught me eyeing the inviting swell of her big, creamy boobs. Just a sweet little hot-pants virgin, I warned myself before I asked what had happened to her friend.

"Oh, her," she shrugged, pursing her pouty red rosebud lips. "She had to get her daddy's car back home before it turns into a pumpkin or something."

That, of course, left her positively stranded, and Karen just giggled and wiggled her cute little butt until I offered to give her a lift. Her nipples stiffened as she accepted my offer.

She flirted and squirmed up a storm as we drove, and by the time I pulled into her dark, hedge-lined driveway, I had a hard-on from the scent of her juicy body. She batted her long black lashes in the moonlight, and hit me up for a copy of the cassette we'd been selling the night she'd seen my band play.

"What do you want for it?" she asked innocently after I'd reached into the backseat and fished one out.

I leaned over impulsively and brushed her moist, red lips with mine. "I want to see the flowers on your bra," I heard myself croaking, and my dick slithered up my belly like a snake.

Karen blushed with becoming modesty, her dark eyes gleaming with suppressed excitement, and then slowly lifted her soft gray sweater to reveal her hungry young jugs. "Like this?" she whispered.

We kissed again, deeply this time, and my hand strayed up to cup her sweet, warm fullness. Karen cooed and squirmed around to offer herself more completely, and I teased her hard brown nipples through the pink-and-blue-flowered cotton of her brassiere.

"Oh, gosh," she moaned softly as I licked and suckled at her tits. "Oh, please, I—Mmmm!"

I slid my hand down between her plump, willing thighs and stroked her pussy through her damp designer chinos. She groaned with pleasure and splayed herself for me like the hottest little whore in town, frantically grinding her snatch against my pressing, probing fingers. I put her hand on the thickness of my big, stiff dick, and she started shaking and squealing with delight, practically creaming in her jeans. "Oh, baby! Oh, honey! Oh, please!" she gasped, her plump, firm ass wriggling wantonly. Then she stiffened and clutched my hand to her crotch as her cunt exploded. "Oh, honey, that feels so good!"

I kept probing her muff until she'd humped herself dry. Her fingers shyly caressed my cock as she dreamily rested her head in the hollow of my shoulder.

"Oh, shit," she suddenly hissed in dismay, a guilty blush creeping across her face. "It's really late. I gotta go now." Before I could move a muscle, she was yanking down her soft gray sweater, snatching up her purse and the tape and disappearing into her house like a shot.

"Fuckin' virgins," I muttered in frustration. I had to haul my raging hard-on back home, wait patiently for my wife to get home after working the second shift and then bang the living daylights out of her until three in the morning, trying to screw the silly little squirm out of my system.

I couldn't stop thinking about her, though, and I guess little Karen must have been feeling the same way, because three days later I got a call from her just after my wife had left for work. She told me she'd gotten my number from a friend of a friend who books the bands at Joe's, and added that she just had to talk to me one more time.

"So talk." I shrugged.

"Not on the phone," she pleaded prettily. I acquiesced, and an hour later she was standing in my living room, fidgeting with the hem of a skirt and apologizing "for acting like such a baby the other night."

"It's just that I never . . ." she stammered, rocking her hips to and fro. "I mean I just never let anybody get me that, um . . . you know . . ." She looked up at me, shame-faced. "You m-make me want to . . . do things," she barely whispered.

I got up from my easy chair and kissed her. "What kind of things?" I asked, pulling her close.

"Everything," she sighed, the scent of her mounting excitement rising from between her legs.

"Then take off all your clothes," I told her.

Karen hesitated for a moment, then slowly eased that same gray sweater over her tousled black hair. She'd left her flowered bra at home, and her naked tits stood out full and creamy above the smooth, flat tautness of her trembling tummy.

"I've got goose bumps all over," she giggled, beautifully abashed, her long brown nipples fiercely erect as she let her short, flared skirt drop down around her ankles. She stood there shyly in her scanty, blue cotton briefs.

I sat down in front of her on a low leather ottoman. "You are a beautiful young woman, Karen," I murmured, sucking each of her big, tender breasts in turn. She shivered involuntarily when I grazed my tongue across the salty-sweet skin just above the waistband of her panties, which were quite moist.

"Oh, oh, oh," she mewed softly. "What are you gonna do?"

She whimpered just a little when I pulled down her panties and exposed her surprisingly thick black bush. I began to kiss and nibble lovingly at the sensitive flesh of her hot, moist thighs.

Soon they were quivering with passionate desire, and Karen moaned and spread her legs to steady herself.

I cupped the plump, buttery globes of her ripe, round rump, and licked along the length of her glistening gash. "Oh! Oh! Ahhh!" she blushed, thoroughly embarrassed and totally aroused now.

She was shaking so hard that she could barely stand up. I wiggled my tongue deep into her juicy twat, and started sucking up her pearly essence.

"Oh, lick it! Lick it! Oh, my God, I've never felt anything so yummy before!" she panted with guilty delight, her sweet teenage nectar flowing freely down her legs. Her pussy bucked and squirmed in an erotic frenzy against my face the whole time. "Oh, God, honey, you're gonna make me come!"

I stood up quickly, pushed her gently to her knees and began to unbuckle my belt. "Oh, my," Karen blushed, moistening her pouty lips in uneasy anticipation as I squeezed a drop of clear fluid from the tip of my steaming peter and watched it roll down one of her proud, young boobs. "Oh, honey, I had no idea your cock was so big!"

"Do it, Karen," I urged her, running my hands through her short, tousled hair. "Suck my dick, you sweet little bitch."

She slowly took me into the heavenly wet warmth of her mouth and swirled her tongue experimentally around the swollen purple head. "Mmmm, mmmm, mmmmphh," she grunted happily as my rampant rooster slurped noisily in and out. As she wrapped her soft hands firmly around the thick base, she admitted, "I've never been this turned on in my life."

The sight of her red lips stretched around my cock drove me wild, and the sweet little cocksucker let me fuck her mouth until I was slick enough to stick it up her tight cunt—and too damn horny to put it off for another minute!

I spread Karen out on our Persian carpet and gave her heaving tits one last lick. "Oh, yes, it feels so good!" she squealed when I rubbed the tip of my dick all along her creamy slit. "Oh, honey, fuck my pussy!"

I was shaking with the effort to control myself as I eased my cock into her hot, wet honey-hole, and Karen only increased my excitement by instantly coming all over my cock. She babbled and cooed and encouraged me ardently as I buried a couple of inches in her eager snatch. She shrieked with pleasure when I lifted her knees up over my shoulders and plunged into her up to my balls with one quick, forceful thrust.

"Oh, yes!" she hissed, clamping her pussy muscles around my cock and grinding her pelvis into mine. Soon we were screwing each other urgently. Karen's legs were wrapped tightly around my back while I held on to her ass-cheeks and buried my cock in her dripping quim again and again.

"Oh, fuck me, honey. Fuck me!" she begged me, her sweet face shining with perspiration as she writhed and humped shamelessly beneath me.

Then I pulled out and positioned her on all fours. I entered her from behind while she glanced back over her saucy little bottom with a blush of bashful reproach and passionate abandon. I dicked her like a corkscrew, my balls tight and churning, and she cried out ecstatically with the thrill of her umpteenth long, hard orgasm when I started squirting wads of jism into her luscious cunt.

Karen let me have her one more time before she left, crawling shyly into my lap as I sat in my easy chair. Straddling me, she squatted down lewdly on my stiff, slick shaft and stroked us slowly into sweet oblivion.

But then she had to get home for dinner. I gave her a band T-shirt, and she gave me a long, lingering soul-kiss. After walking her to her car, I went back up to my apartment and thanked my lucky stars for rock and roll.—*T.M., Muncie, Indiana*

Three-for-all

BUBBLE, BUBBLE, WIFE TAKES ON A DOUBLE IN THE HOT TUB

I thought I'd write and tell you about the most erotic adventure that my wife and I have ever had. For years we've been avid fans of your magazine. One of our most exciting fantasies, which we'd talked about for years, has been for my wife to suck my cock while my best friend fucks her. We'd talked about it for years, and it finally became a reality the other night.

After an exciting weekend of fucking and sucking, Helen and I decided that we would finally broach the subject of a threesome with Matthew, my best friend. We invited him over for a dip in the hot tub. I wanted to skinny-dip to help set the mood, but since my wife is a little shy, we started out wearing our swimsuits.

After relaxing in the tub for about fifteen or twenty minutes, I decided it was time to break the ice and get the ball rolling. I looked at Helen and then at Matthew and said, "This is the first time that we've been in here and haven't fucked our brains out." Everyone just kind of looked at each other and smiled. I figured I needed to help things along just a little more, so I turned to my wife and said, "Don't you owe Matthew a blowjob?"

Helen replied, "I don't know. Maybe." I pulled my wife over on top of me and started to bury my tongue into her mouth. While I was hugging her and kissing her, I began to rub my hands over her tits. At first she pushed my hands away, but as I continued to kiss her she placed one hand on my dick and the other arm around my neck. I lifted myself up to the edge of the tub and started to untie her bikini top. As I did that, Matthew maneuvered himself around behind her and started to rub her back. And as he worked his way down to her ass he grabbed her bikini bottom and began to pull it down.

As I continued to knead her tits and squeeze her nipples, she began to moan and started tugging down my trunks. She stiffened momentarily as Matthew inserted his fingers into her pussy and began to slowly finger-fuck her. As she moaned louder and neared her first orgasm, Matthew picked her up, turned her over and started to tongue-fuck her.

She reached the most intense orgasm that she has ever had while I cradled her head in my lap and continued to play with her tits. All at once my wife turned over and started to suck my dick like never before. She sucked my cock deeper into her throat than she ever had. She stopped long enough to glance over her shoulder and say to Matthew, "Shove your cock into my cunt now!"

Matthew grabbed her hips and began to fuck her hard. Even though she had my dick in her mouth, she started to scream with the most intense and vocal orgasm that I have ever witnessed. Her orgasm triggered mine, and as she came, I started to fill her mouth with my semen. She eagerly swallowed every drop, even though she usually doesn't swallow.

But Matthew hadn't finished yet, and he continued to pump her cunt. My wife met each of his thrusts with one of her own. I held her in my arms as Matthew continued to fuck her. All at once Matthew stiffened and shot his come into her.

After all that, I thought my wife would be finished, but she turned around and said to Matthew, "I guess I do owe you a blowjob." Well, that started everything up again. We probably tried at least twenty different positions before we'd finally had enough, but that's another story.—*L.K., Topeka, Kansas*

CURIOUS COUPLE TAKES A LOOK AT THE SWINGING SIDE OF LIFE

My wife and I have been married about fourteen years. With two kids and the challenges of parenting, our sex life had been pretty boring and mundane. One day a close friend of mine confided that he and his wife had tried swinging and found it to be a boon to their love life.

During a somewhat mechanical lovemaking session with my wife Ivy, I whispered the revelation my old college pal had shared with me. All of a sudden Ivy came alive as my hand rubbed her beautiful mound. She asked me what I thought about the idea. As we talked, our passion increased, and her juices flowed as I fucked her with one and then two fingers. She was out of control as her nightgown climbed over her hips, exposing her glistening pussy. I asked her who she would select to swing with, and to my surprise she hissed the name of a close mutual friend, Chad.

We spent the following weekend at Ivy's parents' beach house. Chad and his wife also had a house close by. We all spent Saturday on the beach. I managed to get Chad alone for a few minutes, so I broached the subject of swinging with him. He told me that he was sure his wife would never agree to it, but that he would sure be game. He said that Ivy and I should meet him later in the evening, adding that he would bring along a canister of nitrous oxide that he had brought home from his dental practice so we could enjoy the sensual high it provided.

I mentioned Chad's invitation to Ivy later in the day, and she was eager to try the new sensation. Chad stopped by our place about ten, and we got into his car for a drive down to the beach. It was a beautiful night. Ivy sat up front with Chad, and I sat in the backseat. We shared a joint, and then Chad broke out the nitrous oxide. I inhaled the gas first. I couldn't believe the erotic sensation that came over me. I passed the canister to Ivy, and she immediately sucked in a lungful of nitrous oxide. I reached up to the front seat and began rubbing her tits through her loose-fitting shirt and kissing her ear. She responded immediately.

With the tube still between her lips and my hands all over her tits, I told her we were being unfair to Chad. With that she reached over and began to massage his prick. Chad reacted by sliding his hand up the miniskirt she was wearing. We passed the canister of nitrous oxide around while Chad and I ran our hands all over Ivy's quivering body. Ivy managed to release Chad's huge prick from the constraints of his jeans. To my amazement she bent over and started eagerly sucking it. After a few minutes she came up for air, turned and kissed me on the mouth. Her tongue flicked in and out of my mouth as she kept repeating that she loved me and she wanted to make both Chad and me very happy.

The intoxicating fragrance of her womanhood filled the car. I suggested that we take a walk on the beach. It was a dark, moonless night and, as we walked, Chad and I took turns kissing and feeling up Ivy. We fell on the sand in a tangle of limbs and mouths, licking, sucking and groping. Ivy kept repeating that she wanted to fuck and suck us at the same time. I watched Chad pull up her skirt and pull down her laced-trimmed bikini panties. She moaned as Chad's prick entered her soaking pussy. I loved watching my friend fuck my wife. Ivy was in ecstasy as she moaned, "Fuck me. Fuck me."

I pulled out my cock and rubbed it across my wife's lips. Her mouth responded instantly as she licked at it with a wild passion. As her mouth, tongue and saliva engulfed my cock, Chad's movements quickened. We responded in unison. As he fucked her and tweaked her exposed nipples, Ivy sucked greedily on my cock. I watched the action and enjoyed the sensations. When Chad warned that he was about to come, Ivy's hips pumped faster. All at once we all moaned uncontrollably as Chad and I shot our wads.

Since that summer night, Ivy has gotten more in touch with her womanhood. Together we have seduced a close friend of hers, and she recently admitted that she'd gotten it on with a friend of ours who was visiting from out of town. She described in detail how she'd let him fuck her in the garage after she picked him up at the train station.—*R.V., Mobile, Alabama*

THERE'S MORE THAN A SUMMER SAUSAGE IN HER PICNIC BASKET

The telephone rang as I stepped out of the shower early one Friday evening last summer. I had been expecting my girlfriend Dot to return my call, so I rushed to the phone. It was good to hear her sexy voice. I'd been out of town for several days and was horny as hell. I was really looking forward to being with her that night.

"I'll be right over," she said. "I'm bringing supper and a surprise, so don't dress up."

"I don't have anything on, but I am getting a hard-on talking to you," I admitted. "Hurry over before I jerk off."

"Don't do that. I'll be there in a few minutes," she replied.

I put a couple of bottles of our favorite red wine on ice and straightened up the apartment. I had just finished putting clean sheets on the bed when the doorbell rang. I knew it was Dot, so I slipped on a lightweight robe, letting it hang open so that my cock poked out.

I opened the door. "You certainly are hot to trot," exclaimed Dot as she stared at me. She put down the basket of goodies she was carrying and hugged me. I wrapped my arms around her, pressing my dick into her crotch. Our tongues danced in each other's mouth. My hands sought and caressed her breasts. I heard someone chuckle and looked over Dot's shoulder. A tall, slim, blond guy was leaning in the open doorway. He wore tight white slacks, a T-shirt and a big grin on his face.

"Hey, what's going on, Dot?" I exclaimed. "Who's this guy?"

"He's the surprise I told you I was going to bring," Dot replied. "He's a good friend of mine. Come on in, Adam. I'd like you to meet Jordan."

Adam walked in, closing the door behind him. We shook hands. He was very well built and spoke in a soft voice. I suddenly felt almost naked as his eyes roamed over my body.

"Well, you certainly did surprise me, Dot. Make yourselves at home while I put on some clothes. There's wine in the ice bucket."

"Don't dress on my account, Jordan," Adam said. "I'm a stripper. In fact, that's how I met Dot. I met her at a birthday party I performed at. I hung around and went home with her that night. We still get together once in a while, but there's nothing serious between us—just fun and games."

I opened a bottle of wine and got three glasses. "This is going to be fun," said Dot. "I've always wanted to have two good-looking studs at the same time." She glanced hopefully in my direction.

"It's okay with me," I said. It wasn't what I'd had in mind, but I was game. "But I don't want to be the only one who's half naked."

"Come on, Adam, show us how you strip," said Dot. She pulled me down on the couch beside her.

"Okay, but I usually wear a costume. How about some music?" Dot turned on my CD player. Adam began gyrating to the beat of the music. Twisting and turning, he kicked off his loafers. Then he ran his hands over his hips and rubbed his crotch. He caressed his chest and slowly pulled his T-shirt over his head. Then he undid his belt and opened the waist of his slacks. As he did bumps and grinds, he slowly pulled down his zipper.

I'll admit it was fascinating. Dot stroked my thigh, then opened my robe and tickled my swelling cock.

Adam lowered his pants and kicked them away. He danced around the room in only white bikini briefs, moving closer and closer to Dot. He was obviously becoming aroused.

Dot reached out for him as he thrust his crotch at her. She put her fingers inside the waistband of his briefs and pulled them down until the base of his cock was exposed. Adam pulled them off and pointed his hardening dick at Dot. It was massive, thick and long, at least seven or eight inches. She grasped it in both hands and leaned forward. Her tongue ran over and around the head before her lips encircled it. She sucked in about half its length.

I wasn't sure how I felt about seeing Dot with another man, but it was still very exciting. I threw my robe on the floor.

Adam pulled back. "Not yet, Dot. We want you naked first. Jordan, let's strip her." Dot stood and we had her bare in a heartbeat. She looked more beautiful than ever. Hungry lust shone in her eyes. Our hands were all over her. Adam kissed her nipples and fondled her tits as I caressed her ass and slid a finger into her warm pussy. She sank to the floor. I placed a cushion under her head and spread her legs. She was writhing in ecstasy.

"Fuck me," she moaned. "Give me your big cocks. I can't stand it."

I aimed my rod at her pussy and leaned over so that the head touched her clit. I slid it up and down her slit before penetrating her cunt. Adam continued to tease her tits. She was going wild, thrashing and bucking, lost in the throes of passion. I'd never seen her so hot. I pumped into her faster and faster. "Give it to me. Don't stop. Harder, harder. I want it all!" she exclaimed. Then her body spasmed violently as she came. Her whole body tensed and convulsed. I kept on fucking her, trying to hold off my orgasm.

"Feed me your cock, Adam. I want you both at the same time," she begged. He held his dick so that she could suck it into her mouth. He slid more and more of it in as she tried to devour him.

I couldn't hold back any longer. The sight of Dot sucking Adam's huge cock as her cunt muscles tightened around my cock sent me over the edge. I spasmed and filled her with my come.

I leaned back, still plugged into her pussy, and watched as Adam's dick exploded in her mouth. Streams of come ran down her chin. Adam gave her a deep kiss and licked it off. We collapsed in a heap of arms and legs.

A glass of wine helped revive us. "Anyone getting hungry? For food, that is," I asked.

"Let's have a naked picnic," suggested Dot. I spread out a

blanket, and we were soon sprawled out on the floor, eating the food Dot had brought. I kept the wine flowing.

"Lie on your back, Jordan," said Dot. She poured wine into my navel and sucked it out.

"Save some for me," said Adam, and he did the same. Some of the wine ran down my stomach and into my pubic hair. Adam's tongue lapped it up. My cock began to enlarge as his face brushed against it.

"Your turn, Dot," I said. I poured wine on her tits, and Adam poured some in her navel, making sure that some ran onto her pussy. He lapped at her cunt lips as I licked her tits. Dot clamped her legs around Adam's head. He licked and probed with his tongue, bringing her to climax in just a couple of minutes.

My rigid cock strained for attention. "Adam, why don't you blow Jordan?" asked Dot. "I know you want to."

"If it's okay with Jordan," replied Adam.

I said, "Sure," as I leaned back on my elbows and spread my legs. My cockhead almost reached my belly button.

He gave me just about the best blowjob I've ever had. He knew just where and when to lick and suck in order to bring me to the brink of orgasm. He would stop, squeeze and then start again, taking me to an even higher level of excitement. I felt like my cock would burst each time, and then he would find a new way to drive me crazy. I couldn't take it any more when he sucked me into his throat. I convulsed and exploded. He took every drop of my come.

Dot had been fingering herself as she watched us in action. "Come here, Adam, you haven't fucked me yet," she reminded him. She got on her hands and knees. Adam rubbed his dickhead up and down her pussy lips, then plunged it into the hilt. Dot squealed with delight. Back and forth they rocked. Adam would pull almost all the way out and then slam it back into her as far as it would go. Finally he held her hips and pulled her to him tightly. The expression on his face told me that her cunt muscles had massaged him to climax. At the same time, Dot exclaimed that she was coming.

After they recovered, we showered, washing and drying each other.

Dot and Adam left soon afterward. Although I was bushed, I was happy and very satisfied. What a night! I went to sleep wondering what surprise Dot would bring the next time. Maybe a bisexual girl?—*J.L., Omaha, Nebraska*

HER SECRET WISH IS GRANTED WHEN LOVER SHARES HER FANTASY

I've always enjoyed making love to Garnet. What I really like is her willingness to explore all of her sexual feelings and expand her horizons. Recently, however, I took her to a plateau of excitement that even she didn't think was possible. Many times when we were reading *Penthouse Letters* I'd noticed that she got particularly excited by the pictorials and letters involving two women. She never actually came out and said that she wanted to experiment with another female, but I can usually read her pretty well, and I intuitively knew that she was definitely interested.

One day I got to thinking about this predilection of hers. Coincidentally, seeing two women in action had always been one of my fantasies, along with having a threesome with two women. I thought that it would be fun to live out this fantasy and thereby kill two birds with one stone.

I knew that our female friends would never consider such a scenario, so I was in a predicament. One day I picked up a swingers magazine at the local newsstand and turned to the personal ads. I scanned them, hoping to see a personal ad describing my fantasy. Sure enough, I found the following ad: "Bisexual woman seeks open couple to explore a threesome fantasy. I'm in my late twenties and athletic, with a good figure." There was a number to call to leave messages, so I dialed the number, punched in her mailbox code and left my name, number and a brief message asking her to give me a call.

A couple of days later I received a phone call. The lady on the other end of the line had a very sexy voice and explained that I had answered her personal ad. Her name was Monique. We talked for a few minutes and agreed to meet for drinks later that day. I couldn't wait, and had a hard-on for the rest of the day, fantasizing about what our meeting might lead to.

Monique looked very good in the sexy black miniskirt she wore to the bar that night—good enough to eat. Her tits were shapely and she had long, lean legs. Her black hair flowed down her back and served as a nice contrast to her pale white skin.

We hit it off well, and I told her my plan to introduce Garnet to some sapphic lovemaking. I was very careful to ask Monique the questions that I knew Garnet would want me to ask, since Garnet was still unaware of my plan and wouldn't have the opportunity to screen Monique. I was quite satisfied with all of her responses, and I decided that Monique would be the perfect addition to our bedroom.

Monique was quite excited by the prospect of joining us in bed, and gave me a fantastic blowjob in the car before I left. She told me that this was just the beginning of some exciting experiences between the three of us. We arranged for her to come to my place the next weekend.

That weekend I explained to Garnet that I had a new fantasy that I hoped she would allow me to fulfill. Garnet, her eyes quizzical, asked me what my fantasy was. I went on to tell her that I wanted to blindfold her and pleasure her body with my hands, my tongue and my long, stiff cock. She agreed immediately. What she didn't know is that I had arranged for Monique to let herself into my apartment and then join us in my bedroom at a prearranged time.

I told Garnet to lie on the bed with her arms and legs spread-eagle. I could see her pussy dripping with excitement and passion burning in her eyes. I knew that this was going to be quite a night. Her body looked fabulous. Her nipples were hard as erasers, and I lightly teased them with my tongue. Then I blindfolded her. We kissed passionately, our tongues battling each other. Starting with her face, I ran my hands lightly all over her body, tantalizing her with the touch of my soft hands exploring her body from head to toe. She was beginning to thrash on the bed as my fingers penetrated the wet folds of her pussy. I plunged my fingers in and out, rubbing the inside of her pussy, then reaching up to caress her clit again and again. Soon my pace quickened, and she came all over my fingers. My cock was as hard as a rock, and I wanted to be inside her, grinding her to yet another orgasm. The walls of her pussy were pulsating as I opened her up with my manhood. I went in all the way with one stroke, shivering with delight as her pussy engulfed me.

Looking up, I could see Monique standing in the doorway, watching us. I slid my fingers into Garnet's mouth so that Monique could see how much she loved the taste of her own juices. Garnet sucked on them eagerly, as I knew she would. I knew this excited Monique, because she started touching herself.

Garnet was in another world as I thrust in and out of her. The intense pleasure my rod provided for her caused her to scream out in ecstasy. The next chain of events was an incredible exchange of sexual passion. I pulled my cock out of Garnet and straddled her chest to feed it to her. It was coated with her come, and she really loved the taste. I could feel her jump in surprise when she felt another tongue slide across her pussy lips and Monique's hair caress her thighs. She paused as if to protest, but then succumbed to the pleasure Monique was giving her. She resumed sucking my cock with such force that I exploded in her mouth. At the same time, Garnet came all over Monique's face. It was clearly an intense orgasm from the way that her body spasmed and writhed.

I moved off Garnet's chest as Monique moved her lips up Garnet's body, tonguing her skin as she headed toward her lips. Garnet, in seventh heaven, licked and sucked her juices off of Monique's lips while feeding tastes of my load to Monique. Seeing the two of them together, pale skin contrasting with tan, black hair with red, and two pink, tongues clashing in heated passion, made my cock spring to life. Oh, what a sight it was! My eyes greedily drank it in.

I wanted to fuck Garnet again. But first I removed her blindfold so she could see the source of much of her pleasure. Then I sank my cock into her. Monique positioned her pussy over Garnet's mouth. Garnet got her first taste of another woman as I entered her. Moving and grinding and touching, in a tangle of arms and legs, it was obvious Garnet quickly got the hang of licking pussy as Monique's squeals of pleasure filled the air. We all came simultaneously in a rip-roaring triple orgasm.

We tried all kinds of positions that night. The girls straddled me, taking turns riding my face and cock as they fondled each other's breasts and kissed each other passionately. Garnet later thanked me for setting it all up by making mad, passionate love to me for the rest of the night.—*Name and address withheld*

MR. MANNERS' GUIDE TO PROPER THREESOME ETIQUETTE

I was filled with anticipation as I walked toward the house with the package under my arm. Although I had often fantasized about taking part in a threesome, this time it was for real. My friends Tal and Robin had invited me over to join them in a ménage à trois, and I was eagerly anticipating a night of total sexual bliss.

I knocked on the side door as I had done so many times before. Tal answered with a big grin on his face and asked me to come in. His wife Robin got me a wine cooler and we sat down to talk and listen to some music. Robin is a pretty woman, standing about five feet nine inches tall. She had a playful smile and beautiful tits. They were a nice size (36C's according to her husband), but I think it was more the shape that held my interest. They were always perky, with just the right amount of erect nipple to be noticeable. She was wearing a tight-fitting T-shirt, and I kept sneaking looks at her as we talked.

We'd only been talking for a few minutes when one of my favorite songs came on. I asked Robin to dance, and we ended up dancing through two or three songs. As we paused to catch our breath, she noticed the package I had brought. "What's this?" she asked. I told her it was a little something I had bought for her because I'd thought she'd look good in it. She opened the box, revealing a sexy black negligee. I had fantasized all week about seeing her in this negligee. It left little to the imagination, with a see-through inset for the breasts with spaghetti-strap supports. She blushed as she held it up. Tal and I agreed that she'd look great in it, and we convinced her to model it for us.

After she finished her drink, Robin excused herself. I noticed that she took the box with her as she left the room. It seemed to take a long time for her to return, and our anticipation was really building. When she came back she was wearing a robe, but I could see the top of the negligee underneath it. Tal immediately started teasing her about being inhibited, and we all laughed again.

Another good song came on. Tal and Robin started dancing as I watched. As they danced, Robin's robe loosened up. She was really getting into it. As she shimmied and gyrated through the song, I caught quick glimpses of her firm breasts. I was really getting excited. I could hardly wait for what was to come.

Just then a slow song came on. Tal turned down the lights. He held her close throughout the song. He was kissing her and running his hands all over her body. It gave me a great opportunity to really look her over. She had long, tan legs and a nice, tight ass. Robin works out frequently and it really shows. Suddenly Tal asked me if I wanted to dance with Robin while he got fresh drinks. Boy, did I! I took her tenderly in my arms.

We started swaying slowly to the music. Robin smelled wonderful. I closed my eyes as my member started to grow. I wondered if she could feel me getting hard. As the song progressed, we slowly explored each other with our hands. Her robe was completely open now. My hands slid up and down her sides. I caressed her back with long, slow strokes, moving closer to her ass each time. Her tits felt fantastic against my chest. My cock was throbbing as she ran her fingers up and down my sides, sending a chill up and down my spine.

We were both breathing pretty heavily by now, and I leaned down to give her a kiss. It was the longest, most passionate kiss I had ever experienced. Her tongue darted in and out of my mouth as her robe fell to the floor.

As Tal entered the room, I could tell he was surprised with the progress we had made. He handed me a drink and said something about it being his turn. Then Tal and Robin started really getting it on. She was rubbing his ass and stroking the front of his jeans. He was massaging one of her breasts and kissing her neck. I couldn't believe I was watching this incredible display of passion. He asked her to keep dancing as he sat down beside me.

Robin was slowly and sensually rubbing her body as she swayed and twisted in front of us. A strap had fallen from the negligee. The top of one of her breasts was exposed. Her eyes were closed as she cupped her breast and gently massaged her nipple. Her lips were parted and her head was thrown back. I looked over at Tal. He was stroking his cock and his eyes were glued to her every move.

Robin sashayed over to her husband. He leaned his head back on the couch as she began to lick the tip of his love-muscle. Mine was throbbing at this point. Just watching her suck on him was almost too much to bear. As I reached into my pants to pull out my prick, Robin's eyes were riveted on me. Her eyes widened as I exposed my cock. Although it's not as big as some, my cock is noticeably larger than her husband's. I could tell by her expression that she was excited about the idea of a big cock. She looked up at Tal, and he nodded in my direction, giving her the go-ahead she wanted.

She slid over between my knees. She began to lick my cock. Her husband had told me on several occasions that she was an expert in this department, but I still couldn't believe how good it felt. She slowly licked the head of my cock. She twirled her tongue around and around my cock while gently massaging my balls. I was in heaven! She went up and down my shaft like she hadn't touched a cock in weeks. Her tongue teased and tantalized me as she ran it along the sensitive underside of my cock. Then she sprinkled rapid, sucking kisses all along its length, pausing to give the tip of my cock a tender French kiss. The sensation was incredible as her tongue probed my slit. When she completely engulfed my cock in her mouth and began bobbing her head up and down, I knew I wouldn't be able to last very long. She paused and came up for air for a few minutes, giving me a chance to regain my control.

Tal continued to stroke his member. He was really getting horny watching his beautiful wife suck on my big cock. The pre-come was oozing out of his prick as he stroked. He got behind her and began rubbing his cock up and down her slit. Robin was really getting hot now. She was begging for Tal to fuck her, but he just kept rubbing. Then Tal said he wanted to trade places. I think he wanted her to get the benefit of feeling my cock in her. As Robin wrapped her mouth around her husband's cock, he let out a low moan. I took his place behind her.

I paused for just a moment to take in the sight. Robin's back was arched right in front of me. Her ass was sticking up in the air and her juices were flowing down her thighs. She was driving Tal up the wall with her blowjob, and me out of my mind with lust.

As I held the head of my prick at her opening, Robin began to wriggle toward me. She wanted me. She wanted to be fucked, and she wanted it now! I jammed my meat into her with a powerful thrust. She let out a gasp. Her pussy was so hot and tight that I could feel her pussy muscles gripping my cock like a vise. I hoped I could last long enough to give her the pleasure she so rightly deserved.

As I was giving her the fucking of her life, Tal was really groaning. She was going up and down on him like there was no tomorrow. All three of us were moaning loudly. I started to feel a tingle in my balls, and I knew I was losing control. I screamed "I'm coming!" and began to unload more jism into Robin's snatch than I thought was possible. At the same time, Tal began to shoot his load. Robin's entire body began shuddering, and Tal's cock slipped from her mouth. Tal spurted his love juices all over as Robin screamed in ecstasy. We all collapsed in a heap on the floor.

Finally I got dressed and headed for the door. I turned to take one last look at Robin and Tal. They were curled up on the couch, murmuring endearments to each other. It was an experience I'll never forget, and I'm thankful that I was able to share such an intimate experience with my friends.—*J.M., Saint Petersburg, Florida*

WHAT'S A BEST FRIEND FOR? CONNUBIAL COMRADERY, OF COURSE

Many times while Ronnie and I were having sex that was not particularly inspired, my friend Barry came to mind. And when Ronnie and I got married, I continued to think about threesomes. Ronnie was hesitant, of course, but I knew she'd love it if she'd try it. I made a plan.

One night, knowing we were going to fuck right after dinner, I sneaked into another room and phoned Barry. I told him what I had in mind and asked him to come over. He agreed to watch through our bedroom window, and when he saw us playing around in bed walk right in on us. Ronnie and Barry are good friends, so I hoped she wouldn't be too shocked.

Ronnie and I were soon in bed, on our sides, enjoying a hot 69. As Ronnie kissed and sucked the tip and shaft of my penis, I was applying broad strokes to her pussy that had her dripping onto the sheets.

We were in the throes of passion when Barry walked in. Ronnie's mouth was stuffed, and she was too carried away by sexual ecstasy to complain.

My friend sat on the edge of the bed and removed his T-shirt. His sleek, firm body excited me, and I knew it would excite my wife as well. Barry smoothly stripped the rest of his clothes off, and I gently turned my wife over to face him. He gently caressed her small, warm ass, and ran a finger lightly over her creamy slit. Ronnie seemed in heaven! I felt her up as well, while Barry's free hand was pleasuring his own stiff cock, which was already sticking straight up.

Barry stood up and offered to feed Ronnie his cock. To my surprise, she unhesitatingly guided it into her mouth. My dick was at maximum hardness, and throbbing as I kissed my wife on her cheeks, feeling Barry's cockhead massaging her mouth through them. I gently squeezed his big ball sac, while pinching and squeezing my wife's erect nipples.

Suddenly she popped Barry's cock out of her mouth, spread her legs and cried out, "Somebody fuck me!" Barry glanced over at me for my ready approval, and slid his body between her thighs. Ronnie raised her sexy legs over his shoulders, and I leaned over so I could watch Barry's hot, hard prick slide easily into my wife's dripping pussy. I reveled at the sight of his shaft going in and out of my wife's pussy, her juices shining on it, and dripping profusely in her excitement.

Moments later, Barry announced in a breathy voice, "I'm gonna come!" As she too shuddered all over, she moaned as if out of control. Meanwhile, because I enjoy a bit of a foot fetish, I had been sucking on her toe. Then I fucked the underside of her foot, my head pressing into the bottom of her warm toes. Within seconds, I shot my come all over her toes, grunting involuntarily with pleasure. I sucked the come off, then I slid smoothly into her well-fucked, sperm-filled hole.

We enjoyed our three-way afterglow, and when Barry left I fell asleep.

It's now been about six months since our first time, and we've agreed to let Barry be our only extra lover. Barry and my wife now enjoy sex regularly and often, by themselves as well as with me. Since our first threesome, Ronnie has become entirely uninhibited, sucks our penises better than ever, and has even mentioned to me that she now fantasizes about certain women as well. Sex has become better than ever, and we may try something new, tomorrow.—*A.R., Nashville, Tennessee*

SHY WIFE LETS HER HAIR DOWN AND GOES TO TOWN

I've always enjoyed reading your magazine. My very straight, shy wife, however, used to get pissed whenever I bought it, so I've mostly had to read it on the sly. I particularly like reading about men who share their wives with other men. Since Lynnette has always been very traditional about sex, I thought these experiences would remain fantasies.

But, then, my college roommate Rick separated from his wife and, in order to get away from her, transferred his job to the town we live in. I offered to let him stay at our house while he looked for a place to live. Since I work days and he nights, I didn't get to see him much.

Once he found his own place and moved out, we kept in touch partying frequently on the weekends. During these times I noticed Lynnette would pay close attention to him. It was innocent things, like serving him drinks, giving him back rubs and dressing up more than normal when he was around. In particular, she would wear her more revealing outfits. Most women wouldn't consider them very daring, but for Lynnette they were pretty wild, and not what she'd normally wear for company.

One night while we were in bed, I asked Lynnette why she was paying so much attention to Rick. She said she felt bad for him, because his wife always treated him badly and he deserved much better. She wanted him to feel loved, and to be proud of his good nature and good looks.

I wasn't sure how to take this, so I continued to probe for answers while rubbing her belly and breasts. When pressed about how she felt about him, she said that she loved him as a family member, but finally admitted that she was also physically attracted to him. Lynnette began to respond to my caresses, fueled no doubt by her thoughts of Rick.

My next question was whether she'd ever thought of doing anything about her attraction. Looking at me to gauge my response, she stammered a little, then bit her lip and started talking freely. "One morning," Lynnette told me, "when I went to wake Rick up to go house hunting, I seriously fantasized about dropping my nightgown and climbing in bed next to him."

As she spoke I moved my hand to her pussy, and was surprised to find how wet it was. She was really responding to my attention, and continued to talk in a dreamy voice. "I'd like to make love to him, to show him how loving a woman can really be. But I could never do anything to hurt you."

Rolling on top of her and guiding my hard cock to her entrance, I asked, "Does it feel like I'm hurt?"

Lynnette yielded to my thrusting, and as I stroked in her wet tunnel I kept talking, looking for more answers. As our lovemaking became more urgent, I asked if she wanted to feel his hard cock inside her, and she was panting, "Yes . . . yes . . . yes!" as she came.

My problem then was how to get something going between them. I knew they'd never do anything on their own. One day things just fell into place. Rick called me at work, explaining that he had the day off and wanted to come by my shop and hang around. I called Lynnette and told her to come by for lunch, and that Rick would be there.

Rick was the first to arrive, and I kept talking about how attractive Lynnette was. Rick said she sure was.

Lynnette showed up, wearing a summer dress that buttoned in the front. She'd left it unbuttoned down to her navel and up to her thigh. It quickly became obvious that she had nothing on under the dress. We made some small talk, and I made some drinks and passed them around. As the alcohol took effect, I could see Rick trying to get a peek at her tits.

That was all I needed. Moving behind Lynnette, I reached around and held her dress open so that Rick got a clear look. I told him, "I think Lynnette wants you to see these, and it's pretty obvious you want to as well."

Rick responded by saying, "What, just look?" He knelt in front of her and took one hard nipple into his mouth. I stood behind her, kissing her neck, as I watched my old friend suck my wife's tits and slide his hand up her dress.

Lynnette shifted her weight, to open her legs and give him access to her wet pussy. Rick stopped sucking for a minute to admire her shapely thighs and hairy cleft. She moaned, "You guys can't get me all worked up and then leave me horny like this."

I led her over to my desk and laid her on it, saying, "We have no intention of leaving you any way but satisfied." I kissed my wife as Rick dove into her pussy and started slurping away. Lynnette was very excited, moaning and sliding her ass back and forth on the desk. Her legs kept clutching Rick's head and then releasing it. The eagerness with which she pressed her tongue between my lips had me almost as excited as she was.

After a while Rick and I traded places. I was eating her velvety cunt. Looking up, I was surprised to see Lynnette struggling to undo Rick's pants and free his hard cock. Once she succeeded she took him deep into her mouth without hesitation. That was something she had done for me only reluctantly and after much coaxing. Even then she was always very tentative about it.

Not anymore! Lynnette rolled onto her side on the desk, grabbed Rick's ass in both hands and pulled his hard dick deep into her mouth. She sucked him with wild abandon, her cheeks hollow from the suction she was applying.

I repositioned the group. Rick was sitting on the desk with Lynnette bent over in front of him, sucking his dick. I lined up behind her and guided my cock into her clutching pussy from behind. This was great! My normally timid wife was bobbing her head up and down on Rick's hot prick and at the same time grinding her hot cunt back into me at every stroke. She couldn't get enough dick in her at one time, and kept trying to draw us deeper into her.

Rick looked as if he was going to blow his wad, so I told

Lynnette that if she wanted to have him in her pussy she should hurry up and get it. She climbed up on his lap and sank down on him in one stroke. She bounced up and down on his pole while I held her jiggling tits from behind.

Not satisfied with this, as she wasn't getting him in deep enough, she climbed off and knelt on the desk, with her ass up in the air. Reaching between her legs and spreading the swollen lips of her pussy, Lynnette growled, "Come on, Rick. Give me that dick and fuck me hard." I couldn't believe my ears. Here was my shy wife talking and acting like a slut and really enjoying it. Rick fucked her furiously, and I moved around to get my rod sucked, but she turned away to watch Rick pound his meat into her.

Rick was right on the edge of coming. Lynnette told him not to come inside her, as she hadn't inserted her diaphragm, so he pulled out. Seizing the opportunity, I took his place, sinking into her to the hilt in one stroke. In fifteen years I had never felt her this wet before. Lynnette ordered Rick to come to her mouth and feed her some more of his delicious dick. He quickly obliged, and we were soon pumping her full of prick from both ends. I came first, which triggered her orgasm. She loves a spurting dick in her snatch, and it almost always brings on her own climax. Then Rick started to grunt, and muttered "Oh, great Christ I'm coming!" When he tried to pull back, Lynnette grabbed his ass and pulled him hard against her. His dick slid down her throat, and she swallowed his tremendous load, which continued to flow for a long time.

As we all were catching our breath Lynnette kissed me full on the lips, working her tongue into my mouth. I could taste Rick's come in her mouth.

We got dressed and everyone left without saying much of anything. Later that night I asked why she sucked him dry so enthusiastically. Lynnette replied that he couldn't come in her pussy, but that she wanted him to come inside her someplace. She added that his smaller cock was more comfortable to suck, that she could relax and enjoy it, which she's never been able to do with my larger rod.

Rick has since moved out of state. We never repeated our original scene. I'm still hoping, and always on the lookout for some other stud whom she might like enough. I can't wait to see her once again transform into the wanton slut that she was that day in the shop.—*W.D., Denver, Colorado*

SEXY INGENUE RELIVES THE MEMORY OF HER FIRST TRIO

When I was eighteen I went to spend the summer with my sister, who lived in an apartment complex. My bedroom faced a swimming pool, and beyond the pool a construction crew was working on the apartment across from my room. I was hypnotized by their lean, tanned bodies, and sat there for days watching the men come and go from that apartment.

One day, after a long hot shower, I lay on my bed with only a towel on and began watching the men at work. As it turned out, two of the men were already watching me.

Standing up and letting my towel fall to the floor, I stretched my arms as if tired, and lay back down on the bed. A few minutes later, when I looked up from the book I was reading, the men were still standing on the opposite balcony watching me. It turned me on knowing they were staring at my body.

As I lay there, fantasizing about what it would be like to have these two men in the room with me, I began touching myself. I began rubbing oil on my breasts and then all over my body. When at last I looked up, the men were walking across the complex toward my window.

By the time the men reached my window my whole body was covered with oil. My nipples stood as erect as two soldiers. I looked over at the men, then nodded lazily at the door, as if to say, "Don't just stand there. Come on in here and show me what you can do."

They took the hint at once, disappearing from the window. I went to the door and unlocked it, then returned to my room. Lying on the bed, I ran my hands impatiently over my firm skin and waited for my suitors to arrive. The door opened, and I looked up to see them standing in the doorway of my bedroom. For such big, strong men they seemed awfully shy. They kept shifting from one foot to the other and clearing their throats. I was still rubbing oil into my supple hips.

One of the men walked over to me, sat down by the side of the bed and just watched me touch myself as he caressed his own manhood. The other man was taking off his jeans as he watched my fingers nibble at the lips of my hot, wet pussy, avoiding direct contact with my most tender parts. I was so turned on by the thought of having these two men. They still hesitated to make a move, and it pleased me even more to feel that I controlled this sexy situation.

I looked up, acknowledging them for the first time since they'd entered. "The bathroom is through there," I said, pointing with one finger. "I insist that you both shower before you touch me. But hurry!"

They practically tripped over each other getting to the bathroom, running the water, finding the towels. Listening to them scrub the sweat off, I continued to caress myself all over, still trying not to touch the most sensitive spots, saving those for my two lovers.

When they reentered the room I looked at them both appraisingly, then asked, "Who wants to eat my pussy first?" They both began rubbing my body. I was so hot that I couldn't stand it. I made an O with my mouth, and the taller guy, getting the message immediately, slipped his long, thin dick between my lips for a blowjob. The other guy planted his tongue inside my pussy. I threw my legs apart and ran my hands through his damp hair, encouraging him to drive his tongue deep inside me.

After a few minutes they changed places. I was so hot I couldn't stand it! I said that I wanted one of the men to lick my pussy while the other man fucked it. The guy who had been in my mouth moved into position to tongue my clit, while his companion slipped his prick into my wet, wet tunnel. It was especially exciting for me to see this big, masculine guy with his tongue brushing against his companion's penis as he worked my knob. I was already having little contractions that ran up and down my spine. Soon my whole body would be spasming uncontrollably.

The dark-haired construction worker, the one who was pumping my pussy, pulled out too far, and when he tried to drive back into me his prick missed my opening and buried itself instead between the lips of his coworker. After that one stroke, he got straightened out and slid back into the right channel, but the look of surprise on the blond guy's face when he suddenly found his mouth full of hard dick had pushed me to climax. I came hard, making it almost impossible for the poor guy to keep his tongue on my button.

I looked at the blond, and told him that I wanted to suck his hard cock. He stood on the floor beside my head. I turned over on my hands and knees and began sucking him while the brunette kept fucking. The blond guy had a longer dick than his friend, and I wanted it in my pussy. I told them to trade places.

While sucking on the dark guy's hard cock I begged the blond to give it to me hard, and he did. He fucked me as I'd never been fucked before. Panting hard, I begged him not to stop, as I was going to come a second time. The harder he fucked my pussy the harder I sucked the other guy's cock. The final, perfect detail of my fantasy came true as we all came at the same time.

Afterward we all went into the bathroom and got into the shower at the same time. Both men began rubbing soap all over my body. I was getting turned on again. I told them if they didn't stop they would have to fuck me again. They kept on rubbing me. My pussy was throbbing.

My blond got down on his knees and began licking my pussy while his companion stood behind me rubbing my breasts. I was so excited I was soon ready to come again. This time I wanted my other lover inside me, so I reached back with my hand and directed his bobbing erection into my cunt from behind. The other man stood up and started kissing me. His tongue felt so good that my pussy was still throbbing. He took over playing with my tits, tugging on my nipples and squeezing the whole of my breasts. I couldn't stand it anymore. I was so hot I began to come for a third time in the last fifteen minutes.

We got out of the shower and went back to my room. As my boys were now fully erect again, but hadn't had a second come, I had them lie on their backs and I took turns sucking their cocks.

I heard my bedroom door open and I turned around and another of the construction workers had come in. I just turned back and started sucking those two hot cocks in front of me.

That was when my little affair turned into a once-in-a-lifetime orgy. While sucking the two men, I felt a hard cock rubbing my pussy. The new man inserted his dick, and I began to moan, letting the blond guy's dick fall out of my mouth. I'd never been so turned on in my life! I turned to the man who had been fucking me and started sucking his hot cock.

Then I decided I didn't want to do any more work, but simply put my body at their disposal. I lay on the bed and let all three men lick me and touch my body.

One of the men lay down on the bed and pulled me on top of him. He put his hard cock in my pussy. While he was fucking my pussy one of the others stood in front of me begging to be sucked. The third guy jerked his dick with his hand and rubbed the tip of it all over my skin. I came again and again.

I asked them all to try to come at the same time, all over me and inside me. After a short while my dependable blond beauty started to spray his come into my pussy. I ran my hand rapidly up and down the shaft of the second guy, and in a few seconds was drinking his milky nectar, just as I felt my third lover begin dribbling his load onto my heaving ass-cheeks.

We fell asleep after a while. I woke up that next morning thinking that it must have been a dream, but when I rolled over I found my blond lover still lying next to me. I finally asked him his name, and he told me it was Robert. I think I fell in love that day.

While lying there, I said I had something to tell him. He just looked at me and waited to hear what I had to say. I thanked him for the great time and I let him know that before he and his coworkers had come to visit me I was a virgin.—*D.W., Omaha, Nebraska*

CARELESS CLEANING LEADS TO CAREFREE FUN

A year ago, just before we were married, I took some pictures of my wife Kira nude. I left them all over the house. I even had posters made of some to hang on the walls of my study. On our honeymoon, we rented a camcorder to make live sex films.

One day my best friend Dan and I went to my house for lunch. He found a few of the pictures, which I had carelessly left out, and right away he was lusting for Kira. I ended up showing him all of them.

For my birthday this year we made another video, and during the filming we talked about having someone else film us. This really made Kira hot. She asked who I would get to film the video, and after talking about it, I told her I would ask Dan to film it.

We decided to have Dan watch the film we had just made, to make sure we were all comfortable with each other. The next day I asked Dan if he would film us. He was game. Then I told him about the video, and we went by at lunchtime to see it. We all took our seats, Kira in the middle, and the show began. It started with a striptease. Mild as that was compared to the rest of the film, at the first sight of titty Kira's face turned red as a beet. I reached up and started unbuttoning her shirt.

Before long Dan was helping me fondle her big, soft breasts.

On the television, Kira gave me a quick blowjob and a long, slow fuck—and by then it was late enough that Dan and I had to sprint unwillingly back to work. Not long after I got back to work, Kira called. After some hemming and hawing, she asked, "Would you like to try a threesome?"

After thinking about it, I called her back and told her to be waiting for us after work and to wear a tight shirt and no bra so we could fondle and suck her. We decided not to have intercourse until later, after we had a chance to talk about it.

When Dan and I arrived, she had on a black, tight muscle shirt, with her nipples straining out of the thin fabric. She was already breathing hard. At first we sat on the couch. Kira had always been very conservative and shy, but now a strange hand was feeling her right tit, and I had her left between my fingers.

Soon we ended up on the bed, Dan sucking one breast and I the other. We were both feeling her pussy and rubbing her body. She reached down and started rubbing our dicks. It wasn't long before Kira was sucking Dan's dick. I was so turned on by watching that I came as soon as I entered her pussy, then went limp. Dan soon came in her mouth, and Kira drank every little drop. I moved up to get a blowjob, while Dan ate and then fucked her pussy. I watched him give it to her, their bodies slapping together, until he came again.

The glow from this session lasted a long time. That week was filled with so much fucking that Kira and I decided to set up another threesome. We chose the following Monday night.

This time Kira enjoyed it even more. She sucked her own titties, and Dan fucked her first. I was supremely excited from kissing her and sucking her tits while watching Dan fuck her pussy. He moved slowly at first, then slammed into her faster and harder. I was still wearing my pants, and came in them while watching his dick going into her soft little cunt.

We now have an understanding. We talk about who she wants to fuck. She won't do it if I ask her not to, and never sleeps with anyone without me.—*B.R., Boise, Idaho*

LIFELONG MEMORIES OF HER ONE WOMAN

I met Peter when I was about eighteen years old. We saw each other occasionally, and often ended up in bed. While there, he would always tell me about a special person he wanted me to meet—his girlfriend, Anita. He said he would love to get both of us in bed at the same time.

A few weeks later, while I was talking to Peter on the phone, he told me Anita had just returned from Europe and he was dying for me to meet her. He arranged for me to visit the following Friday.

Friday arrived, and I was quite nervous and excited. I had no idea what Peter had told Anita. I had no idea what she even looked like.

I got to the apartment about eight, and took the elevator up to the seventh floor. Uncertain of what the evening might bring, I knocked on the door. When the door opened I was surprised to see one of the most beautiful blonde women I'd ever encountered. She invited me in, offering me a seat on the couch.

I learned that Anita was twenty-six, eight years older than I was. She was also more aggressive than I was, and knew exactly what Peter had in mind. Before I knew what had happened, Anita had taken me into the bedroom and started showing me magazines with pictures of threesomes and two women together. This had me dripping wet with anticipation. Anita sensed my arousal and, gently bending over, kissed me softly on the mouth. That's all it took. Before I knew it we were both lying on the bed, wrapped in each other's arms, minus our clothes. Anita had the most beautiful set of tits I had ever seen. They were nice and round, like a couple of cantaloupe halves, but soft and silky to the touch. I couldn't keep my hands or mouth off them. Anita massaged my tits in return, slowly kissing her way down my stomach to my aching clit. She knew just where to suck and where to nibble. In no time at all she brought me to a huge orgasm. I soaked the sheets.

Then it was my turn to taste forbidden fruit. I was a little apprehensive at first, but I slowly worked my way down to her waiting pussy and took my first taste of her luscious mound. She was much tastier than I had expected, and I soon found myself wrapped up in giving her what she had given me only moments before: a tremendous orgasm.

Suddenly, Peter appeared. He had been standing off on the sidelines watching, waiting for the right moment to join us. Noting our relaxed state, he dove in. While Anita once again buried her beautiful blonde head between my legs, Peter fucked her from behind. Once again his gorgeous lady brought me to climax. At about the same time, Peter emptied his load into her.

Well, that was eighteen years ago, and to this day I dream about Anita.—*S.W., Houston, Texas*

Crowd Scenes

FIREFIGHTERS' HOSES CAN PUT OUT ANY FIRE—EVEN THE FIRE DOWN BELOW

I am a twenty-nine-year-old firefighter. The firehouse where I work receives relatively few calls, so the crew and I are always looking for something fun to do when we're not busy.

One evening Timothy, one of my crew members, mentioned that his brother had just fucked a beautiful twenty-year-old Asian girl who had recently broken up with her first real boyfriend. She'd told Timothy that she wanted to catch up on all the fun she'd been missing out on while being tied down in a relationship, and mentioned that she found firefighters very sexy.

Timothy invited her up to the station for a visit. The four of us on duty that night were sure that Tim had been exaggerating and that nothing would happen. It just sounded too good to be true. Kim arrived shortly after dinner and was dressed conservatively, reinforcing our belief that she was to be no more than an ordinary visitor.

After being given a tour of the fire station, Timothy and Kim joined Matt, Jesse and myself in the recreation room to watch television. After some idle talk, Matt and Jesse decided to retire for the evening. They left for the bedroom, not knowing what was about to happen.

Timothy and Kim were on the sofa while I sat in a recliner. I watched her make her play on Timothy. She asked me to turn down the lights and I readily complied. I realized that this girl was finally getting down to business with Timothy.

In the glowing light from the television, I watched as Kim's mouth moved deftly from Timothy's lips to his zipper. She began to expertly suck his cock, apparently oblivious to my presence. Just when I had given up hope of getting some of the same attention, Timothy asked Kim, "Will you take care of my buddy too?"

After removing Timothy's dick from her mouth, she rotated her head toward me and said teasingly, "Well, maybe . . ." It was then that I suggested we move into the kitchen.

As we headed toward the kitchen table, Timothy and I were already working feverishly on removing Kim's clothes. As her black lace bra fell to the floor, I was awestruck by the length and hardness of her beautiful brown nipples. She took it upon herself to remove her panties and lie on her back on the table as Timothy and I hastily took off our clothes.

"You can do anything you want to me," she said as she turned her head to the side to take my engorged cock into her mouth. Timothy moved to the other end of the table and entered her abruptly, prompting a squeal of delight from our horny guest.

As Timothy fucked her, I tweaked and sucked her nipples, all the while watching her suck my cock and moan in pleasure. Timothy and I decided to switch places, so I reluctantly pulled my cock out of her mouth and plunged it into her soaked pussy.

After we fucked her for a while, I decided that we shouldn't deprive Matt and Jesse of all this fun. Besides, I knew they probably wouldn't believe the story if they didn't see it for themselves.

The three of us walked into the dorm and woke up Matt and Jesse. Kim went right to work on Jesse's dick while Matt fucked her hungry snatch from behind. Timothy and I had no trouble getting hard again as Kim had us move into place for a double handjob.

Just when we had all begun to moan in unison for a group climax, the harsh reality of our occupation fell upon us like a brick. The lights came on, and the blaring tones from the loudspeaker signaled that we had an emergency medical call to respond to.

We immediately stopped what we were doing, pulled on our coats and boots and hurried to the fire engine without so much as a word to our new friend. We just didn't have a second to spare.

We returned from the call some forty minutes later, fully expecting that Kim would have left the firehouse. But when we entered the sleeping quarters, she was lying naked on Matt's bed with her fingers deep in her pussy. She said, "You guys are my heroes. Now take off your clothes and finish fucking me." It was a firefighter's dream come true.

After the four of us had fucked her in every way and place imaginable, including on the hose bed of the fire engine, we sent her on her merry, albeit slightly bowlegged, way.—*P.E., Boston, Massachusetts*

TWENTIETH HIGH SCHOOL REUNION REUNITES SOME FRIENDS LONG LUSTED AFTER

When the invitation came in the mail for our twentieth high school reunion, my wife Alexandra and I decided to go. We thought it would be fun to see some of the old faces again. I wondered if the other women had aged as well as Alexandra had. At thirty-seven, she still has a youthful face and figure.

During the weeks before the reunion, Alexandra talked about her old friend Ken a few times. Ken had been the quarterback on the football team and was known as "The Bear." I know Alexandra was wondering if Ken would make it to the reunion too.

I don't think my wife fucks around on me, but after a few drinks she does get pretty horny. At more than one party, I've seen guys grab her ass or a tit while dancing with her. Such a sight always turns me on, and I have often entertained thoughts of Alexandra getting it on with another man. I knew she'd had the hots for Ken once, but that was years ago. I thought that maybe, with a little coaxing from me, something would happen at the reunion.

We arrived in our hometown on Friday night. Once Alexandra unpacked, she called a girlfriend who still lived in town. After finding out where the old gang was congregating before the reunion, we went to meet up with them. Alexandra wore a short, white dress. She really looked sharp, and I knew she would get plenty of admiring looks.

When we got to the reunion, we started to mingle. Some of the women looked good, but most of them had put on weight. Alexandra and I separated for about an hour while we sought out friends we hadn't seen in a while. When I ran into her again, she was standing at the bar with Ken and Sid, another ex-football player. Both men had kept themselves in very good shape.

From the look on Alexandra's face, I could tell she'd had a lot to drink. She said, "I was just going to look for you. Ken invited us to go to his house for a drink." I said that sounded great, and the four of us headed out.

When we arrived at his house, Ken gave us the grand tour. When we reached the patio, Ken suggested, "Let's take a dip in the hot tub." Alexandra looked over at me, and I told her it was up to her. She said it sounded good to her. Ken and Sid stripped down to their shorts as I unzipped Alexandra's dress. She stepped out of her dress and climbed into the tub. Her nipples were rock-hard, and I could see her dark bush through her white panties. Ken said, "Wow, Allie! You look great!"

Alexandra sat next to Ken, and I sat on the other side of her. Alexandra's tits floated on the surface of the water, and I could see Ken's fingers lightly caressing her nipples. Alexandra leaned her head back and closed her eyes. I kissed her deeply, my tongue exploring her mouth. Suddenly I stood up and told Sid to take my place. I sat across from them and watched intently as the two men played with my wife.

Sid lifted one of her tits out of the water and sucked on her hard nipple. After a few minutes, Alexandra's panties floated to the surface, followed by two pairs of briefs. Ken started kissing her and, by the way his arm was moving, I could tell he was fingering her cunt. Alexandra began moaning loudly, clutching Sid's head to her breast.

Ken then stood up and lifted Alexandra up onto the deck. He put her legs over his shoulders and started feasting on her cunt. Alexandra wrapped her hand around Sid's cock and started jerking him off, but he had a better idea. He moved his cock to her lips, and her tongue flicked around the head before she slid the entire thing into her mouth. I'd never seen her so horny, and I was glad I had the best seat in the house to watch the action.

It wasn't long before Alexandra's legs were quivering. She pulled her mouth away from Sid's cock to say, "Oh, God, I'm coming. Don't stop!" Her legs tightened around Ken's neck as she had her first orgasm of the night. She stuffed Sid's cock back into her mouth and sucked him dry.

Then Ken stood up straight, and his cock came into view. I couldn't believe what I was seeing. Ken's cock was at least ten inches long and six inches around.

I don't think Alexandra knew what she was in for when Ken grabbed his cock and rubbed the head up and down her slit. She moaned, "Put it inside me. Please put it inside me."

Ken started fucking her nice and slow, pulling out on each stroke until just his cockhead was inside her, then sliding it all the way back in. After a few minutes she screamed that she was coming again.

Ken picked up the pace. Soon I could see the muscles in his ass contract, and I knew he was pumping his load into her pussy. I watched in awe as trickles of bubbly white come oozed out of her hole.

Ken said, "Baby, that was great," as he sat back down in the tub. I was sitting on the rim of the hot tub, rubbing my cock. Alexandra said, "Let me do that." She came across the tub to me, leaned over and started sucking my cock. Sid came up behind her and slid his cock into her doggie-style. I lasted about three seconds before I shot my wad. Sid unloaded in her cunt a few seconds later.

By this time the four of us were pretty waterlogged, so we went inside to resume the action on Ken's king-size water bed. We sucked and fucked the night away. It was dawn before we finally fell asleep. I woke up around noon to find Alexandra riding Ken's cock like a cowgirl. That was the best reunion I have ever been to. Now I'm looking forward to our thirtieth reunion!—*C.K., St. Petersburg, Florida*

SUNNING IN THE GREEK ISLES: HOW SWEDE IT IS!

My girlfriend Frannie is tall, blonde and beautiful. Among the many interests we share are sex and sunbathing in the nude.

Last summer we went on vacation to the Greek islands, mainly because we had heard so much about the nude beaches there. We had a wonderful time, thanks to great weather, gorgeous beaches and beautiful people. We are both pretty uninhibited, but one day Frannie really outdid herself.

We had been in the hotel lobby one evening when a group of Swedish men checked in. We later met a group of them in the bar, and they told us that they were members of a rugby team who had come there to train. They were all well-built young men in their early twenties, many of them blond and blue-eyed. Frannie was soon surrounded by an admiring group of a half dozen handsome young men, all competing for her attention. After a while I heard Frannie telling them that we had found a beautiful, secluded nude beach that was only about a twenty-minute walk from the hotel, and offering to show them where it was after they finished their workout the next morning.

The next day at about noon we set out with fifteen of the young rugby players. Frannie has been all excited the night before about seeing these young hunks nude on the beach. (And, quite frankly, so was I. I am bi and also love to see my sexy girlfriend get it on with other guys!)

When we reached the beach it was almost deserted. We walked down to one end, away from the other sunbathers. There was fierce competition among the young men to spread their towels on the sand as close to Frannie's as possible. Then we all stripped and went for a swim. I could tell that Frannie was in heaven—the only girl on the beach, with sixteen nude guys around her. It seemed that everywhere we turned there were muscular bodies, hairy legs with big thighs, well-developed pecs and, of course, cocks and balls of all shapes and sizes, which Frannie was unabashedly checking out (as was I). Some were bigger, some were smaller, but all were exciting and all were uncircumcised, as is the norm with Europeans.

We all frolicked in the ocean, and there was a lot of splashing and horseplay, especially around Frannie. I even got to grab a few handfuls of muscular butt and grope a couple of crotches (which was not unfavorably received—in fact one guy made a point of doing the same to me several times).

After a while things quieted down and I saw that one big guy had hoisted Frannie onto his shoulders. She was pretending he was a horse, spurring him on with her heels. She was bouncing up and down as though she were horseback riding, and I could tell from her erect nipples and flushed face that what she was really doing was rubbing her pussy against the back of his neck! She waved to me and winked. Then she said, "Come on, Hans, take me back to my towel!"

Hans splashed through the shallows to the beach, and we could all see that his big cock was sticking straight out from the nest of golden hair at his crotch. He carried her to her towel, then crouched down to allow her to slide off his broad shoulders. She turned to him and said, "Thanks, Hans." Then, looking down, she continued, "My God, you are a horse! At least you're hung like a horse!"

Sinking to her knees in the sand, she kissed the foreskin-covered end of his big tool. Then, grasping the shaft in one hand, she pulled back his foreskin and wrapped her lips around his fat knob. There were some cheers and applause from the other guys as they crowded around to watch. Several of them were already sporting hard-ons, as was I.

Hans stood, muscular legs apart, the sun glistening on the golden hair covering his head and his well-developed chest, and watched my beautiful girlfriend go to town on his prick. I could see it jump and throb in her mouth as she caressed the shaft and his big, dangling balls. I was in the front row as the crowd pressed closer around them. By now everyone was in a state of sexual arousal. I could feel someone's cock throbbing against my leg. The guy on my left had casually thrown one arm across my shoulders, while his other hand idly slid his foreskin back and forth over the head of his very large, very erect tool.

Frannie continued to suck and stroke Hans while the fingers of one hand danced across her clit and probed the wetness between her legs. She lifted her mouth off him, allowing his rigid pole to slap up against his goldenhaired belly. Then she rolled back onto her beach towel, her knees spread wide so that we could all see her golden bush framing the open, pink wetness of her cunt. Hans needed no second invitation. Kneeling on the towel between her spread legs, he grasped his big tool and ran the fat, pink head up and down her slit a few times. Then, pushing forward, he was soon all the way into her, up to his balls. This elicited another cheer from the crowd.

Somebody began stroking my cock, but I was too busy watching my beautiful Frannie being fucked by this big stud to take much notice. Frannie was now thrusting up her hips to meet his, her eyes glazed over with lust and her hands caressing his muscular back. Supporting his weight on his arms, Hans started to fuck her in earnest, his hairy buttocks rising and falling as he worked his tool in and out. Before long he increased his tempo, and Frannie's breasts jiggled to and fro as she met his every thrust.

As she shrieked and thrashed through an orgasm, he threw back his head and roared while he spurted jism into her. Hans collapsed across her heaving breasts. After a moment he stood up, his dripping cock still erect. Frannie moaned as she stroked her swollen, gaping cunt with one hand. Hans's come flowed out, matting her bush. "Who's next?" she gasped.

In an instant another hunk was poised over her. This time it was one of the few dark-haired members of the group. His long, thin cock throbbed above a pair of balls that hung low in his pendulous scrotum. His well-muscled body was almost hairless except for a dark tuft above his shaft. As he mounted Frannie, she wrapped her legs around his firm little butt and thrust her cunt up to meet his every stroke.

The hand on my cock had been replaced by a warm, wet mouth. Looking down, I saw that Hans had his lips wrapped around my shaft. He glanced up at me, winked, and then went back to work on my rigid rod. One of his hands was busy at his own crotch, where his huge tool seemed to be as hard as ever. Looking around, I saw that there was a lot of indiscriminate sexual activity going on. Some of the guys were intently watching their buddy fuck Frannie while stroking their own cocks, others were lending a hand or a mouth to the pleasuring of each other.

The guy fucking Frannie soon shot his load and was replaced by a third guy—another blond whose tool was not very long, but extraordinarily thick. I saw my girl mounted and vigorously screwed by all fifteen guys while she had orgasm after orgasm.

I was beside myself, kept just on the brink of orgasm by the expert fellatio of Hans, who would never quite let me come. A couple of times I almost went over the edge, but he firmly squeezed my dick until I came back down from the peak. The guys had incredible staying power—their cocks never seemed to get soft after shooting a load into Frannie. After screwing my girlfriend, they went right back to playing with themselves or each other.

Finally Frannie's cunt had been penetrated by all fifteen cocks, and she lay spread-eagle on the towel, exhausted but happy.

Hans finally released my aching rod and said, "Now you!" Hard as steel, I plunged straight into Frannie's sloppy, come-filled vagina. As I slowly stroked in and out, savoring the sensation of her warm, well-fucked pussy, I was aware that Hans and his friends were watching us intently. I wanted to put on a good show, but I was so overcome with lust that I knew I wouldn't last long. All around us the guys were stroking themselves, their eyes fixed on us. I felt Frannie start to spasm under me, and as my own orgasm built I didn't even try to hold it back. I shouted in ecstasy as my spunk spurted into Frannie's pussy. What a day!—*A.C., Denver, Colorado*

FUN-LOVING FOURSOME GOES WILD WHEN WIVES STRIP AND SHOW OFF

I guess it all started when my wife Amelia met Dawn in the laundry room of our apartment complex. We had just moved in, and Amelia was glad to meet some of our new neighbors. She was especially happy to learn that Dawn and her husband Joey live just a few doors down from us.

Over time Amelia and Dawn became very close friends. Both are slender, petite redheads, and many people mistook them for sisters rather than friends. Joey and I got to be good friends as well.

We all like to party and have a good time. One night we were returning home rather late after a night of drinking and dancing. We were all in a somewhat wild mood. Dawn suggested it would be fun if she and Amelia rode topless. There was little traffic at two in the morning, and my wife Amelia was all for it. Dawn and Amelia slipped off their blouses and bras, proudly displaying their chests. Both had nice, firm tits, with large nipples.

Joey was driving, and he managed to get caught at several red lights in a row. Both Joey and I were getting turned on, knowing that other drivers were enjoying the sight of our wives' nice tits. Joey dared his wife to take off her skirt and panties. Dawn said she would if Amelia would too. We soon had two naked women seated alongside us, revealing their matching dark red bushes. Needless to say, both Joey and I soon had hard, throbbing cocks.

Finally we arrived home. The girls walked from the parking lot to our apartment totally naked except for high heels and fishnet stockings. Dawn was even daring enough to stop at a newspaper vendor and ask for a newspaper. He gave it to her for free.

When we got to our apartment, we all stripped naked. Dawn and Amelia lay side by side on our king-size bed with their legs spread wide. Joey and I commented that their pussies looked identical. Then Joey fucked Dawn and I fucked Amelia. It was fun watching another couple make love and being watched ourselves. All four of us came at about the same time. Afterward both women had come oozing from their cunts.

We all decided to take a shower together. Joey soaped up my wife, and Dawn and I lathered up each other. Joey paid special attention to my wife's tits and pussy, and she to his cock and balls. Dawn and I were drying off when Joey suggested that we fuck each other's wife. Both Amelia and Dawn were all for it. I knelt between Dawn's spread legs as she guided my aching cock to the opening of her cunt. I eased it in gently, and her hot, tight cunt grasped my cock like a fist. She wrapped her long, shapely legs around my hips to pull me in even deeper. She raised her ass to meet each of my thrusts as she rotated her hips and ground her cunt against my crotch. I vaguely heard my wife begging Joey to fuck her harder.

After a sweaty, passionate fuck, Dawn and I reached our peak. She pulled me tightly against her. Her tits were smashed against my chest as her cunt muscles milked every last drop of come from my throbbing cock. Both Joey and Amelia were totally exhausted from fucking so furiously. They lay there panting, trying to catch their breath. Soon Joey mounted Amelia again. Eventually we all drifted off to sleep.

I awoke to the sensation of the bed shaking gently. Joey was fucking Amelia doggie-style. Dawn got up to go to the bathroom. When she returned, I mounted her in the missionary fashion. Again her hot, pulsating cunt milked every last drop of come from my balls.

We discussed our night over breakfast, and we all agreed it had been a lot of fun. We continued swapping on a regular basis for almost six months. Then Joey and Dawn moved to another state. We hope to get together again over the summer.—*E.N., Fresno, California*

WEEKEND GETAWAY AND RAGING HORMONES BRING ON CABIN FEVER

It all started out innocently enough last summer when our best friends Roy and Lucy invited my wife and me up to their cabin in Vermont for the weekend. Since my wife Joelle and I both needed a break, we decided to make the six-hour trek the next day.

When we arrived, Roy and Lucy were out on the deck, sunning and drinking beer. Their cabin was on the shore of a beautiful, crystal-clear lake, and the view was stunning. But I was more interested in checking out Lucy than the lake.

I have always lusted after Lucy. She is of Latin descent, with dark hair and an olive complexion. She has large tits that still stand up nice and firm when she goes braless. Her tummy is flat and her firm butt flows right into her long legs. I felt my seven-inch dick twitching in my shorts.

Joelle went into the cabin to change into her bikini. When she returned, I was already in the water trying to hide my rising cock. We swam around for a while, then we hopped into Roy's speedboat and cruised around the lake for a bit.

When we got back to the cabin, we dressed and went out for a lobster dinner. The girls were dressed to thrill in short, tight dresses. They got me so turned on, I couldn't wait to get back to the cabin so I could screw my wife.

On the way back, Lucy suggested that we go skinny-dipping. I said I was game, but I didn't think Roy would ever let it happen because he's always protective of his wife.

When we got back to the cabin, we started a fire in the fireplace and broke out the beer. Someone suggested a game of Quarters, and soon we all had a good buzz going. Lucy brought up skinny-dipping again, and I was quick to say I was game. Joelle and Roy weren't so sure, but after a few more beers we convinced them to try it.

The next thing I knew, we were all standing out on the deck with only towels on. We slipped into the lake in almost total darkness, and the water felt great against my bare skin. Afterward, as we made our way back to the cabin, I was a little disappointed that all I'd gotten was a quick glimpse of Lucy's ass. I'd been hoping for a nice tit shot.

We all sat around the fire wrapped in our towels. We smoked a joint as we joked about our adventure. Suddenly both our wives dropped their towels and got on their knees. Joelle started licking my balls, and I got hard in a hurry as I watched Lucy sucking Roy's swollen cock. Her beautiful tits swayed back and forth as her head bobbed up and down. Then Lucy crawled up onto Roy's lap and sank her wet snatch onto Roy's pecker.

I watched as her pink pussy slid down his pole, then back up again. Her juices were flowing down onto Roy's balls. I shot a huge wad of come into my wife's mouth just as Roy exploded in his wife's tight snatch. Lucy was shaking in the throes of orgasm.

We all lay down in front of the fire to rest. Then Joelle and Lucy started sucking Roy's cock. My wife was bobbing up and down on his big shaft while Lucy had both his nuts in her mouth. I sat on the couch to watch, and it wasn't long before Roy shot his wad all over. Then the girls both looked over at me, and the next thing I knew I was getting the same treatment. What a feeling! This was a fantasy come true.

I figured I might as well go for broke, so I asked Lucy if I could tit-fuck her. Lucy got on her back. She sucked my pole deep into her throat to get it all slippery. Then she squeezed her tits together, and I slipped my pecker right between them. When the head poked through, my wife gave it a lick with her tongue. As you can guess, it wasn't too long before I was coming all over Lucy's tits.

We spent that whole night in front of the fire, and the next day as well!—*P.B., Stamford, Connecticut*

THEIR FIRST ORGY STARTED SLOWLY, THEN TURNED INTO THE BIG BANG

The night was wet and windy. We were hoping that the weather wouldn't discourage our guests. As we prepared for the party, Rosa and I knew that this gathering was going to be different from any we'd had before. We had invited five couples to join us for an evening of dancing, movies and games of all sorts. We had asked people to dress formally, but without any underwear. Rosa chose to wear a black velvet dress with black silk nylons, a lacy garter belt and black velvet pumps with four-inch heels. I had chosen to wear a black tuxedo, a white shirt and a red tie.

The house was decorated with white bows and draped red sheets, and lit only by candles. We wanted a warm and romantic evening. The guests began arriving at about eight. They included an accountant, the receptionist from my office, the owner of our local health club, a college classmate and our mail carrier, each bringing a spouse or lover.

Everyone was dressed to the hilt. My accountant Pete's wife wore a white, silk see-through top and matching latex miniskirt. Pete had on a white tux, white shirt and black tie. Celia had on black knee-high boots, black shorts and a top that covered less skin that most bras. Her long blonde hair ran over her shoulders and down to her knees. Stu, her husband, had on a navy blue tux and shirt.

My receptionist Susie is twenty years old, and reminds me so much of a peach that my mouth waters every time I see her enter the office. For this occasion she had worn a red nylon body suit.

Her husband Keith had a baggy silk suit on. Mike, the gym owner, had a light blue suit on, with a black turtleneck. Lisa, Mike's girlfriend, was wearing black spandex pants, black pumps and a white blazer. Kelly, the postperson, came in a red evening dress with red pumps. Her man Cory had on a red blazer and white pants.

The room was warm from the fire on the hearth and the candles lighting the room. After dinner, Rosa steered the conversation to the question, "How did you meet your mate?"

Pete was eager to start, saying, "When I met Rhonda, we were dancing at a strip club. We danced together in a strip-and-sex show." He added, "That's how we worked our way through college." This piece of information got everyone interested.

Susie said, "I wish I'd seen that show."

Rhonda responded, "It's never too late." And we were off to the races. This was going to be a lot easier than Rosa and I had imagined.

We went into the living room, where Pete said, "If we do the show, you all have to join in." None of us knew what that was going to entail, but everyone seemed titillated at the prospect. I went to start the music as everyone settled on, in and around the furniture. When I returned, Pete was already dancing for the group. Rhonda was lying on the floor with her legs up in the air. Pete started to take off his clothes.

When he was down to his pants, Rhonda stood up and, after a little teasing, took off her white blouse. Her tits were as fine as any I've had the pleasure of seeing. I looked around the room and saw everyone in a trance. Then Pete removed his pants. His solid penis pointed at Rhonda as she removed her miniskirt. She started to lick her lips as she moved toward him, taking his penis in her hand and kissing the head of his dick.

I looked for Rosa, only to find her with my receptionist Susie. Rosa had her hand between Susie's legs, playing with her pussy. They watched the show, licking their lips. Keith came behind Rosa to feel her tits. Rhonda crossed to me and hit me with a passionate, lustful kiss. When, after some time, I again looked around, Rosa was completely nude. Pete had his left hand on her breast, massaging it as she sucked on his penis. I dove tongue-first back into Rhonda's mouth, my hands beginning to wander over her warm skin.

Suddenly the music stopped. Rosa had stopped it because some of our guests still weren't joining in. She decided to try another expedient. Rosa said, "Thank you, Pete and Rhonda, for the show. My pussy is so wet I'm going to have to have it pumped out by the D.P.W. Our next entertainment is a game called strip musical chairs. The rules are simple: When the music starts, you start dancing. When the music stops, if you don't have a chair, you strip for the group. And once your clothes are off, they stay off! Pete and Rhonda will start and stop the music, as they've already done their show."

Pete started the music, and Rosa removed a chair from the circle. The group danced, most of them giggling so hard that when the music stopped they stumbled toward the chairs. Susie was left standing, and so became the first to strip.

The music began again, and Susie started to dance. I could see a spot on her red body suit from where Rosa had been rubbing her pussy. She turned her back to us, removing the strip that held the top of her body suit. She faced the group again, showing her small, firm breasts. She went on to remove the body suit, and when she pulled it past her hips we saw that her pussy was completely shaved.

After dancing and taking her applause, Susie went to sit with Pete and Rhonda. The music began again, and Pete removed another chair. The next winner/loser turned out to be Stu, Celia's husband. He started with his jacket, then his shirt, in order to show his hairless, muscular chest. When he dropped his pants we had another surprise: He was wearing a cock ring. The sight of his swollen schlong kicked the party into overdrive. We all jumped up and started to do our own strip act.

The group did the strip in record time. Rosa has big tits, and as our guests disrobed she started to kiss and suck on her own breasts.

Lisa, not surprisingly for a gym owner's girl, is a female bodybuilder with very large, muscular legs and a powerful butt. She and Stu began kissing. Stu's dick was hard, and Lisa started to masturbate herself using Stu's dick, rubbing it on her clit.

Keith, Susie's young husband, was all over my wife's tits. Rosa was enjoying this young stud and the attention he gave her boobs. Susie was kissing Keith's cock at the same time. I went to help Rosa out of her dress. Susie got on all fours and Keith entered her from behind. Rosa started to masturbate, licking Susie's pussy and Keith's cock as he plunged in and out of Susie's box. Before I could get into Rosa, Cory moved in and inserted his dick into Rosa's hot twat.

Celia came over to me with her boots on, and we started to get on all fours. I entered her from behind. Her pussy was amazingly tight. I asked her why, and she said, "Stu is never home to fuck me. If you and Rosa ever want to come over and get it on, just give me a call." After that all she said was, "Fuck me, fuck me, fuck me hard." Soon she wasn't making words at all, just pushing her hips back against me and grunting. I reached around to feel one of her breasts as I fucked her from behind. I loved the way they moved every time we slammed together. Celia started to come, and the tensing of her cunt muscles caused me to fill her love-nest with my come.

Celia disengaged from my satisfied penis. When I looked back at Rosa, she was bucking as Cory poured his come inside her. Cory pulled out, and Lisa started to lick Rosa's pussy clean. In a few minutes, Rosa had a powerful orgasm.

When I turned from looking at that scene, Kelly and Mike were fucking on the kitchen counter. Pete and Cory headed into the dining room, and I followed. Pete lay on his back on the table, his head hanging off the end, and started sucking Cory's dick. The rest of the guests lined up for their turns. Rhonda got on top of Pete and started riding his cock, her heavenly pussy grinding away as fast as she could go. Rosa started everyone, giving each of us head (both men and women), then Pete would finish us off. I'd never had sex with a man, but Pete gave head almost as well as Rosa does. I looked at Rosa as I was getting my blowjob from Pete. The loving look on her face was all I needed to let go and come. Pete took it all without spilling a drop.

Rosa came over to kiss me after I had come, and asked me if I wanted to see whether Lisa and Mike would stay with us. I said, "That would be awesome." Rosa asked Mike and Lisa to stay. As our other guests began to leave, she asked each man to let her give them a final blowjob, for she is truly the best. She sucked each of them, and they all came a last time. After each one came, I slid my tongue into her mouth to taste what she had just enjoyed.

When just the four of us remained, we moved to the hot tub to clean up and enjoy the feeling of satiation. We started to relax and talk about the evening. We all felt brilliantly tired when we finally climbed out and toweled each other off.

As exhausted as we all were, we'd gotten so excited by everything that had happened, it was hard to stop. We went up to the bedroom and piled all the blankets and pillows we own on the floor. Then the four of us fell down in a big puppy pile. As our recap of the night continued, hands inevitably began to roam. It wasn't anything very sexual, just a lot of patting, petting, and rubbing of exhausted muscles.

After a while we ended up pairing off, Mike with Rosa and I with Lisa. We got into a lot of deep kissing and feeling of breasts. It was a little like being in high school all over again. No one had the strength to fuck, and it was really fun to just be making out and rolling around on the floor.

We switched back to our own partners. I have to admit, after all the action with other partners it was great to feel Rosa's familiar size and shape in my arms. Everyone likes to have some variety in their lives, but there's also a lot to be said for knowing how someone likes to be kissed and touched. My hand slowly slid down to Rosa's crotch, and one finger slipped between her pussy lips. She was still plenty wet inside, and I lazily moved two fingers up and down her opening, circling her clit each time I reached the top of her slit. This went on for a long time, until she let out a long sigh and clamped her legs around my hand. Her orgasm was deep rather than violent, and it pulled the last of her energy out of her. She fell asleep with my hand still clutched between her thighs. I drifted off soon after.

We all slept together on the floor until noon. Mike and I were awakened by the sounds of Rosa and Lisa eating each other's pussy. After Mike and Lisa had gone, Rosa and I held each other until we fell asleep again. She said, "I love you. Do you want to call Rhonda so she can come over next week?" I had to say yes. I love my wife, and I'm so grateful she's mine.—*D.K., Lincoln, Nebraska*

SHE MAKES UP FOR LOST TIME AFTER THE WHISTLE HAS BLOWN

Two years ago, after my five-year marriage ended in divorce, I enrolled in night school to obtain a certificate in secretarial science. I supported myself and paid my tuition by working days as a cocktail waitress and weekend evenings as a go-go dancer. My social life took a nosedive with the hours I was keeping, and my sexual activity was virtually nil. I finally graduated seven months ago and started working with an agency that specializes in temporary secretarial help.

About two months ago I was given a four-week assignment

with a small company that sells and services heavy machinery. My boss, Roland, was a man in his early fifties, a burly Italian who acted gruff but was really just a big teddy bear. The guys who worked around the office and in the shop were young and studly. Every single one of them made a pass at me in the first week, and I don't mean that we just flirted. As I mentioned before, I've been a dancer, and my body often attracts a lot of attention. Still, none of the guys followed through. I figured maybe Roland enforced the old adage, "You don't get your meat where you earn your bread and butter." At any rate, I found myself getting rather frustrated having all these great hunks wandering around. I had been celibate for two years.

Well, on my second Friday at the job I was headed home after work when I realized that I had left a birthday present for my sister inside my desk drawer. I turned around and went back to the office. When I got there I found, to my surprise, a number of the guys' cars still in the lot. Usually they trip over each other on the way to the door at five o'clock.

I let myself into the office. As I made my way to my desk, a lot of laughter and catcalls drifted out of Roland's office. My curiosity got the better of me, and I quietly made my way over to the open door. From the doorway I could see Rory, Teddy, Rick and Warren sitting around with drinks in their hands, watching Roland's oversize TV set. On the screen was a naked blonde, sitting on a kitchen counter with her legs spread wide open. In front of her was a well-built guy, also naked, who was busy sucking and fingering her cunt.

When I walked in, the guys froze. Then Warren reached over to turn the set off. "Don't do that," I said, "it looks like it's just getting good." That broke the tension. Rick asked if I wanted to join them for a drink and watch the movie. I eagerly accepted the invitation and took a seat on the sofa between Rory and Rick. Warren poured me a stiff Jackie D on the rocks. I settled down to see how the action would develop—on and off screen. I figured that if I didn't get laid now, something was definitely wrong.

The movie screen changed. There was a beautiful redhead with giant tits getting done by two guys. One was fucking her doggie-style while the other stood in front of her and fed her dinner through a big, fat straw. The guys were trying to watch the screen, but kept stealing looks at me out of the corners of their eyes. I loved knowing that my being there was making their breathing even heavier than the video was. For my part, my tits were already heaving pretty hard. Their rise and fall was indicated by my nipples, which were threatening to tear a hole in my flimsy bra.

This went on for a good twenty minutes, and still these guys hesitated to make a move. Eventually I reached over to my right and placed a hand on Rory's crotch. The bulge I felt was most impressive. I moved my left hand over to Rick and felt about the same thing. "You guys must really be enjoying the movie," I said. "I don't know how men can stand having something that hard pressing against their pants. It's got to be uncomfortable." They both muttered in agreement. "Well, dear hearts, why do you insist on suffering?"

I stood up, moved in front of Rory and leaned down to unzip his fly. I had trouble fitting his cock through the opening, so Rory helped me. It stood before my eyes like a flagpole. I squeezed it briefly in my hand, my fingers barely covering the knob. My eager mouth captured the head of his penis as I began to twirl my tongue around the top few inches of his mighty tool. Rory threw his head back and let himself enjoy my cocksucking.

I felt a pair of hands on my hips, and realized that Rick was behind me. He rubbed my hips and ass with his strong hands. It felt great. Soon I felt Rick's hands move down to the bottom of my skirt and raise it gradually above my hips. Rick massaged my ass in earnest. As he squeezed my ass-cheeks against each other I could feel wetness on my pussy lips, and I knew that my panties had already soaked through.

I continued to suck Rory as Rick pulled my panties down to my ankles and I obligingly stepped out of them. Rick's hands slid down the cleft of my ass. He began to move his fingers up and down the length of my cunt lips. My joy-juices were running like a stream now, and his entry into my pussy with his finger was heavenly. The twitching of the dick in my mouth signaled that Rory was ready to come. He gasped, "Please don't let me come yet. I want to save it for your cunt."

I obliged by giving him the squeeze treatment, then disengaged my mouth and stood up. I bent over at the waist, my hands on Roland's desk, and positioned the tip of his cock at my opening, my knees quivering just a little at the thought of finally having a good, hard dick inside me. When I lowered myself onto that magnificent piece of meat, it was like going to heaven. Unable to control my speed, I rode Rory like he was a racehorse. It didn't take long before he let out a moan and spurted his hot come inside me. My orgasm came almost simultaneously and, with a shout of joy, I let go the sexual frustration of many, many months.

I slipped Rory out and turned to see the other three guys standing naked, big grins on their faces. This is what I'd wanted, and I decided to make the most of it.

Rick was next, and he too did me doggie-style, as I stretched over the arm of the sofa. While he was working in and out of my slick cavern I took Warren in my mouth, trying to be careful not to make him come.

Rick was good—very, very good. He lasted a long time, churning along at an even, steady pace, and I came twice before his load joined his buddy Rory's. My orgasms were just like Rick's fucking—long, strong and steady.

I was so satisfied after Rick that I told the guys it was time to take a break. "Don't worry," I winked at the other two, "everybody gets fucked tonight."

We watched the movie for another half hour and had another drink. By then I was as horny as when we had started. Warren asked if he could be next. He took me missionary style while I lay on my back on the wall-to-wall carpet. The other guys stood around us in a circle, cheering us on. Warren knew a lot of moves. He not only varied his tempo, but also swung his ass in almost a corkscrew pattern, causing his cock to reach some out-of-the-way places in my cunt. When I came, I thought my head was going to fly off. It was a tremendous turn-on to be fucked while three studs stood there naked, waiting their turns.

Good old patient Teddy was the last in line, and I decided to give him something special. "Do you like to tit-fuck?" I asked him.

"Who doesn't?" he responded, grinning.

"Well, I think you deserve that little treat for waiting so long." One of the guys came up with a tube of hand lotion from Roland's desk. "Oh, I don't think that's going to be necessary," I said and took a huge scoop of male and female come from between my legs with two fingers. I ran my hand over my cleavage, smearing the moisture everywhere. "There, that should do it. If not, there's plenty more," I said to Teddy. He led me back over to the sofa and sat me down so that my breasts were at the right height for his prick.

Teddy was gentle as he took his dick in his hands and used it to finish spreading love-oil on my tits. He then took one globe in each hand and squeezed them together around his shaft. He caressed my nipples with his thumbs as he began to slide up and down in the lubed groove. The feeling was incredible, and I added to it by reaching down to play with my clit. The other three guys stood close at hand and watched as Teddy began to pump away at my slick cleavage. It didn't take long before he began to geyser great sprays of hot come into the air. I leaned over and caught the first spurt in my mouth.

When Teddy was done, and had reluctantly pulled away, I sat up on the sofa. Rory, bless him, had brought me a dampened towel so that I could clean up. After I got dressed, I gave each guy a kiss and told them all what a great time I'd had.

The last two weeks of my assignment were really something. Whenever possible, without Roland knowing it, one of the guys would get me into a hiding place where we could have a quickie. Sometimes it was in the supply room, sometimes in the little coffee room and other times in the shop tool crib. Believe me, I was making up for my past two years.

When my final Friday arrived, Rory told me that the guys wanted to take me to a farewell dinner and that they would pick me up at my apartment at seven o'clock. I figured it was going to be another fuckathon, but I was wrong.

They picked me up in a rented limo, complete with champagne and assorted snacks. We went to a fine restaurant and they ordered me a superb meal. Then they revealed that they had tickets to see *Phantom of the Opera*. What an evening! When it was over and they took me home, each guy stood in line at my door, kissed me on the cheek and wished me luck. Then Rory handed me a small gift-wrapped box. "From the four of us," he said.

When I was alone in my apartment I opened the box and found inside a beautiful, delicate, gold necklace with a locket attached. I opened the locket and read the inscription. "To the best typist in the world," it read. What else can I say?—*S.L., Brooklyn, New York*

THIS MOTHER IS NAMED THERESE, BUT SHE'S NO MOTHER TERESA

My name is Therese. I'm a forty-two-year-old mother of three. I keep in good physical shape through regular exercise, although

I'm never completely happy with how my body looks. This is probably why I have always ignored my husband Ralph's suggestions that I engage in sex with other men. I've often fantasized about it, but never wanted to take my clothes off in front of someone other than my husband. This all changed, however, shortly after I began working at a local department store.

One of my coworkers is a twenty-six-year-old woman named Lucille. Lu loves to have a good time, and one day she and her friend Lilly were telling me about some of the places they go for entertainment. They asked me what I do for fun, and I said I usually just go home and watch TV. Lu said, "What a drag. You need to get out of the house, girl." They both insisted that we all go out some night and have a good time. I laughed at this, figuring they were just trying to be nice.

When I got home that night, I related the conversation to my husband Ralph. He laughed too, then became serious, saying, "You know, you really don't have that much fun. You ought to take them up on their offer." Well, it wasn't long before Lu asked me to go out with her and Lilly after work one night. I almost said no automatically, but then a little thrill went through me at the idea of doing something different, and I decided to go along.

I wore a print dress with a full skirt to work on the big day, so as to feel comfortable in either a casual or more formal environment. I confess to having spent a long time picking my clothes that morning. I also filled my purse with all sorts of extra makeup so that I could change my look depending on where we ended up. Ralph was as excited about my night out as I was, and gave me a big, warm kiss before we both went off to work. "Have a good time," he told me. "Be careful, but don't be too cautious." He winked at me."And give me a call if I shouldn't wait up." I blushed and gave him another kiss.

After work I rode with Lu in her car, because I didn't know how to get to the place she told me we were going. Heck, I hadn't even heard of it. I felt good about my outfit, though, because Lu was also wearing a dress.

We arrived at the nightclub and found Lilly already there. We sat around drinking wine and talking about men. Both Lu and Lilly seemed to have extensive sexual histories involving a number of different men. That fascinated me, having married Ralph when I was nineteen and a virgin. As the evening went on and the drinks went down, these women began to really open up, comparing their men and their stories. I started to feel my sexual juices flowing. Lu told us about an old boyfriend who could go for an hour or more without coming. Lilly tried to top that, saying that she had a boyfriend who could keep getting it up after he'd come. "How many times?" Lu wanted to know.

"I don't know," Lilly replied, "I always wore out before he did."

They asked me about my experiences, and I admitted that I had only ever had sex with my husband. They thought that was a terrible shame, and suggested that someday they fix me up with one of the young studs they know.

We left soon after, to go to Lu's apartment. She said she had some good wine there. She wanted to kick back and relax more than she could in the bar.

Soon after we arrived, we heard a knock on the door. I thought I saw Lu give Lilly a look before she answered it, as if they were both in on some kind of secret. Lu came back leading three young studs. They were friends of Lu and Lilly, and had rented a videotape that they wanted to watch with us. I was surprised to discover that it was a homemade X-rated video. It showed some guys dancing suggestively around a room for a small audience of women. The ladies on the tape were going wild, pulling at the men's G-strings and feeling them up.

One of the young men with us, Chad, stated that he had often thought about becoming a male stripper. This received a wild response from Lu and Lilly. Chad is really built. He's about twenty-four, with black hair and a lot of muscles. I could tell by the way his chest hair spilled out of the top of his shirt that there was a lot more hidden away. Chad's chest is smooth, and I've often fantasized about fucking a man with a hairy chest.

The girls kept encouraging Chad to stand up and strip for us. At first he coyly said no, but after the guys started in on him too, he stood up and began to dance for us. At first he just gyrated, moving his hips around and then back and forth in a fucking motion. This was exciting enough for me—I was creaming my chair and hollering. Lu and Lilly, though, had started chanting, "The pants, the pants, the pants!" Chad released his belt, eased his fly open and slowly gyrated his hips while his pants slithered down his legs. He kicked them off and they landed in my lap.

At this point I could get a good look at his bulge, which appeared to be enormous. It was straining his underwear, the head peeking up past the waistband. Obviously he liked the attention. Chad approached each of us and danced right in front of us, his crotch at face level. He rocked his hips back and forth in a fucking motion in front of my face. I swear I was drooling. I unconsciously put my tongue out, and he brought his cotton-clad cock just close enough for me to touch with my tongue-tip. The smell of his manly sweat was everywhere.

The other guys, Greg and Cole, didn't like Chad getting all the attention, and they soon joined in. Now we each had our own private dancer, and they switched places every few minutes, so that each woman got a one-man show from each man. Before they started around the circle the second time, Lu pulled off all their underwear, exposing their raging hard-ons to full view. She also gave each of them a quick caress to make sure they were in their full glory. My husband's cock was the only one I had ever seen before, and the sight of three beautiful erect dicks at once made me sweat.

Chad's dick was about seven inches long and quite thick, with dark pubic hair surrounding it. The head glistened with drops of come, as though it was crying to be sucked. Lu took pity on Chad and quickly engulfed his member. I watched as it slid in and out of her mouth. I could not watch for long, though, as Greg was thrusting his prick into my face, and it too begged to be put in a warm, moist place. I opened my mouth and slowly eased his rampant dick past my lips. I love the feel of a man's cock in my mouth, and at that moment Greg's felt as good as anything I'd had in my life. Greg lurched back and forth, pumping his cock into my mouth. My pussy seemed to just keep getting wetter and wetter.

After a few minutes Greg removed his dick from my face and went to Lilly. I felt like my puppy had been stolen, until Cole's erection bobbed toward me. My eyes shut, my mouth opened, and Cole shoved his cock between my lips. I pulled him out for a minute and rubbed his cock all over my face, making incoherent but happy sounds, then began licking his balls. Each of them disappeared into my mouth and got a good sucking. I then reinserted his prick into my mouth and began sucking for all I was worth. I was desperately trying to see how much of his pole I could shove into my mouth and throat when, with very little warning, Cole sent a load of hot semen flowing down my throat.

This was the first time a man had ever come in my mouth. Ralph had always wanted to, but I had resisted, preferring to take his load in my cunt. But Cole had given me no warning, so I experienced for the first time the taste of hot come. Who knew it would be so good? Next came Chad, and he too shot his hot wad into my eagerly waiting mouth. There was so much that I had trouble swallowing all of it, and some dripped onto my dress.

Greg had delivered his spunk to Lilly, so by this time the boys were all temporarily satisfied. I'd had three different men without even removing my clothes!

That changed in a few minutes, as the boys started saying that it was now our turn to dance for them. Lilly was the first on her feet, and Lu and I weren't slow to join her. We all had on long dresses, and we removed our undergarments before we began dancing in front of the guys. They sat on the floor in front of us. We took turns raising our skirts, exposing our cunts to them one at a time from a distance of about five feet. We worked our way slowly toward them until we were just inches from their faces. I could tell they were enjoying the show, as their dicks were all hard again. My pussy was aching to be touched, fucked or sucked—it didn't matter which.

On a signal from Lilly we each raised our skirt and dropped it over the head of the man in front of us. I happened to be standing in front of Cole, and as I dropped my skirt over his head he instinctively rose up to get a closer look at my dripping cunt. He then grabbed my ass, pulled me to him and treated my pussy to a soft, sensuous kiss. My juices were flowing all over his face as he began to lick and kiss my slit. He rolled my clit around with his lips, and inserted his tongue into my steaming love-canal.

Lilly signaled again and we all switched. This time I put my dress over Greg's head. The feeling was just as good, as Greg licked and kissed my pussy and tongue-fucked me until I screamed with delight. Next it was Chad's turn, and he gave me a tongue-lashing I'll never forget. I began convulsing, and came while he was sucking on my clit.

At that point my knees grew weak and I slid backward onto the floor. Chad ended up on top of me, my motion pulling him forward as he held on to me to ease my landing. He was lying on top of me, and I felt his hard cock against my swollen pussy lips. I adjusted his prick so that its head lay at my entrance. He quickly entered me and began pumping away, using a smooth, steady rhythm. This was just what my aching pussy needed. The excitement was intensified by the fact that this was the first time I had ever fucked a man other than Ralph.

Chad pumped in and out of me for the longest time, and I became even more aroused, something I would have said up until then wasn't possible. I loved the feel of his hairy chest. Wanting to feel his hair rub against the soft skin of my breasts, I pulled down the top of my dress and unhooked my bra. I also love having my tits sucked during sex, so I pushed Chad's head down until he took one of my pointy nipples into his mouth and began vigorously sucking on it. I told him that I liked having my breasts licked all over, slowly and softly. He was a quick learner, and I leaned back to fully enjoy the exquisite pleasure of a hard dick in my moist cunt and soft caresses on my ample tits.

Soon Chad pulled his cock out of my cunt, slid it up to my chest and began fucking my tits. Cole quickly filled the spot between my legs, licking my soaking pussy before turning me over. Chad was under me, still fucking my tits, when Cole entered my pussy from behind. I was in heaven. Here for the first time I was enjoying two men at once, and I quickly went over the edge. As I convulsed in my second orgasm of the short evening, Chad began coming between my tits. I licked up all that came close to my mouth. Cole then arched his back and came in a flood. He filled my pussy to overflowing with hot semen. I was ecstatic with pleasure.

Before the night was over I had sucked all the guys, had had my pussy eaten and had been fucked no fewer than three times. I enjoyed every minute of it. When I got home I told my husband Ralph of the evening's events, after he noticed a come spot on my dress. To my delight he was not angry, and even suggested that I try to see them again sometime soon. I know that I will. Lilly, Lu and I talked at work the next day about trying to arrange our schedules so that we all had an evening off together. Next time I think I'll take Ralph along. He would enjoy the show and maybe even join in. Lu and Lilly have met Ralph and said they would love to show him the ropes. Ralph is delighted at my change of mind. When we all do get together, you can be sure my fellow *Penthouse Letter* readers will be the first to know.—*T.M., Columbus, Ohio*

SHE ASKS EBONY BALLS TO CUE UP FOR HER AT THE POOL TABLE

I've read *Penthouse Letters* for years looking for interesting new ideas to experiment with. My husband and I have enjoyed a wide variety of interesting sexual experiences, but recently I was able to participate in my all-time favorite fantasy.

My husband and I were at a local club having a drink and talking to a really nice black guy named Lawrence. (My husband and I are both white.) One thing led to another, and before long I told Lawrence about my favorite fantasy—being fucked by a group of black guys on a pool table.

Within thirty minutes we were driving behind Lawrence on the way to his house. He served us drinks, made some phone calls and then suggested we sit in his hot tub. The three of us got undressed and proceeded to do just that. I was getting really turned on when the doorbell rang and Lawrence said, "That must be my friends." Then he looked at me and said, "Cindy, would you like to answer the door?"

Without any hesitation I got up and went to the door, dripping wet and naked. I opened it and found four very surprised black men. I stood in front of them, holding the door open and letting them get a good long look before I coyly invited them to come inside. Then I calmly went back to the hot tub.

Lawrence had music playing and one of the new arrivals asked me to dance so I got out of the tub and slow-danced in the nude with a guy who was fully dressed. The feel of his cold brass belt buckle against my stomach and the coarse material of his shirt against my straining nipples was driving me crazy. My pussy was throbbing and I just couldn't wait any longer, so I said to Lawrence, "I'm ready if you are."

Six men with hard-ons followed me into the den where the pool table was. When we got there Lawrence picked me up, put me on the pool table and told me to spread my arms and legs out toward the corners. I couldn't help touching myself as I watched the other guys undress. I was in heaven, and my hips were grinding like crazy, when Lawrence took my hand away from my wet snatch and said, "That's my job."

Lawrence then got on the table and began to fuck me. I went crazy and kept yelling for more. There was a mirror on the ceiling above the pool table, so I just lay back and watched myself getting fucked. It really looked hot seeing Lawrence's ebony form pumping between my pale white legs. I think Lawrence fucked me for fifteen or twenty minutes. Finally he exploded inside of me. Then he stepped aside and watched as each of his friends took their turn. I'd had so many orgasms that I was becoming weak and dizzy, but I found the situation so exciting that by the time they had all had a turn I was ready for them again. Each one of them took a very quick second turn—just long enough for them to shoot their second loads into me. But I didn't mind. I just kept coming and watching myself in the mirror.

When they were done, my husband got on the table and was going to help me up when I said, "I want you to fuck me too!" So he got on top of me and fucked me. I had so much come in me and was so wet that I could barely feel him. He, however, seemed to feel me just fine because he came with a loud cry after only a few quick strokes.

On our way home I was so exhausted that I fell asleep in the car. But as my eyes closed and I drifted off I smiled because I knew that I had finally gotten to live my greatest fantasy and that after some rest I would discuss every little detail with my husband.—*Name and address withheld*

CHECKING INTO A HOTEL GETS HER CHECKED OUT—THEN MATED

I have been married for ten years to a wonderful man who earns a good living, has a sweet disposition, is quite handsome and, most important, is a superb lover. Nonetheless, three years ago I developed an irresistible urge to experience some other men. While my husband and I regularly had intense and exciting sex, it just wasn't enough for me. I wanted variety.

While my husband and I always fantasized together about me dressing like a slut and picking up other men, I knew he would never accept me doing so in reality. I had purchased some erotic outfits to entertain him with in the bedroom, but I never wore them out of the house, even though I felt terrific in them. I'm five feet four inches tall and weigh one hundred and fifteen pounds. I have 36C breasts, a twenty-eight-inch waist and thirty-five-inch hips. I knew then as I do now that I have a smashing figure and a beautiful face with tempting lips and eyes.

My husband travels out of town for a few days at least once a month. During one of his absences a while back, I decided that I just couldn't stand being without a man. The first morning he was away I must have brought myself off a half dozen times with my fingers, a vibrator and a huge dildo—but I was still unsatisfied. My daughter was at school and was planning to sleep over at a friend's house that night. I had the house to myself for the evening, so I decided to do something about my frustration.

I put on a black leather miniskirt, a black garter belt, fishnet stockings, high-heeled black pumps (to accent my ass), a black, deeply-cut lace bra and a sheer black blouse. I didn't put on any panties. I made my face up heavily with red lipstick, mascara and foundation, and put on a good dose of Obsession perfume. I looked and smelled like every man's wet dream. Looking at my outrageously sexy outfit in the mirror and imagining the lust it would inspire in men got me so excited that I fingered myself to yet another orgasm before leaving the house.

My plan was to rent a room at one of the hotels just outside of town where I knew there would be a crowd of businessmen attending a meeting. On my way to the hotel I rented a couple of X-rated movies. Before going into the hotel, I covered myself up with a light raincoat so that my intentions wouldn't be quite so obvious to the hotel staff.

After checking into a room, I went down to the lobby without the raincoat. After ordering a drink I sat down at a table expecting to catch someone's attention fairly quickly.

I wasn't disappointed. Within five minutes three guys who had been talking together approached me. They looked about thirty years old and were all well-built. They asked me if I was staying at the hotel and I told them I was. I then explained that I had been bored sitting alone at home and had decided to go out and see if I could make something happen. I uncrossed and opened my legs to give them a quick preview.

With their pricks beginning to visibly harden, I knew they were more than willing, so I invited them up to my room. I learned that day that what I really like is group sex—and lots of it!

In the elevator on the way up to my room I began to playfully rub against the guys and give them kisses. By the time we got to my hotel room door they were touching and squeezing me all over.

Once inside I told them all to get out of their clothes. I kept mine on, though my nipples already had nudged out over the edge of my bra and were sticking out quite a bit through my sheer blouse. After they had stripped I started licking their cocks and balls. When they were good and hard I proceeded to slowly strip my clothing off and throw it at them a piece at a time. Once I was nude I told them that I wanted them all at once.

They began to suck and lick me all over, from my clitoris to my nipples to the nape of my neck. Having three tongues and six hands going all over my body at once was an unbelievable turn-on. While they were working on me I intermittently squeezed and sucked their cocks and balls. All the time they were talking dirty to me—asking me how I would like being fucked by them in a public place like the corner of some dark restaurant, or whether I'd enjoy doing it with a half-dozen guys on a table in a dingy bar. I felt incredibly dirty, sexy and turned on. After about a half hour of foreplay I got on all fours, took hold of the longest, thickest prick of the three and guided it into my dripping cunt. I motioned for the other guys to lie on the bed in front of me, and I alternated between sucking and jacking off their thick, hairy pricks. The experience of having three pricks moving in and out of me was exquisite. I began to tremble and shake. We did this for what seemed an eternity until, one after the other, we all exploded in orgasm. My orgasm was absolutely incredible. I must have twitched for five minutes, totally enraptured.

We then took showers together and did lots of touching. They stayed with me the rest of the afternoon and all evening. We even watched the X-rated movies to stimulate our imaginations. One of the guys went out and got some fast food for us, but other than that we only ate each other. I must have had twenty orgasms, each one quite powerful. For the first time in ages I felt sexually satisfied. By the time they left the next morning, I knew for sure what I had always suspected—that I was a fucking nymphomaniac!

I never told my husband about this episode, or all the incredible ones which have since followed. We still have great sex together, but nothing like the sex I have when I'm on my own. I advertise in swinger magazines and have started enjoying women as well as men. When my daughter is in school and my husband is at work I spend most of my day getting quickies at some neighborhood bar. I now have quite a wardrobe of slutty clothes and have become quite an exhibitionist. When my husband goes away on business, I check into my favorite hotel. All the employees there now know me—in every sense of the word!

This is one woman who can say she has her cake and eats it.—*L.E., Walnut Creek, California*

FROM CONTRACT BRIDGE TO STRIP POKER TO STRIPPED POKERS

Like most people who read *Penthouse Letters*, I never believed that the stories in it were true. Well, I've finally had some experiences which make me question this conventional wisdom.

My wife June and I are blessed with some very good friends. Two such friends are Reed and Lucille. Both are younger than we, and both really love a good time.

It all began when the four of us were playing contract bridge. We had been playing bridge every Saturday night for the previous six months, and after all that time it was getting a little boring. So, on this particular Saturday night, Reed and I thought it would be great if we could talk the girls into playing strip poker. I left it up to Reed to approach the girls on the subject.

"I know! Let's play a little strip poker for a change," Reed blurted out as soon as we had sat down to play cards. Much to our surprise, the girls agreed. (Maybe the grain alcohol and orange juice we were all drinking had something to do with their answer.)

It didn't take long before we were all naked as jaybirds, and believe me I was enjoying the scenery. Lucille is a large gal, standing about five feet, eleven inches tall. She's a natural blonde and has a great body and long, sexy legs. Her pubic hair is light brown, which contrasts nicely with June's jet-black pussy hair.

Since we were all nude, Lucille asked, "What should we play now?" Well, we all put our heads together (so to speak) and came up with a new game.

These were the rules: First we'd each take a card from the extra deck we had and place it facedown on the table in front of us. That card would be our bet, with different cards representing different sexual acts. Cards of any suit between two to ten represented a fuck, with the number of the card standing for the number of strokes that would be made. An ace meant you would have to let your spouse fuck you while you sucked on the genitals of the member of the other couple of the opposite sex. For the ladies, a Jack meant being fucked doggie-style—either by one of the guys or by the other girl with a strap-on dildo. A king or a queen meant the winners could do whatever they wanted to whomever they wanted.

Making up these new rules was getting us all turned on, but fast! Reed won the first hand and only June called his bet. Reed had a full house and June had three of a kind. Slowly, he turned over June's bet card. It was a jack of spades, which meant that June was going to be fucked by Reed doggie-style! Slowly June got up and bent over the card table exposing her ass and cunt, while Reed got up from his chair. Then, gently stroking his nine-and-a-half-inch prick, he stepped up behind her and began rubbing the head of his cock all over her glistening cunt.

He placed the head of his huge cock between her cunt lips and started slowly thrusting into her. Just then Lucille started yelling, "Fuck her honey, fuck her! Push that big prick of yours all the way in!" And fuck her he did. I never thought that I would get so turned on seeing another man put his meat into my wife!

Reed fucked her until they were both on the verge of orgasm. Then he stopped. June begged him to finish what he had started, but he refused, saying, "We still have a long night ahead of us."

Lucille won the next hand. When she turned her bet card over she revealed a queen, which meant it was her choice to do whatever she wanted. With a gleam in her eye she turned to me and said, "I want you to eat my cunt."

"How long?" I asked.

"Until I tell you to stop, of course!" She went over to the easy chair, sat down and spread her legs, exposing a juicy pink cunt. I knelt down in front of her and began running my tongue up and down her slit. I gently sucked her clit as she moaned and squirmed. It wasn't long before Reed and June came over to watch. Reed had his meat in his hand and was stroking it, while June was busy pinching her nipples and fingering her cunt. Then, card game forgotten, Reed reached over and began finger-fucking June. Every now and then he would withdraw his fingers and lick them.

This went on through most of the night until we had all fucked and sucked one another.

When it was all over we got dressed and had a bite to eat. We all agreed we would get together for more card parties like this one in the future.

After that we had many more encounters with Reed and Lucille. One I remember especially well occurred on Lucille's birthday. June was away on business, so I went alone when Reed and Lucille invited me to dinner.

After dinner we had some drinks and sat down to watch a little TV. Soon the drinks had the three of us feeling pretty good and we began to loosen up. We all knew what we wanted; it just took us a little while to get started.

First Reed and Lucille started smooching. Then Reed went into the bedroom and came back wearing a shirt and nothing else. He then sat back down beside Lucille and went back to making out. Lucille then grabbed his prick and began stroking it. It didn't take long for it to get hard.

I was getting pretty horny watching the two of them, and was wondering how to join in, when Lucille came over to me, reached inside my pants and took hold of my stiff prick. Boy, did that feel good!

After getting us both good and hard, Lucille went into the bedroom and came out holding something behind her back. She asked me, "Do you want to see what Reed gave me for my birthday?" I nodded and she pulled out the biggest dildo I'd ever seen. It must have been twelve inches long and a good two inches in diameter. It was chocolate brown in color.

"Give us a show, Lucille!" Reed said.

"Wait, I have to get some K-Y jelly from the bedroom so it will slide in easily," she replied.

Soon she came out of the bedroom with that large dildo hanging between her legs. She then sat on the easy chair, spread her legs apart and began slowly fucking herself with that dark brown dildo.

What a sight! Reed and I couldn't help stroking ourselves as we watched that massive dildo disappearing into her.

Lucille then said, "I want the two of you to jack off and shoot your come at the same time all over this big dildo."

We were more than eager to shoot our loads in front of this sexy woman. The only problem was managing to do it at the same time. But we did it! As we shot our come onto her cunt and that big rubber dildo Lucille slammed the dildo into herself and came with a loud groan. What an evening! After we both fucked Lucille we called it a night. Later on I told June all about it. Her only regret was that she hadn't been there.

Once June and I had started exploring group sex we couldn't get enough. After a while, making it with just one other couple started to seem limiting. So, together with Reed and Lucille, we planned a big costume party.

Six couples were invited. There was Lucille and Reed, June and myself, Kathy and Joe, Dirk and Sarah, Peter and Jean, and a surprise couple whom Peter and Jean had invited.

The surprise husband-and-wife team was Stewart and Darlene. Stewart and Darlene were black. Steward was built like an athlete, with broad shoulders and a small waist. He was over six feet tall. Darlene looked like a black goddess. She had huge tits and a big, firm ass.

Everyone was supposed to be wearing their costumes under their regular clothes. After we all loosened up with several drinks, Jean announced that the party was going to begin!

The first activity on the agenda was a game she called, "Tie a yellow ribbon round the old oak tree." Jean sent Stewart out of the room and then handed out yellow ribbons to each of the girls. Then, as the strains of "Tie a Yellow Ribbon" came out of the stereo, Stewart stepped into the room, wearing nothing but a bow tie.

That Adonis-like body brought a lot of gasps from the women. His cock was magnificent. Even in its flaccid state it was a good nine inches long. As he walked from one girl to the next, they each tied their yellow ribbon on his oak tree. By the time he had gotten to June, his prick was beginning to come alive, and had grown to nearly twelve inches. By the time he got to his wife, Darlene, it was fully erect and glistening.

Darlene knew what Stewart liked so she licked and tongued his dick for a while, getting the rest of the girls wild with envy. They wanted some of that black meat also. Then, before Darlene's ministrations could bring Stewart off, Jean called out, "Costumes, everyone!" Everyone then stripped off their outer clothes.

Darlene was wearing a red lacy camisole. Lucille had on only a corset that left her large breasts exposed. June was wearing black crotchless panties, and a bra that exposed her nipples. Kathy had on a tight miniskirt which barely covered her ass, and no panties. Sarah was dressed in a short see-through skirt and nothing else. Jean just wore a silk scarf around her waist.

Men's underwear being what it is, the guys couldn't find anything to match the girls' outfits, so we all just went buck naked. I had gone one step further, however, and had shaved all the hair off my cock.

All the women were eager to get at Stewart's twelve-incher and, before the night was over, they had all had that massive cock inside each of them at least once. The rest of the men got their share of pussy as well.

At one point Lucille demanded that Reed put his cock in her

mouth while Stewart's cock was in her cunt. As a matter of fact, all the women wanted the same thing: their mouths and cunts filled with dick at the same time. That was certainly a memorable evening!

Even though we love group sex, June and I still know how to have a good time when we're alone. We must have tried every conceivable sex toy ever made—from skinny six-inch dildos to fat twelve-inch dildos, from cock rings to ben-wah balls.

One day I told June that I was going to bring home an extra-big dildo, one that was about twelve inches long and three inches in diameter. When I got home she rushed me into the bedroom so we could play with our new toy.

Foreplay is all-important for June and me. In fact, sometimes we spent entire nights without getting past foreplay!

We started off this night's foreplay with a wide variety of dildos. After she was nice and wet, I slipped our smallest dildo into her. She moaned with pleasure. Just as she was really starting to get into being fucked by this first dildo, I took it out of her and replaced it with our next-largest dildo. This time she moaned louder.

We continued working our way up until she was finally ready for the big one! Slowly I placed the head of that huge dildo in between June's cunt lips. "Go slow," she said. "This one is a little large and it may hurt."

Following her instructions, I slowly slipped this magnificent instrument into her straining pussy. Before long I had about eight inches of that dildo inside her beautiful cunt. I then began fucking her with it.

Slowly at first, then faster, I fucked June's pussy with the dildo until she started to yell, "Harder! Faster!" I could tell that she was about to come by the way she was bucking her hips. Then she came, letting out a scream of ecstasy. I let her calm down and then slowly inched out the rubber cock. June had the most satisfied look on her face that I have ever seen.

Lately June has been seeing one of my coworkers on the side. I am happy for her, because it has been a while since she has had a strange cock in that gorgeous love-hole of hers.

Just the other day June and I started making plans to seduce a black couple who live across the hall from us. We'll see what happens and let you know!—*Name and address withheld*

ENERGIZED BEACH BUNNIES—THEY KEEP COMING AND COMING

The Saturday before my wedding day I had my last sexual fling as a bachelorette, and my best friend and maid of honor, Debby, joined me in the festivities.

Debby is five foot six, weighs one hundred and twenty pounds and has the most beautiful pair of pointed nipples I've ever seen, perched atop a pair of gorgeous 34B breasts. Her best asset is her shoulder-length, silky brunette hair. I'm five foot eight and weigh one hundred and forty pounds. I have short blonde hair and a firm ass that fills my jeans nicely.

My bachelorette party was supposed to be a very quiet luncheon held by Debby and a few of my friends. That's how it started, but that's sure not the way it ended up!

After lunch I asked Debby if she wanted to go to the beach with me. I knew that if we were out of town she was more likely to get wild and party. At first she hesitated, but then I told her I thought I deserved a real bachelorette party and that if she wouldn't come I'd go without her. That convinced her.

As we drove, I told Debby that even though I loved my husband-to-be and he had a great eight-inch cock, I found him too conservative sexually. "He's the kind of guy who thinks only sluts suck dick," I said. Then I explained that he was only marrying me because he thought I was a good girl.

When we got to the beach we rented a motel room and then went out to do a little window-shopping. As we passed one shop, Debby stopped to stare at a headless mannequin wearing a black string bikini under a sheer cotton blouse. Debby said a girl would have to be headless to wear an outfit like that. I disagreed and went inside to buy each of us the outfit.

On the way back to our hotel room we noticed several college-age guys running back and forth between the rooms next to ours. As we were unlocking our door, one of the guys asked us if we wanted to go to a party with them. Debby coldly told the guy we had other plans and stepped into the room. I stayed behind and told the guy I would change her mind. "Have a few beers and wait for us by the pool," I told him.

I knew if I could get Debby hot she would go along with me to the party, so when I got into the room I started undressing next to her, telling her we should try on our new bikinis.

Debby's eyes widened as I began to unbutton my blouse. We

didn't usually change in front of each other. I think that was because we both felt a certain amount of sexual tension in each other's company. I had taken my blouse and skirt off, and was wearing nothing but a lacy bra and a matching pair of panties. I said to Debby, who was just standing there, "Don't you want to try on your new bikini? Do you need help getting out of your dress?"

I stepped up behind her and started to unbutton her dress. Debby began to tremble as I pushed the dress off her shoulders and let it drop to the floor. Then I removed her bra and stepped around in front of her. Her gorgeous nipples were erect, so I bent over and took one into my mouth and she reached behind me and cupped my ass-cheeks in her cold little hands. We fell on the bed.

Debby had told me that she once orgasmed just from having a guy suck on her nipples. I was determined to prove that I could excite her as much as any guy could and I succeeded. By using my lips and tongue on her nipples I soon had her orgasming.

As she caught her breath I started asking her about the time she was gang banged by five guys. Breathing deeply, Debby described how she had gone to a black tie social banquet and on a dare ended up in a suite with five guys. She had sucked, fucked and let them bang her all night!

When Debby had gotten totally turned on from telling me about that night, I told her I wanted to live out my own sexual fantasy—letting three guys fuck me at the same time. Debby was so turned on by now that she said, "Then let's go find three guys!"

As I finger-fucked her I said, "Let's find three guys for each of us."

Wearing only the bikini bottoms and transparent blouses I had bought earlier, we were soon heading out the door to meet the guys by the pool.

When we got outside I was disappointed to find that none of the guys were there. But then Debby noticed that the door to one of the rooms down the hall was open. Curious, we headed toward the door. When we got to the open doorway I got the surprise of my life. Three incredibly good-looking guys were standing around the bed naked. As soon as they saw us they invited us in.

It seems the guys had been listening at our door while I had been persuading Debby to come out and party. They had heard everything, and were more than willing to fulfill my fantasy.

I was already stripping off my blouse as Debby turned around to lock the door. In moments I was lying on my back on the bed with one of the guys climbing between my thighs.

I was on my back fucking away as I watched Debby strip her blouse off and start sucking another guy's cock. She engulfed it over and over again while playing with his balls. Then she deep-throated him, and her eyes opened wide. I realized then that the guy was coming down her throat. Debby swallowed it all without losing a single drop!

Debby's guy's cock soon grew hard again while watching his buddy fuck me, so Debby pushed him down on the other bed and straddled him. As I watched his massive cock plunge into her tight, wet pussy I started to come. This caused the guy who was fucking me to shoot his load deep inside me.

I then crawled over to Debby's bed and sat on the face of the guy she was fucking. Facing Debby, I started tongue-kissing her and massaging her sexy tits as the guy we were both mounted on worked his tongue deep inside me. Soon all three of us had explosive orgasms.

Leaving the guy Debby and I had just fucked to rest, I then asked the other two guys if they would fuck me. Needless to say, they were eager to comply.

I got on the bed on all fours and Debby guided one of the guys' stiff cocks into my steaming hole. Meanwhile I swallowed the other guy's tool all the way down, letting him fuck my throat.

Debby had one hand on my hip and one hand on the ass of the guy behind me. She was helping us get into a steady fucking rhythm. Watching me get double-fucked from just a few inches away was getting Debby so hot that she started yelling for the guy I was blowing to come all over my face. In a moment, he did.

Debby and I started kissing as the guy behind me drove his stiff cock into my pussy. When I had an orgasm I cried out into Debby's face, causing the guy who was fucking me to climax inside me. After a brief rest I followed one of the guys into the shower.

Once in the shower, I soaped up his body from head to toe, then started sucking on his flaccid cock. When his dick got hard I sent him out to fuck Debby, and he sent one of the other guys into the shower.

As I was giving this other guy the same treatment, I heard someone knocking on the front door. The first guy then came into the bathroom and told me that his buddies were at the door. He wanted to know if it was all right to let them in.

I stepped out of the shower and went into the other room. Debby was lying on her back with her legs spread, gently fingering herself. I asked her if she was ready to handle a few more guys. Her only response was to nod and jam two fingers deep into her soaking pussy.

There was another quiet tap on the door so, not wearing a stitch of clothing, I went to answer it. When I opened the door I found four very surprised guys staring at me. Then their eyes widened even further and their jaws dropped as they saw Debby finger-fucking herself on the bed. They rushed inside and I locked the door behind them.

Debby looked up at the newcomers and said, "I want to be fucked by all of you." The guys were dumbstruck, so I went up to the closest guy and pulled his sweatpants down around his knees. He had an erection that was easily eight inches long. I wrapped my fingers around his cock and pulled him toward Debby. That was all the encouragement he needed.

As the guy with the eight-inch dick fucked Debby, I sat on the bed and looked into her eyes. They were shining with pleasure, and I realized she was experiencing consecutive orgasms. She was gasping and quivering. Her knees were bent, her feet were flat on the bed and her hips were thrusting upward to meet each stroke.

As they stood at the foot of the bed watching Debby get fucked, the rest of the newcomers started to strip. As these guys waited their turn to fuck Debby, I sat down on the other bed and told them I would suck their cocks while they waited.

As I sucked cock and watched each guy take a turn with Debby, I became amazed that she was still going. I guess the fact that Debby is a long-distance runner gave her the stamina to continue. She was in an animalistic frenzy that infected the guys fucking her. Her runner's thigh muscles gave her the strength to lift her ass up off the pillow and meet each stroke of each guy who fucked her. Only the two guys who had come in my mouth lasted any appreciable length of time before coming inside her. She was out-fucking them all!

After they had all been fucked dry, the guys sat watching Debby finger-fuck herself into an orgasm that shook the bed. Then she finally started to calm down. Everyone watched as, shuddering and gasping for air, she came down from her sexual high.

As Debby calmed down she looked around and found herself in a room full of naked guys, her hips propped up on a come-drenched pillow and her spread-eagle legs dripping with come.

She laughed, closed her knees with a groan and ran into the bathroom. I got up and followed her in. I found her sitting on the toilet letting the come drip out of her red, swollen pussy. I sat on the floor and told her she had been awesome. But Debby was embarrassed and didn't answer. She just went into the shower.

While Debby was in the shower I went out and talked with the guys. There were five guys left standing, since two of them had passed out from too much beer and fucking. They wanted me and Debby to join them in the room next door, since the bed Debby had just been gang banged on was drenched with sweat and come.

I told the guys that I was willing to come with them, but that Debby was tired and wanted to go back to our room. The guys agreed, and I borrowed a shirt and a pair of shorts and handed them in to Debby.

When Debby came out she had put on the shorts and shirt. I told her she would find the key to our room under the doormat, and that she should go lie down. I told her I would join her later but that first I was going to go next door and get fucked by the guys some more.

As the guys filed out of the room they all stopped to tell Debby that she was the most sensual female they had ever met. Before following them out of the room I winked at Debby and said, "I think they're absolutely right."

Once we got to the next room the guys started to strip right away. Then Debby surprised us all by walking in and sitting down in a chair to watch. I was determined to make sure she got an eyeful!

I sat down on the foot of the bed and stripped off the jersey I had borrowed from one of the guys. Then I started running my hands up and down my body and massaging my breasts. I asked if anyone had some Vaseline. One guy said he did, and jumped up to get it. I stood up, leaned back against the desk, spread my pussy lips enticingly and told the guys I wanted them all to fuck me.

The guy with the Vaseline came back and stood next to me, greasing up his cock. I told them that if they did what I wanted first, I would do whatever they wanted afterward. The guys all nodded agreement, so I took charge and started positioning them the way I wanted.

I had the guy with the Vaseline on his dick lie on his back. Then I straddled him so that he could fuck my big tits. I then had the guy with the biggest cock mount me and fuck me from behind. I then told the last three guys that I would suck on one of their cocks while giving the other two handjobs.

When the tit-fucker came I had one of the other guys take his place. Then the guy fucking me from behind came too, and another guy took his place. Each of those guys came in or on me at least twice as they took turns fucking my face, my tits and my pussy.

As the five guys took turns fucking me, I discovered I could make them come faster by tightening my cunt muscles. I did this trick over and over again, milking the last drop of come out of each of them.

After the last guy shot his load deep into my pussy I looked over at Debby, who, in the meantime, had taken off her shorts and fingered herself to another orgasm while watching the hot action.

Debby stared at me wide-eyed, as if she couldn't believe what I had just done. She asked if she could do anything for me. I just leaned back, spread my pussy lips and let the come drain down my inner thighs.

Meanwhile, the guy with the big dick was hard again, and told Debby he wanted to fuck her once more. Debby took me aside and said she was sore, that the only sex she wanted was for me to tongue-kiss her swollen pussy lips. I thought this was a great idea, so I told the guy and his buddies to go out for a swim while Debby and I took a shower. When Debby and I were in the shower I squatted down and started licking her very red, swollen pussy. Suddenly we realized we weren't alone. The guys had snuck back into the room and were watching us make it in the shower.

I told them to get out and wait for me in the next room. Then I wrapped a towel around myself and told Debby I would go get rid of them.

As I was talking to the guys Debby walked in, also wrapped in a towel. The guys were begging me to let them watch Debby and me get it on, and they promised not to interfere. I didn't think Debby would want to, and I started to say so, but she surprised me again. With a nervous look she kissed me, then, asking me to be gentle, she led me to the bed.

Licking my lips, I told her to get into the 69 position. As the guys watched Debby crawled up on the bed and lowered her pussy onto my face. We were really getting into tonguing each other's come-soaked pussies when the guys broke their promise.

Lifting her up as if she were no heavier than a doll, they lowered her onto me pussy-first, and started sliding her back and forth over my face. I gripped her ass-cheeks and started licking her entire come-drenched crotch.

When Debby saw that the guy with the big dick was hard again she took a deep breath and said, "Fuck me again, but be careful!" She went down on me while the guy lubed her aching pussy with Vaseline. When he slipped his big cock into her lubricated cunt, she moaned, her face rising for a moment out of my crotch. That triggered a convulsive series of orgasms in me, and I came and came as I watched two more guys take turns fucking her from behind.

As I drove home the next morning, I told Debby that I planned to write down the details of our gang bang and send them to *Penthouse Letters*! I also told her that in one year we were going to celebrate our first anniversary with a second gang bang!—*L.S., Gainesville, Florida*

Girls & Girls/Boys & Boys

SHE WENT LOOKING FOR PUSSY AND GOT SNATCH GALORE

I'm a sexy twenty-one-year-old secretary. I recently moved out of my parents' house and into my own apartment. Like many women today, I've been curious about what it would be like to make it with another woman. My desire for girl-girl sex has long been fueled by the sapphic pictorials appearing in your magazine every month.

One night I decided it was time to shut up and just do it. I decided to try a gay bar. It was the first time I had been in one, and I expected to see lots of masculine-looking women. Instead I saw some rather beautiful, very feminine ladies. After a couple of drinks, I lost my timidness and noticed a gorgeous blonde sitting alone at a table. Her shoulder-length golden hair was parted in the middle. She was wearing tight jeans and a sheer blouse, and her large, round breasts were braless, the nipples poking through the gauzy material.

I stood and walked over to her table, feeling my own small but cute 34As bouncing freely under my sweater. I asked if I might join her. She nodded. I sat down and the two of us chatted amicably. Her name was Beth. A little later I asked her if she would like to go back to my apartment, as I had better-quality whiskey. She smiled and told me she would be delighted.

I drove us to my apartment. I fixed us both a drink and then joined Beth on the sofa. Neither one of us was feeling any pain at this point. I brazenly put my arm around her and drew her close to me. She leaned her head on my shoulder while I ran my fingers through her hair. Then she looked up into my eyes, as if she wanted to be kissed, so I obliged her. It was the first time I had ever kissed a woman, and it was great. Her lips were so small and soft. The whiskey had made me high, and Frenching Beth made me even higher. I was flying, and my pussy was wet and open. I reached down to her blouse, fumbled with the buttons and was soon cupping her warm breasts. They were so large, firm and soft, and her nipples were really long and thick. Her breasts were so different from mine.

My head was spinning. Sensing my giddiness, Beth held me in her arms and guided her nipple to my lips. While I worked on the hardening nub, she pulled my sweater completely off, exposing my little tits. Her caress was so gentle and tender that I shivered all over.

At this point Beth suggested we go to my bedroom. We staggered in and I flopped onto the bed. Beth unfastened my jeans and pulled them off, along with my drenched panties. I watched as she removed her blouse, then unsnapped her jeans and slowly pulled them down until her thick, blonde bush was visible. Obviously Beth didn't much care for underwear.

I lay flat on my back, and Beth got on top of me and French-kissed me, crushing my breasts against her own. Shortly thereafter, she pried my legs apart and guided her pretty face between them. While her nimble mouth sucked and nibbled my pussy, I erupted in a great, surging climax.

Beth wanted me to go down on her. Realizing that I was more than ready for her, she sat on my face, which allowed me to tongue her with minimal effort. Even in my overly anxious condition, I was able to bring her off.

After she regained her strength, she fingered me and sucked my stiff nipples at the same time. I grabbed her ass-cheeks and fondled them. We were very tired, so we soon fell asleep for the night. Since we both had to get up for work the next morning, we woke, showered, ate breakfast and left.

I truly love being with her, and at this moment she is my number-one lover. As long as I can have a sexy, warm lady, I'll be completely satisfied.—*Name and address withheld*

AFTER MUCH FRUSTRATION, HE FINALLY GOT HIS MAN

I am writing this letter to let your readers know that even their wildest, most perverse fantasies can come true, as they will find out from my experience with my best friend Mark.

First I would like it to be known that I am not gay; in fact, I don't even think I'm bi. I simply have this uncontrollable desire to be intimately close with very good friends, male and female. I find it very hard to undress in front of my buddies without getting sexually aroused, and I wonder what they think when they see my cock growing hard. It can be very embarrassing.

Mark has been a friend of mine for three years now. Our experience happened only a few months ago, right after he turned eighteen. One night we went out looking for snatch. We couldn't pick anyone up, so we proceeded to his house, where I was to drop him off. As we turned down his street my tire went flat, so Mark invited me to spend the night.

We had finished off almost a case of beer while looking for girls that night, so I was feeling pretty good—and horny as hell. I had always fantasized about getting into Mark's pants and was hoping that maybe he wanted to get into mine.

We went straight to Mark's bedroom to smoke some herb. His room was furnished with a thick carpet, tables and chairs. There was no bed. A few sleeping bags were strewn on the rug instead. We sat around and got high, listening to music and talking about how horny we both were. I was praying that something sexual would happen between us.

The next thing I knew, Mark was sound asleep. I thought, Why not see what it feels like? I squeezed his dick through his jeans. He woke right up and I quickly pulled my hand away. He did not seem too upset. I asked him if he had ever been in a circle jerk. He said "No," adding that he couldn't get off on anything like that. Then I asked him if he had ever jerked off in front of a mirror. I told him that I had and that I found I had better orgasms watching myself beating my meat, with my balls flapping against my inner thighs. He laughed and admitted that he occasionally used a mirror while jacking off.

I asked, "What's the difference between watching yourself and someone else? Either way it should feel better."

"I guess so," he replied. "But I still don't think I could get into it."

Afraid that I had already said too much, and not wanting to lose Mark as my best friend, I suggested we crash before I put my foot in my mouth yet again. He crawled into his sleeping bag wearing his jeans, but I took mine off. Of course, my cock was ready to rip through my shorts. Mark looked right at it, and I explained that I was so fucking horny I could jack off right there. He told me he wouldn't care if I did.

I was still a little leery of what he would think, so I crawled in my sleeping bag before pulling my penis out of my shorts. I made a point of stroking it straight up and down so that Mark could see the length of it even though it was under the covers. I looked over at him and saw that he was jacking off also.

I put my peter back in my shorts, climbed out of the sleeping bag and said, "It's better to do it out in the open. That way I won't get come all over your sleeping bag when I shoot my load."

"Good point," he said.

I asked him if he had something we could catch the come in, and he told me where the paper towels were. I got a bunch and lay back down on the sleeping bag, rubbing my balls through the fabric of my shorts and groaning about how good it felt. Mark was still beating away under his sleeping bag while watching me play with myself. In order to heighten his excitement, I raised my hips up off the floor and slowly pulled my briefs down to my ankles. Staying in this position, I furiously pumped my rod, opening my mouth and pointing my prick toward my face.

By now I was so turned on, it didn't matter to me what he thought. All I knew was that I wanted to see what Mark had under the sleeping bag, so I sat up, pulled the sleeping bag off him and waited to get punched for invading his privacy. He was still wearing his jeans. They were unzipped and his cock poked through the open fly. It was exciting to finally see Mark's cock fully erect and ready to explode.

"Take your pants off all the way so I can watch your balls bounce," I said. He was reluctant, so before he could say anything I quickly pulled them off. Now we were both stark naked, lying on our backs, pounding away on our love-muscles.

Then something happened that I didn't expect. Mark looked into my eyes and asked me if I wanted to suck his dick. I quickly moved toward his beautiful, pulsating hunk of meat, wanting to taste the juices oozing from the tip before he changed his mind. I pounced on his stiff rod, licking the head of his prick with my tongue and tasting his salty fluid. This was a first for me, and I loved it.

I worked my tongue down his shaft to his hairless testicles. When I looked at his face, his eyes were closed in ecstasy. (He later told me that while I was sucking him off he was imagining that it was a beautiful woman chowing down on his meat.) I put his testicles in my mouth, and then grabbed his cock with one hand and mine with the other and jerked us both off. When our pumps were nice and primed, I moved closer to him, rubbing my cock and balls against his knees and taking his dick into my mouth. I sucked his peter, sliding it in and out of my lips and tonguing the head.

Wanting him to see how large I was, I grabbed my cock at the base and hefted it before his eyes. "Wow!" Mark exclaimed. "What a fuck-rod you have!"

I couldn't hold back any longer and, keeping both hands on my bursting cock, ejaculated my first shot, which almost hit the ceiling. Mark watched as my rod kept jetting thick white sperm out of its tip.

After the deluge finally ceased, I sat up and looked at Mark, feeling embarrassed. There was come all over my hands, balls and belly. He smiled and asked, "Did it feel good?" I answered, "Yes," and as we rolled over to go to sleep, Mark said, "Thanks a lot."—*Name and address withheld*

THIS EVE DIDN'T NEED AN APPLE TO TEMPT HER LOVER

My name is Lynn, and I've been divorced for two years. I am an advertising executive for a large firm. My sexual experiences started when I was young. I got married when I was only nineteen. My husband was a lot older than I and showed me a lot of different things. I will not forget those experiences.

I am a practicing bisexual. I want to tell you about my sexual encounter with Eve, a beautiful blonde from Sweden who is working as a model in New York. Her 36-24-35 body would melt you on the spot.

I met her at a dinner party and we became close friends. We had a lot in common, and I found out it was her first time in our city.

The next night we hit the town and ended up at my place. I made a couple of drinks and put something nice on the stereo, then excused myself to change my clothes. I wore a T-shirt, no bra, and a tight pair of jeans that let her know I was no slouch myself when it came to having a good figure.

When I returned, Eve was staring at me. I lit up a joint and we got really high. I showed Eve my art collection, which included a nude portrait of me that was a birthday present from my ex-husband. She said she loved it. While we were standing there looking at it, I grabbed her hand and gave her a quick kiss on the mouth. For a split second my skin crawled with fear, as I didn't know how she was going to react. But then she put her arms around me and gave me a deep kiss, making all my fears dissipate. Our bodies were afire and they melded lovingly together. We must have French-kissed for about five minutes.

We made it to the bedroom and undressed. Naked, we embraced. Then I fell onto my water bed, pulling her down on top of me. Eve massaged my beautiful breasts, and in a flash her mouth was all over them, kissing, sucking, licking and nibbling me. Her hot lips slowly moved down my body until they were dancing over my thighs. She spread my legs and stared at my dripping-wet pussy. She started to play with my clit, driving me into ecstasy. Then she plunged her middle finger into me, and I started having orgasm after orgasm. She finally lowered her head to my love-button, making me orgasm so many times I almost passed out.

After I'd calmed down, Eve gave me a deep kiss and held me in her arms. Then it was my turn to please her. We were in bed for hours, but the highlight of our lovemaking was when we positioned ourselves in a 69 and started eating each other out.

The next day I woke up in Eve's arms. We made love in the shower that morning, and went at it again that night too. It was a long weekend I will never forget.

Eve and I keep in touch by phone. I know that when she comes back to our beautiful city we will be lovers again. I love my lifestyle.—*Name and address withheld*

FILMFEST TURNS INTO SUCKFEST WHEN NEIGHBORS HOLD A PRIVATE SCREENING

Last week I had an incredible experience that I'd like to share with you. I'm a married man in my early thirties. My wife and I enjoy sex and are fairly open sexually. We've discussed having another person or couple join us in bed, but for various reasons we've never acted on it.

Last summer a couple about our age purchased a home several houses down from ours that had been vacant for several months. We were glad to see someone finally moving in and taking care of the yard and so forth, bringing it back up to this neighborhood's high standards.

We met the couple briefly after they moved in, and would occasionally stop to chat with them if they were out when we took our evening walk. Fletcher and June are probably about a year or two younger than Naomi and I, and both of them are attractive and in good shape. Fletcher and I have both admired each other's wife with subtle, furtive glances.

Last fall I began thinking that Fletcher and June might be the perfect couple to join Naomi and I for an evening of unabashed fucking and sucking. I mentioned this to Naomi, and although she was receptive to the idea, she felt it might be prudent to get to know them a little better before proposing anything like that. She was afraid we would seriously alienate our neighbors if they weren't amenable to our proposition. I agreed that a little discretion was in order, and we should adopt a wait-and-see attitude. With our busy schedules and the colder weather, we didn't see much of Fletcher and June except an occasional wave as we were coming or going, so our plans were temporarily postponed.

Last week, though, I was off from work for a few days. One morning I decided to go rent a couple of adult videos for Naomi and me to enjoy that evening. One of the local video stores has a separate room filled with nothing but X-rated movies of all varieties, so I went there. As I wandered from one aisle to another, who did I run into but Fletcher. At first we were both a little embarrassed by being caught red-handed renting fuck films, but we soon overcame it and admitted to doing so once or twice a month. Fletcher told me he was also off for the day, and invited me down to his house to watch a couple of the films we were renting. I accepted his invitation, in the back of my mind thinking that it might be a perfect opportunity for me to bring up the idea of a threesome or foursome.

After Fletcher left, I made a few more selections, then headed home. I parked in our driveway and walked down to Fletcher and June's house, bringing the videos I had rented along with me. When I arrived, Fletcher was dressed in a pair of cutoff sweats and a T-shirt, and was drinking a beer. He offered me a cold one, and even though it was only eleven in the morning, I accepted. What the hell, I was on vacation, right?

He popped one of my tapes into the VCR and fast-forwarded to the opening scene. A busty blonde was taking on two guys at once. The rest of the movie was filled with hot, steamy sex, and

I had to discreetly reposition my uncomfortably hard cock a couple of times. I began to regret the fact that I hadn't changed into shorts or something more comfortable. I noticed that Fletcher's cock was also obviously erect, but the loose-fitting shorts he wore weren't nearly as constricting.

I don't know if Fletcher noticed me checking out his bulge, but shortly thereafter he repositioned his cock so that his shaft rested along his leg with the head almost peeking out the leg hole of his shorts. I couldn't help but notice from the size of the bulge in Fletcher's shorts that his cock was considerably larger than mine. I made a mental note to mention that to Naomi!

When the video ended, Fletcher ejected it and popped in one that he had rented. We discussed the obvious enthusiasm the star of the previous film had for sucking cock as he fast-forwarded through the opening credits. The film opened with an attractive blonde licking another blonde's pink pussy. I've always been immensely turned on by the sight of two beautiful women enjoying each other's body, and I hoped I'd get to see Naomi and June do so. As the scene progressed, the second blonde rolled the first one over and began sucking her gorgeous tits before heading down toward her pussy. Both Fletcher and I had gotten to the point where we were giving our cocks gentle rubs through our pants from time to time. The sight of these two babes going at each other was really something. But just as the second blonde got to what should have been the first blonde's pussy, she wrapped her fingers around a cock and began sucking for all she was worth! The first blonde was a she-male, and a gorgeous one at that.

Fletcher commented that he had always wanted to see a she-male. I agreed that the she-male sure had me fooled. As the movie progressed, so did our horniness. Fletcher's cockhead was now protruding from the leg of his shorts, and I could hardly keep my hand off my own bulge. Fletcher pulled the leg of his shorts back and began to openly fondle and stroke his cock. Seeing this, I unzipped my pants and freed my own stiff dick.

The two blondes on-screen had been joined by a guy who was having his substantial rod licked by both of them. The combination of the video, my hand massaging my own hard-on and the sight of Fletcher stroking his was an incredible turn-on. Fletcher's cock was not only larger than mine, but had a perfectly smooth shaft with not a single vein protruding. He was undoubtedly enjoying this whole incredible scenario as much as I was.

As the guy on-screen began fucking the second blonde's

pussy, the she-male positioned her cock so that both the girl and the guy were able to lick and suck it. Just then, Fletcher reached over and replaced my hand with his.

The sight and feel of his hand on my cock was wonderful. Without hesitation I reached over and began to stroke his big cock, reaching into his shorts to cup his balls with my other hand.

From this point on, things got wild! Fletcher leaned over and began kissing me. He sucked my tongue deep into his mouth, then pulled away and let go of my cock. He slipped off his shirt before standing up and dropping his shorts, fully exposing himself for the first time. His balls were absolutely hairless, and his cock was thick and perfectly smooth, with a slight upward curve. It wasn't really much longer than mine as I had originally thought, but it was considerably thicker.

This incredible sausage was no more than a foot from my face. Without the slightest hesitation, I reached out and pulled it into my mouth. The warm, fleshy texture on my lips and the musky aroma in my nostrils were unbelievable. I couldn't get enough as I sucked and slurped hungrily at his cock. As my enthusiasm calmed, I began to instinctively suck it the way I liked Naomi to suck mine. Fletcher was enjoying it as well, and as I worked my tongue around the sensitive underside of his cockhead, he moaned in pleasure and told me how good it felt. When he placed his hands on either side of my face and began to slowly fuck my mouth, I could tell that he was approaching orgasm. I wrapped one hand around his shaft and cupped his hairless balls in the other as I continued to hungrily suck his cock. I felt him tense and spasm, and then his hot, thick come flooded my mouth. I continued to suck and swallow as he shot at least seven or eight spurts into my mouth, not allowing a single drop to escape. When he was through coming, I continued to suck his cock, releasing it from my mouth only after I had licked it clean.

As soon as I released his shrinking organ, he leaned down and kissed me, tonguing me deeply as he unbuttoned my shirt. We separated to finish undressing me, and I was soon as naked as he. He positioned me in one corner of the sofa, cupped my balls in one hand and guided my raging erection to his mouth with the other. He sucked me deep into his mouth, almost burying his nose in my pubic hair as he gently rolled my balls in his hand. I couldn't hold back, and held his head, my cock deep in his mouth, as I pumped out what felt like gallons of come.

As my erection subsided and slipped from his mouth, he

looked up and told me how fantastic the whole episode had been for him. I agreed, and we began to talk about it. He told me he had experienced one other homosexual encounter while he was in the navy, and he commended me on my performance, which of course had been my first. We sat around in the nude, and began to openly discuss how nice it would be to do this again with our wives. I mentioned that Naomi and I had discussed the possibility of swinging with them, and he was ecstatic. He thought his wife might need some convincing, but said that he would begin subtly working on her. He pulled out some nude photos that they had taken of each other, and I was pleased to see that June was even better-looking than I had imagined. She had pert breasts with upturned nipples, a nicely trimmed bush and a beautiful round ass. He explained that she liked his balls to be hairless when she sucked them into her mouth, so for this reason he kept them shaved.

The erotic conversation and nude photos soon had both of us hard again, and he leaned over to French kiss me. Then, moving downward, he licked and sucked at my nipples before heading for my stiff dick. He gently sucked one ball into his mouth, and then the other. Suddenly he was sucking my dick deep into his mouth. I turned and positioned myself so that his cock was directly above my mouth. I pulled downward on his butt, burying his dick in my mouth, sucking sloppily on it as my own orgasm erupted in his mouth. It was incredible!

Fletcher and I have talked several times since then, and we fully intend to get our wives involved in our fun if at all possible. But even if they can't be persuaded to join us, I know that Fletcher and I will somehow find a way to repeat our afternoon.—*N.R., Butte, Montana*

LOOKING FOR LOVE LEADS BLACK BOMBSHELLS TO SAPPHIC SEXPOTS

It all started when I went to visit my girlfriend Peggy. Peggy is a very attractive black woman with an extraordinary body and a dynamite personality. I myself am a single, twenty-three-year-old black female of average height who has been blessed with a perfect 36-24-36 figure.

Well, I got to her place, and after the formalities, a few joints and a few glasses of champagne, we decided to go to a local bar to find a couple of eligible young men to round out the evening. So, dressed to kill, we began the hunt.

As we sat in the bar, getting more tipsy and very itchy for some excitement, I noticed two young ladies in a nearby booth, obviously also on the prowl. One was an attractive redhead with beautiful green eyes. Her brunette friend was equally attractive, with a bulging set of tits that almost spilled through the V-neck of her blouse. This made me giggle. I pointed them out to Peggy, and a smile crossed her lips. "Angie!" she exclaimed. She jumped off the bar stool and ran to the two girls, hugging the brunette first and then the redhead. Peggy then introduced them to me as Angie and Laura, friends from college.

We joined them and the four of us sat there drinking and giggling until the bar closed down, at which point Peggy invited us all back to her place. We got back to the apartment, quite loaded, laughing and carrying on like a bunch of schoolgirls. Peggy turned on some music and lit up a joint. We talked and partied for the next hour and eventually got around to men and sex. As the conversation got more involved, I found myself getting excited, and I could tell the girls were too. At that point I excused myself to go to the bathroom to freshen up. While inside the bathroom, I found myself fantasizing about the redhead and her beautiful body.

When I returned to the living room, Peggy and Angie were sitting on the couch locked in a French kiss. The slit in the front of Angie's skirt was being passionately parted by Peggy's roaming hand. This stunned me at first, but then my disbelief quickly turned to excitement. I looked at Laura, who was watching from the corner chair, obviously very turned on and hot to trot. I walked over and began nibbling on her ear. At this point I knew there was no turning back. I worked my way around her neck to her full lips, which were trembling with anticipation. We were soon sharing the best French kiss I've ever had. She put down the magazine, which left her hands free to explore my body through my thin dress.

By then Peggy and Angie were completely naked and tangled in a passionate 69 position. At that point I stood up and slowly lifted Laura's shirt over her head, exposing a perfect pair of tits with pink, erect nipples. I immediately went right to work, exploring them with my hands, and then my tongue.

She then, in turn, removed my dress, leaving us both very excited. Next I slowly reached down and unzipped the tight pair of jeans my lover was wearing. As she stepped out of them, I was pleased to see that she was not wearing any panties and was a natural redhead. I reached down to fondle her bush and realized she was as wet as I was. Out of instinct I immediately knew what she wanted. I slowly sank to my knees and parted her moist, pink lips with my tongue. She put her hands on the back of my head, moaning, "Eat me, please. Please, do it."

This increased my excitement, and with childlike enthusiasm I ventured forth and had my first taste of a woman. At that point she was putty in my hands, and I was able to bring her to a wild, frenzied orgasm. As soon as I pulled my come-drenched face from her sweetness, she dropped to her knees. With renewed vigor and sensitivity, her knowing tongue found my clit, sending me to dizzying heights I'd never before climbed.

Wanting more of each other, we positioned ourselves in the most fantastic 69 of my life! But more surprises kept coming. I suddenly felt Peggy's hands on my breasts and Angie's tongue licking my ear. That was all I needed to have the most mind-shattering orgasm I'd ever experienced. We then moved to the bedroom, and there we stayed until the next afternoon, enjoying one another in every way we could.

Peggy has now moved, and I haven't seen Angie or Laura since. Men are still on the top of my list, but when I masturbate, it's the thought of that love-filled, fun-filled evening and afternoon that really gets me off!—*Name and address withheld*

COUNSELOR AND CADET EXPLORE EACH OTHER IN TENT FOR TWO

I'm a student at a southern university. I do some work as a counselor in a local military youth auxiliary. Our cadets are high school seniors. Once a quarter we go on a weekend training bivouac. Our last trip was in September.

It was a cool Friday when we started setting up camp at a state park. After dinner, the list of assignments for our two-man tents was posted. I was to keep an eye on a new cadet named Daniel, a good-looking guy with large brown eyes. He wrestles at school and has an attractive, well-built body. I had noticed him at the meetings, but knew better than to go after a cadet.

As the night closed in, it got very cold quite fast. I suggested that we combine the sleeping bags to conserve body heat. After the jokes and snickers were over, the commander said it was a good idea.

Settling into the tent that night, I moaned about how cold it was. I stripped down and crawled into our joint sleeping bag. We talked, then went to sleep.

It must have been the movement of the bag that woke me up. When I opened my eyes, I saw that the sleeping bag was moving up and down right over Daniel's hips. My cock snapped to attention and I lay there watching him. Forgetting all discretion, I moved and grabbed his weapon. When I asked him if he could use some help, he gave me no answer. He just grabbed my rock-hard cock and yanked me toward him. I started caressing the head of his prick, then moved my hand up and down, using slow, tight strokes. He did the same to me. We picked up the tempo, and he leaned over and gave me a red-hot kiss on my mouth.

The handjobs were moving too fast, so I dove under for a taste. His weapon was in desperate need of a good cleaning. Daniel moved around and started nibbling on my balls. He was no beginner, and his tongue nearly drove me over the edge. I was still deep-throating his cock and could not stop when he said he was about to come. Before I could react, his warm seed was trickling down my throat.

He increased the intensity of his sucking, smacking the back of his throat with the tip of my cock. I came in a shattering explosion.

We kissed, fell into a gentle, snug embrace and slept.

During breakfast the next morning someone asked Daniel why he had not eaten much. He looked straight at me and said he had had a snack earlier. I nearly died! Need I say that the rest of the weekend was festive?—*K.L., Nashville, Tennessee*

ONCE HIS GIRL GOT A TASTE OF SALLY, DAVE DIDN'T HAVE A CHANCE

I am a twenty-three-year-old college grad now working in New York. Three years ago an event took place that shocked and surprised me so much that I've been trying to sort it out ever since.

My boyfriend of my early college days, whom I'll call Dave,

was the first real love of my life. But after about two years of a happy and fiery relationship, our sex life, which I thought was great, began to slow down. Then one day Dave brought me home an issue of *Penthouse Letters*. That did the trick for a while. I come from a strict home and have always been straight, but your girls and articles brought me to new heights.

Finally, one night I broke down and confessed to Dave that the nude girls in your magazine were driving me absolutely wild. I even told him that I bought a few magazines on my own and spent many nights masturbating with those lovely bodies and sexy poses before me. He suggested exactly what I wanted to hear, and after I heard him out, I agreed to let him help me find a woman to make love with me.

One week later Dave picked me up after explaining to me over the phone the night before what he thought we should do. We drove to a large house, where a girl Dave had been friendly with lived. I knew Sally, and even though I found her attractive, I still didn't know if I'd be able to go through with our plan.

Dave and I walked in, and Sally was very friendly. She told us to make ourselves at home because everyone in her family was away for the weekend. We had a few drinks, and within an hour things were very relaxed. I mentioned that my back was sore, and Sally quickly picked up on that line. Within moments she was sitting on my ass, giving me a great massage, while Dave was watching television. She asked me to take my shirt off so that she could do a better job, and I obliged. I was feeling fantastic. She rolled me over, and although I was a little uptight, I didn't say a thing. She began to play with my breasts, squeezing my nipples and licking and sucking them until I was shivering and tingling all over. I was loving every minute of it. I felt my clit grow and my cunt get wet. I whispered into her ear that she should take off my pants, and with a smile, she said, "Yes, I think you're ready."

Dave sat down on the floor next to the bed and watched. Then what happened was simply amazing. I was completely nude, my pussy aching for pleasure. Sally licked her way down to my dripping cunt, and within seconds I was experiencing sensations that I had never felt before. When she touched her cool tongue to my steaming clit, I arched my back and let out a scream. I was going absolutely crazy. Her tongue was magic.

For the next hour Sally ate me out and brought me to at least ten shattering climaxes. And these were no mild climaxes. Sally's mouth and fingers had me in absolute spasms. I never thought sex could be so satisfying. My body literally went into fits of ecstasy. My cunt was convulsing, the muscles actually pulsating while my love juices poured like a fountain.

Then I asked for something I never thought I would have the nerve to request. "Please take your clothes off and let me taste you," I said. She removed all her clothes except her white silk panties, which looked very beautiful against her tanned skin. "If you want what's under here bad enough, you'll have to take these off yourself," she said. I pulled her down on top of me, humping and kissing her desperately.

After sucking on her tits, which brought me to the brink of orgasm, I resumed my trip down to the place where I wanted to be. I smelled her soaking pussy through her panties and licked around the edges and over her crotch. Then I couldn't hold back. I took her panties off and saw a cunt that was prettier than any I had ever seen in a magazine. I dived into it with complete abandon. I licked it to orgasm after orgasm, lapping up every drop of her nectar. At some point, while I was loving her, Dave left. I couldn't stop to say good-bye. I ate her for over an hour; I could have done it forever. The taste, the smell, the feel, the warmth—it all transcended earthly experience. We sucked one another until we collapsed. I passed into a deep slumber, with my face close to Sally's pussy.

We made love a few more times after that night, mostly by ourselves, but also once with Dave. The loving was great every time.

I am now enjoying a relationship with a guy. We have fun together, but every once in a while I need to find a good woman to help me really get my rocks off. I think sex between two girls is just incredibly hot! In my guess, plenty of women think about doing it, but they're scared. Too bad!—*Name and address withheld*

AIR FORCE HUNK TAKES RANDY LIEUTENANT ON FANCIFUL FLIGHT

I am twenty-three and a lieutenant in the army, stationed in Germany. I am married and have always kept away from trysts out of respect for my wife. I'm no prude, just loyal.

Anyway, about six months ago I was ordering supplies at an

army depot when a young air force sergeant came in. Since we were inside, he didn't have to salute me, but he did anyway. As I returned his salute, I noticed that he had the bluest eyes I'd ever seen. They seemed to be looking right through me. His staring unnerved me. He had a handsome Nordic face that reminded me of a Viking.

I finished my order and went outside. The guy's eyes followed me as I left. He came out just as my truck was getting warmed up, so I offered him a lift. He climbed into the cab and offered to buy me a beer. Intrigued, I accepted, and drove us to the nearest bar. His name was Bruce and he was from Oregon.

Well, one beer led to another, and we talked about everything in the world. It was the best conversation I'd ever had. After about three mugs of suds, he asked me if I smoked. I could have had his stripes for asking me, but instead I asked him if he had any. He showed me a huge hunk of hash, saying it was from Turkey. "It's the best," he added.

He said he lived nearby on a farm and invited me over. I was supposed to have returned the truck by then, but I knew I could straighten it out later with the motor pool, so I accepted. Somehow I knew something very unusual was happening, though I didn't know just what. The prospect of getting stoned after going so long without any hash was exciting in itself.

We drove to a small stone farmhouse. The owners, an elderly German couple, only came out there on weekends, I learned. We went inside, drank some more beer, smoked several bowls of sweet black hash and got really high. We were stoned and drunk when he reached over, laughing, and suddenly squeezed my crotch. I fell backward, chair and all, and he fell on top of me. My hand brushed against his crotch, and I felt his hardness and heat. Waves of desire and passion churned through me.

Without a word, he stopped struggling and lay back, pulling me with him. His lips sought mine, and I found myself kissing him, our mustaches rubbing together. He kissed much harder and stronger than a woman. I couldn't think about anything because I was too excited. His arms went around me and squeezed me so hard that my back almost popped. I pressed my body against his, and we rubbed cocks. I didn't know what to do next, so for a while I just lay there, grinding and panting, getting more and more excited and horny by the second.

Finally his hand went to his crotch and he took out a very hard, very smooth six-incher. I proudly pulled out my own erection, which is closer to eight inches. His was thicker, though, and he wasn't circumcised.

In one motion he pulled my khaki officer's trousers down to my knees and started licking my belly button. My meat oozed in anticipation, and I fumbled with the buttons on my shirt. He took his green fatigues down as well and started playing with his swollen, throbbing cock. His mouth finally went to my dick, and it was the softest, warmest mouth I've ever felt there. I'd never been too crazy about blowjobs before, as I had never been able to climax from one. But this guy knew how to treat a dick—probably because he has one of his own. He gave me such good head that I was ready to come in a couple of minutes. He knew that too, and shifted his body around so that his cock was nodding in my face. I stared at it, licking my lips.

I reached out and grabbed it. He was eagerly licking my balls, his skillful tonguing blowing my mind and making me tremble. Then his beard-stubbled face grazed my thighs, making me quiver and shake. Lost in the intensity of our lust, I took his meat into my mouth. We rocked back and forth in a heavy, sweaty 69. It was very different having sex with someone who was so strong. When his arms squeezed, it almost hurt, and when his hands massaged, I felt the sensation all the way down to my bones.

After a while I was sure he was about to orgasm. Even though this was the first time I'd ever sucked dick, I could tell that he was going to lose his load. He moaned and started pumping his hips.

Just then I realized that I was getting there too. We started sucking each other faster and harder. I ran my hands over the hard, hairy cheeks of his ass and pulled his cock into my throat. I gasped for breath because of my own excitement, and this only made me more aroused. For the first time in my life I lost touch with reality during sex. For a second I actually forgot who I was and where I was. The room seemed to turn bright orange, and the color deepened as my orgasm approached. Suddenly he groaned like an animal and shoved himself against me. I felt sprays of warm semen trickling down my throat as he shot his load. At that moment I let go too, and he sucked me dry before his climax even ended.

Now there was peace. All my muscles trembled and twitched. It had all been so wild.

We lay there on the floor for a long time, not speaking, enjoying the afterglow. Then I got dressed. When I left, I told him I'd see him around, but he only smiled and looked at me with those steel-blue eyes of his.

As it turned out, he and I did run into each other again. It was one Friday evening, in a bar away from the base. He saw me first and approached me while I was drinking a beer. I invited him to sit, and bought him a beer. It only took a few moments before the heat started building between us. He told me about a quiet little park on the other side of town, and asked me if I would like to see it.

"Sure," I replied. I got my wallet out of my back pocket and left money on the bar. Then we left.

It was a warm night, without the slightest breeze to ruffle the heat. We walked silently through the streets, dark, silent houses rising up into the night all around us.

We reached the park and, of course, the gates were locked. Not that that was going to stop us. I climbed first, and then helped him over. We walked across the grass, listening to the crickets chirp in the dark distant trees. There was no one in sight, and the sounds of the night were free of man-made noises.

We found a patch of grass behind some bushes. We undressed and lay down side by side on the cool turf. A gentle breeze had arisen, cooling our stiffening cocks.

He turned onto his side so that he was facing me, and leaned his head toward mine. His warm breath gushed onto my lips, smelling mildly of tobacco. I felt his hand wrap itself around my cock and begin slowly pumping it. I lifted my face to his and crushed our lips together.

We kissed and grasped each other's hard-on, then we assembled into a 69. I was amazed at how exhilarated it was to be having sex there in the open, under the star-sprinkled sky. I was not the least bit self-conscious of getting caught.

Then my lover grunted under my touch and fed me his semen. At his request we got out of the 69 and I lay on my back. He masturbated me to orgasm, licking up the warm sperm that had landed on my chest.

I haven't told anyone except my wife about those two experiences. To my surprise, she was very understanding and supportive when I told her of my encounter. She has even encouraged me to look for Bruce.

I don't think I will, but I'll never forget Bruce or the time we had together. For all you guys out there who think homosexuality is just for queenie hairdressers, I want to tell you that you're absolutely wrong. Sexual contact with another human being, no matter what the gender, is a very precious thing. I am "straight," whatever that means, but I am glad to have had that experience. It stirred me from muscle to marrow, and I'll never forget it.—*Name and address withheld*

FROM STRICTLY BALLROOM TO DIRTY DANCING IN ONE EASY LESSON

Not long ago my girlfriend and I signed up for a ballroom dancing course. The instructor is a young man named Craig. He is tall, slim and graceful. I would guess his age to be about thirty. My girlfriend and I figured he was gay, but that didn't matter to us.

My girlfriend was out of town for a few days, so I went to one of the classes alone. It didn't make any difference since we often switch partners anyway. After class, Craig joined a group of us at the bar for a drink. As the crowd was breaking up, Craig asked if I would give him a ride home since his car was being fixed.

When we got back to his house, Craig invited me in for a drink. I accepted, since it was still early and I was in the mood to keep partying. His apartment was very well-furnished. On the walls were photos of celebrities with whom he had performed. Craig fixed a couple of drinks and turned on the stereo. We sat there talking and drinking for a while.

I went to the bathroom and, when I came out, Craig was nowhere to be found. But a few minutes later he returned, wearing only a white leotard that really showed off his physique, especially his crotch. The considerable size of his dick and balls was very obvious. He explained that he liked to wear leotards at home because they were so comfortable. Then he began to gyrate around the room, striking various ballet positions and doing other dance steps as well. It was fascinating to watch him perform.

"You're my best student," he said. "Why don't you show me what you can do?" I declined, saying that I would rather watch him.

"From what I can tell," he said, "you have a good body. I'd love to see you naked—or at least in a pair of leotards. I have another pair you can try on. Don't act shocked," he went on, flashing a smile. "You must know that I'm gay."

"I'm not shocked," I said. "But I'm not gay."

"Well," he said, "I'd still love to seduce you." He looked longingly into my eyes. "Look, I've already got a hard-on." His prick stretched the front of his leotard. He moved closer to me. His hands squeezed my thighs, and my heart began to pound.

"Come on, at least take off your shirt," Craig urged. "It's hot in here." He unbuttoned my shirt and spread it open. I leaned back as he ran a hand over my chest. "Feel good?" he asked. I did not answer, but it felt wonderful.

Craig unbuckled my belt and opened my zipper. He felt inside for my swelling cock. "It's huge," he murmured. "Let's get these clothes out of the way." He stood and stripped. His big dick jutted out as he thrust his hips forward. I then raised myself up and allowed him to pull off my pants and briefs. My hard shaft sprang free. It felt strange letting a man undress me. Craig then pulled me to my feet. He put his hands on my waist and our pricks touched. It felt like a bolt of electricity running through my body. I took his hand and let him lead me to his bed.

"Lie back. I'm going to feast on that beautiful bone," he said. Craig crouched between my spread legs. His strong hands were on my feet, then my ankles, calves and thighs. I wanted him to touch my throbbing dick, but he took his time. He caressed my chest and stomach. I was thrashing about on the bed, my body on fire as he licked every place that his fingers explored. "What do you want me to do now?" he asked.

"Suck my cock," I said.

My prick was twitching. He nuzzled my balls and sucked each one into his hot mouth. Then he lifted my shaft with his fingers. "I'm going to suck you off, but you'll have to do the same to me. Do we have a deal?"

"Deal," I said, suddenly hungry for cock.

He licked me from base to knob several times before twirling his tongue around the tip.

"Don't tease me," I said. "Make me come."

That was just what Craig wanted to hear. He went at me with vigor, taking my cock all the way into his throat. I humped upward to meet the motions of his bobbing head.

"I'm coming right now!" I screamed. My whole body convulsed as I exploded into Craig's waiting mouth.

Craig kept sucking until I was drained dry. To my amazement, my cock stayed hard. "Okay, now it's your turn to do me," he said. "In fact, let's do each other. Looks like you've got another orgasm left in you." With that, he spun us around into a 69. He took my cock back into his expert mouth. I looked at his bone-hard shank, told myself it was now or never, and wrapped my lips around it.

The taste of his flesh made my entire body tingle. I'd never had a dick in my mouth, but at that moment I realized all the fun I'd been missing. It was great to explore the silky surface of his penis. The different textures of his spongy cockhead, smooth shaft and hairy balls were an incredible turn-on. I knew it would be only a minute before I was shooting off once again.

I pressed my face into his groin, taking in only four inches or so of his massive rod. He began to jack off into my mouth as I continued to lick. "Now!" he cried. His cock emptied into my mouth, blast after blast of tangy sperm shooting onto my tongue. Craig's spunk didn't taste foul, as I was afraid it might, so I gladly swallowed it all down.

We got cleaned up and then I left, thanking Craig for introducing me to a whole new way to get off. When my girlfriend returned, I told her all about what Craig and I had done. She was delighted, and said that next time she wants to watch us get it on.—*R.P., Charlotte, North Carolina*

OLD FRIENDS MEET, TALK ABOUT OLD TIMES, SUCK A LITTLE COCK . . .

It was late July and I was in Chicago on a business trip. I was heading for the hotel lounge to quench my thirst, when I heard a familiar voice behind me say, "Vince, is that you?"

I turned to see my old college classmate and best friend, Paul. We hadn't seen each other since graduation many years earlier. I wanted him to have a drink with me, but he explained that he had to attend a business dinner that evening. We agreed to meet at the hotel lounge at midnight.

I got there at about midnight and had several drinks at the bar while waiting for Paul. By one in the morning he still had not arrived, and I was getting drunk, so I headed upstairs to my room.

I was just climbing into bed when there was a knock at the door. It was Paul, explaining that he'd had to meet with his boss after dinner and apologizing for not showing up at the lounge. Since we were in the same hotel, he decided to drop by and see if I was still awake. I noticed that he had an unopened bottle of whiskey in one hand and a bucket of ice in the other.

I was wearing only my boxer shorts, and reached for my pants as Paul poured us two drinks. "No need to dress," he said. "I'm not modest." I certainly didn't need another whiskey, but I took it anyway. I leaned back against the head of the bed, and Paul sprawled himself across the foot.

We talked for over an hour, until I got so tired I couldn't keep my eyes open. As I started nodding out, Paul began to massage my feet. It was very relaxing. Then I must have dozed off, because when I came to a few minutes later, he was rubbing my calves.

"I thought I'd lost you," he said, rubbing my leg. "Does this feel good?"

"Yes," I mumbled. "But if you keep it up, it's going to make my dick hard."

"Good," he said. "Relax and enjoy." He placed my foot against his crotch and began to rub my thighs. My cock began to swell in my shorts. In a few minutes I felt Paul's hand on my crotch. He started lightly stroking my dick.

Paul got up and undressed. I closed my eyes, pretending to be asleep, but actually I peeked at him while he stripped. His body was strong and firm, a work of art. He came over, sat beside me and carefully removed my shorts. His fingers tickled my balls, and my already hard cock lurched in response. Pre-come oozed out. He lifted my dick and licked off the clear drops of sperm.

"It's beautiful," he whispered. "I'm going to suck you off. I've wanted to blow you ever since we were in school. You like it when a man sucks your cock, don't you?" he asked. I moaned my approval.

Paul ran his hands over my chest and stomach, making me even more aroused. He blew hot breath on my cock and balls. I twisted and turned but did not resist.

"Relax and let me please you," he murmured. He held my rod and took the head into his mouth. His tongue swirled all over the turgid flesh, and his lips tightened around the shaft. I couldn't help but thrust upward into his mouth as he sucked. He was driving me crazy with lust. I tangled my fingers in his hair and pushed his head down. He pumped the base of my cock with one hand and caressed my balls with the other. Every nerve in my body tingled, and my dick felt as though it might burst.

Paul could tell I was about to come, so he removed his mouth and squeezed my cock with his fist. Soon he began to suck again, and this time I could no longer hold back. My juices begged for release. My prick jerked in Paul's mouth as he sucked on all seven solid inches. I could feel the knob pushing against his throat. My body convulsed, and I shot my load into his mouth. He continued to suck until my cock was fully drained and beginning to soften.

Paul turned off the light and lay beside me. "I know you liked that," he whispered. He held my cock in his strong hand as we fell asleep.—*V.T., Columbia, South Carolina*

DORM BUDDIES: WHY JUST SHARE A ROOM WHEN YOU CAN SHARE EACH OTHER?

I am a nineteen-year-old student and, like all young men my age, have an ever-present, overwhelming thirst for sex. In my first year of college my roommate Kenny and I spent much of our time commiserating about how tough it was for freshmen to get laid. Most weekend nights we would come back to our room without having boned anyone. We'd stay up all night, smoking dope and complaining about how horny we were.

One night after the usual dead-end search for pussy, we returned to our room. Kenny said he was so horny that if he jerked off, he would probably come in less than a minute.

As we turned off the lights, Kenny asked me how long I thought I'd last if I jerked off. I told him I suspected that I wouldn't last a minute either. He said that although he was dying to come, he wanted to see how many times he could get himself to the brink of orgasm and then stop, in order to intensify the pleasure. I felt awkward about discussing masturbation in such detail, though, and stopped talking.

I was restless and could not sleep. I lay in bed for at least ten minutes, thinking about our conversation. I had a major hard-on and wanted to jerk off, but was too nervous to consider jerking off in the same room with Kenny, even while he was asleep.

After a while I heard Kenny turn over and pull his covers down. I could see his silhouette, and could see that he had pulled down his shorts. He had a tremendous hard-on sticking straight up in the air. He must have assumed that I was asleep, because he immediately started to stroke his erection. My dick was hard as a lead pipe as I watched his hand slide up and down his six-inch shaft. I could feel his sense of urgency as his strokes became more intense.

From the speed of his strokes, it was obvious that he was about to shoot his wad. But just when I was sure he was at the point of no return, he stopped. He waited about half a minute, then gripped his penis and slowly started to pump his shaft once more. I could hear the rhythmic strokes as his hand slipped up and down the full length of his manhood. He pumped his cock right to the brink of orgasm, then he stopped once again. Even though I was across the room, I could sense the incredible energy that was building up inside him.

Kenny started jerking off for the third time. He must have finally reached his limit because he went ballistic, pulling his pud with wild, feverish strokes. His hand was a blur as it slid from the base of his pole to the tip. He raised his butt off the bed and arched his back as he frantically pounded his tool. Every muscle in his body tightened as his load squirted into his palm. My cock throbbed feverishly as he continued to milk his member long after the last drop of come had oozed out. After leaning back into his pillow for a few moments to recover, he got up, washed his hands and then went back to bed and slept.

As soon as I thought he was sleeping, I pulled down my covers, pulled my shorts down to my knees and grabbed my aching dick. The thought of disciplining myself to stop just before I shot my load was out of the question! I was so excited that I came in only about ten strokes. It was the most intense orgasm I'd ever had.

The very next night we went out and partied at a local heavy-metal club. We both met attractive girls. They wouldn't come back to our dorm room to get high, but they did say they might do so in the future. After Kenny and I dropped them off at their dorm, we went home, excited by the prospect of fucking these two lovely ladies sometime soon.

After the lights were out, I couldn't wait for Kenny to fall asleep so I could jerk off. His breathing soon became slow and barely audible. I figured he was asleep and that it was safe to beat my meat. I slid my shorts down and started to rub my throbbing penis. As my excitement grew, I decided to try to stop just before my orgasm to extend my pleasure, the way I'd secretly observed Kenny doing the night before. My stroke was rapid and my heart was racing. My balls started to tighten as I approached orgasm,

Just as I felt my groin begin to spasm. I forced myself to stop—and just in time too. The feeling of holding off orgasm at the last second was so intense, I couldn't resist doing it again.

I took my hand off my cock, closed my eyes and let myself settle down. Just before I was going to start pumping again, I felt a warm hand grip my penis and begin stroking it. I was startled to realize that Kenny must have been watching me jerk off. Now he'd quietly snuck over and was kneeling beside my bed in the dark, jerking me off! Without saying a word, I lay back and enjoyed it.

Kenny expertly played with my penis. His hand slid up and down my shaft, and he pulled the skin up over the tip of the very sensitive head. I was surprised at how unashamed I was to have a man yank me off.

The next thing I knew, Kenny slipped into bed with me. I could feel the warmth of his naked body. A thrill shot through me as his rock-hard penis touched mine. My excitement got the best of me. I ran my hands up and down his muscular chest, and felt him tremble with excitement as I ran my fingers through his kinky pubic hair and gently squeezed his big, sperm-filled balls. I wrapped my hand around his prick and pumped it up and down. He grabbed my member again and matched my movements stroke-for-stroke.

We explored each other's cock and balls, taking each other to the brink of climax several times. After about half an hour of this, I sensed that we both were ready to come. As I felt my balls tighten, I could feel Kenny's body quiver with anticipation. We both were trembling as we pulled each other to climax. Kenny's hard penis pulsed several thick jets of sperm into my hand. In turn, his hand was the recipient of my own creamy love-milk.

We were so exhausted from the workout that we fell right asleep. When we woke the next morning, we decided that we would never repeat our experience of the previous night, but we agreed that we were glad it happened once.—*Name and address withheld*

THE ONLY SINGLES BAR HE'LL EVER NEED IS RIGHT BETWEEN HIS LEGS

I am forty years old and recently divorced. My sex life over the past decade has been quite ordinary, with the frequency of sexual activity much lower than I care to admit. This has been due to my having committed myself to career advancement, civic responsibilities and raising a family. I don't have any regrets about the life I've chosen, but I'm amazed at how much I've changed since I went to college in the early 1970s.

I attended a very small, liberal, four-year school in New England. Drug use and sexual experimentation were the norm then, and I experienced everything I could. My hard cock found its way into a wide variety of things ranging from men and women to fruits and vegetables. Many nights were spent in dark rooms in the midst of some sort of group grope, being rubbed, licked, sucked, stroked and fucked to orgasm by the hands, mouths, feet and genitalia of males and females alike.

Anyway, I thought those adventurous days were behind me. My attention and energy had been redirected to the more serious pursuits of career and security. But a couple of things have happened since my recent divorce that have made me realize I haven't changed all that much.

As a newly single man, I had to find a place to live. I approached a male friend of mine who is my age and has never been married. He agreed to let me move into his apartment with him. Joel is a landscaper and a triathlete. Although he is in his early forties, he has the body of a twenty-year-old. I run twenty-five miles a week, so I'm in great shape myself. Joel is proud of his body, and spends much of the time at home in his boxer shorts or totally nude. He never gets dressed in the morning until he has to go out. I found this odd at first, but grew quite used to it within a few weeks. In fact, I took up nudism in the apartment too, and found it to be a lot of fun.

When I first moved in, Joel and I talked a lot about lifestyles, philosophies, sexual experiences and the common bond we shared: keeping our bodies healthy through rigorous exercise. Joel's girlfriend, Wanda, is a beautiful blonde who is always tan and is also quite athletic. Joel asked me to help give Wanda a special birthday present: a ménage à trois! I surprised myself by quickly agreeing. I knew it would be a fun experience for all of us. Joel set the stage for the evening's activities. It was to be a surprise for Wanda, who had years earlier mentioned to Joel that her biggest fantasy was to enjoy two men at the same time. The plan was this: Joel and Wanda would go out to dinner, then return to our apartment at midnight. I was to stay at home and get into Joel's bed before midnight. I bought a large bottle of red wine and rented three X-rated videos in preparation for the big night. I got into Joel's bed at about nine o'clock, drinking wine and watching the videos.

Joel had made up the bed with black satin sheets. They felt terrific against my nude body. All three videos I'd rented were bisexual films. I drank wine and watched these films for two and a half hours. My prick never went soft! On several occasions the action on-screen got me so hot that I thought I would have to jerk off to relieve the sexual tension. But I wanted to save my big load for Wanda, so I held off.

Precisely at midnight I heard the apartment door open. I got a little nervous about what was to happen next, but I was too sexually aroused to either chicken out or, for that matter, lose my hard-on. I heard Joel say, "Wait out here for a few minutes, then come into the bedroom."

Joel walked into the bedroom and gave me a big, broad grin. He stripped to his underwear and asked if I was ready for a really fun evening. I told him I'd been getting ready all night long. Joel was now wearing only his blue paisley boxer shorts. He turned toward me and pulled them down. His cock was already stiff. He pulled the shorts down slowly, revealing his fat penis an inch at a time while looking me straight in the eye. As the waistband cleared the head of his penis, his erection sprang back up so that it was pointed at the ceiling. The head was shiny and huge.

"Should I keep the shorts off or put them back on?" he asked. I replied that Wanda would probably like to take them off for him, so he pulled them back on, slid between the sheets and lay down beside me.

"Are you ready?" he asked. Without waiting for my reply, he slid his hand down and gently grabbed my hard shaft. "I guess you are ready!" he said. He told me how much fun we were going to have, and what a big surprise this was going to be.

Then he said, "I have good news and bad news. First the bad news. Wanda drank too much before, during and after dinner. She ended up getting sick in the car on the way over here. I had to take her back to her place to sleep."

Disappointed, I said, "What's the good news?"

"The good news is that I am still prepared to make your evening fun," he responded. "That is, if you're up for putting a little variety in your sex life."

While Joel was telling me this, he had begun to slide his hand up and down my stiff prick. I didn't tell Joel that I'd slept with several men in my younger days, but the fact that I didn't back away from his caress was encouragement enough for him. He began rubbing and stroking my cock with more intensity. I knew I was going to go along with whatever he wanted to do. I was just too sex-crazed at this point to stop!

Joel played with my hard-on for quite a while, rubbing it, tickling it, pumping it and holding it. He moved his head down to my crotch and began to lick every inch of my penis and balls. He teased the head until I thought I was going to explode. Finally he took my cock deep into his mouth and pumped it, stroking the shaft each time it emerged from his lips. As I approached orgasm, Joel pulled my cock out of his mouth, pumped it with his fist and licked hard on the crease on the underside of the head. When I came, it spurted out over his head! The volume of come I shot was unbelievable—it could have filled a juice glass. Joel placed my spent organ back into his mouth and gently sucked it until it was soft and drained dry.

He then asked if I had enjoyed getting the blowjob as much as he'd enjoyed giving it. I told him I certainly had. "Are you up for returning the favor?" he asked. Without hesitating, I gave him my answer—but with actions, not words. I reached down between the satin sheets and wrapped my hand around Joel's hard, hot cock. Although, as I've said, I'd been with many men when I was in college, I was young then, and nervous, and in a hurry to get those encounters over with. But I was in an entirely different frame of mind with Joel. I found the feel of his hard-on very enjoyable, and wanted to prolong the pleasure for both of us.

I pulled the sheets away so that I could see his prick and watch what I was doing to it. His penis was about the same length as mine, but a little thinner. His shaft was very light, shiny and smooth, and the head was pronounced and reddish pink in color. I moved down until I was resting my head on his stomach so that I could look at his prick while I played with it. I stroked it, pulled the skin up and down over the crown and cupped his warm balls in my hand. In short, I spent a good twenty-five minutes exploring Joel's beautiful and sexy erect penis.

Joel was loving the attention. I moved my head down on his

belly so that I could stick my tongue out and touch the head of his prick. I licked a clear drop of pre-come out of the slit. It was sweet as candy. I licked the head for several minutes, working my tongue up and down the fleshy tube like it was a lollipop.

The effect of my attention was visible on Joel's face. I sensed he was approaching release, so I stuffed his fat cock between my lips and all the way into my wet mouth. I rolled my tongue around the silky-smooth head and pumped the skin of his shaft up and down. Within seconds, Joel unloaded a gusher into my mouth. I held it all in my mouth until he was finished ejaculating. Then I kissed him on the lips, sharing his load of semen with him. We caressed as we swallowed down his come. It really tasted good.

I don't know if your readers will understand this or not, but I don't really have sexual feelings for Joel, no more than I have true sexual feelings for my hand, or for the cantaloupe I jerked off into once at college. I lust after women. I love women. But I also love the feeling of having my hard cock rubbed, licked or stimulated to orgasm, and I guess it doesn't matter who's doing it. As long as I get off, that's the only important thing.

Joel and I are completely at ease with each other in the apartment. The other night I was reading *Penthouse Letters* while lying nude on the couch. I had a full erection and was not ashamed of it. Joel walked over and said, "Here, let me help you with that." While I continued to read the magazine, he gently played with my hard-on, eventually pumping it to orgasm. I thanked him for beating me off, and he said, "You owe me one." Believe me, I've returned the favor—and then some.—*Name and address withheld*

MASSEUR TEACHES NEOPHYTE THE INS AND OUTS OF THE BUSINESS

I am a single bisexual male living in a small rural town. Although it's near to two bustling major cities, things are pretty dead around here. Nightlife is almost nonexistent, and you can't even get any action with the ladies. If anyone around here even suspected I like men, they'd probably lynch me, so I do my best to be discreet about my proclivities. Mostly all I can do is fantasize fondly about my experiences of the past.

I had my first bisexual experience several years ago in California. At the time I had recently been discharged from the military and was working nights as a bartender in a bar that attracted a mixed crowd: professionals, models, bodybuilders, bikers and so forth. I had done quite a bit of weight lifting while in the military, and even though I'm only five feet ten inches, I didn't have an ounce of fat on my one-hundred-ninety-five-pound body.

I had one customer who came in every night—sometimes two or three times a night—who was a particularly good tipper. He was young, tanned and very well built. He would order a shot of Wild Turkey on the rocks and sip it until his beeper went off, at which time he would give me a twenty-dollar bill, say "Keep the change" and leave. Naturally curiosity was killing me as to what his line of work was! I thought he must be dealing drugs or something, as he always had a lot of cash and kept very much to himself.

One night he came in for the third time just at closing time and ordered his usual. As I cleaned up and prepared to close the bar, he struck up a conversation with me for the very first time.

After the usual small talk about sports and the weather, he asked me how much money I made in tips and salary. I admitted that more than half of my money came in tips from him. He laughed and told me that I was wasting my time. He said I should consider quitting my job and getting into his line of work. When I asked him what he did for a living, he replied that he gave massages to people in their homes or apartments, and smiled. When pressed for details, he said it would take a while to explain and invited me back to his apartment for a drink if I wanted to hear the rest of the story.

I agreed, locked up and followed him to a very nice apartment in an exclusive section of town. He said he shared the place with a coworker who was on vacation at this time.

As we settled down to talk and sip bourbon, he explained that he worked for an out-call massage service that beeped him whenever he had an appointment. Most of his customers were older women or men who paid very well to have him massage their nude bodies while he was also nude—several of the older men actually paid him to allow them to give him blowjobs!

He added that he had a very few married men—bankers, lawyers, doctors—who wanted to have a young stud suck them off, and that he could easily make two- or three-hundred-dollar tips for doing so. He also said that they were in the minority, and that I may never run into one of them.

Well, the combination of Wild Turkey and wild talk, combined with the promise of money, got me real excited. He said that he made more than two thousand dollars a week and only worked about four hours a day. He told me that he knew the owner of the massage parlor well enough that he could practically guarantee me a job if I wanted it. I was so fucked up that I called my boss at home, cursed him out and quit! Too drunk to drive home, I slept on his couch that night.

The next evening, as I was preparing for my job interview, he dropped a bombshell on me—part of the interview was to give the boss a blowjob!

I explained to him that I had never done that before and didn't know how. Since I had already blown my other job, I was in quite a panic! He tried to reassure me, telling me that he'd show me how to do it.

We both stripped naked, and he sat me on the couch and began to nibble and lick at my cock and balls—I never felt anything so good in my life! He then had me try the same technique on him.

He finally worked me up to taking most of his cock into my mouth. It was long and very big around, circumcised with a beautifully soft, red head. I sucked until he came, and even though I tried to swallow it all, some of his come ran down my chin.

He told me that the boss wouldn't hire me if I was sloppy like that, and said I needed more practice. Since he had to save himself for his clients that night, he said he'd call up a friend for me to practice on. He got on the phone, and about fifteen minutes later his friend Biff showed up. Biff, a blond surfer-type, had the situation explained to him and was quite amenable to serve as my guinea pig. I soon found myself on my knees in front of him, eagerly gobbling down his cock, which was at least eight inches long and almost as thick as my wrist. When I finished sucking Biff off, I was proud of myself as I hadn't spilled a drop of his delicious joy-juice. The two of them, however, decided that I needed more practice and got back on the phone.

Within twenty minutes, two gorgeous muscle men arrived. After hearing of my predicament, they stripped, exposing beautiful cocks. I carefully and lovingly gave my best effort yet. I was beginning to really enjoy sucking cock. After finishing both guys off, they all decided that, despite my sore jaw, I was ready to meet the boss.

Since the boss was an older man with a very short, skinny dick, I passed my interview with flying colors.—*T.P., Dallas, Texas*

BUSINESS TRIP TURNS INTO PLEASURE JAUNT WHEN HE'S RUBBED THE RIGHT WAY

Last month I attended a marketing seminar in San Diego. I flew in about midafternoon and took a taxi to my hotel. It was a luxury hotel located right on the beach. My room, which was quite large, overlooked the ocean. After I unpacked, I stretched out on the bed and read the material describing the facilities available to the guests of the hotel. Since I had plenty of time before the opening reception that night, I decided to check out the men's health club on the top floor.

A tall, thin young man with longish blond hair, pale blue eyes and a sensuous mouth greeted me when I walked in. He wore tight white slacks and a T-shirt that was a size or two too small for his broad, muscular chest. His name tag read Byron. I requested a massage, but he explained that they were fully booked for the rest of the afternoon and suggested a sauna instead. He led me into the changing room, where I stripped, and then to the sauna. Several other men were inside. In about twenty minutes sweat covered my body and I decided I'd had enough. Byron ushered me into the shower room and sprayed me with cool water. He then suggested that I go onto the private sundeck and relax in the late-afternoon sun. I joined several others who were stretched out nude on lounge chairs.

The warm sun felt good on my naked body. I was about to doze off when Byron brought me a large glass of cold fruit juice. He said that if I still wanted a massage, he would stay late and give me one. I said that would be great.

The other guests began to leave as closing time approached. Byron led me into an alcove, and I lay on my stomach on the massage table. He helped the other attendants close up. I heard him say good-bye to them and ask them to lock the door.

"I really appreciate this," I said when he returned.

"I'm glad to do it," he replied. "I get tired of massaging fat, hairy, old men with short, ugly dicks all day. Once in a while someone like you comes in, but not often. You have a good body—very well proportioned, with long, lean muscles. You must be a runner."

"No, but I swim a lot," I admitted.

"Your shoulders and back are well developed, and your ass is quite firm," Byron commented as he spread warm oil on my shoulders and back. He began working on my neck and shoulders, then down each arm. He rubbed and kneaded my hands and snapped the joints of each finger. Turning his attention to my back, he began squeezing muscles I didn't even know I had. His strong hands worked their way down my spine. He poured oil on my lower back. Some ran into the crack of my ass. Slowly he pressed and rotated my buns, massaging them thoroughly.

"How do you feel?" he asked.

"Great, but you're about to give me a hard-on," I told him.

"That happens sometimes. I hoped it would with you." Byron patted me playfully on my buttocks. Spreading my legs apart, he massaged my thighs, allowing his hands to occasionally brush against my balls, before working on my calves and ankles. He rubbed my feet and pulled and pumped each toe like it was a little prick. Sexy sensations shot up to my crotch. I moved to adjust my swelling cock.

"Okay, now for the front. Turn over," he instructed. I obeyed and opened my eyes. Byron was staring at my crotch and smiling. "It's big, beautiful and not even hard yet," he said gleefully. He had removed his T-shirt and pants. His bikini briefs bulged suggestively.

Byron stood behind my head and massaged my shoulders. He tweaked my nipples as he worked over my chest. He squeezed and manipulated my stomach muscles, brushing against my hard cock occasionally.

"Now it's long and thick, and curved like a big banana," Byron remarked.

"Hey, you got me this way," I reminded him. "It doesn't get harder than that."

"Do you want me to take care of it for you?" Byron asked eagerly.

"What did you have in mind?" I teased.

Byron grinned and ran his tongue over his lips. "You know what I want," he said.

I grasped my rigid pole and held it up. "Come and get it," I teased him.

"I'll get it, but you'll come," he laughed.

Byron tickled it lightly, then gripped it in both hands and pumped it several times. He leaned over and licked off the pre-come that drooled out. His face nuzzled my crotch. My balls were licked and sucked. He gently nibbled along the length of my shaft and twirled his tongue around the knob. I was going crazy. Every nerve in my body tingled. My cock pulsated. He sucked in a couple of inches and pumped the rest.

Suddenly he pulled away and removed his briefs. His big dick jutted out of a tangle of kinky blond hair. Byron placed my hand on it. "Jerk me off while I blow you," he requested. I pumped him slowly.

Byron lowered his head, opened his mouth and sucked in my cock. I put my free hand on his head, urging him to take more. I thrust my hips upward, and my cockhead hit the back of his throat. Byron could tell that I was getting close to orgasm. He stopped sucking and squeezed my dick sharply under the head.

"That will slow you down a little. You don't want to shoot off too quickly. I'm just getting started with you. I'm going to drive you crazy," he promised. And he did. His hands played over my body, exciting nerves I didn't know I had. My body quivered. He caressed my balls as he sucked on the knob of my dick.

I knew I couldn't hold back any longer. "I'm coming," I groaned. My muscles tightened. I could feel come rush from my balls and surge into his mouth. Byron kept sucking until I was drained and my cock softened.

"Now do me," he begged.

I sat on the edge of the table. Byron stood between my legs, his throbbing cock standing straight out. I pumped it slowly with oil-slicked hands as I played with his big balls. Pre-come made his cockhead glisten. If I was ever tempted to suck a dick, that was the time. I held him with both hands, and he fucked my fists. Byron moaned and streams of his juice squirted into the air.

"You were tempted to suck me, weren't you?" Byron asked.

"Yes," I admitted.

"Have you ever sucked off another guy?" he asked me.

"No," I answered.

"Why not? Are you afraid to? Sucking a cock isn't going to turn you off girls. You ought to try it—you just might like it."

"I might," I agreed.

"Will I see you again? I hope so," he said eagerly.

"I don't know," I told him as I got dressed.

"By the way, no charge," he called out as I left.—*L.D., Muncie, Indiana*

HOLIER-THAN-THOU GLORY-HOLE AFICIONADO DOESN'T PRACTICE WHAT HE PREACHES

Not long ago, I paid a visit to my good friend Carl, who's been married for several years. When Carl and I were younger, we would often go out together and frequent strip clubs, X-rated theaters and adult bookstores. Being single, I still visit these places on occasion. However, Carl's wife takes a firm stand against him indulging in such activities. But the weekend I was visiting, Iris was staying overnight at her sister's with the kids, which allowed Carl amnesty from her rule. After all, what she didn't know wouldn't hurt her.

We went out and hit a few go-go bars. We were having a great time cutting loose and catching a buzz. Carl suggested we stop at an adult bookstore to watch some loops, since X-rated videos were also taboo in his house. He commented that he hoped there weren't any "damned cruisers" there, as he put it. We'd never discussed our sexual experiences, so he had no way of knowing about the encounters I'd had with men, and I figured there was no need to bring it up now. Nonetheless, many adult bookstores have become seedy over the years.

We bought several dollars' worth of tokens and separately set out among the catacomb of video booths. There were indeed cruisers roaming about, and most of the viewing stalls sported glory holes—openings about the size of a large coffee can in the walls between the booths for anonymous oral trysts. After declining a few propositions, I was left alone and began to enjoy a particularly hot video. I lowered my jeans to stroke my stiff erection.

Through the hole I noticed someone enter the booth next to mine. From the slacks and shoes revealed through the hole, I knew it was Carl. Glad that I wouldn't be bothered or interrupted again, I continued to jack myself off. After a while I became curious and leaned down to peer through the hole. Although I couldn't see his upper body, Carl had also lowered his pants and was pumping his big, hard dick. I was amused at the thought of both of us whacking off surreptitiously right next door to each other. Then suddenly Carl got up and struck his turgid shaft through the hole.

I was startled and thought at first that he had recognized me and was just teasing me. After several seconds I heard him say, "Suck it."

I figured, What the hell, and began to stroke his hefty organ. When I licked his swollen glans, I felt him jump and heard him moan. I licked every inch of his hot, velvety shaft and lapped at his heavy, come-filled balls. I then lifted his massive slab and ran my tongue along the vein on the underside. I positioned his throbbing boner against my pouting lips, kissing his soft cock-head. I parted my lips and slowly inserted his pulsing member in my watering mouth, teasing and coaxing at it with my flickering tongue. I'm an accomplished cocksucker, and Carl groaned as I sucked his long schlong down my throat. My talents excited him, and his breathing quickened as he pressed harder against the wall. My own straining erection displayed how turned on I was getting by all this.

Several minutes into his blowjob, Carl began to hump my mouth. I relaxed my jaw, but continued sucking as he fucked my mouth with full, gut-pounding strokes. I reached up to play with his nuts and felt them tighten and swell, indicating his approaching orgasm. I decided to let him come in my mouth and soon felt him quicken his pace. I heard him gasp louder, then exclaim, "I'm gonna come!" At that I sucked harder, prompting him with my swirling tongue.

Suddenly his dick swelled and spasmed. Groaning loudly, he blew his thick wad into my eager mouth. His rigid rocket shot spurt after spurt of hot jism down my throat. So immense was Carl's load, I couldn't swallow or hold it all. Some ran out of my mouth and down my chin. I continued sucking his wonderful organ until he pulled away. I backed away from the portal and watched Carl pull up and secure his pants, then leave his booth. Being extremely aroused by what had transpired, and feeling the cream dripping down my chin, I catered to my own upright prick, bringing myself off and gushing my pearly goo into a tissue. I could hardly believe that I'd just given a blowjob to one of my closest friends. It struck me as extremely ironic that Carl could make such a big deal bitching about "those damned cruisers" when he obviously had enjoyed their favors. I'm sure he would've been completely horrified if he had realized that it was me who was sucking him off!

Back in the lobby, I ran into Carl, who said he was ready to leave. In the car we commented on the different films we had viewed. I asked Carl if his booth had a glory hole. He replied, "Yeah, and it's a good thing those damned cruisers didn't bother me!"

I just smiled knowingly as I tasted his tart come, which still coated my tongue, and agreed.—*T.R., Nashville, Tennessee*

Domination & Discipline

THAT'S WHAT WE MISS ABOUT SCHOOL: ALL THAT PUNISHMENT HOMEWORK

I met Nancy the first week of college. She had light red hair, small breasts and green eyes. The first time I saw her I wanted her more than anything else, but it took me four years to get into her pants. Though we were friends, Nancy never let it get further than that. We stayed "just friends," and I had to suffer through her descriptions of one jerk boyfriend after another. She seemed to go for a certain tough-guy type that just wasn't me. By my senior year I had pretty much given up the chase. I'd even almost stopped fantasizing about fucking her. Almost.

I was an art major, and my senior project was a large metal sculpture. I hadn't mentioned it to Nancy, but she'd heard about it from a mutual friend and asked to see it. So I invited her over. I was sitting outside my front door when she arrived. I explained that to fully appreciate my sculpture, she would have to be blindfolded first. That way, I could present it with the proper amount of dramatic flair. She giggled and said, "Okay."

I blindfolded her with a handkerchief, making sure that she could not see a thing. As I led her into my apartment, she said, "It's a good thing I trust you."

I responded by asking, "Are you sure you can?"

She seemed just a little nervous by my answer and said, "I don't know. Maybe I shouldn't."

We stopped in the middle of the living room and I kissed her. She was definitely surprised, but not displeased. I kissed her again, for a little longer this time. When she opened her mouth, I sank my tongue into it, and our tongues finally stopped talking and met properly.

When we came up for air, she asked, "Why did you kiss me?"

"I should've done it four years ago," I said. She said she

wanted to take the blindfold off, but I told her to wait, and led her to my bedroom, then to my bed, and lay beside her.

After several minutes of passionate necking, I realized that she was no longer asking me if she could take her blindfold off, but instead she seemed very turned on by it. I took both her wrists in one hand and held her arms over her head. She gasped with excitement. With my free hand I shook a pillow free of its case. I straddled her breasts and used the pillowcase to tie her wrists to the bed frame. She was shaking as I unbuttoned her blouse, but she never asked me to stop. When I ran my hands over her breasts, she arched her back so I could unhook her bra.

I unzipped her jeans and started to pull them down over her soaking-wet panties. She tried kicking her legs to help me, but that only made it more difficult. I stood up, grabbed each pant leg at the bottom and pulled them off. She was sweating and almost naked—her panties dark where her wetness had stained them. The stained glass window I'd installed in my bedroom let in red streams of light that fell on her nearly nude body, giving her a magical glow.

I knelt over the bed, with my mouth pressed against her panties, and blew warm air onto her cunt lips. She moaned and said, "Fuck me." I laughed and pulled off her panties. I ate her pussy like a starving man, occasionally tickling her clit with my tongue.

A few minutes later she pleaded, "Please, fuck me now. I want to feel your dick inside me."

"You've made me wait for four years," I said with a nasty chuckle. "Four years of frustration. Well, what goes around comes around."

With that, I left the room and got myself a beer.

When I came back a few minutes later, Nancy was writhing on the bed, trying to loosen the tight knot around her wrists.

"Are you ready to be fucked now?" I asked.

"I told you before, I'm dying to fuck you," Nancy said. Her voice sounded angry, but there was no mistaking the excitement in her hard-tipped nipples, or in the way the juice was dripping from her tight little cunt. I realized in that instant that my approach to Nancy had been wrong all along. I was always a nice guy, sensitive to her needs and unwilling to do anything she might not like. But here I had her tied to my bed, blindfolded, and all she could think about was my cock.

"Beg me," I said.

"Please give it to me," Nancy said breathlessly.

"It doesn't sound to me like you really want my dick. I'm going to get another beer."'

"No, wait!" Nancy cried. "I want to taste your cock. I want to bathe it with my tongue. I want you to fuck my mouth and let me swallow your come."

"That's more like it," I said. It was time to let Nancy know what she'd been missing all these years. I pulled down my pants and straddled her chest. Then I positioned my dick at her mouth and rubbed the head against her lips. She opened them wide for me, and I pushed in my cock and fucked her mouth vigorously.

"Suck it!" I said. She feasted on my organ, her tongue moving all over my shaft like a paintbrush. I was so worked up that I came in less than a minute, filling her mouth with the thickest, most enormous load of spunk I'd ever shot.

"Swallow it," I ordered. "Every drop."

Nancy did as she was told, gulping my sperm until my cock was dry as a bone and totally soft.

"Ready to get fucked?" I asked.

"I want it so bad!" Nancy sighed. "I want your hard cock between my legs. I want you to make me come with your long prick."

"Beg for it," I ordered.

"Please fuck me! Please!" Nancy chimed. She lifted her legs and bent her knees, offering up her steaming cunt. I was almost ready to give her what she wanted—but first I got my camera and took a few pictures of Nancy. I instructed her to keep her legs up high so I could get good pictures of her juice-dripping cunt lips.

After I'd shot an entire roll of film, my cock was ready to burst. I plunged it into her soaking pussy and she wailed with delight. Nancy's fist-tight hole milked my cock like no other pussy ever had. I pounded one last time deep into her and we both came.

I untied her and took off her blindfold, then lay beside her and stroked her sweat-soaked breasts. "Was there really film in that camera?" she asked, somewhat anxiously. When I answered that indeed there was, she asked if she could see the pictures when they were developed.

"We have three years of sex to catch up on," I explained. "You've made me wait all these years, and now we have to make up for lost time. When I think you deserve it, I'll show you those pictures."

The next day I took the film to be developed at one of those one-hour labs. While the film was being processed, I went to Nancy's apartment and tied her up again, giving her another great fuck—this time up the ass. As soon I blasted her rear full of come, I headed off to the lab—leaving her tied, facedown, to her bed—and picked up the film.

I've since showed her the pictures, and they got her so horny she is now more willing than ever to do exactly what I want. All I can say is that it was worth the wait.—*Name and address withheld*

JUST TAKE IT—TAKE ANOTHER LITTLE PIECE OF MY GIRLFRIEND, STRANGER

Last night my beautiful sex-slave Ellie showed how devoted she was by fucking a dozen or so total strangers for me. Ellie is twenty-five years old and has been my totally subservient slave for four years now. She is five feet tall, has long, dark hair and a well-proportioned, athletic body. She is completely trained to please me sexually. She always wears a jeweled dog collar around her neck, and keeps leather restraints handy, putting them on her wrists and ankles anytime I command her to do so.

I began last night by taking Ellie to the sleaziest adult motel I could find. It can be rented by the half hour, but I paid for the whole night: thirty dollars. In the room, I ordered her to strip and put on her restraints. Then I cuffed her spread-eagle to the bed and switched on the closed-circuit TV to the channel that played continuous X-rated movies. I opened the curtains so any passersby could see her naked, helpless body. Then I left the room, telling her that I was going to find some men to fuck her. "Thank you," she lovingly responded.

I went to a poolroom I had scouted earlier to pick up some guys for Ellie. I hung out for a while and soon struck up a conversation with Rory, a crude-talking biker. I told him I knew where there was some action, and that if they brought the liquor, he and his friends could have all the free pussy they wanted. Rory and his buddies—Bob, Drew and Scott—were definitely interested. I followed them to the liquor store, and they followed me to the motel.

When we arrived at the room, Ellie's eyes grew wide with lust at the sight of these four rough-looking characters. Upon seeing her tied up on the bed, her pussy already gaping and wet, the guys whooped with delight.

They were on her in no time. Rory didn't bother to completely undress. He just dropped his pants and shoved his cock into her mouth. Ellie sucked greedily. Drew at least removed his shoes and pants before he dove tongue-first into her spread-open snatch. Scott, Bob and I settled back to enjoy the booze and the show.

Rory came quickly in Ellie's mouth. As he observed her swallowing down his spunk, he pulled up his zipper and announced, "This chick is a good little cocksucker."

Drew asked me to untie her legs to make it easier to fuck her. I obliged, and he roughly pushed her legs back over her head and plunged his hard dick into her pussy. He was slightly overweight, and his ass shook violently as he banged her box without mercy. After about five minutes he groaned, "Oh shit!" as he tensed up and came. He abruptly dismounted, leaving his semen spilling out of Ellie's wide-open twat. His buddies handed him a drink and slapped him on the back.

Scott was a tall, slender black man with a thin beard. "I need to fuck some ass," he said. Contending with my own erection, which by now was as hard as a steel-plated tank, I undid Ellie's wrists so she could get up on her hands and knees. Then I attached a leash to her dog collar.

"Tell these guys why you're here," I said to her, giving her rump a stinging slap.

"I'm a slut," she responded. "I want to suck and fuck as much cock as I can get. If I don't please you, I want to be punished."

I handed Scott the leash and said, "She's all yours."

Scott said, "All right! That's some wild bitch you've got there," and removed his clothes. "I'm going to fuck your tight asshole," he said to Ellie. "I don't want my long, black dick to hurt, bitch, so you'd better lubricate it with your tongue first." He grabbed a handful of Ellie's long hair and pulled her forcefully to his crotch. She slathered all over his limb, getting it shiny and slick with her saliva. Scott was really built. It looked like Ellie was sucking off a stretch limo.

Scott turned her around and pulled her ass to him. Without having to be told, Ellie grabbed her ass-cheeks and spread them apart, revealing a puckered pink hole. Scott placed the head of his prick, dripping with Ellie's saliva, at the entrance to her hole.

With brute force he thrust several inches of his giant cock deep in her butt. Ellie let out a shrill cry of pain. One of my rules is that she is not allowed to express any discomfort during sex. As Scott reamed her ass, she said, "I'm sorry for crying out. Your dick feels so good in me. Please punish me for that. I'm such a stupid little cunt."

"Damn right you are," Scott responded. He was my kind of guy. "The only thing I want to hear out of your mouth is how much you like riding this big black pole." To make his point, he pinched both nipples of her dangling breasts as hard as he could. Ellie winced a bit, but did not make another outburst.

"Oh!" she bleated passionately. "Yes, yes yes! I love getting it up the ass. Come in me, come in my ass right now."

Scott was only too willing to comply. He deposited a load into her chute. Ellie flexed her ass muscles until his cock had been milked dry and slipped out of the tight passage.

As she was catching her breath, we noticed that several men had gathered at the window to watch. I told Ellie to invite them in. She got off the bed, walked to the door and opened it wide. "Hi, guys!" she said enthusiastically. "Would you like to do me too?" Suddenly the room was crowded with men intent on getting the fuck of their lives.

The door remained open for the rest of the night as a steady stream of both men and women used Ellie's body in any way they desired. Most of my time was spent acting like a traffic cop, directing people in and out of her available holes. At one point I announced that what Ellie really loved best was to be fucked in the mouth. This got everyone—even some of the guys who already had come two and three times—hard again. A line of stiff dicks formed beside the bed as one guy after another fucked her face. She took load after load all night long, even enthusiastically eating several hot pussies to the cheers of all in attendance. By the end of the night, Ellie's hair was slicked back and caked with sperm and cunt juice. She looked beautiful!

This morning, after the last satisfied man had headed home, I told her she had been a good slave. I rewarded her by letting her fuck herself with her favorite giant, fifteen-inch dildo. Watching her masturbate got me very hard, so I asked Ellie to show me how grateful she was to me for allowing her to satisfy so many horny people. She responded by crawling over to me on her hands and knees and taking my cock in her mouth. She was exhausted and covered with dried come. Her tits, ass, mouth and pussy were red and sore from all the activity, but she still blew me like an enthusiastic little slut, drinking every drop of my load and begging for more.—*N.F., Detroit, Michigan*

CA-REAR OPPORTUNITY: LOTION PLUS MOTION, AND THEN A PROMOTION!

I am a thirty-four-year-old male lawyer. I have had a succession of beautiful women since I was in my teens, but Nora, my wife of three years, is the prettiest of them all.

Nora is ten years younger than I. She is small and slim, with blonde hair flowing halfway down her back. She has an incredibly cute face and a body to die for. Her ass is a perfectly carved set of soft, rounded orbs, and her tits are firm and bountiful. She was a shy saleswoman at an exclusive store where I used to shop, and it took me months to get her to go out with me. Once she did, I knew a good thing when I saw it and asked her to marry me. Because of her strict upbringing, she was a virgin when we met. I popped her cherry on our wedding night.

Our sex life, though, was strictly routine. Until we met she'd never sucked a cock, and she never really learned to like sucking mine. By the end of our first year of marriage, sex for us consisted of a couple of missionary-position fucks a week, and it was an occasion for celebration if she came from intercourse. But she never complained and, to be honest, I was too committed to my career to care about anything else but getting ahead in my job.

I was gunning for a partnership and met with strong competition. I worked long hours and kissed ass, knowing that making partner would double my already large salary and allow me to do all the things I'd always wanted to do. The partner I worked directly under, Larry, was forty-five years old and average looking, but he was the most influential of all the partners. He was tough to work for and very demanding, but the promise of a partnership turned me into a full-fledged brown-noser.

One afternoon I was leaving from work for a three-day business trip. Since I was returning on a Saturday, Larry told me that he'd be dropping a huge box of documents at my house for me to review when I returned from my trip. It was not exactly what I had in mind for the weekend, but of course I told him it was a good idea. Larry had been sending me on more and more trips, and working me harder than ever. I took this as a good sign, and hoped that the firm had me in mind for the next partner position.

I returned from the business trip a few hours earlier than expected, and noticed Larry's car in front of our house. I didn't know what to make of it. I have always been the suspicious type, but my wife was so prim and proper that I never suspected her of even thinking about being unfaithful to me. I quietly parked down the block and snuck up to my house. I almost had a heart attack when I looked in the window. There was my wife, nude except for a pair of black leather boots. She was bent over the arm of the couch, facedown. Larry was standing behind her with a drink in his hand.

His dick was shiny and limp. He apparently had just come and was telling Nora what to do to make him hard again. I moved closer so I could hear exactly what they were saying.

"Tired yet?" Nora asked. Larry responded by slapping her ass hard with his hand.

"I know what you want," he said to her. Without a word she reached down and picked up bottle of body lotion. She bent over and squirted a glob of the white cream on her asshole. Larry grabbed her arms and stuck his dick—which was hard again and much bigger and fatter than mine—into her back door.

"What do you want me to do?" he asked.

"Fuck me," Nora said. She had never spoken those words to me, and it was strangely exciting to hear her utter them to another man.

"Where do you want to get fucked, bitch?" Larry asked.

"Put it in my ass," Nora said unenthusiastically.

"Beg for it or you won't get so much as an inch of dick," he commanded.

Nora, obviously into Larry's little power trip, said, "Larry, please fuck my ass with your big dick. I want your come to make my asshole nice and squishy."

Larry held Nora by the waist and began to cram his dick into her rump. Once it was all the way in, he released her hands and told her to spread her ass-cheeks with her fingers. He grabbed her long hair with both his hands and pulled it hard as he vigorously fucked her butt. "Now, make yourself come like a slut," he commanded. She began to finger herself feverishly. With her free hand she brought a tit to her mouth and sucked the hard nipple. I had never seen her do either of these things before, and was completely mesmerized. "Come!" Larry urged brutally, slapping Nora's butt-cheeks while he continued to ream her bunghole.

"Yes, I'm coming!" Nora announced, her finger moving a mile a minute on her sensitive clit.

Larry gave her ass a few more hard spanks and then stiffened. "Feel it, baby," he growled. "Feel my come pump into your ass!"

I waited for Larry to clean up and leave before I went inside. My wife was in bed, and needless to say, surprised to see me. She said she was going to take a shower and seemed very nervous. I immediately told her what I'd seen, and she broke down crying and explained what had happened. Apparently, Larry had come over to drop off the documents, just as he'd said he would. But when he got there, he told her that she'd have to be his sex slave for the night or else I wouldn't get my partnership. She said she was devastated by this news, because I had assured her that the partnership was mine. In desperation, she agreed to Larry's terms.

To be honest, I wasn't sure whether to believe her. I suspected that Larry came on so strong to my conservative wife, plying her with flattery and his bold approach, that she was easily seduced into doing what he asked. But I couldn't hold it against her. The fact is, it was incredibly exciting to see my wife with another man, to see her so overpowered that she was begging him to fuck her asshole. But I didn't tell her this. Instead, I told her that if she wanted to get it off her chest, I'd be happy to let her tell me all about what had happened before I got there.

The way she told it, Larry had been adamant about making her his sex slave. She'd tried to refuse, but he kept telling her that there were other men who also deserved the partnership. "And I've already fucked their wives," he said.

"No one will ever have to know," Larry had told her.

"No one?" she'd asked.

"Not a soul," he'd answered, peeling off her clothes.

What followed was a string of commands from Larry to my submissive wife: "Take off your clothes. Crawl over to me. Suck my cock. Deep-throat it. Turn around. Get on your knees. Put your face to the floor and spread your ass-cheeks for me. Tell me how much you love a hard cock." She admitted that after a while, Larry's dominance over her became a turn-on.

"By the time you saw us," she said, "I was begging for him to fuck my ass, but only because I really wanted his cock up there."

Well, I'd never been so turned on in my life. I had an erection that could've sliced through granite. I took Nora in my arms and carried her to our bed. We fucked tirelessly all night long. Nora's pussy was so wet and gooey from the time she'd spent with Larry that she was able to take the most ferocious strokes I could muster up.

About a week later my suspicions about her being a more-than-willing partner for Larry were confirmed. Nora confessed that while I was away at work, Larry had come over with a friend of his. They both had their way with her, and videotaped the entire episode. Nora, who was rapidly beginning to enjoy her role as Larry's sex toy, urged me to watch the tape. What I saw literally made me come in my pants.

When the tape came on, Nora was already naked, as were Larry and his friend Frank. "What do you want to do first to our little whore?" Larry asked Frank.

"I want to fuck those big tits," he said.

"Have you ever tit-fucked a man?" Larry asked my wife. She confessed that she had not, so Larry showed her the way. He leaned beside her, took her hands in his and used them to press her fleshy breasts around Frank's cock. Frank, who had one of those incredibly long cocks that are ideal for a good tit-fuck, pumped the tight gap while Larry casually fingered her asshole.

"Tell him how much you like it," Larry said to her.

"Oh, yeah, Frank. Do my tits," she groaned. "I love the way your cock feels against my skin."

"You're going to make me come soon, you hot bitch," Frank blurted.

"Come on my face," Nora said with a wicked smile. "Give me a sperm bath."

Frank blew a load onto her face that was so thick it dripped down like paint.

"I told you," Larry said to his friend. "See what a slut she is? Just watch how much she loves having a big cock in her asshole.

"Yes, do it," Nora urged, squeezing some body lotion on her anus to keep it moist.

I was shocked, to say the least, by what I was seeing on the tape, but there was no denying that I had the hardest erection of my life. I watched, open-mouthed, as Nora fucked Larry and Frank in every way imaginable. What an incredible conversion! Just a few short weeks earlier she seemed bored by the whole notion of sex. Now she was fucking like a thousand-dollar-a-night whore, taking on two hard cocks and luxuriating in the sweat and semen that, by the end of the videotape, coated her from head to toe.

Things have been good for Nora and me since then. I got my promotion, and Larry treats me very nicely at the office—which is something few of his other coworkers can say. He's been treating Nora nicely as well, fucking her whenever he—or for that matter, she—gets the urge. Sharing my wife with a guy like Larry has taken some getting used to, but as long as she's happy, so am I.—*H.R., Rochester, New York*

WORDS OF LOVE: "KEEP YOUR EYES TO YOURSELF OR YOUR ASS IS MINE!"

I have always been interested in women who can take control and provide the proper discipline I need. I have not been able to establish a permanent relationship with such a woman, but from time to time I get the kind of treatment I crave. This letter is about one of my most enjoyable experiences.

I was out with my girlfriend of the time, Marlene, but I couldn't keep my eyes to myself. I made the mistake of commenting on how good a woman sitting near us looked in her miniskirt. My girlfriend stated that only a slut would wear a skirt that short. Seeing that she was in one of her moods, I dropped the subject.

But when we got back to my house that evening, Marlene told me she was going to teach me a lesson for having a roving eye. She led me to the dining room and told me to lean across the table. She then got two short ropes and tied each of my wrists to a table leg. I was bent over the table with my feet just touching the floor. My ass was in a very vulnerable position. She then produced a neckerchief and rolled it into a blindfold for me to wear.

So there I was, bound and blindfolded, with no hope of escape. The next thing I knew, she was undoing my belt, unbuttoning and unzipping my jeans. She pulled them, along with my underwear, down to my ankles. Then she told me she was going to get some "toys." My bottom was starting to get goose bumps. I was already very excited, and had a full hard-on before she even returned.

When she came back into the room a few minutes later, she said, "You were very bad in that restaurant tonight, looking at that slutty woman. You're really going to get it tonight." With that, she started spanking me with a wooden paddle about a foot long. I'd designed the paddle myself. It has holes drilled in it so that it can move swiftly through the air without any resistance.

Marlene really let me have it. Starting at the top of my right butt-cheek, she reddened my entire ass. Not one to overlook any opportunity to give me pain, she made sure to give equally harsh treatment to both sides of my tortured ass. The stinging of the paddle on my bare flesh was glorious, but I was able to keep quiet until she landed a particularly sharp blow on the inside of my right thigh. I let out a loud yelp to let her know she'd hit one of my favorite tender spots.

"That hurts, doesn't it?" Marlene asked. She must've been in a real devilish mood because, when I said it did, she gave me another twenty whacks in the same area. By that time I was moaning and groaning from the blows of the hard wooden paddle.

Although I was blindfolded and couldn't see anything, I was sure that my poor bottom looked like a brand-new apple, all shiny and red. She stopped long enough to caress my bottom and judge how hot it was, then teased me by running a finger up and down the crack of my ass. Once or twice she encircled my anus with her finger, but that too was just a tease. There was no way she would indulge me with that kind of pleasure. "Your behind isn't even that hot yet," she announced. "I think you need a little more spanking, don't you?" Just hearing those words gave me a rush.

I heard Marlene put down the first paddle and pick up another. When the first of many swats landed dead-center on my ass, I knew which paddle she was now using. It was an eighteen-incher I'd fashioned out of an old bookshelf. Marlene was able to smash this paddle against my skin with much more force than the foot-long one, and that's just what she did. She made sure that every inch of my poor ass was treated to dozens of hard whacks. Some of the best licks she delivered were on the top of each thigh. My favorites were the ones that managed to land on both ass-cheeks at once, causing extreme, irresistible pain.

She alternated from one cheek to the other, occasionally pausing to ask me about the woman I'd been looking at earlier in the evening.

"Did you think she was pretty?" Marlene would ask.

"No," I said contritely, my answer rewarded with a savage blow of the paddle and another question.

"Then why were you looking at her? You did think she was pretty, didn't you?"

"Yes," I confessed, to the sting of another swat.

"And did you think that little slut was sexy? Did you want to fuck her greasy pussy?"

"Yes, I wanted to fuck her."

It was just the answer she was waiting for. She paddled me severely until it seemed the skin of my ass had been stripped away and all that was left was bare muscle. My cock was hard from the beating and on the verge of orgasm. A couple of strokes would've been all that was necessary to make me come. But Marlene wouldn't let me come, no matter how much I begged. She made me pull up my pants and drive her home.

Sitting in the car was as painful as getting whacked. The burning in my buns, in fact, did not subside for several days. Each time I sat in a chair, or lay on my back, I was reminded of the glorious beating I'd received at the hands of my domineering girlfriend.

Marlene and I are no longer together, although I think of her often. I am still looking for my perfect mate, a woman who knows how to dish out punishment in a most sensuous manner, and is willing to do it as often as I like. She would have to be the kind of woman who can reduce me to a crying, sobbing, kicking, spoiled brat who is happy to receive the long-overdue punishment for his actions. I hope to find her while I still have some mischief left in me.—*S.G., Atlanta, Georgia*

DESPERATE MAN DISCOVERS HIS SECRET SIDE WHEN HIS EX TAKES CHARGE

When my girlfriend Delia told me she was leaving me, I thought I wouldn't be able to live without her. I knew that I had to get her back to survive. I decided that I would do anything—even beg if necessary!

I met her for coffee one Friday morning and explained that I had to have her back. I said that if only we could reconcile, she could call all the shots. She said she would call me at my office by three o'clock and let me know what her decision was.

I waited on pins and needles all afternoon. A minute before three, the phone rang. Delia told me that if I was sincere and truly wanted a second chance, I had to follow her every instruction to a tee. As I had stated that she could call all the shots, I was to go to her apartment and follow the instructions I would find under the doormat.

I immediately left for her apartment. I found the instructions where she said they'd be. I let myself into the apartment before reading them. The first line read, "Shave off all hair!" I thought, Hell, no! But as I read on, I saw that she had stipulated that I only had to shave below my sideburns, and I breathed a small sigh of relief.

My next thought was that there was no way that I would let her do me this way. Then, suddenly, I realized that maybe I did have a chance to win her back. I figured that no one but us would ever know and that it might even be fun to win her back this way.

On the kitchen table I found a pair of scissors, a can of shaving cream, a razor and a bottle of Neet. There was also an envelope with my name on it. Of course, more instructions were inside. I was told to go to the bathroom and "comply fully" with the additional instructions I would find.

In the bathroom I found another envelope with the message "Open only after the first step is completed!" on the front of it. I really didn't want to go through with this dumb request, but I knew that I'd never win her back if I didn't. Slowly and very, very, carefully, I shaved off all my body hair. I felt really naked as I stepped out of the shower, my task finally completed. I felt like a guy who had forgotten to zip his fly and didn't have any underwear on.

I read the next set of instructions, which informed me I was to go into her bedroom and jack off into a washcloth she'd left on the bed. The note stated that she didn't want to see me with a hard-on, so she expected that I would take care of that now, before she came home. She added that if I wanted to back out of the deal, I should leave now. I decided to go ahead with her little game.

Just after I had finished my second task, she walked through the bedroom door. First she laughed and said I looked like the little wimp I really was. Then, with a smirk, she explained that she had video monitors in every room in the apartment and now had a cute flick that she was sure I wouldn't want the guys at work to see. At this point my dick, which had already shrunk down to the size of a pencil, suddenly shriveled down to the size of a tadpole. I knew I was in trouble then!

By now it was six in the evening, and of course she had more instructions. I was told to get my little slave prick into the guest bedroom and stay awake for six hours, jacking off each hour on the hour. She promised to join me at midnight. I followed these instructions only to wake up alone the next morning with a sore prick. She appeared shortly after dawn and told me it was time for another jack-off session. With a big grin on her face, she watched as I brought myself off yet again.

When I was through, she said we were going for a ride to the beach. I couldn't believe my ears. I had shaved off all the hair on my body below the shoulders and this was my reward?!

We drove to the beach and she pulled into the parking lot adjacent to the nude beach, which was a three-mile strip of sand just south of us. She parked and got out for a moment, saying she had a surprise for me. Two minutes later she returned, and we drove south.

Now I sensed that I was in trouble. She drove to the opposite end of the beach and told me to follow her down to the water. She handed me the tote bag and started walking off. I felt I had gone too far to turn back, so I followed her.

About fifteen feet from the edge of the water, she laid out a beach towel. Then she removed her cover-up, revealing that she was wearing only the thong bottom of a skimpy bikini. I handed her the tote bag, and she retrieved a pair of sunglasses and lay down.

She looked up at me and told me that this was a nude beach, so I wouldn't need my trunks anymore. When I protested, she reminded me of the video she had made and the fact that a lot of people I knew would probably love to see it. I grudgingly removed the trunks as she watched, and then she tucked them into the tote bag.

I had never thought that I would be standing on a nude beach, completely naked. The situation felt worse, because here I was, hairless and bare as the day I was born, with a limp, two-inch prick dangling between my legs. I glanced around and realized that I was really out of place. Some of the other men on the beach were sporting nine-inch trophies!

My next instructions soon followed. I was told to walk up to the north end of the beach where we had first parked. I was to locate the pint-size milk container she had left there and follow the instructions inside it.

I turned and headed north to the other end of the beach. I was fully aware of the eyes of both men and women watching me. Some would giggle and whisper to their friends while others pointed at me. The walk seemed endless, but I guess that was because of the circumstances. Being devoid of body hair, and sporting a prick that most teenagers would be ashamed of was rather embarrassing for a grown man like me.

When I reached the end of the beach, I looked around until I spotted the milk carton. I opened it up to find yet another surprise. Inside it was a note with instructions and a ball harness with a dangling tag that said "Slave," on it. A ring was attached at the base. Underneath it was a temporary tattoo that also said "Slave," and a moist towelette.

As I read the instructions I couldn't believe it. I was to apply that tattoo to my right ass-cheek and strap on the harness. I looked around to see if anyone was nearby and was relieved to see that the coast was clear.

I complied with the orders and headed back to the southern end of the beach. To my surprise, the harness caused a semierection that I was well aware of. I thought, At least that's better than the two-inch joke I walked north with. I'm not sure if it was my hard-on, the harness or the tattoo that made me feel like I was the center of attention, but I soon found out!

A naked young woman was the first one to approach me. She grabbed me by the harness tag, wanting to see what it read. She got down on one knee to get a better look. As she read it, she smiled and motioned me on, but slapped my ass hard as I passed. To my amazement, this made my prick even harder. I was even more surprised when a lady of forty or so walked up to me and handed me a business card. A note on the back said to call her if my mistress ever gave me up.

When I finally got back to where Delia was lying, she asked me to give her the instructions. I told her I'd put them back in the container, which I had left where I'd found it. She told me that I had made a really dumb mistake and had to go back and get them. She told me to take off the harness and start walking. I started to worry that this thing would never be over. I dropped the harness in her hand and headed north once more.

At the end of the beach I again located the container and retrieved the instructions. I saw that there was yet another piece of paper in the carton. I dreaded what it would say as I pulled it out. I almost cried as I unfolded it. The note read: "Your trunks are buried in the sand about four inches below where you picked up the container. I hope you read this before moving away or you might be searching all night! Don't return without them!"

Well, let me tell you, I was really relieved that I hadn't moved the container! I dropped to my knees, dug in the sand like a terrier and found my swimsuit. I hurriedly put it on, glad to be covered up again. All of a sudden I heard a horn blow in the parking lot. I turned and saw Delia's car slowly headed in my direction.

When she realized she had my attention, she stopped and motioned me over. As I reached the car, she simply told me to get in. As we drove away she informed me that she had thoroughly enjoyed her day at the beach. She added that she was really glad I got all that sun, and that I would probably peel like a snake, right down to my worm!

I glanced down and realized that she was telling the truth. I was as red as a lobster. I had been on the beach for hours, totally naked, and I hadn't even used any sunscreen. To make matters worse, I could feel that the sand in my trunks was only complicating the problem. I was going to pay dearly!

What she said next really floored me. She told me that she had a new lover, and that her lover had made another video of me while I'd made a fool of myself on the beach. She added that I would have to meet her lover sometime, and that it might as well be now. She told me that I'd soon be viewing the tape as well. I was also informed that I was going to be given to a mistress named Vicky.

When we pulled into the parking lot of Delia's apartment, I was instructed to go in and shower. I was to then wait naked in the living room for my orders. I knew that it wouldn't do any good to argue. As I dried off after the shower, I realized that I was badly sunburned. I had blistered from head to toe, and the pain was just beginning.

I waited in the living room as instructed. I'd been there less than a minute when the doorbell rang. Delia told me to answer the door, that it was probably her new lover and my new mistress.

My prick would have crawled up inside me if it could have as I answered the door. You can imagine my surprise when I saw the young woman and the lady in her forties whom I had met at the beach standing in front of me.

Delia explained that the older woman, Brenda, was her new lover, and Vicky was one of Brenda's friends. Brenda was in the process of teaching Vicky to be a real man-hater. The three of them grabbed me and, within seconds, had cuffed my hands behind my back. Vicky opened her purse and pulled out the same ball harness that I had worn at the beach. She encased my balls and attached a leash to the ring that the tag dangled from. Pulling on the leash, she led me across the living room and told me to sit on the floor at her feet.

They turned on the television and announced that it was show time. I was forced to watch myself as a slave, from shaving myself bald to parading down the beach. Then I was forced to watch the three of them have sex with each other. After a while, Vicky stood up and tugged hard on the leash as I tried to quickly scramble to my feet. I managed to stand, and Vicky knelt in front of me, kissed my cock and slowly proceeded to blow me. My prick grew harder and harder, and I was about to explode when she suddenly stopped. I was left with a raging hard-on, and for the moment there was nothing I could do about it.

Vicky pulled me by the leash down the hallway, led me into the spare bedroom and pushed me facedown on the bed. I lay sideways across the bed as two of the three women tied my ankles to the bedposts. The cuffs were then unhooked by a removable link and reattached to chains on the opposite side of the bed. Next two pillows were placed under my hips and a four-inch vibrating dildo was greased and shoved up my ass. One of the women turned it up on high just before they left the room. I lay there with a throbbing hard-on and a stuffed ass for who knows how long. It seemed like at least three hours had passed, and I wondered if the batteries would ever run out.

Vicky finally came back into the room by herself. She asked if I thought it was time for her to take the dildo out. I told her that it was way past the time. She walked around in front of me and slowly stripped off the robe she was wearing. She opened a dresser drawer and pulled out a six-inch, strap-on dildo. As she strapped it on, she said that it wasn't time for the vibrator to be removed, but time for it to be replaced. She then pulled out a cock-shaped gag and ordered me to open my mouth. I kept my mouth shut in protest, so she reached over and spanked my sunburnt ass with her bare hand. Needless to say, a small plastic prick was soon shoved into my mouth and secured around the back of my head with a cloth strap.

She asked me if I had ever fucked a girl up the ass. I knew that Delia had probably confided in her that I had, so I nodded. Next she asked if I had ever wondered what it felt like to be screwed that way. I could only shake my head no as she pulled out the vibrator. She said it was high time I found out what it felt like.

When she went to plunge the dildo in, I realized she hadn't even lubricated it. I muffled a scream as she invaded my backside. Tears began to flow from my eyes as Vicky tugged on the leash of the ball harness and shoved the dildo in to the hilt. She fucked me for what seemed like an eternity.

When she finally got bored of this, she removed the dildo along with my gag. She turned around and instructed me to kiss her ass to show my appreciation for losing my anal virginity. After I kissed each cheek, she said she would see me in the morning and left. As she closed the door she told me to get a good night's sleep.

I was left facedown, spread eagle, and with the ball harness and leash still attached. I have no idea how long I lay there like that before finally falling asleep. It must have been most of the night, because I didn't feel well rested at all when I was awakened the next morning by Vicky.

My hands were reattached behind my back and my ankles were freed. I managed to get to my feet, and I was led by the leash back into the living room. While I walked I felt a soreness in my ass and an aching in my balls. I glanced down and realized why my nuts hurt so bad. I still had a raging hard-on, and my nuts were full and trying to break free of the harness. I wondered if I would ever get any relief.

As we entered the living room, I saw Delia and her new lover fondling each other on the couch. I was taken to the center of the room and instructed to stand still. The leash was then removed from the harness and Vicky told me to turn around, which I did. My back was now to the couch. Vicky informed me that the temporary tattoo would be replaced by a permanent one just like it. She said a tattoo artist would be over around two that afternoon.

I was told again to do an about-face. Vicky told Delia to set up the camcorder because she wanted another video. Then she asked if I wanted to get my rocks off. I was at her mercy, as my cock and balls really ached for relief. As Delia manned the camera, I was told to beg for relief. I pleaded for an orgasm and was made to promise to be Vicky's slave for life.

Finally my harness was removed. Vicky knelt in front of me and proceeded to give me a blowjob. As she sucked my prick, she fondled my balls, and in no time I found myself ready to shoot my load down her throat. She sensed my imminent explosion, and just as I reached the point of no return, she released my cock from her mouth. She grabbed it with one hand and pumped my prick dry, catching my sperm in her other hand. Then she raised her come-filled palm to my face and squeezed my nuts with her other hand, telling me to lick her hand clean. Since I wanted to keep my balls, I complied while they got it all on videotape. As a finishing touch, Vicky shoved a butt-plug up my sore ass.

Delia then stood up and took over. She told me to call my boss and tell him I'd be out sick all week. She produced a pair of crotchless panties, and as I stepped into them, she pulled them up. Next she removed the cuffs, freeing my hands. She handed me the phone and I made the call. She said that I would find similar panties in the bedroom, and for the next week that was all I could wear. I was to shave my body every other day and refrain from beating my meat. If I didn't comply with the instructions, she told me that every person I knew would be sent a copy of the video.

Promptly at two the doorbell rang, and I had to answer it in my crotchless panties. Of course, it was the tattoo artist. I was told to show her the temporary tattoo and request a permanent one to replace it. The girl seemed to enjoy her job of applying the tattoo. In fact, everyone viewing the process seemed to enjoy it, and of course they got it all on tape.

I would have thought I'd be totally humiliated by all that I went through, but I was surprised to find that I actually had enjoyed it. It was really quite a turn-on. I must have been born a true slave without even realizing it. I'm so grateful to Delia for exposing this side of me. I love my new life, and I love catering to Vicky's every whim. I feel totally satisfied.—*R.O., Tampa, Florida*

LESBIAN DUO'S EXERCISE REGIME LEAVES COLLEGE BOY HANGING

I attend college in Virginia and I had a unique experience last summer that I have to share with you. I am a five-foot-eight-inch one-hundred-fifty-pound male who is still a virgin, but now I'm a much more contented virgin.

I had rented the upstairs apartment in a house owned by two ladies who lived on the first floor. Jill was twenty-seven and

Angela was about thirty, and I got the impression they were both lesbians.

After I had lived there for about three weeks, Jill invited me down to see their basement. They were both in great shape, the reason being that the basement was full of all kinds of exercise equipment. She told me I was welcome to work out with them that night. Now, exercise isn't really my thing, but I didn't want to refuse and hurt their feelings.

So later that night I put on my jockstrap, shorts and a T-shirt, and met them in the basement. They both had on spandex leotards, which really hugged their bodies. Jill's erect nipples were quite noticeable.

After showing me how several of the exercise machines worked, Jill demonstrated how the gravity boots were used. She slipped her feet into the boots and strapped them on. Then she hooked them onto the rod above her and secured them so that she was hanging upside down. Angela taped her hands behind her and told her to do a few sit-ups. She did about five, which really impressed me because it looked rather difficult. Then Angela cut off the tape and released her. They asked me if I wanted to try it, and I said I did.

So I slipped off my sneakers, put the boots on and asked them to help me up on the pipe. Jill told me to take my shirt off so it wouldn't fall in my face, so I pulled it over my head. They helped me hook the boots onto the pipe and put the pins in so I wouldn't fall. Then Angela taped my wrists together behind my back and told me to start. I did about three sit-ups before I was exhausted. I relaxed, just hanging there. That's when I realized my face was right at the same height as Jill's and Angela's pussies.

Angela gave a little laugh, knelt down and asked if I was doing okay. She then started to rub my nipples with her fingers, telling me that she wanted all my muscles to be hard. Well, I could feel my penis stiffen up to a full erection but there was nothing I could do. I felt somewhat intimidated, so I just mumbled to them that I was ready to get down.

Jill grabbed the scissors, and I thought she was going to cut the tape off my wrists. But, much to my surprise, she just cut through the waistband of my gym shorts, and they fell on the floor. I looked up. All I had on was a jockstrap, and you could plainly see my erection sticking up in it.

The girls started to rub their hands all over my body, exciting me even more. I could feel the pre-come dripping from my penis, and they hadn't even touched my genitals yet. My dick was straining against the elastic of the jockstrap when Jill picked up the scissors again and told me it was show time. She walked behind me, and I could feel her cutting away my last piece of clothing. All of a sudden my jockstrap fell off, and my hard cock popped out. My dick was hard as a rock, sticking out at a forty-five-degree angle, and by now I was dying to come.

I yelled at Angela to please touch me, and they both stopped. Then Jill bent down and told me that every time I opened my mouth, this would happen. She then snipped off a big chunk of my pubic hair and let it fall in front of my face. Angela came up to me, and I could see she had two long peacock feathers in her hand. She and Jill both started to lightly tickle me all over. Every time I begged them to stop, one of them would snip off another tuft of pubic hair until there wasn't any more left.

They tickled me everywhere except my cock and balls, which they purposefully avoided. Even though I was dying of laughter, I not only retained my erection but got even harder. My cock was almost purple, and I could feel that it was ready to explode, but they wouldn't touch my genitals. Finally Angela bent down and said that they would let me come if I begged them to shave off my pubic hair. I immediately began to beg, and after a few minutes they both started to tickle my penis with the feathers. They ran the feathers over my balls and down my shaft. My penis, which was sticking straight out, now started to jerk uncontrollably. In about thirty seconds, I started shooting a huge load of come. It was really strange, because since I was upside down, my come was shooting toward my face. Jill grabbed my head and tilted it upward, allowing several streams of come to hit me square in the face. Finally my cock stopped spasming, and they wiped me off with a soft cloth.

Jill disappeared for a minute, and when she returned a razor and a can of shaving cream were in her hands. She rubbed shaving cream onto my pubic hair and all my body hair, then they both shaved my entire body. The feeling was indescribable. When I looked up, I saw a limp, naked cock absolutely bare of pubic hair.

After admiring their handiwork for a few minutes, the girls started to take off their clothes. I guess all the action had made them pretty hot. I could feel my cock start to stiffen up again, and by the time they were naked my cock was totally stiff again.

They both looked absolutely beautiful. Jill had small tits and a blonde pussy, while Angela had big tits and a brunette pussy. They got into a 69 and licked each other to orgasm after orgasm while I hung upside down with a swollen cock between my legs and nothing to rub it against. I kept thrusting my hips forward, but all I could do was fuck the air.

Jill and Angela finally noticed my predicament and started to laugh at me. Finally Jill got up, walked over to me and took my cock into her mouth, at the same time positioning her pussy over my face. She grabbed my head and made me lick her pussy. Whenever I licked her the way she wanted, she would suck on my cock harder, but never hard enough to get me off.

Then Angela decided it was her turn. She pushed Jill away and slid a rubber onto my cock. She began blowing me while Jill got on her knees and started to lick my balls. I could feel my penis get even harder and the come start to move up my shaft. I couldn't hold back any longer, so I shot my load into Angela's mouth. It was incredible to be upside down and have no control over my body. It was such an intense orgasm.

After that they took me down, and we all took a shower together. As they were washing me off, they told me that although they were primarily lesbians, for fun they occasionally enjoyed dominating a man and having sex with him. They told me that if I kept my body shaved, remained naked in their presence and did whatever they said, I could play their game.

Angela said that she knew I was interested, and when I asked why she was so sure, she pointed at my erection, which had grown to enormous proportions in the shower. Well, I agreed, and to seal the bargain I had to masturbate for them right then, shooting come through the shower spray. The rest of the semester was great, and my new semester starts tomorrow. Jill tells me they were easy on me and this semester will be harder.

I can't wait.—*L.P., St. Paul, Minnesota*

I'LL WHIP YOUR ASS AND HAVE IT TOO—REFLECT ON THAT

I'm a thirty-six-year-old petite blonde, with a very round bottom that is the delight of my boyfriend. He is a confirmed butt man, and also the most sensuous and imaginative lover I've ever had.

We both have a taste for light S&M. Until I met Robbie I'd

never felt comfortable enough with anyone to act on any of these desires.

Even with Robbie it took a while for me to really express myself. Occasional blindfolding followed by some light spanking with his hand was the most we ever ventured. These special lovemaking sessions were sometimes followed by some anal stimulation. We discussed sodomy, but he had never gone as far as penetrating my back door.

One evening, after I'd complained to Robbie about a particularly dreadful day at work, he instructed me to dress in my black stockings and merry widow, black stiletto heels and black Fedora. I was then to put on an overcoat and drive to his house. I did as I was told.

When I arrived, his living room had been decorated for what promised to be an evening exciting enough to make me forget my troubles. The only light in the room was cast by the candles that flickered on the living room table. A large mirror had been set up on the coffee table, arranged so that anyone on the couch opposite it could see themselves. A small pot of incense was burning.

Despite all these delights the thing that really grabbed my attention was the assortment of spanking objects laid out, believe it or not, on a silver platter. A riding crop, a black, silky cat-o-nine-tails and a black leather belt were artfully arranged on the tray. I must admit I felt a little nervous. Robbie suavely removed my overcoat and inspected my attire with approval.

As we embraced and kissed, he massaged my nipples through my lacy merry widow. Then he lifted my breasts out of their covering and lightly circled my areolae with his tongue. My arousal was all the more delicious because of my slight anxiety about what he had planned.

His next move was to bend me gently over the couch so I was facing myself in the mirror. As I watched, he rubbed my shoulders, then my back, finally sliding his fingers gently inside my pussy. We both knew then how turned on I was, because I was incredibly wet. To my surprise, after a couple of swift but gentle plunges of his finger, he withdrew. He disappeared from my view in the mirror.

I started to stand up and turn around, but I heard him say sternly, "Stay right where you are!" I did as I was told, and he quickly reappeared. The next thing I knew I felt a dildo, which had been lubricated with warm oil, sliding into my ass! I gasped.

It hurt slightly at first, but I was so hot that I found myself relaxing and actually pushing against his thrusts.

After a few minutes, he pulled out the dildo, quickly enough to make me gasp. Again his image disappeared from the mirror. This time he walked in front of me and picked up the riding crop. I felt myself tighten up with apprehension, but I also yearned for whatever was to follow. As the riding crop struck my bare ass I cried out. It really stung! I felt myself becoming wetter still, but after about ten swats I begged him to stop. Robbie began to smack me hard with his hand for being naughty and for asking him to stop. By this time I was so horny that even his hardest swats felt good.

Stopping momentarily, Robbie slipped a vibrator into my hand and told me to use it. As I rubbed my clit with it, he walked in front of the couch again and picked up the cat-o'-nine-tails. He began to whip me while describing how red my behind was getting and telling me he wouldn't stop whipping me until every square inch of my ass was properly red and burning. As I felt it lash my bottom, occasionally flicking right on my exposed asshole, I came in an incredible, jaw-clenching orgasm.

As soon as I was done grunting and writhing, Robbie dropped the whip and plunged his cock into my ass! His gorgeous cock had never felt so big, and when it penetrated my ass I thought I was being torn in half. He plunged into me with complete abandon, as if oblivious to my pain. He must have known, however, how much I would really enjoy it. Sure enough, I started thrusting back against him, taking his cock all the way up my ass with no problem. I came again, at the same moment that he released a rush of hot come into my ass. My orgasm seemed to roll on and on, and I felt the spurting and contracting of his penis more clearly than I ever had in my pussy. Even after he stopped moving I clutched my cheeks tightly, in a vain attempt to keep his shrinking erection from slipping away.

Although we now indulge in fantasy play and S&M on a regular basis, I'll never forget that first time.—*A.W., Baltimore, Maryland*

TEACHING AN OLD SOLDIER NEW TRICKS: LOVER, TAKE YOUR LICKS

I hope that my beloved Maria will read this, as she has long been a devoted reader of your Domination and Discipline letters.

I am a white male in my early sixties, retired from the military, previously married but divorced for over twenty years. For about ten years after my divorce I wasn't involved with anyone. During that time I became a workaholic, keeping at it both day and night. While on a business trip to Jersey City, I met Maria. We instantly became friends and soon started going out. At that time I was living with my sister. As I didn't get along with her, Maria suggested that I move in with her. Since I'd already had a bad marriage, I was skeptical about the idea, but she convinced me that we'd be happy. She was right, too. We shared everything: expenses, food shopping, cooking, cleaning.

She did have one habit that put me off. If we were out clothes shopping she would hold pieces of sexy lingerie up in plain view of all the other shoppers and ask my opinion of them. People would look at me with silly grins on their faces, probably the same expression I was wearing myself. I told Maria that I could no longer go into the ladies department with her. She just looked at me, smiled and replied, "Don't worry. You'll get used to it. Who cares what other people think?"

Even I had to admit this was a pretty small complaint, and as each day went by I found I loved her more and more. Maria asked me once if I'd ever had oral sex with anyone, and I said, "No, and I never would!" This was something my mother had taught me was wicked.

Our sex life was very good, though. Maria knew just how to excite me, often waking me up at night by rubbing my lips with her index fingers, saying, "I love you," calling me affectionate names, and so forth. Then she would play with my pecker and get me going.

Until I met Maria I'd never made love to anybody but my ex. My sex life with Maria was completely different. She drove me wild, often wearing just her panties and bra around the house, teasing me, rubbing herself all over me. Once she knew she had me excited she'd French-kiss me, sticking her tongue deep in my mouth. Or she'd run her tongue around the rim of my ears. Maria never stopped experimenting with new ways to turn me on. From time to time we'd come back to the subject of oral sex, but I would never give in and eat her. She wanted just as much to do it to me, but I always stopped her. When I objected she listened to what I said, never showing anger. Instead she'd tease me about it and continue trying to find out what excited me most.

One night Maria woke me up, as she had done so many times. Rubbing my lips with her index finger, and tickling my ears with her tongue, she suddenly slid her tongue right inside my ear. Right away I was powerfully turned on, and Maria knew that she had finally found my most sensitive spot. Keeping her tongue in one ear, she moved her finger up to drift over the other. That really got me going! I was moaning and squirming right away. Normally I'm not so out of control, and it embarrassed me. I kept begging her to stop, but she ignored me. My penis got so hard that it was lying flat on my stomach, the tip of it even with my navel.

All of a sudden she had my penis in her mouth, and I just couldn't stop her. Overwhelmed by a wonderful series of feelings, sensations I'd never experienced before, I could only lie there and take it. My fists kept clenching and unclenching, and I'll be damned if my toes didn't do the same! Maria was going up and down so fast that I exploded in her mouth.

Come still dripping from one corner of her lips, she climbed on top of me, put my penis inside her and began pumping. She leaned forward, put her tongue once more in my ear, and took control of me again. Without letting me slip out Maria rolled onto her back and wrapped her legs around me. We were both slamming away with our hips, and before long we both came at the same time. Her cunt muscles squeezed my cock, sucking out my load.

We held each other for a very long time, and I fell asleep on top of her. What a beautiful experience I enjoyed that first time oral sex was ever performed on me.

In the morning I felt ashamed that I couldn't stop her from sucking my dick. I felt that I had degraded her, and couldn't look her in the face. While we were drinking our coffee Maria looked at me and said, "I want to be sure you know that I love you very much. Last night was the most beautiful night we've shared together yet, and things are only going to improve. Tonight will be even better—for both of us."

That night, after I was asleep, Maria again woke me up. She gave me a big hug and told me, "Tonight, I'm going to be the specialty of the house." Maria began to fondle my penis, her tongue at the same time playing around with my ears. At first I tried to move my ears away from her tongue. Letting go of my penis, which was already erect, my honey put a finger in my right ear, her tongue in my left, and sent me spinning into orbit.

I tried to move away by shaking my head back and forth, but she held it in place. Giggling, Maria said, "Tonight you belong to me, and I will do as I please with you. Now you shut up and listen, or you can start packing."

Frightened by that, but still excited, I gave in to her, thinking she was going to suck me again. I got the surprise of my life when she got on top of me and sat right down on my face.

I tried to move my face away, but Maria grabbed my head with both hands and pushed my mouth right into her vagina. She kept rubbing it in my face, holding me tightly. With the fingers of one hand she held open her vagina, then pulled me closer to her. "Put your tongue out as far as it will go!" she commanded. "Now work it around inside. Touch me all over. Slide it out of my vagina and lick all around the outside. Gently! Just your tongue, no teeth! That's right. Oh yes, that's definitely right!" Maria moved up a little and told me to work my tongue real fast up and down. I could hear her moaning, and breathing faster and faster. "Keep going," she moaned. "Faster, faster, faster!" The pressure of her hands on the back of my head kept increasing. "Open wide, lover," she sighed, "I'm going to come!" I tried to move my head away but couldn't move. Maria was moaning much louder now, and saying, "Oh that feels so good! I'm coming! Keep my juice in your mouth and don't swallow it until I tell you to." My mouth was filling with juice, both my own saliva and the love juice that was squeezing from her ripe fruit. Maria kept twisting and rubbing herself all over my mouth, holding me tight against her with both hands. Finally I heard Maria telling me to swallow her love-juice.

When she finally released me, Maria sat next to me on the bed and calmly informed me, "Starting today, I'm going to teach you how to be my slave." Then she lowered herself on top of me and put my penis inside her. She began rapidly rising and falling. As she came down I met her with my own hip thrusts. She stuck her tongue into my ear and took control of me, whispering that from now on I would be her slave and she would be my mistress and I would have to obey her without question. "Is that what you want? Make up your mind!" Maria demanded I reply right away, and I gave in to her, agreeing to do whatever she demanded of me.

She rolled off me to her side of the bed, reached onto the floor and picked up her red panties. She said that from this moment on I would have to wear her soiled panties, and wouldn't be allowed to wear my shorts anymore, in the house or anywhere else. Even when I went to work I would wear her panties. Then she slipped her dirty panties on me and smiled.

In the morning I discovered that she had already hidden all my boxer shorts. Until then I thought I could fool her, because she works days and I work nights, and I figured I could change when she wasn't home. Scrounging around in the laundry bin I found a pair she'd missed, and wore them that next day.

When I got home from work at around one in the morning, Maria was awake, waiting for me, and asked me to hand her my key to the house. I asked her why, and she bluntly told me that I hadn't worn her panties to work, so I would have to leave. My pleas fell on deaf ears. She said that she would give me one last chance, but only if I would listen to her and give in to her demands. Also, to show my sincerity I would have to agree to be punished first. Once more I gave in.

We went to the kitchen and she made coffee, then told me to take all my clothes off. Before I could sit down to have coffee she took off her short black negligee and told me to put it on. She helped me, then took her black panties off and told me to put them on as well. I figured that this was my punishment, but she had something else in mind. After we had our coffee she put on a shocking pink negligee and told me to get on my knees. She made me recite a promise never to disobey her anymore, and always to accept whatever punishment she felt I needed. I was getting excited by Maria's request, and my penis was getting hard from wearing her clothes.

Maria turned around and told me to raise her negligee. Bending over, she told me to kiss both of her cheeks and say I was sorry, which I did with a growing pleasure. She then instructed me to lick her asshole, trying to push my tongue into her butt, then slowly circle my tongue inside her hole. The smell was very clean and sweet. She had obviously bathed and perfumed, knowing what she had in mind.

After several minutes of this, Maria turned and smiled, telling me that I was a good listener. She took a towel and put it around my neck, saying, "Now you're going to eat my cunt until I tell you to stop, and I'm going to fill you with love juice." As I began my work, not nearly so unwilling as I'd been the night before, she explained just how she liked to be eaten? "Flip your tongue back and forth on my lips. Make me good and wet. Now put your tongue in deep. Move it around in circles." Her breathing kept growing heavier and heavier. Her legs were holding my head very tightly, and trembling. "Oh, lover!" she shrieked. "I'm getting ready to come in your mouth. Open your mouth and drink my honey." Then she let out a scream and twisted back and forth, rubbing her love juice all over my face.

Maria finally stopped, looked at me lovingly, gave me a kiss and told me to swallow her love juice. Then she told me to lie on my back and make sure the bath towel covered my chest and my neck. She let out a squirt of urine and rubbed my face with it. She instructed me not to wash or shave the next day.

In the morning, Maria didn't go to work, and I asked her if she was sick. "Not at all," she replied. "I just want to make sure you have my panties on when you go to work. I'll be waiting at the door tonight when you get home, too, and you'd better have them on." Believe me, I did.

Maria has moved to another state, so we don't see each other anymore. I've never had such an exciting relationship with anyone else, and I miss it desperately. If I could find someone who wanted to dominate me as Maria did, I'd be in heaven.—*N.W., Trenton, New Jersey*

HAPPY BIRTHDAY HUMP WITH HUBBY AND A HORDE OF HUNKS

It was to be Cerita's big birthday party. For over a year she'd been telling me what she wanted: lots of friends, food, dancing and naked, beefy men. "I like hard-bodied male strippers," she'd tell me. "And that's what I want at my party. With maybe some baby oil and a hot tub."

I'd had a huge birthday party myself the year before, but the only gift I'd asked for had been a stripper. It was mostly a joke, but Cerita had made good on my request. Late in the evening a lovely girl had arrived and performed a striptease for me. The performance had been videotaped, complete with me sitting alone in the middle of the floor watching, while my wife, mother and in-laws watched. My excitement was dampened by all the spectators, and the girl only stripped to her bra and bikini. It was fun, but nothing like what my wife had in store for her party!

Her friend Marge was my accomplice. On the night of the party, Marge arrived early. She and Cerita almost immediately started sucking jello shooters and giggling. As they dressed for the party, Marge explained to Cerita that we hadn't been able to afford male strippers for the party. She had found a club nearby, though, that had some very hunky men, and Marge said that they could go there after the main party was dying down. Cerita likes to stay at a party until the bitter end, so she wasn't sure about leaving. Marge had brought some pot with her, though. I'd told her that it makes Cerita hot as a pistol, and after a couple tokes she's flushed, panting and ready to skip right to the naked part.

Cerita's family is huge, with dozens of children, so I'd rented the local Lions' Club hall for the party. It was a lot of fun—music, food, presents, happy people—but Cerita seemed a little agitated. She left the hall a number of times with Marge. They would return each time a little more giggly, and Cerita kept getting more and more flushed, so it was pretty clear to me what was going on. Marge was acting sillier than usual, probably because she knew something Cerita didn't. You know how that is.

At about ten I announced that we were going to take the kids to a local bowling alley. It's connected to a dance club and bar, and would be open until very late, so both the kids and the adults could have a good time.

Everyone piled into cars, and Marge made sure that she and Cerita took a car by themselves. They were going to dress for a different club, she explained. I gave Cerita a great big birthday kiss and told her to have a good time.

They drove to our house, and Marge encouraged Cerita to shower and think about what to wear to a sexy strip show. Just as Cerita was emerging from the shower, the doorbell rang.

Marge didn't answer. Swearing, Cerita opened the door, wrapped in a towel that barely covered her large tits. Her pussy was clearly peeking out below. It nearly fell off altogether when three huge, handsome men asked for her. She yelled for Marge, but got no response. One of the guys handed Cerita a note that read, "Happy Birthday! Ask these men to unwrap your presents! Love, Marge." It was like offering cream to a hungry kitten. She let them in.

The first one, Sean, held her tightly and started to dance as

Chaz put a tape in the stereo. While she ground her naked pussy into Sean's bulge, Cerita saw Chaz and Gordon, the third man, begin a slow striptease. She moaned when Gordon finished stripping and pressed his naked body tightly against her back. Without skipping a beat, Sean was replaced in front of her by a naked Chaz. He pulled her towel away to reveal her beautiful body—quivering, clean and naked.

Cerita stared at Sean's well-practiced strip routine. Gordon was massaging her ass with his huge hard-on, licking her earlobes and roughly pinching her nipples. Marge and I had let the guys know that Cerita likes to be touched firmly, even roughly. Chaz was on his knees in front of her, his tongue lightly tickling her pussy. Without the men to hold her up, she would have collapsed from pleasure. Cerita moaned when she saw Sean's huge cock.

"Do you want it?" he asked.

"Yes," she sighed.

"What do you want? Tell me," he ordered.

"I want your cock. All your cocks."

"What will you do for them?" Sean questioned her.

"Fuck you. Lick you. Dance on your beautiful cocks," she moaned.

"You have to beg," he told her.

"Please fuck me!"

"Not me . . . him!" and with his eyes Sean indicated someone over Cerita's shoulder.

She turned to see me standing with my arms crossed, fully dressed, trying to look convincingly angry. Her face turned such a bright red I thought she was going to explode right there.

"I see you've been very bad," I admonished her. "You know that you're mine. If you want something, you should ask properly. Now get on your knees," I ordered. The men backed away enough to let her kneel before them. Three huge cocks bobbed inches in front of her hungry mouth. "Ask them sweetly," I told her.

Looking straight into Chaz's eyes, she purred like a kitten, "May I lick your cock? Please?" She turned to Sean. "Please fuck me!" The men all nodded, and Cerita wrapped her lips around Chaz's member. Her head bobbed up and down the length of his shaft and her hands began to stroke the cocks of the other two. In a moment she shifted from Chaz's cock to Sean's, then Gordon's, keeping a hard cock in each hand and one in her mouth.

While this was going on, I stripped and positioned myself behind her. Cerita moaned loudly at my touch, and raised her ass a little to allow my fingers easy access to her pussy. She had shaved her pussy in the shower, and it was like touching living silk. I immediately drove three fingers into her and tickled her G-spot. She growled. Swallowing the cock in front of her even more deeply, she humped my hand like crazy.

"Do you want to be fucked?" I asked.

"Yes, fuck me!"

"Ask sweetly," I ordered.

"Please fuck me. Fuck me hard!" She almost screamed.

"Are you mine?"'

"Always!"

"Show us your beautiful pussy," I said.

She stopped sucking and stroking and lay on her back. Her legs opened wide and her fingers spread her sweet pussy lips for all to see. The four of us stepped close, stroking our cocks.

"Show us how hot you are."

Her hands were a blur as they stroked her pussy wildly. She licked her lips and whispered urgently, "Now! Take me now! Please!"

Sean knelt at her head to let her suck on his hairy balls, while Chaz and Gordon spread her legs wide. I lay on her belly and drove my rigid cock into her waiting snatch like a piston. Over and over I shoved, harder and harder. With every thrust her back arched and her ass jumped to pull me in deeper. Chaz and Gordon pulled her legs back toward her head as they knelt to lick at her hard nipples. Her hands snaked out between their legs to grab and pull on their swollen rods. In minutes I blasted into her like a geyser, which sent her over the edge.

Normally, Cerita can only come once in a session. Often she has to stop altogether. She clenches so hard that her pussy gets sore. But she was so wild with passion she didn't miss a beat when Chaz took my place between her legs. She was so wet that his cock slid all the way in to the hilt on the first thrust. Gordon was now enjoying her hot mouth, and Cerita was jerking on Sean and me while we sucked at her nipples.

As soon as Chaz came, deep inside her, he and Gordon traded places. Her screams and moans made it clear how much she was loving being passed around.

Sean was the last to take her on the floor. His cock was the largest of all, and Cerita almost choked on my rod when he slammed his into her. She came again almost immediately, nearly fainting. Sean stopped then, without coming, and got up.

"Do you have some wine?" he asked.

"Good idea," I replied. "Cerita, serve us some wine."

"Oh, please," she begged. "I want him to come for me."

"You will serve us now," I said sternly. She stood and reached for her towel. "No!" I commanded. "A woman as beautiful as you are should remain naked for us to enjoy." She grinned and walked to the kitchen with a wiggle in her ass that promised much more fun to come.

She returned in a moment with four glasses of wine. Sean was lying on the floor, and poured some of his wine on his cock.

"Lick it off," I commanded her.

She dutifully knelt, and with a grin began licking at his huge dick like a kitten with a treat. I poured my wine on the crack of her ass and began to lick and nibble her succulent butt.

She arched her back and moaned, "Do you want to fuck my ass, baby?"

"Ask sweetly."

"Mmmm, please fuck my ass."

"Make him come," I replied. She immediately climbed onto his manhood and lowered herself slowly. Once he had reached bottom inside her, she began to rock and buck with abandon. Chaz and Gordon moved in front of her. Cerita first took Chaz's, then Gordon's shaft into her eager mouth. I moved in behind her. As soon as she felt my cock rubbing the crack of her ass she stopped and bent forward, to give me easy access to her tight butthole. I put only the head in at first, waiting for her muscles to loosen before slowly shoving my whole penis into her ass.

"Yes, yes, yes!" she screamed. As soon as my cock was as deeply buried in her ass as it could go, she began to buck and hump. Our two cocks were driven into her ass and pussy as far as she could take them, and she was pumping them faster and faster.

"Suck their cocks!" I growled, and she grabbed at Chaz and Gordon. First one then the other cock slid easily into her throat. With a scream like a banshee she stuffed both cockheads into her mouth at once, sat down hard on Sean's and my cock and convulsed in the biggest orgasm I ever saw her experience. Her spasms made us all climax. What seemed like buckets of come shot into her pussy, her mouth and her asshole.

She rolled over onto her back and moaned quietly to herself as she rubbed their come into her skin. Her sticky hands slid from her tits to her neck to her belly.

I stood and told her, "I'm going to clean up. Entertain these gentlemen until I return."

"Mmmm, yes," was all she could say.

I returned after a short shower to find Cerita alone on the couch drinking wine. I asked if she was okay. She grinned and said that she was great. I had to agree.—*A.S., Philadelphia, Pennsylvania*

Serendipity

FIVE TIMES WITH MOE! BALLPLAYER SCORES BIG WITH WAYWARD WIFE

I am a twenty-five-year-old woman. Two years ago I married a very wealthy, forty-year-old sports attorney. With my husband Oscar usually busy making deals and meeting with his clients, I spend most of my time working out at the local spa and sunning by our pool.

On a recent Saturday, my husband and I were planning to go out on his partner Todd's boat, which we often do, along with Todd's beautiful wife Sondra. Just as we were leaving, my husband received an emergency phone call from a client, and immediately had to meet him at his office. I was going to stay home by the pool, but Oscar encouraged me to go with Todd and Sondra. Sondra has a knockout body and loves to show it off by wearing skimpy outfits. We always have a good time together, so I decided to go after all. Under my cutoffs I wore a skimpy white bikini that you could see through when it was wet, even though I knew that next to whatever Sondra would have on, it would still look plain.

When I got to the boat, Todd was there with a friend of his named Moe, who was a professional baseball player. Moe is tall and black, and had a reputation with women. After I explained that Oscar could not make it, Todd told me that Sondra couldn't come either. I was a little embarrassed to be dressed as provocatively as I was, and tried to tell them to go off without me, but they insisted I go along with them.

When we got out on the ocean, I lay on my back to get some color. Moe and Todd sat up front, steered the boat and had a few beers. After an hour of so, they dropped anchor just off the shore of a local beach. I was getting slightly sunburned and decided to roll over. I asked Todd to rub some lotion on my back. He came over to do it, and noted that I was still wearing my shorts.

Partially because it was a beautiful day, and partially because I was in the mood to do a little teasing, I took off my shorts and lay down on my stomach. My thong bikini left my ass-cheeks fully exposed. Todd and Moe were speechless at first. Then Moe insisted that Todd needed help with the lotion.

I lay there while these two gorgeous men rubbed lotion all over me. Todd had untied my top and was massaging my back while Moe rubbed my legs. Moe became very bold and spread lotion all over my ass. Instead of stopping him, I was getting wet between the legs. I could not stop thinking of how I had heard from many women at my club that Moe was a great fuck. When Moe asked me to roll over, I didn't even pause. I was now topless, and halfheartedly tried to cover up by putting my elbows over my breasts. Moe confidently told me to move my arms down because he liked seeing my beautiful body. I did just as he said.

Todd then began rubbing lotion on my tits while Moe spread my legs and rubbed lotion up and down my thighs. I was hoping he would rub between my legs, when he suddenly pulled my bikini bottom right off! I had never fooled around on my husband before, let alone with two guys. I think that's what had me so wet.

I was no longer the one doing the teasing. They were teasing me! Moe began to say to Todd, "Doesn't she have the hottest body?" He then said to me, "You must be a great fuck."

I replied, "I may be, but you'll never know. I'm going swimming now."

The two men just laughed. Moe then said, "You can go swimming if you like, but you don't really want to, do you?" I knew the answer to his question, but I couldn't bring myself to say it. Moe then whispered, "No one has to know, except the three of us."

I had to shut my eyes to stop from screaming out, "Yes, fuck me!" I had never been so wet or wanted anything more in my life than to fuck both these guys. I quietly whispered, "Stop, we can't do this," but Moe could read my mind and his hands continued touching every part of my body. I felt a finger push into my moist pussy.

By now my eyes were closed and I was sighing in ecstasy. When I opened my eyes, Moe was standing in front of me, stark naked. His cock was gorgeous and dark brown, and his body was awesome. I couldn't believe what was happening, but I didn't want it to stop. Todd whispered to me, "It won't bite—touch it," and guided my hand to Moe's cock.

I was a little scared, but I couldn't take my eyes off his luscious cock. I grabbed it. It was so much longer and thicker than Oscar's. I had never sucked Oscar's cock, but I was so mesmerized by Moe's body that I grabbed his huge prick and began feeding it into my mouth. My small hands could only cover two-thirds of its length. I wanted so badly to please him that I managed to get his entire penis into my mouth. I was lost in ecstasy, licking and sucking his big, black cock. All I could think of was giving him the best blowjob he'd ever had. It made me even more excited to know that Todd was watching.

I looked into Moe's eyes and said, "I want to drink every bit of your thick come. Fuck my mouth." I couldn't believe I'd said it, but I was out of control. Sex with Oscar had always been so conservative, with him on top for five minutes or so until he came. I never knew I could be like this, so horny and free.

As I sucked Moe's cock, I could sense he was about to come. The thick come began to shoot into my mouth. I was determined to keep sucking till I swallowed every bit of his load. As he shot off, I got even hotter. I came just from the excitement of what I was doing to his beautiful cock. I sucked him down to the last drop. When I pulled away, his creamy spunk was still dripping from my mouth.

I then turned to Todd and said, "Are you next, or do you just like to watch?" He seemed shocked at my boldness (and so was I) as I unzipped his fly and pulled out his beautiful cock. It was thick, but not as big as Moe's, which was a relief. I didn't think I could take another gigantic cock right then.

I was so horny that, after tearing off Todd's shorts and sucking his cock for a few minutes, I pulled him down to the deck and jumped on top of him. I was bouncing wildly on top of Todd. My tits were shaking and I was screaming in ecstasy while Moe watched and stroked his growing erection. I couldn't get enough! The sensation of a cock inside me that was much thicker than Oscar's was pure pleasure. I felt Todd shoot his load inside me and thought of what Oscar might say if he saw what I was doing. The thought made me come uncontrollably.

After we'd both come, I fell back in exhaustion. I soon felt kisses on my stomach. I opened my eyes to see Moe above me, that huge cock of his sliding up my thighs. I told him I didn't think I could take all of him in my pussy. He just laughed and said, "Todd was just a warm-up. I'll have you coming like you never dreamed."

He then started teasing my cunt with his cock. I soon lost my head and begged him to stick it in my gash. "Please do it!" I moaned.

He began to stick it in. I couldn't see how it was all going to fit, but he kept sliding it farther and farther inside me. In a minute it was buried in me up to the balls, and we were fucking hard. His awesome black cock had me coming again and again. He must have fucked me for over thirty minutes. I don't think I ever came twice with Oscar in my life, but in that half hour I must've come five times with Moe. When he finally came, I had to ask him to stop. I felt my body would explode if I let myself have another orgasm.

Since that day I haven't been able to get enough of Moe's dick. I've been sneaking over to his apartment almost every day. When Oscar's away on business, Moe comes over to sleep with me. I am addicted to his cock, and he knows it. I never knew sex could be this great.—*P.E. Los Angeles, California*

HOT BAHAMA MAMA ENSURES THAT THIS MAN IS NO ISLAND

I arrived in the Bahamas on a Sunday evening. The only thing I could think about was pussy. I was looking for some of that sweet Bahamian beaver to make my vacation extra special. But after days of looking and flirting, I couldn't find a local woman who'd give me the time of day.

On Thursday I decided to write my friends back home some postcards. When I went to the post office to mail them, a surprise was awaiting me. The Bahama mama I'd been looking for all week was behind the counter. When she asked, "Can I help you?" I became speechless for a few moments. She was the most attractive woman I had ever seen. She had a perfectly shaped body, with a thin waistline, small, round buttocks, shapely legs and skin the color of milk chocolate.

She said again, "Sir, may I help you?"

I managed to pull myself out of my daydream about her and reply, "Yes, please." I asked her for some stamps, and when she gave them to me, I handed her the money along with the telephone number of my hotel room. I thought she would have gotten offended by me being so direct, but it didn't seem to bother her. She took the money and the note, then smiled and told me to have a nice vacation.

About seven o'clock that evening the phone rang. I answered it and was pleased to hear a pleasant female voice say, "Hi, this is Kim, the woman you met in the post office today."

I said, "It was a real pleasure to meet a woman as beautiful as you. Do you have any plans this evening? I have just one day of vacation left."

"I have no plans tonight," she said, "and I have tomorrow off from work too."

I suggested that we have dinner at my hotel, and asked if she liked seafood. She said she loved it. We said good-bye, and then I called the hotel restaurant and made a reservation for two.

Kim came to the hotel at nine o'clock. Boy, was she hot! She looked good enough to eat. She had on a black biker outfit. I greeted her with a big smile and told her to make herself comfortable while I opened the wine.

I put on some nice romantic music and dimmed the lights. As we sat and talked, I felt myself becoming powerfully aroused by this beautiful woman. I took one of her perfect fingers and dipped it into my wineglass. I gently licked her finger up and down, and sucked on it as though it were a nipple. She started to smile and let out a sexy moan. I started to lick all over her tender body, and she responded with pleasure to my sensuous tongue. I knew then that we were going to miss dinner.

By now she had started to squirm around on the sofa, and began breathing rather hard. My dick was so stiff it was practically undoing my zipper all by itself! Kim wasn't one to beat around the bush. She said in a very soft voice, "Take me, honey. Plant your pleasure in my wet pussy."

We quickly undressed each other and I carried her to the bedroom. I placed her toes in my mouth, licking and sucking each one the way I hoped to suck her clit in the moments to come. As I worked my way up her beautiful thighs, I poured some wine near her pussy and began to lap it up very slowly. I kissed her belly button and worked my way up to her breasts. She was moaning deeply from the pleasure I was giving her.

I moved back down her body and buried my tongue deep into her sweet pussy. She was feeling so good that she started to squeal. She came and came, her juices dripping down my chin like rain. My tongue was buried so deep in her pussy, she told me it was touching parts of her that had never been touched before.

"Wait until you feel what my dick can do," I said.

"Do it now!" she begged.

I turned Kim around. She propped herself up on her elbows, lifting her ass to the level of my ten-inch dick. I guided my cock into her cunt, working in very slowly, inch by inch, until it disappeared completely in her pussy. She screamed from pleasure and then started to moan really loud. "Fuck me, fuck me," she chanted, shoving her rump against me like a battering ram. When I came, which didn't take long, it felt as though I'd released enough jism to fill a bucket. We both fell asleep with my dick still inside her pussy. We had breakfast the next morning and then picked up where we left off the previous night. Later on that afternoon she took me to the airport. We both agreed that our short time together was the best sex of our lives. We parted at the airport with a final, long kiss.

As I started to go through the metal detector, Kim yelled out, "Hey, honey! Do you need a license to carry that big dick of yours?" We both had a good laugh about that.—*Name and address withheld*

CUB REPORTER GOES BARE FOR THE DAY'S BIGGEST STORY

The news business is full of surprises, and not just the kind that wind up on the front page. At the small news service where I work in California, for example, I was more than surprised to find that my steamy romance with one reporter there would be such a source of tongue-wagging for my coworkers. I'd assumed they were all adults whose nose for news could be put to better use, but I was wrong. However, one of the women who gave us such a hard time about our affair was to provide me with the biggest surprise of all.

Molly is a young graduate of an Eastern journalism school, a bright, aggressive, hardworking reporter who I have no doubt will go far. Unfortunately, Molly also seemed to be obsessed with my recent dalliance with Elise, another reporter at the bureau. Elise is beautiful, sexy, hot-blooded . . . you name it. But Molly herself projects an astonishing sexuality. She's a tall, slender, ivory-skinned brunette who has a great sense of humor and exudes a cocky attitude that suggests she's used to getting what she wants. When she was first hired, she was politely flirtatious with me, peppering our conversations with indelicate innuendoes, and I was pleased to see such a dirty mind on someone almost a dozen years my junior.

One morning at about five o'clock, as Elise and I were fucking in her bed, the phone rang and Elise picked it up. It was Molly, at the office. Several propane tanks had exploded near a marina. Molly wanted me to get on the story at once. The only catch was that I'd have to stop by the office first to pick up the cellular phone, in order to relay stories to her from the scene. I said good-bye to the beautiful, naked Elise, patted my erection woefully and got dressed for work.

When I got to the office, Molly was sitting across the desk from mine, smiling and leaning back in her swivel chair with her feet spread apart up on the desk. Her shoes were off, and her runner's legs went on for about a mile before disappearing into a black velvet skirt. Her burgundy blouse was unbuttoned between her breasts. It was extremely warm in there. Or maybe it was just Molly.

"Where's the cellular phone?" I asked. She just smiled at me. "You're an experienced reporter," she said. "You'll have to find it." She tossed her head back and spread apart her legs. I knew the phone wasn't in there, but I sure wanted to look. It appeared the young reporter wasn't wearing panties.

"Look," I said, straining to be serious even though I felt the stirrings of an erection. "I'm not in the mood for games. Where's the phone?"

She shrugged and spread her legs even wider, hiking her skirt up over her lean hips and revealing the unmistakable pattern of a pubic bush.

"Maybe there isn't a phone," she said. "Maybe there isn't even a fire. Not where you think, anyway."

I felt myself blush slightly. "Journalism ain't what it used to be," I said as I began to walk toward her, my hard cock about to split my jeans.

"Maybe I just want to see what that pretty little Elise sees in you. Maybe I want to see it in me for a change," Molly said, sliding a hand under her skirt and fiddling with her pussy. She then leaned forward and took hold of my tie, pulling me to her and burying my face in her sopping pussy. I felt her intoxicating wetness on my lips and nose.

"Hurry, we're on deadline," Molly cooed as I curled my arms around her thighs and parted her succulent folds with my tongue.

"You mean there really is a fire?" I managed to ask.

"Like I said, we have to hurry. Wouldn't want to miss a good story, would we?" she laughed.

I submerged myself in her, munching her delicious rosebud with all the energy and vigor I could summon—and I had a lot of both. I thrust my hungry tongue inside her, then jiggled it against her throbbing clit, every so often swallowing a mouthful of her dripping honey. Meanwhile, my hungry cock bulged against my jeans. And then—you guessed it—the phone rang. I should've remembered that the phones always ring at the wrong time in a news office.

Worse yet, it was Elise, calling from the scene of the fire. She'd taken it upon herself to go there on her own. Molly, while quietly humping my face, commended Elise for her journalistic enterprise. As Molly pulled my lips harder against her, Elise asked her why I wasn't at the fire. Molly replied, "I changed his assignment. He's doing some . . . inside work on the story. Working the, uh, phones." She was flustered and out of breath—after all, I had two fingers up her twat and my tongue was dancing against her clitoris—and said to Elise, "He's right here. Should I put him on?" She smiled and handed me the phone.

Elise was pretty excited about going out on the story. She told me it looked like the whole marina was going to be destroyed, and an apartment building next to it might also catch fire. She asked me if I could take some dictation from her, because she hated to talk with Molly. I positioned myself in front of a computer terminal. As Elise's first adrenaline-flushed words filled my ear, I felt Molly's hand pull at the button fly of my jeans. The dripping tip of my firecracker-red cock sprang free. Molly greeted it with a giggle, followed by several lingering licks up the shaft.

If you ever have the opportunity, I recommend getting sucked off by a sex-starved cub reporter while you type out a story being dictated over the phone by your girlfriend. Of the many thrills I've had in my fifteen years in the news business, none has been as exquisite as taking in Elise's first dispatch while Molly went down on me as if both of our lives depended on it. I was typing and fucking her mouth at the same time! I'm sure my spelling was off, but we have proofreaders for that. Apparently Molly'd learned a lot more at journalism school besides the theory of the triangle lead.

With one hand cupping my balls, she ran her mouth up my prick as though it were a cob of hot buttered corn. She then closed her eyes and put the entire head in her mouth. I watched her large, dark-red lips move up and down my cock, while inside her mouth her tongue polished my cockhead with dozens of quick, hot lashes. Unfortunately this is where it became especially difficult to type, and also where I began to moan. Over the phone, Elise asked me if I was feeling all right, and I told her I was just yawning. Molly's brunette tresses splashed around my belly button as I typed with her head in my lap.

All of a sudden Molly got even more playful and rocked me way back in my chair forcing me to extend my arms to their limits in order to type in Elise's report. Just as Elise was finishing up, Molly began to suck my balls.

"Oh . . . shit!" I exclaimed in ecstasy.

"What was that?" Elise asked.

"Um . . . nothing. I just, um, hit the wrong key," I said. I realized it was a pretty stupid thing to say, while at the same time realizing it would be only a matter of minutes until I flooded Molly's mouth with jizz. She moved her mouth back to my cock and took several zesty slurps on it, taking in all seven hard inches, until her nose was pressing into my pubic hair.

Thankfully, Elise finished dictating her story, and I finished typing. She said good-bye to me and hung up to return to her work. At that point my balls were groaning, demanding release, and my cock was as engorged and tingling as it had ever been. Molly was obviously no stranger to this sort of thing. She returned to my balls with her teeth and lips, pulling on my sac and stroking me vigorously. Think whatever you want to about declining standards in the news business, but take it from me—the talent is still there.

Suddenly, however, we heard the elevator door open down the hall. I couldn't believe it—someone was coming! In a panic, Molly pulled away from me just as I came. My come erupted in wild spurts that shot high in the air and descended like large blobs of hail.

"Who can it be?" I gasped.

Molly's cheeks were flushed with alarm as we frenziedly wiped my jism off the pile of press releases. "I forgot," she said.

"Russell said he was coming in early today. That's probably him now."

She pulled down her skirt, buttoned her blouse and began to search for her sandals. I didn't know where to go. The supply room down the hall seemed to be the best bet so, stuffing my slippery, still-erect cock into my jeans, I limped to the supply room and closed the door behind me. In a few seconds I heard Russell enter the office.

He and Molly exchanged greetings, and I heard him inquire about the fire. She told him Elise and I were at the scene, and he grunted approvingly. I wondered how I was going to get out of there. Russell was one of the biggest office gossips, and I feared he'd really enjoy being the one to tell Elise that instead of covering the fire, I'd been covering Molly's tongue with my sperm.

It was Russell himself who saved the day for both of us by going out for some coffee. I heard the door close behind him.

I walked out with my head spinning. "You'd better go interview the fire chief, and fast," Molly said. From her desk drawer she produced the cellular phone that had, in a way, started this whole thing.

I walked quickly toward the door. "Listen," I said to Molly. "This is between us, right?"

"Don't worry," she said. "One of the first things we learned in school was always to remain true to your confidential informants."

Like I said, news can be a surprising business, and sometimes the best stories don't even get in the paper.—*Name and address withheld*

WHY JUST COVET THY NEIGHBOR'S WIFE? GO AHEAD AND DO HER

I'm twenty-two years old and married to a beautiful woman. This story isn't about my wife, but about Vickie, her longtime friend. Vickie is also married. I'd always dreamed of getting inside her pants, but never thought it would happen.

Every Saturday night I go down to a local club to have a few beers, listen to the music and look at the young babes. I usually meet up with some friends and stay until closing. This particular night, Vickie was there without her husband, who I knew was out of town for a few days. Vickie and I sat and talked, and then I asked her to dance. This was nothing unusual, as we always dance together when her husband and my wife are there. It was getting late and we were both pretty drunk, but we stayed to dance the last slow dance of the night. As we danced, my cock was rubbing against her hip, which she seemed to enjoy because she looked up and gave me a sexy smile.

After we left, I told her I'd follow her home to make sure she got in safely. After we arrived, I walked her to her door and she invited me in. I, of course, accepted. Once inside, Vickie turned on the TV and lay down on the couch. I needed no more coaxing. I walked over to her and kissed her. She drove her tongue deep inside my mouth as we fell back on the couch. For the next twenty minutes we kissed and felt each other up. I slipped my hand inside her blouse and exposed her beautiful tits. Vickie is a small woman with small tits, but they are beautiful, and have huge nipples that stick out at least half an inch when she's aroused.

My mouth and tongue instantly went to work on those beautiful mounds. My hand worked open her jeans, and they were off in a second, followed by her panties. I reached for her hairy pussy and felt that it was dripping wet. When I buried my finger in her cunt, she went nuts, humping my hand and begging me to make her come. I played with her clit for a long time. It stood out as far as her nipples!

After she'd come a few times, it was her turn to please me. She pulled my pants off and took my seven-inch dick into her mouth. I almost went through the ceiling. First she just put the head in her mouth, then slowly took all seven inches down her throat. I almost exploded, but held back to make it last. She sucked me for ten minutes, and then I went down on her. What a beautiful cunt Vickie has—nice and wet and fleshy, just right for eating. I licked her pretty labia until she was moaning with excitement, then nibbled on her clit.

I ate her for at least twenty minutes before getting down to fucking her. She was moaning for me to stick my cock in her, so I gave it my all. God, was she a great fuck! She never stopped moving, which gave my cock sensations I'd never felt before. We fucked until she came, and then she climbed on top of me, sat on my cock and continued pumping away. I came after about five minutes but I never went soft, so we just kept fucking.

I'm sure that we fucked for at least two more hours, during

which time Vickie came several more times. The only reason we stopped was that I had to get home before my wife started worrying about me. What a night that was. We're both looking forward to another two-hour fuck session.—*Name and address withheld*

WHAT WORD BEGINS WITH F AND HAS MANY VARIATIONS? RIGHT—FASHION!

Early one Friday evening I was alone in my apartment when I heard a knock on the door. I answered it and was greeted by the woman who lives next door. She and her husband had lived next to my wife and me for about four months, but we'd never officially met. She introduced herself as Stephanie and asked if my wife was home. I apologized that she wasn't. She'd gone to her sister's and wouldn't be back until late the next day. I asked if I could be of any assistance. Stephanie laughed and, with some embarrassment, said she'd bought a dress for a party the next evening and was looking for an opinion as to how it looked.

Stephanie was the prettiest woman I'd ever seen at that apartment complex. I had often seen her in the hallway and parking lot. She apparently had a good job, as she always dressed in expensive outfits that showed her beautiful legs and calves, and made the most of the huge set of tits with which she'd been blessed. I quickly offered to give my opinion of her party dress.

She invited me into her apartment, then went into her room to change. After about five minutes she came out wearing the dress. It was a snug-fitting black number that accentuated her firm legs and tits. I complimented her on her appearance, adding that she looked as wonderful as she always did.

Stephanie thanked me for the compliment, then offered me a soda. We chatted awhile. She told me that she wasn't looking forward to the party, as her husband was out of town and wouldn't be able to accompany her. Then she said she'd bought a couple of more things and wanted my opinion on them as well. I agreed, and again Stephanie disappeared into her bedroom to change.

When she returned in about five minutes, I couldn't believe my eyes: Parading in front of me was Stephanie in a red lace teddy, garters and stockings. In awe, I couldn't say a word as Stephanie walked by me, turned around, looked at me and said she'd be right back. My head started to spin with thoughts of the beautiful body barely concealed by that outfit. My fantasies were enhanced greatly when Stephanie reentered the room, this time wearing a similar outfit in blue.

Her parade across the room was much slower now. She took her time and showed off her luscious body. My cock stiffened and throbbed as she turned her back to me, bent over and grabbed her ankles. Meanwhile, the teddy revealed more of her ass-cheeks than I'd ever dreamed of seeing. She ran her fingers up her legs, over her calves and toward her thighs. As her hands closed in on her inner thighs, she stopped, turned around, looked at me and said, "I'll be right back."

By now the bulge in my pants was throbbing and my breathing was becoming heavy. This woman wasn't blind. I know she knew how much I wanted to fuck her. Moments later she entered the room wearing a black teddy ensemble. She stood directly in front of me, and our eyes met. We stared deeply into each other's eyes for what seemed to be an eternity. She bent over, and my gaze dropped to the wondrous spot directly between her huge, round globes. They were putting an incredible strain on that black lace teddy!

Stephanie's stare, meanwhile, dropped to my pants, where my growing bulge was very evident. She said, "It looks like you enjoy this color best."

I spoke my first words in a while, saying, "I love them all. You are a beautiful woman."

She returned to the bedroom. A minute later she called me in to join her. As I entered, I saw that the outfits she'd tried on were piled on the floor. Stephanie was lying on the bed, totally naked. Her legs were spread and her tits were pancaked against her chest. She motioned me to the bed, and I had no hesitation in doing what she wanted me to do. I knelt down, put an arm around each leg and buried my face in her glistening pussy.

"Oooh," she shuddered as my tongue touched her velvety folds. I hadn't even known this woman an hour, yet the first part of her I was touching was her cunt. Wow!

I quickly realized I was in for one fun sex session. Stephanie quickly became wild. She loved to talk dirty. "Oh, yes, oh, yes, lick me. Eat me!" she sighed. Her hot talk urged me on. I reached out and found her tits, which were as soft as they were big. Stephanie begged for more. "Fuck me with your tongue, baby. Use your mouth on my pussy. Eat me—eat me and make me come." My fingers squeezed her nipples as she fucked my mouth with her boiling pussy. Stephanie screamed aloud as she reached her first orgasm.

After about thirty seconds, she stood up, put her arms around me and slowly undressed me. It was a huge relief for my cock, which had been throbbing for what seemed like hours. She grabbed a pillow, threw it on the floor and told me to lie on the pile of lingerie she had modeled for me. "You made me come, now it's my turn to fuck you. Just lie there and let me do my magic."

She lowered her pussy over my cock and whispered in my ear, "I'm going to fuck you and talk dirty to you. I want you to squeeze my nipples and play with my tits. I'm going to slide my pussy up and down your cock. You've checked out my body in the parking lot many times, and now you're going to have all your fantasies fulfilled."

"Oh, yes," she went on. "Your cock feels so good in my cunt, and your hands feel so good on my body. I'm going to fuck you hard now." She pumped up and down on me. "I'm fucking you, baby. Come on, lover, fuck me back!" I fucked Stephanie as hard as I could. We both came quickly and collapsed in each other's arms.

I gathered my clothes and went back to my apartment. After an hour I couldn't stand it anymore. I knocked on Stephanie's door. A minute after she let me in, I was fucking her on her couch. This time she fucked me until I was about to come, then took my load down her throat.

After fucking Stephanie for the second time, I went back to my apartment, thinking our quick affair was over. I was wrong. Later that evening there was a knock on my door. It was Stephanie. All she said was, "I can't sleep, and there's nothing on TV." In a flash we were in my bed, fucking again. "Give me that cock," she urged. "My pussy needs to be filled up. Fuck me harder, harder. I just love fucking your prick. Don't forget my tits—suck them, do my nipples. Oh yes, yes yes!" Stephanie's hot words led me to pour yet another load into her soaked cunt. Again, we collapsed in each other's arms.

I was awakened early the next morning by the sublime feeling of Stephanie's lips on my cock. I turned her around and we went at it in a 69. After a little of this, Stephanie took me by the hand and said, "Come with me into the bathroom. I want you to fuck me in the shower." We made the water as hot as we could stand it. Stephanie stood in front of me, and I rammed her from behind. She groaned with every stroke and begged for more.

When it was over, Stephanie gathered up her stuff and thanked me for a wonderful evening. I thanked her in return, kissed her, squeezed her tits and rubbed her pussy once more before she left. That was two months ago. Our spouses never found out, so my memories of that night are still good ones. We haven't slept together again since then, and probably won't, but when our eyes meet, we both still smile.—*Name and address withheld*

IT WAS A DARK AND STORMY NIGHT IN WHITE SATIN . . .

It was one of those nights perfect for curling up on the couch in front of a warm, cozy fire and escaping into a good book. I needed the time to relax after the week I'd just had. Working as a nanny for a wealthy Boston family was a lot more exhausting than I'd imagined when I took the job a year ago.

After reading the children a bedtime story and tucking them into bed, I was relishing the idea of a relaxing evening. The sound of thunder and the lightning flashing outside the windows set the perfect mood for my night as I walked over to add another log to the fireplace. The chill in the room caused my nipples to become erect as they brushed up against my blouse. The sensation gave way to a longing that I was all too familiar with since my recent breakup with my boyfriend. Although I'm an ace at satisfying myself, masturbation is just a temporary relief and not nearly as good as the real thing. What I really wanted at that moment was a slow, sensuous fuck. Just thinking about it was driving me crazy? Maybe a nice hot bubble bath would help ease the tension and chase away the horny thoughts that were running through my mind.

I poured myself a glass of Chablis, grabbed my novel and headed upstairs to the Jacuzzi. As I started up the stairs I smiled, thinking about the delightful times I had spent making love on that magnificent staircase when I had the house all to myself. I've always had a thing for "stair sex," as I liked to call it. In my mind, I could see my ex-boyfriend Roy and me getting it on as he stroked me with his fingers and fucked me from behind. I could still hear my moans of pleasure echoing off the cathedral ceiling.

The lightning and thunder continued outside as I lowered myself into the hot, stinging water. Suddenly the rain began beating down on the roof. I was glad that I was safe and warm inside, feeling sorry for whoever had to deal with Mother Nature at her worst. I sipped my wine, opened my book and began to read, remembering that I had left off at the beginning of a hot, steamy love scene. Just what I needed!

I found myself holding the book with one hand while I spread my thighs apart to allow the warm, pulsing water from the jet spray to hit my clitoris. So much for the book, I soon decided as I reached under the water with my other hand to play with my hard nipples. I felt at any moment that I was going to explode, and soft moans escaped my lips.

At that exact moment the lights flashed once, the jets on the Jacuzzi stopped and everything went pitch black. Great timing! I groped for a towel, slipped on my bathrobe and went in search of a candle. It wasn't difficult finding my way through the house, since the lightning was getting stronger, illuminating everything as though it were daytime. After locating a candle, I went to check on the kids to make sure they were okay. Even with all that thunderous racket outside, they were still sound asleep.

Just then I heard what sounded like something or someone pounding far off in the distance, but it was difficult to tell if the sound was due to the storm wreaking havoc outside, or if someone was actually knocking on the door. Then I heard it again between the claps of thunder. It was definitely someone pounding on the door.

My heart began to race as I wondered who on Earth would be out on a night like this. Mr. and Mrs. Kelvin weren't expected back for several days, and I was sure that their family and friends knew this, so who could it be? I was a little scared and apprehensive as I slowly made my way downstairs, unlocked the door and opened it a fraction of an inch. There, standing in the small halo of light cast by my candle, stood a long-haired man who looked like he'd just taken a shower with all his clothes on. In a pleading voice he said, "My car broke down about a half mile from here, and I was hoping I could use your phone to call for a tow truck."

I'd seen this scenario before in dozens of horror movies. Somehow, though, the look on his face, and his expensive clothing, wet as it was, made me trust him. I let him in, and we stood looking at each other while a puddle of water formed around him on the floor of the foyer. "The phone is in the den," I said as I led the way. I wasn't about to leave him alone, so I watched while he made the phone call. What a body this guy had! I've always had a thing for long-haired guys, and I saw that his fell well past his shoulders. I started stoking the fire and, when I turned around, his eyes were glued on mine with a burning intensity.

"It will be a few hours before a truck can make it out here," he said. "The storm has stranded motorists everywhere. Do you mind if I get out of these wet clothes?"

"No, not at all," I replied, hoping that he would feel free to get all the way out of them. My heartbeat quickened.

He started to undress, still piercing me with those emerald green eyes, and I felt the heat rising up through my body. I couldn't help but notice that his huge cock was fully erect, and I instantly felt the moistness between my legs. He walked over to me and untied the sash holding my robe closed. He knelt down on the floor in front of me, slowly licked and kissed his way down my stomach, then moved on to my thighs. I spread them for him and felt the gentle play of his fingers, followed by his hot, moist tongue on my clit. This man knows what he's doing, I thought as I heard myself moan.

He sucked me with a passion that was unbelievable. It was as though he didn't want to waste a drop of the juices that were flowing from my pussy. I felt myself coming close to an orgasm, and he must have sensed it because he started sucking harder. At the same time he began fondling both my taut nipples until I felt myself coming all over his face. I moaned and pushed his face against my wet pussy as I hard as I could. I knew right then and there that I wanted to please this mystery man as much as he was pleasing me.

I led him over to the staircase, sat him down on the steps and began to suck his engorged cock. He moaned, which told me he was enjoying it as much as I'd hoped. While I sucked him, I felt his hand reach between my thighs to play with my swollen clit. I came several times until I couldn't stand it anymore! I think at that moment we both wanted to fuck.

I took his hand and led him halfway up the stairs. I knelt down on my knees with my ass raised in the air, while he stood one step below me. He guided his cock into me, pumping it in and out slowly at first, moving it in little circles. Then he started going deeper and deeper into me, playing with my nipples and stroking my clit faster and faster until neither one of us could hold back any longer. He pounded into me with such strength that it gave me a feeling of pleasure I'd never before experienced. I was in total ecstasy!

When it was over, we quickly ran up the stairs to the master bedroom, and jumped into Mr. and Mrs. Kelvin's enormous bed. We busied ourselves beneath the satin sheets until the tow truck came for his car nearly three hours later. Long after the time the stranger left, I could smell his come in my pussy, and taste it on my lips. Just as he was leaving he said to me, "Now that's what I call riding out a storm!"—*Name and address withheld*

SEMPER FUCK! MARINE'S WIFE IS LOYAL TO THE CORPS

I'm in the marines, stationed in the Washington, D.C. area. I admit I've often fantasized about watching my wife Kathy make it with a well-hung guy, preferably a black man, or watching her take on two horse-hung studs at once. Talking about it with her, and visualizing her satisfying a bunch of sex-starved guys, turns us both on.

Recently I was away on temporary duty for six months. When I finished my assignment, my friend Paul had a welcome-home party for me at his house. He got a keg of beer and some smoke, and a bunch of guys came with their wives and girlfriends.

By three in the morning, all the couples had gone home. Paul, four single guys and I were still drinking and carousing in the basement. Paul's wife Liz was upstairs with Kathy. One of the guys suggested we put on an X-rated video, and popped a tape in the VCR. Paul jumped up as soon as it started, yelled, "Not that one!" and hit the Eject button with super speed. They all seemed to act a little strange, and it seemed they were all looking right at me. I asked what was going on, and Paul said, "You wouldn't be interested. It was just a tape I made myself. Let me put on a real juicy one instead." After he'd reloaded the VCR, I noticed that he didn't put the first videocassette back with the others, but went to a storage closet and tossed it in there.

We finished off the beer and watched the video, and then the last of the partiers departed. Paul was upstairs in the kitchen. I hollered up and asked him if I could borrow one of his sexy tapes. "Sure, help yourself," was his reply. Naturally, I took the tape from the storage closet.

When we got home, I was keyed up and couldn't sleep. Kathy went to bed and dropped off instantly. My curiosity was aroused, so I put Paul's tape on to find out what it was about it that made all the guys act so strangely.

Suddenly a picture came on the screen. It revealed my wife dancing seductively, stripping and coming on to Bill and Charlie. Bill and Charlie are two big, tough, well-developed Marine M.P.s who happen to be black. Kathy was dancing around them, moving her hands over their shoulders and chests. Nearly nude, she next leaned over them, running her hands over her thighs and their bulging cocks. She was really turning them on.

My cock was steel-hard and getting cramped in my trousers. I had to release it in order to continue watching the tape. Now nude and standing in front of Charlie, Kathy allowed him to insert a long black finger in her pussy while his left hand caressed her ass. Bill stood up behind her and cupped his hands over her tits. He began massaging them, then twisted and tweaked her nipples while Charlie stuffed two fingers up her twat. Kathy was hot, and so was I!

Bill took Kathy by the shoulders and turned her around to face him. He lowered his head to kiss her passionately. Bill's hands moved from her face, which he was holding between his hands while he Frenched with her, to her shoulders. He gently pushed her down to her knees. He undid his belt and fly, then dropped his trousers around his ankles. My wife reached for the waistband of his shorts and pulled them down, revealing the biggest, fattest, darkest cock I'd ever seen. It was throbbing right before her eyes, just inches from her mouth. She gingerly planted a soft kiss right on the tip of the large purple cockhead, then ran her tongue over the slit to taste the pre-come that was already oozing out.

On the sidelines, Charlie was stripping. When he was naked, he stepped up on the far side of Bill, stroking his monster cock and bringing it next to Bill's big dick. By now my wife was avidly sucking all she could of the first black cock. The head alone filled her beautiful mouth. Charlie rubbed the soft, rubbery knob of his cock on my wife's face while she desperately struggled to suck more and more of Bill's long shaft. What a fabulous sight! It was more thrilling and exciting for me to watch than anything I'd ever imagined.

After a while Kathy released Bill's shining black pride and turned to suck Charlie's cock. Charlie's was huge and a little thicker, but not quite as long as Bill's. Trying to suck Bill's cock was a challenge, but trying to manage with Charlie's even thicker rod was quite a task for Kathy. But she did it, and soon was moving from cock to cock, going wild over that double portion of dark meat. What a fabulous wife I have. I'm sure those guys envy me a hell of a lot.

The scene switched from our living room to our bedroom. There was my wife spread-eagle on the bed, holding her pink, juicy pussy lips open while Bill dived in to eat her out. I could hear him slurp up her juices. Charlie got into position and nibbled on her nipples. My wife was writhing around on the bed like a woman possessed. She started screaming, "Fuck me! Fuck me, please! I need a big fat cock in my cunt!"

Bill provided what she so desperately needed. He eased his shank into her cunt, stretching her pussy so it could accommodate the biggest cock she'd ever had inside her. Then he began fucking her in a slow, easy rhythm, sliding his monster all the way in, then almost all the way out. She was moaning and cooing, and I could see that this fuck was the best she'd ever had. You don't know how pleased, proud and turned on I was watching these two athletic studs treating themselves to my wife's sexual gifts.

Charlie's need to sink his fat cock in my wife was too great to allow him to wait any longer. He told Bill to move aside. Kathy let out an anguished "No!" as she felt Bill withdraw. But then Charlie got between her legs and started rubbing his cockhead up and down her pussy lips. Kathy begged him, "Put it in, put it in me now. I want a cock in my cunt!"

Charlie said. "You want it? You got it!" and rammed his meat all the way up her pussy. Charlie was really ripe to fuck, and he pounded Kathy's pussy relentlessly. Her moans had turned to grunts and screams of "Yes . . . yes, harder! Deeper! Fuck me harder!" I saw Charlie stiffen, and I knew he was pumping his load into my wife's pussy. She scissored her legs open and closed while he emptied his sperm-filled nuts into her box.

Paul got a close-up of Charlie pulling his slimy black cock from my wife's pink pussy. Kathy seemed eager for more, and she was not to be disappointed. Bill turned her over, lifted her ass, spread her cheeks and fucked her doggie-style. He was able to slide his black beauty right into her come-filled pussy without any effort whatsoever.

Charlie watched for a few minutes, then took his semihard cock in hand and scooted in front of my wife's mouth. He guided her lips onto his cock and urged her on. "Suck it, baby. Get it nice and hard again. Think about how turned on your husband would be if he knew what you were doing now."

Kathy fed on that cock like a starving woman. The sight of her sandwiched between two muscular black studs, fucking one and blowing the other, was what did it for me. I shot my load all over the television screen. As my semen dripped down the glass, Charlie and Bill each shot a huge wad. Kathy gulped down Charlie's thick spunk, and let Bill fill her pussy with his.

Paul then evidently gave the camera to one of the men, because in the next shot, he was sticking his dick into Kathy's come-enriched cunt. Kathy was so horny, she even seemed to enjoy the fuck she was getting from Paul's dick, which was no more than half the size of Bill's and Charlie's cocks.

After Paul shot his load, the scene changed. Now it showed big, brawny Bill slouched in our bedroom chair with his muscular thighs spread wide, waving his erect, ten-inch dick and telling my wife to come suck him off. Kathy crawled between his legs, anxious to get that cock down her throat, no matter what. She did gag a bit, but she was obviously turned on and determined to do her best. She actually did suck him down to the base a few times, but she couldn't keep that much cock in her mouth for long. When Bill suddenly grabbed her head, lifted his ass and rammed his cock deep into her mouth, I knew she was about to drink another big load of his liquid protein. When he relaxed and slumped back in the chair, my beautiful, sexy wife let a few drops of his come leak from her mouth, and smeared them all over her lips with his glistening prick.

I'd shot a second load of come by that point. The television screen was a mess. I cleaned it off and tried to figure out what to do about this tape. I decided to get it back into Paul's storage closet as soon as possible. I wasn't angry, jealous or upset that three of my buddies had used my wife for sex. I was thrilled and pleased, and thought it best not to mention the fact that I knew about it to them or my wife. I did make a copy of the tape for myself before returning it, however. It's the best fuck tape I've ever seen, and never fails to make me come at least twice.

My wife is better in bed since she took on those extra-large dicks. I hope that Charlie, Paul, Bill and my wife will soon have another wild get-together. But next time, I'd like to participate.—*S.U., Richmond, Virginia*

Head & Tail

DONNA SHOWS OFF A VACANT APARTMENT—AND OTHER PRIME REAL ESTATE

A couple of years ago, when my wife Donna and I were still in college, we lived in an apartment complex near the university. One afternoon I skipped my last two classes and went home early. After searching through the apartment and not finding Donna anywhere, I went out the back door to continue looking for her. The apartment next to ours was vacant, and just for the hell of it I went up to the window and peeked inside.

Donna was lying on the couch, wearing a tank top and nothing else. A giant dildo was buried inside her pussy. I had bought the dildo for her myself, months earlier, but she claimed she never used it.

She was carefully working herself over, sliding the huge dildo all the way in and then slowly all the way out. Very much turned on, I pulled my dick out and started jacking off, when suddenly I heard a vehicle coming down the driveway. I quickly slipped my cock back into my pants and hid behind a bush. From there, I could still look through the window and see inside the apartment.

My wife was in such a state of ecstasy that she didn't even hear the car pull up. Then a man got out of the car, walked up to the door of the vacant apartment and knocked. He must have read about the place in the newspaper and was interested in renting it. My wife was stunned when she heard the knock. She slipped into a skimpy pair of shorts that exposed most of her glorious ass. I couldn't believe what she was wearing!

Donna hesitated before answering the door, but then got the nerve to do so. I could hear her talking to the person, but I couldn't see them. Then my wife walked back into the living room, with the guy right behind her. I could see that he was looking at her ass more than the apartment. Needless to say, he had quite a bulge in his pants.

I couldn't believe my wife was walking around in such a skimpy outfit in front of a total stranger. He immediately noticed the dildo and baby oil next to the couch, but didn't say anything. Instead, he asked Donna where the bathroom was. When he returned, his back was to me, but it was evident that he had pulled his cock out and was stroking it. The expression on Donna's face was that of anger, but she still kept looking down at the guy's tool. He must have asked her if she wanted him to take the place of the dildo, because she removed her shorts and gestured for him to sit on the couch.

When he sat on the couch, I couldn't believe my eyes. This guy's cock was longer than the dildo and certainly much thicker. For a moment I felt jealous and wanted to rush in and stop them, but then the idea of seeing Donna take that entire cock inside her gave me an instant hard-on, and I pulled my cock out and started stroking it slowly. Donna then straddled the guy, guiding his giant cock between her pussy lips. She slowly worked her way down his pole until it was all the way inside her.

They fucked for about ten minutes. Then the guy told Donna to get on her hands and knees. He stuck his finger in his mouth, wetting it nicely with saliva, and said he wanted to fuck her ass. And she said yes! I couldn't believe it! She never let me enter her from the rear. After getting her hole nice and wet with his finger, he slowly inched his cock into her ass. He only pumped her about a dozen times before I saw come dripping out of her ass. After viewing all this, I shot my load in no time.

Donna told me about this episode two weeks later while we were making love one night. I told her that next time she has to tell me about it sooner.—*Name and address withheld*

ONE SUNNY SATURDAY THEY MOUNTED A COUPLE OF HORSES—THEN EACH OTHER

I am a twenty-year-old single male. A couple of weeks ago I needed a haircut. My barber was on vacation, so I decided to visit a beauty salon. It was there that I met Edna. She has shoulder-length blonde hair and one hell of a figure. When she told me she was in her thirties, I didn't believe her. She looks so much younger.

We talked while she cut my hair, and I found out that she lives with her husband on a farm. When she mentioned that they owned a couple of horses, I told her that I loved horseback riding, but that I rarely got a chance to do it. Edna then invited me to go riding with her on Saturday. I jumped at the opportunity.

Saturday finally came. I arrived at Edna's farm around nine in the morning. Edna told me that her husband was attending a farm show and would be gone until Monday. She looked absolutely delicious, dressed in a pair of tight jeans and a flimsy T-shirt, with no bra underneath. I would have much rather enjoyed riding her than the horse.

We saddled up the horses and spent the rest of the morning riding.

Around noon we went back to the farm and washed down the horses. It was hot out, so after a while Edna took the hose and let the water run down the front of her shirt, allowing her nipples to be seen through the thin, wet material.

"Let's go in the house," Edna suggested. I didn't need a second invitation. Once inside, Edna pulled off her shirt and hugged me, kissing me on the mouth. She pulled her lips away and said, "Suck my tits, lover." I wrapped my lips around her hot nipples one at a time while rubbing her crotch, getting her hotter by the second. Then we went into her bedroom and peeled off the rest of our clothes. We got into bed and arranged ourselves in a 69.

My tongue danced into Edna's sweet pussy, and she sucked my cock like a vacuum cleaner. We both came, Edna sucking down every drop of my come while her cunny-honey flooded my wanton mouth.

My cock was still hard, and Edna told me to fuck the living hell out of her. While my cock pumped in and out of her hot box, she pressed her fingers into my back and screamed out that she was coming. After a few more strokes, I let a big load of come loose deep inside her.

We rested for a while, then Edna went and got a candle out of the dresser. "Have you ever been corn-holed?" she asked. I told her I was game, as long as I could return the favor. "Anytime," she agreed.

Edna dipped the candle in a jar of cold cream and told me to get on my hands and knees. I did as she said, and Edna slowly slipped the candle up my ass while stroking my cock with her other hand. It felt really good, and before long I was as hard as a flagpole again. Edna continued to fuck my ass and beat my cock until I exploded all over the sheets.

"My turn," I said. "I'm gonna ride your ass like a stud." I dipped a finger into the cold cream, lubed up Edna's red-hot ass and slowly inched my cock into her. I fucked Edna's asshole for about ten minutes before I filled her bowels with love juice.

We spent the rest of the weekend fucking.

Edna and I get together often to ride horses, as well as each other.—*Name and address withheld*

PAULA PASSED OUT, BUT A GOOD TIME WAS HAD BY ALL THE REST

My wife Fran and I met five years ago when she was in college. Our sex life was great. The better we got to know each other, the more experimental we became. We tried numerous positions and lots of oral and anal sex. We fooled around with video cameras and every sex toy known to man. Then something happened that really slowed our sex life down: We got married!

Although I am almost always ready to go, Fran doesn't seem to be into sex the way she was before we were married. I'm not saying that sex is *always* boring, but it is nothing compared to what we used to have. If we ever do anything new or exciting, I have to initiate and direct the events and hope that she's agreeable. That is until recently, which is why I am writing.

A few months ago some close friends of ours, Doug and Paula, moved away. We recently had a business engagement to attend in a city near where they live. The trip included a free hotel room for Friday night, so Doug and Paula asked us to visit them on Saturday.

After a late-morning workout on Saturday, we met them for lunch and some afternoon sight-seeing and bar-hopping. Since we had bought them lunch, they decided to cook us dinner. Not wanting our afternoon buzz to end, we picked up several bottles of wine to go with dinner. While Paula cooked, the three of us toured the house and started in on the wine. We had more wine with the meal, then for dessert we had yet another bottle. We finished the several bottles we had purchased that day, and had to break into Doug's private stock.

We were all buzzing pretty good, especially Paula and Fran. I knew this because when the conversation turned to our morning workouts and getting in shape, both girls started flashing their tits, showing off what good shape their bodies were in. Paula teased Doug, only flashing her boobs when I wasn't looking. But Fran found it exciting and flashed hers when we could both see her, although she seemed to be more interested in Doug than me.

A short time later Fran and I paired off on the sofa while Doug and Paula spread out on the carpet. Fran and I began some heavy kissing and petting, which is very unlike us to do in front of people. Unfortunately for Doug, the wine was having a different effect on Paula, who began to pass out. Doug sat on the floor and teased us. "You're going to fuck right in front of me," he said, "and I'm going to have to sit here and watch." This only excited Fran more. She grabbed me, occasionally showing her tits to Doug.

Fran asked if my feet were sore. Before I could even answer her, she was sitting on the floor massaging them. I soon figured out what she had up her sleeve. While she rubbed my feet, Doug sat behind her and rubbed her back. Before long, they both became tired of this and lay down, with Doug on his side and Fran's head resting on his legs. I placed my foot between Fran's legs and rubbed her crotch.

The sexual tension developing between Fran and Doug was obvious. There was lots of massaging and caressing going on between the two of them. Fran gave me a devilish look and a wink, as if asking me if it was okay for things to continue. In the past we had discussed and fantasized about having another person in bed with us. Even though I had hoped it would be a female, we had both agreed to give it a try if the situation ever arose. So when Fran looked to me for guidance, I let her know that she could do whatever she wanted.

With that, Fran moved her hand to Doug's crotch. Seeing that things were going to start happening fast, I decided to make a quick trip to the bathroom to relieve my kidneys. I returned to the living room a few minutes later to find that Doug and Fran were gone. I went over to check on Paula. She was out like a light. I thought of trying to wake her by putting my tongue on her nipples or between her legs, but I wasn't sure if she would go for that. And since I had a pretty good idea that Doug and Fran were already going at it, I decided that I'd better not wake her. There was no telling how she would react to the sight of her husband fucking my wife.

I proceeded to walk up the stairs to the guest bedroom, not really sure what would be going on. I had a good idea, but not much time had passed, so I didn't think they would be very far along. How wrong I was!

I went up the steps, walked down the hall and took a look inside the guest bedroom. Fran was sitting on the bed, with Doug standing in front of her. They were both completely naked, and Doug's cock was in Fran's mouth. Doug looked at me with a big smile on his face as Fran continued to suck him.

Feeling out of place, I went into the room, stripped off my clothes and massaged one of Fran's breasts while Doug massaged the other. Fran took turns sucking our cocks. Then she decided that she wanted some between-the-legs action. She had Doug get on the bed so that she could suck him in a kneeling position, which gave me access to her pussy from behind. I stuck my face between her cheeks and licked her crotch.

After licking her for several minutes, I decided to give her something she had often fantasized about: two cocks in her at once.

As I fucked her from behind, she sucked Doug and he played with her tits. Doug soon yelled that he was coming, and Fran swallowed every drop. Fran motioned for me to switch to the missionary position so she could get some friction against her clit. She came quickly, but continued to bang away. Doug decided to go check on Paula, so he left and closed the door while we continued to fuck. Fran came two more times, but all the alcohol was helping me hold off. While we were fucking, Fran told me that when I had gone to the bathroom earlier, she and Doug had started kissing, grabbing and stripping each other right in the living room. She didn't mean to start things without me, but when she started to suck Doug off in front of Paula, he thought it would be best if they went upstairs.

Fran told me she wanted Doug to come back so that she could be with both of us again. I went to check on him, leaving her masturbating. Doug was putting Paula to bed, and once she was under the covers, he was ready for more action. When we returned to the guest room, Fran let us watch while she played with her clit and nipples. She then turned and got on her hands and knees, asking if one of us would like to fuck her. Doug quickly obliged. I don't think I'll ever forget the sexy look on Fran's face as my best friend pumped her from behind. She licked her lips and motioned for me to come closer so that she could suck my cock. Once again she had both our cocks in her.

Doug was pumping her hard and said that he was going to come soon. Fran flipped around and stuck his cock in her mouth so that she could taste his come again. With one hand she pumped the base of his cock and with the other she massaged his balls. Doug soon groaned and filled her mouth with come.

Doug was beat and decided to go to bed. I had yet to come, so I was definitely ready for more, and so was Fran. The first thing she did when Doug left the room was kiss me hard, forcing me to taste some of his come, which she had saved in her mouth. She had done this before, after blowing me, and I have to admit that his come tasted much different than my own. Soon we were fucking in many different positions, but I still could not come. Alcohol often does this to me. I stayed hard because of all the excitement, but could not spurt.

Then Fran said she knew of something that would excite me enough to get me to come. She rolled onto her stomach, spread her legs and told me to fuck her ass. Although I had tried to do this several times, we had not had anal sex in three years. Now she was begging for it. She even got her finger wet with saliva and pussy juice and slid it into her butthole. I climbed aboard and positioned my cock at her anal entrance. I slowly, steadily slid my cock into her tight hole. She moaned loudly. I was worried, and asked if I had hurt her. She said, "Are you kidding? It feels great!"

She begged for more. I pushed in until my balls touched her pussy. I began with long, slow strokes until she asked me to go faster. I pumped her ass hard and could feel the come building in my balls. She begged me to come in her ass. I pumped as hard as I could, and she soon yelled that she was coming. I filled her ass with as much come as I have ever produced.

We both collapsed, with my cock still in her butthole. As my cock softened and slid out, Fran moaned and said that she had never thought ass-fucking could be that good, and that we would have to try it again real soon. After cleaning up, we fell asleep, only to wake up and fuck three more times before Doug and Paula rolled out of bed.

Before we left that day, there were many knowing looks passed between Doug, Fran and myself, while Paula seemed to know nothing of the previous night's events. There has been talk of us getting together again, but I would like to do it with another female next time. Fran thinks it's a good idea and can't wait to give it a try herself. I guess I'll be writing again.—*Name and address withheld*

HUNGRY FOR REAR ENTRY, DIVORCED MAN MEETS WILLING PARTNER

I had been married for twenty years and my sex life was okay. During that time, my ex and I tried anal sex about a half-dozen times or so. Each time, the result was the same. She would put her ass up in the air and prepare to receive me. As soon as my lubricated, six-inch dick slightly penetrated her, she would cringe and let me know that she couldn't stand it. I would always pull out, feeling frustrated. One time I came from having only the tip inside her ass, but it was more from excitement than anything else. I finally accepted the fact that anal sex was one of life's experiences that I would never sample.

About a year and a half ago I was fortunate enough to meet up with an old high-school sweetheart. We quickly discovered that our attraction for each other had not died, even after thirty years of being apart. We also discovered that we are extremely well matched in our sexual desires.

We live far away from each other, so we are only able to get together once a month or so. Each time we get together, it's non-stop sucking and fucking as we push the sexual envelope a little further. She had had an extremely boring sex life in her marriage, so everything I teach her is exciting for her.

On several of our meetings we talked about trying anal sex, but aside from fingering each other's asshole once in a while, I had never tried to penetrate her with my cock.

Absence truly does make the heart grow fonder. Our monthly trysts are always very loving and passionate, and the last time was no exception. I picked her up at the airport and took her back to my place. In no time we were rolling around naked in bed. She loves to suck on my cock, so before long she had her sweet, loving lips pumping my pole, which was leaking pre-come. I spun her ass around, and we locked into a tight 69. She has a very wet and tasty pussy, which I love eating. I especially like the 69 position because I love to embrace her while we eat each other. One of the advantages of being in my forties is that I can go a lot longer than I used to, and this makes for a better time for both of us.

After an hour or more of kissing, sucking and fingering, I decided it was time to do it. She was ready, but she had no idea what was coming, so to speak.

I gently rolled her onto her stomach. I kissed my way down her back, slowly nibbling and massaging her spine until I reached her ass. I then got on my knees between her spread legs and continued to massage her sweet cheeks. I spread her ass and saw the object of my desire. She still didn't know what I had planned. I then pulled her to her knees and got out some K-Y jelly. I put a little around her hole and a lot on my dick. I moved forward to enter her. As I started, she clenched the pillow, and I saw that her knuckles were white. I thought, Here we go again. I asked her if she wanted me to pull out. Through clenched teeth, she said, "Go for it." I was stunned and filled with gratitude.

I lovingly pushed my shaft into her tight hole. Once fully in, I remained motionless for a while. She slowly began to relax. I bent over and kissed the back of her neck. Her knees then relaxed under my weight, and soon she was flat on her stomach. I let my reflexes take over, and I began to slowly hump her loving ass. I took long, deep strokes, nearly pulling all the way out before plunging back in. It felt as good as I thought it would, but what felt better was the intensified love I felt for her. Anal sex strengthened the bond between us. I continued to pump until we both reached a warm, satisfying climax. I then collapsed on top of her, and we stayed in a loving embrace for a long time.

Since then, she has told me that in some ways she finds anal intercourse more pleasurable than vaginal. Our favorite place to ass-fuck is in the shower. While embracing her with one hand, I use a bar of soap to get her hole ready. First I insert one soapy finger, then I wait. When I feel that she is relaxed, I insert a second finger. In no time, she is ready to accept me. She then turns around, bends over and readily takes my soapy dick inside her backdoor. I can pump her as hard and as deep as I want, and she loves it. We laugh because the bubbles fly everywhere. Another side benefit of shower butt-fucking is that if I choose not to come in her ass, I can pull out, rinse off and let her suck me until I do. As we like to say to each other: "We just know how to have fun."—*L.K., New York, New York*

THEY PLIED HER WITH DRINKS—THEN WITH A COUPLE OF OTHER THINGS

First off, to set the stage, it's a hot, sticky summer. The sun had just set, but the humidity was uncomfortable. My best friend Frank and I were sitting in his apartment with Ginger and Camille. Ginger is a plain-Jane brunette, with big tits and an attitude problem. Camille, on the other hand, is a tall redhead, with perky little tits, legs to die for and a deep love for partying.

Since my mom and dad had gone to their summer house for the weekend, we decided to go to my family's house where we could cool off and party. All of us except Ginger, that is, who refused to go. So we left her. Camille was game because she knew my buddy Frank had some cocaine. When we arrived at the house, I went right to the bar and asked Camille what her favorite drink was. "Peppermint schnapps on the rocks," was her reply. I got a bottle of the stuff and a bucket of ice, and the three of us went into my bedroom.

Once there, I poured the drinks. Frank pulled out his blow and we cut some thick lines. We sat on the bed, laughing and talking for hours.

I'd like to add at this time that Camille is model material, while Frank and I are just average-looking guys.

I had already made up my mind that she was not going to put out for us, so I started downstairs. Before I reached the bottom of the stairs, I heard her moaning softly. I went back to take a peek, and there she was, before my very eyes, naked and looking good enough to eat, giving my buddy Frank a blowjob. He saw me looking and waved me in.

Then she looked at me and said, "Don't just stand there! Let that monster of yours out of his cage and put him wherever he feels most fitting!" When she said that, I just about came on the spot. I got naked and joined the fun.

She was on her knees, with her arms around Frank's waist. All I could see was her long red hair covering Frank's middle. I called her the Flaming Flash, because all I saw was a flash of red hair as her head bobbed up and down on Frank's cock. This chick was hot, and knew her business. Within a few minutes she had Frank screaming and shuddering as he shot his load down her throat.

Her beautiful red bush was dripping cunt juice. Just looking at her wet cunt made my mouth water. I had to suck that juicy pussy, so I dropped to my knees and went to work. I started by sucking on her clit, and the very first taste was like biting into a big, juicy apple sprinkled with salt. I lapped up all the cunt juice she could put out.

Before long I had her trembling and shaking. Suddenly she stiffened and screamed, and I knew she'd just had one of the best orgasms ever. I have never seen a woman come as hard or as much as she did, and the sight of her excitement got me so excited, I thought I was going to have an orgasm.

I put my mouth over her whole cunt and sucked it as she came. She poured out so much juice, I thought I was going to drown.

I had to fuck her. Spreading the folds of her cunt lips, I rubbed the head of my cock up and down that soaked gash. Then, in one hard thrust, I rammed my rock-hard cock all the way in to the hilt and just held it there for a few moments, savoring the feeling of that hot, juicy cunt sucking on my cock.

Meanwhile, Camille was slurping hungrily on Frank's cock, never missing a beat. I started to slowly pump in and out of her quivering body, trying not to come too soon, but I was caught up in the heat of the moment and couldn't hold back. I started pounding that pussy so hard and deep, pussy juice was squirting all around my cock. The harder I fucked her, the better her pussy got. No doubt she was being fucked like she had never been fucked before, and she was loving it.

She stopped sucking Frank's cock and pushed me off her just as I was getting ready to come. It was her turn to do the fucking, she said. I lay back on the bed. She stood over me and pointed her ass at my face and asked me if I liked what I saw. Before I could say a word, she had swooped down, her cunt taking the whole length of my cock inside.

She sat there, not moving for a while. Then she started to do a slow grind. Her motions gradually intensified until she was at a fevered pitch.

By this point she was out of control and was grinding my meat like a well-oiled machine. I exploded inside her like a blast from a shotgun. Bright lights exploded inside my head.

I came, washing her insides with my come. She got off me and licked my cock, trying to get it hard again. It was no use, though. She started whimpering, sliding my flaccid cock between her lips. Then Frank jumped behind her and fucked her doggie-style. After watching them for a while, I went to get some sex toys that I keep in my room.

A few minutes later I was back with a twelve-inch dildo. As soon as I neared the bed, she stuffed my cock inside her mouth. My prick was as hard as steel again. I told her that I wanted to fuck her back door, and she said that she loved the idea of having a cock up her ass. I took my cock out of her mouth and lubed it up with K-Y jelly.

"I want that big cock of yours up my ass," she said.

I held the cheeks of her ass apart and shoved the head of my prick in. Then I leaned back so I could watch my cock slide in and out of her ass. She reached behind me and grabbed my ass, helping me move back and forth.

She had orgasm after orgasm. This was the first time I had ever seen a woman have multiple orgasms. She was screaming, moaning, groaning and loving every minute of it. She started to scream, "Fuck my ass with the rubber pecker!" I pulled out of her, grabbed the dildo and slid the entire thing inside her butt. To my surprise, she was able to take the whole thing.

Then the dildo disappeared inside her ass. She loved the feeling, and told me not to touch the thing. I stood back and watched her writhing in pure ecstasy. I've never felt so much pleasure in my life, and I'll never forget our girl Camille.—*Name and address withheld*

ROCK 'N' ROLL SINGER SAVES A FEW HOT LICKS FOR HIS NUMBER-ONE FAN

I'm a twenty-one-year-old guy, and I'm the lead singer for a rock 'n' roll band. Last week we did a show at a bar in Austin,

Texas. While I was on stage, I noticed a cute auburn-haired lady at one of the tables near the stage. She sat with two other pretty women. She kept her eyes glued on me throughout the whole evening and was obviously enjoying the music my band was performing.

After the show we packed up our equipment and started loading it onto the bus. A couple of giggling girls came over and invited us to a party. Since we had no other plans, we decided we'd go check it out.

The party was well under-way when we arrived. To my surprise and delight, the cute girl from the bar was there. She came up to me and told me that she enjoyed the show and was very attracted to me. By this time we were both a bit high from all the drugs and booze we'd consumed at the party. I suggested that we find a quiet place to sit and talk, and she said that sounded like a great idea.

We went out to the backyard and sat on a bench secluded behind some bushes. After we'd talked for a few minutes, she leaned over and kissed me, probing my mouth with her tongue. I, of course, responded in kind.

As we were kissing, I felt her hands on the top button of my button-fly jeans. My twitching cock began to stiffen as she hastily unbuttoned my fly and rubbed my cock through my undershorts. We briefly stopped kissing so she could pull off my pants and undershorts. My rock-hard eleven-inch rocket sprang into view.

She caressed my penis with both hands and started blowing it. She had a talented mouth, and she soon had me writhing in ecstasy. She alternated between quick flicks of her tongue and long, languid licks. Then she slowly engulfed my entire cock in her mouth, and I could feel her clench and unclench her throat muscles to further stimulate me.

As she sucked me, she pulled off her blouse. She wasn't wearing a bra, so her wonderful champagne-glass-shaped tits were exposed to my view.

Not able to resist the temptation, I pulled her off my shaft so I could suck on her tits. As I sucked, I reached down to pull off her miniskirt and panties. When she was naked, I kissed my way down to that beautiful mound of pubic hair. I sucked and licked her pussy until she had come three times. Then I mounted her, and we fucked to a beautiful simultaneous climax.

Exhausted, I collapsed on top of her, my penis still lodged in her hot, wet love-box. We then got dressed and rejoined the party. A few months later we got married, but that's another story.—*R.T., Austin, Texas*

BLIND DATE WITH AEROBICS INSTRUCTOR LEADS TO A TONGUE WORKOUT

Recently I went on a blind date that turned into an incredible sexual experience. Some friends set me up with a girl named Janetta. She was described as a cute thirty-year-old blonde who works as an aerobics instructor. Since I wasn't in a relationship, I welcomed the idea of meeting someone new.

Janetta and I met at a local restaurant. When I first saw her, I thought to myself, Oh no, it seems like my trusty friends failed to give me a complete description. She was cute, blonde and thirty, but she also looked to be rather short and plump.

Nevertheless we hit it off pretty well. Besides being intelligent, she was friendly, vivacious and a good conversationalist. After an enjoyable meal she invited me back to her place for a drink. Since Janetta had turned out to be such a nice person and we were enjoying each other's company, I happily agreed. But, I must admit, I never expected things to go as far as they did.

Back at her place, Janetta turned on the TV, told me to make myself at home and went into the kitchen for a few beers. I loosened my tie and sat on the couch. When she returned, she handed me a cold beer and sat down next to me on the couch rather than sitting on the recliner. I was surprised by this, but even more surprised by how close she sat to me.

As we watched television, we sipped our beers and made some idle chitchat. It was hard for me to keep the conversation going, because I was distracted by the great perfume she had on. Perfume really makes me horny, and its earthy fragrance was really driving me crazy. And to add to the distraction, Janetta removed her shoes and started to massage her calves.

When she did this I couldn't help but notice just how muscular her ankles were. My early assessment of her plumpness may have been a bit rash—she seemed to be pretty solidly built. As she rubbed her legs she complained that her muscles were really sore due to her constant workouts at the health club where she was employed.

Then she moved her right leg behind my left leg, rubbing the back of my ankle. While she did this she leaned over and whispered into my ear, "I would really like you to do the honors. There are some places I just can't reach." I was stunned. I never thought I'd see action on the first date.

But I wasn't about to pass up a golden opportunity. Wordlessly I moved to the floor in front of her. Janetta reclined back on the couch and I began rubbing her legs. As this was happening, I became aware of two things.

First of all, this big blonde had very shapely, feminine legs with extremely well-toned muscles. Also, she had on stockings and a garter belt—no panty hose for this lady. As I continued my massage, Janetta lay back and closed her eyes, sighing in bliss. Since things were going so well I decided to push my luck.

I flipped her dress up past her knees and started to rub her thighs. They too were large but well-shaped. At this point I kicked off my shoes. Janetta kept her eyes closed and started softly murmuring, "Yes, yes."

I worked my way up to her waist and started to play with her belly button, probing it lightly with my finger. As soon as I slipped my hands under the waistband of her panties, Janetta lifted her hips and I easily slid them down. Staring me right in the face was her beautiful, clean-shaven muff. It's musky aroma invited me in for a taste.

I kissed her tummy and continued downward until I reached her pussy lips. I teasingly kissed around her clitoris and vulva. Janetta yelled out, "Tongue me! Tongue me!" To oblige her I licked her pussy lips and dipped my tongue into her love-canal.

Janetta moaned in pleasure as I drank down her love juices. While my head was between her legs, I took off my tie and began unbuttoning my shirt. After rolling my tongue around inside her, I slid two fingers into her snatch. As I finger-fucked her, I darted my tongue around and then finally right on her clit.

This finger- and tongue-action caused Janetta to buck up and down, screaming in ecstasy. Needless to say, this woman was very orgasmic. About half an hour and countless orgasms later,

Janetta slumped on the couch, totally spent. Now it was time to see if she would return the oral favor.

I stood up, took her hands in mine and placed them on my naked stomach. Janetta explored my chest, pausing to tongue my nipples, which I took as a good sign. Then she dropped her hands down to my pants and rubbed my inner thighs. As my cock stiffened, she worked her way up to my belt buckle.

After unbuckling my belt, unbuttoning the button and unzipping the zipper, she tugged my slacks to the floor. By this time my raging slab was desperate to get out of my briefs. Janetta stuck out her tongue and, in one incredible motion, swiftly pulled down my underwear. When my pulsating pole sprang out, it plopped effortlessly right on her waiting tongue.

Janetta swirled her talented tongue around my engorged cock while I rotated my hips. While she was busy slurping away, I was moaning in pleasure. Taking advantage of the situation, I reached behind her and unbuttoned her dress.

I knew I was close to orgasm. Not wanting to waste my load, I took a step backward and withdrew my dick from her mouth. At this point Janetta stood up, allowing her dress to fall to the floor. I quickly discarded my shirt as I took in the sight of this near-naked beauty.

Janetta was about five feet two inches tall. Although nobody would describe her as petite, the extra pounds she carried were erotically proportioned around her ample frame. From the bottom up she had muscular legs, hips that flared out and a narrower waist that was topped out by an enormous pair of boobs. They were barely contained by Janetta's voluptuous black lace bra.

Janetta stepped toward me, and we wrapped our arms around each other. During a long French kiss, her cantaloupe-size breasts pressed against me, while her long blonde hair spilled over her shoulders and across my arms and chest.

As our tongues darted in and out of our mouths, I opened the clasp on her bra. I was rewarded with the sight of her huge, creamy-white jugs capped with mouth-watering pink nipples that were standing at attention, just waiting to be sampled. Words can't describe the thrill I got holding her full-cupped bosom.

Janetta pulled away from my embrace and fell back onto the couch. She threw one leg on the top of the back of the couch while stretching the other down toward the floor. The gate to heaven was open. Her pussy seemed to unfold before my eyes. I quickly mounted her, and in one fluid motion my hard cock sank deep into her tight warm womanhood.

Her box was unbelievably hot and wet. My hips were pumping away, allowing Janetta to feel every inch of me. Meanwhile I caressed her tits. As I sucked on her left nipple, I tweaked the right one with my fingers. After a while I reversed the order.

All the while Janetta was crying out at high decibels. Occasionally she would yell out, “Faster, faster,” or “Fuck me! Fuck me!,” or “Oh my god, I’m coming!” During this time I would change the pace from a quick, frantic motion to a long, drawn-out penetration.

Finally Janetta threw her legs up over my shoulders, allowing me to penetrate her even more deeply. My hands grasped her titties. They were soft and heavy to the touch. In this position I felt my balls tighten up as the urge to shoot my load increased. I quickly spread her legs farther apart. They now stood straight up in the air. My hands slid down to her prodigious hips, and I pounded away.

Finally I knew I couldn’t last any longer. I pulled out, grabbed my poker and gave it a few more strokes. Every drop of semen that I had in my body came firing out in a massive salvo. Janetta’s whole chest was bathed in my goo.

After I climaxed, Janetta got on her hands and knees on the couch. My come dripped off her hooters like the morning dew off a melon. She leaned over and licked my manhood clean, keeping at it until I got hard again. As soon as I had some lead in my pencil, I positioned myself behind Janetta. I entered her doggie-style as her ass swayed enticingly back and forth. As I slid in and out while holding onto her bulbous hips, I was really getting into this position. Janetta howled out in bliss, “Ohhh, I’m coming.”

I responded by moaning out, “I’m about to join you.”

When Janetta pleaded, “Please shoot your sperm inside me,” I was at the point where I couldn’t say no. The next thing I knew we were in the throes of a titanic simultaneous orgasm. Stream upon stream of my come jetted forth, flooding the lovely Janetta.

After this we stumbled to the shower. After working up quite a lather, we rinsed ourselves off. It was the most exciting shower I’ve ever taken. Afterward we felt clean and refreshed. We proceeded to the bedroom, where we both took turns giving each other full-body massages.

During this time we got each other off orally one more time. Then, completely exhausted, I wrapped my arms around Janetta, gave her a huge kiss, and we both drifted off to sleep. Needless to say, this became the start of a beautiful relationship.—*A.H., Stamford, Connecticut*

HE'S JUST WILD ABOUT HARRIET, AND SHE'S JUST WILD ABOUT SEX

Your magazine, which is read in our home almost daily, continues to serve as a wonderful source of inspiration and new ideas for me and my wife. Your readers and their wonderful letters have brought new life and new excitement to our marriage. Thank you for continually reminding us, as well as the rest of the world, that humans are innately sexual. Now let me get to the real reason for writing.

Let me start by saying that my wife Harriet is the most beautiful woman in the world, and I love her dearly. Right now she is away, so all I can do is look at her picture and wish she were here.

I have traveled around the world and met many beautiful women, but none more beautiful than she. In my opinion, she is the world's most perfect woman. In short, I am deeply in love with my wife. To me, she is life itself.

For the past three years, we've rarely left each other's side for more than a few hours at a time. We haven't even worked apart. We opened a restaurant (I am a chef) so we could be together every day. There we work, side by side, throwing the occasional French fry at each other across the kitchen, and playing touchy-feely games whenever we can.

I have a cock that is somewhat larger than average. It's just over eight inches long and about seven inches around, with fairly large balls. This often leaves a rather conspicuous bulge in everything I wear, but I have learned to live with the problem.

Harriet is of Penthouse Pet quality. Standing five feet eight inches tall, she weighs one hundred fifteen pounds and fills out a 36C cup very nicely. She has a slim waist that tapers to a very beautiful, clean-shaven, sweet-tasting pussy. Her pussy sports a large clit and full lips that she loves to have lightly rubbed and licked. She doesn't like direct contact on her clit until she is really aroused. Rounded hips taper exquisitely to shapely legs and slender ankles. All of this topped off with long, wavy, windblown hair and a perfect movie-star smile is rather like placing the cherry atop an ice-cream sundae.

Harriet really enjoys showing off her body, and I enjoy it too. Sometimes Harriet will wear a very low-cut top so that she can bend over for good-looking men at opportune moments to give them a good view of her ample breasts. Lately she has even taken to wearing loose-fitting short shorts so that she can flash her blonde beaver when the mood strikes her.

My pride really soars when she gets some other man's dick hard while we are together. It really makes for some hot sex together later. She gets so wet when she's been flashing her body. My cock slides in so easily, and pumps in and out effortlessly.

Harriet is multiorgasmic, and in one hour can have as many as twenty or twenty-five orgasms, each one coming in quicker and quicker succession. Sometimes we have to stop because her clit gets too sensitive. My problem is that I enjoy being buried inside her for as long as possible every time we make love, which is at least once a day, and sometimes several times a day.

Recently Harriet asked me if I would mind if she found another man, or possibly even another woman, to join us in a threesome. The idea excited me, and we talked about it while we made love. We both achieved spectacular orgasms. Afterward we lay together, and while my dick was still hard and dripping with come, Harriet licked it clean. We talked some more, agreeing upon the terms of this encounter. We then set about deciding who, when, where, and so forth. After tossing several names back and forth, we finally settled on a guy we had befriended only two weeks before. His name is Walter.

Walter is a fellow we met at an automobile dealership. He wanted to buy the very same convertible that we had just bought. After ordering our cars, we went out for cocktails to celebrate our new purchases. Then we all had dinner together. We hit it off real well with him and made promises to get together again soon.

Being the man of the house, it was my task to broach this subject with Walter. I invited him out for lunch the very next day to discuss the possibility. Walter almost swallowed the olive in his martini when I told him what we had in mind. He practically jumped out of his chair in excitement and asked, "C'mon, are you for real? I mean seriously?"

I assured him that I was completely serious, and his retort was, "But your wife is so fucking beautiful. I can't believe this. Yes, of course I'm interested. When? Where? I'll take the rest of the afternoon off, man!"

After calming him down, we made arrangements to meet at the cocktail lounge in a nearby hotel at eight the next night. He said he'd be there and that he couldn't wait.

The whole next day Harriet and I were both quite nervous. I imagine that Walter probably felt the same way too. We arrived at the lounge a little early, and after what seemed like forever, Walter walked in.

After we all had a drink, I went to the front desk to get a room. On an impulse, I opted for the honeymoon suite. After retrieving Harriet and Walter from the lounge, we all went upstairs.

As I closed the door behind us, Harriet made a mad dash for the bedroom. I tried to tell Walter that since Harriet and I had never done this before, he should take things kind of slow. But before I could get all the words out, Harriet was calling to us from the next room. Walter and I went in to find that Harriet had already removed her blouse, slacks and panties, and was now standing in front of us totally naked. She was evidently ready to dive right into the action. We were both speechless, but Harriet sure wasn't. "I need a tongue in my pussy and a cock in my mouth, men, and I need it now!" she announced imperiously. Walter looked at me, and I looked at him. Well, if she was ready, so were we!

We raced to get undressed and over to Harriet. Walter won, but only because one look at his big dick stopped me dead in my tracks. I could see that Harriet was shocked too. Neither of us had ever seen an eleven-inch cock before. It was a magnificent tool, and it looked as if it had been carved out of ivory. Rock hard, it reached up to his belly button. It had a huge purple head, with large distended veins running along the shaft, and he had a smaller set of balls than I had. Nevertheless, I wasn't sure that Harriet could take all of that meat. It was going to be a tight fit.

Harriet has what I'd call a milking pussy. She can fuck a man and not move an outward muscle, yet make herself come again and again. She has incredible control and is really an artist at manipulating those inner muscles.

Upon seeing Walter's cock, Harriet told me to wait and just watch. I did as I was told, standing off to the side with my dick in my hand as I watched Harriet take control of this huge cock.

She took hold of it as if in awe of it and hefted it in her hands, as if she were guessing its weight. After running her hands over it and exploring every ridge and vein, she started jacking him off. Walter shot off immediately, and Harriet let his creamy come shoot all over her tits. Then she got up and told him to lick his sperm off her until it was all gone. He did so without hesitation, licking her tits with gusto and playing with her pussy the whole time.

Harriet was really getting into this and asked me to masturbate for her so Walter could lick up my come too. I moved closer and jacked off as quickly as I could while she massaged my balls. When I was about to explode, I pulled Walter away from Harriet's pussy lips, which he was licking, so that I could shoot my load all over her pubic hair. Harriet then asked Walter to lick up my come too. While he licked her clean, she again stroked his cock, telling him how much she wanted it in her hot, tight pussy.

When he was almost done, she stopped him and lay down on the bed. She had us get on either side of her, and she kissed both of our cocks and played with our balls. She told us that she wanted us each to fuck her three times in succession, and then she would give us a treat. She asked us if we thought we could handle that, and of course we said yes. Since she had never been fucked by Walter before, she asked that he go first. I said that was fine with me.

Walter got down between her legs to finish licking her clean, but Harriet told him to go ahead and fuck her right away. That way the love juices from all three of us would mix as he shot off in her for the first time.

Walter took his big cock in his hand and guided it toward her entrance. He rubbed the head up and down her slit, and over her clit, until she begged him to fuck her. She pleaded, "Give me your big cock now! Please, fuck me before I come!" She sounded so sexy! How could he refuse?

Walter spread her lips with his left hand and guided his cock into her tight love-tunnel with his right. He worked it in slowly as Harriet gasped at its girth, but she grabbed his hips and pulled him into her ever so slowly until he hit bottom. Harriet reached down to feel his cock and realized there were still a couple of inches of it outside her pussy. She instructed him, "Put it in the rest of the way, or as far in as you can." She was determined to get it all in, and when my wife sets her mind on something, she usually gets it.

Walter started thrusting his huge cock in and out of her pussy slowly, pumping a little faster every few strokes, and also pushing into her a little deeper with each of those strokes. Before Walter got his cock all of the way in, he came again and pulled out to shoot the last spurts onto Harriet's tummy.

I hadn't realized it, but Harriet had me coming too. I had been so turned on by watching Walter fuck my wife that I shot my load right after he did. I probably would have even if Harriet hadn't been jacking me off, and man did I come. It felt like my balls exploded. I let out a huge moan as the pressure released with such force that my sperm hit the wall several feet away.

My cock stayed rock-hard, so in compliance with Harriet's wishes, I mounted her. Walter took a break and watched us fuck. I thought Harriet's pussy would be all stretched by his huge cock, but to my delight she felt as tight as she always had, only better. It was a real turn-on fucking my own wife with Walter's come in her pussy and between us on our stomachs. All of my senses were heightened. I came within ten minutes and almost fell off the bed from pure exhaustion afterward.

Harriet asked Walter if he was ready for round two, because she wanted more of his cock in her. Walter jumped up, his cock as hard as before, and got between Harriet's legs again. This time when he pushed into her, he kept at it until only a little over an inch was left outside of her very willing pussy. I got up and sat on the edge of the bed to watch. Then I slipped my hand between them and played with Harriet's clit as I leaned over and sucked on her nipples. My wife looks so beautiful while she is being fucked. I watched every muscle in her body tense and scream for sexual release as he fucked her faster and deeper, until his entire cock was buried in her tight, wet, warm pussy.

I couldn't believe it. She had taken all of him. When he announced, "I'm going to come again," I surprised myself by reaching down and squeezing his balls. He came very forcefully, grunting out, "Oh fuck, that feels so good." They lay together for a few minutes, and then Walter moved aside for me.

I instructed Harriet to get up on her hands and knees so that Walter could lick her pussy while I fucked her. We got into position, with Walter on his back, Harriet straddling his face and me behind Harriet. I slid into her doggie-style. She felt even hotter than she had the last time, and Walter's come dripped out of her pussy and into his mouth as I fucked her. This time, though, it took much longer for me to come, and I really enjoyed feeling Harriet come so many times while I fucked her.

After I pulled out, Walter fucked her again. This time he slid easily into her and gave her a royal fucking. When he was through there was a huge pool of come on the sheet beneath her. Then, to complete the sequence, I also fucked her for a third time.

After that, we found out what Harriet's surprise was. Unbeknownst to Walter or I, Harriet's best friend Delia, who was now standing at the bedroom doorway frantically fingering herself, had videotaped the entire encounter. Of course, at that point we had to turn our threesome into a foursome, but that's another story. It was an experience I will never forget, and one I want to try again real soon.—*R.N., Detroit, Michigan*

WIFE GOES OUT ON THE TOWN TO GIVE THEIR SEX LIFE A LIFT

I want to tell you about my ultimate fantasy, which finally came true recently. I'm twenty-three years old, married and I just had a baby. To help rekindle our sex life, I encouraged my husband to open up to me so we could discuss our sexual fantasies. We talked about what would really turn us on. I confessed to my husband that it would be a tremendous turn-on for me if I could go out by myself, pick up a guy, let this guy fuck me, and then come home and tell him all about it. I even added that I really wanted him to go down on me afterward and eat the stranger's come from my pussy. After I related my fantasy, we were both very horny and had great sex. Later we talked more about it and decided that we should give it a try sometime.

One day I decided it was time to fulfill my fantasy. I told my husband that I was going out that night and would have a surprise for him when I got home. I got all dressed up in my sexiest outfit and had my husband drop me off at a nearby dance club.

Not too long after I arrived, a really handsome guy came over to my table and asked me to dance. Right away I knew he was going to be the one. After we danced to a couple of songs, I told him I needed to take a breather, so he joined me at my table.

As we talked, I gave him my full attention, hanging onto his every word. I did my best to let him know that I was interested in him, and he evidently caught on. Soon our conversation was sprinkled with double entendres, and I could see the bulge growing in his pants. Since it was getting late, he asked me if he could drive me home. I said okay.

When we got into his car, he was all over me in an instant. I was nervous but hot and horny at the same time. We kissed passionately for some time before he started the car. We were already on the freeway when I finally got up the courage to tell him to pull over. He got off at the next exit and pulled into a deserted parking lot.

I started playing with his dick, which was rock hard. I could almost feel it throbbing. I lifted my skirt up around my hips. I could tell he was more than ready. I pulled his dick out to expose it completely. Then I crawled over and straddled his lap, guiding his dick into my snatch. He immediately started pumping. I knew it wouldn't be long before he shot his load. The whole time he was fucking me, I kept hoping he would shoot a really big load so my husband would have a lot to eat out of me. When the guy came, I climbed off and clenched my legs together so none of the come would run out.

We got back on the road, and I directed him to our apartment complex. When we got there, he asked if he could fuck me again. I said sure, excited beyond measure that I was going to be fucked by a stranger practically on my own doorstep! This time he crawled over and got on top of me. I could feel he was rock hard again as I guided his cock into my pussy. I was thrilled to think that there was going to be a big serving of come for my husband to eat. As soon as he came, I thanked him, and jumped out of the car.

I quickly ran into the building and headed straight for our apartment. My husband was already asleep, so I hurriedly got undressed and climbed into bed. My panties were soaking wet. I eagerly exposed my husband's dick, then got on all fours and began sucking him off. He immediately opened his eyes. I told him I had a surprise for him as I straddled his face. I could tell he was a little apprehensive, but after he kissed my wet pussy a few times while I was explaining what the other guy's dick had felt like inside me, it was as if he couldn't get enough of my hot snatch. I kept telling him to soothe my aching pussy and to clean it all up for me. The whole time he was licking me I was stroking his dick. When my husband came, he shot a huge load high into the air. That told me that he had enjoyed playing out my little fantasy as much as I had.—*P.B., Los Angeles, California*

JAILBIRD SOARS WHEN HE'S BLOWN DURING A VISIT AS A CROWD LOOKS ON

My name is Christopher, and I'm twenty years old and very horny! Unfortunately, I am currently incarcerated. I read your magazine every month and I just love the letters.

When I came to prison two years ago, I had a girlfriend named Jill. She was always good to me and did whatever I wanted. I'd always had a fantasy to get a blowjob in public, and I finally made it happen!

One day Jill was supposed to come visit me, so I made arrangements with a friend of mine to block the officer's view of me and my girl while we were having our visit. When the time came for my visit, I got my pass and off I went, with my friend the lookout in tow.

When I got to the visitors' area, it was packed with lots of people, which helped advance my scheme. I walked over to Jill, kissed her and sat with her on a small couch. As we had prearranged, my friend stood in front of me to block the view.

Jill could tell I was hot when I walked in, so as soon as we sat down, she started rubbing my cock through my pants. She licked her lips as she stared at the huge bulge that was getting larger by the second. She loved to jerk me off, so she slowly unzipped my pants and let my cock slip out. Jill surreptitiously wrapped one hand around my throbbing manhood and slowly started pumping my rod. She was licking my ear and sucking on my neck at the same time. All the sucking noises she was making in my ear was driving me insane.

I wanted her big, red lips wrapped around my fat cock. I wanted her to suck me off in front of all these people, some of whom were now glancing over at us because of all the noise I was making. I then leaned over and whispered in her ear, "Suck me off right now!" To my surprise, she looked around at all the people staring at us, then looked at me and smiled. She slowly lowered her moist lips to my engorged cock, not caring about our audience.

The shining tip of her tongue wrapped around the head of my dick, and she swirled it around and around inside her wet mouth. She gazed up at me with seductive, yet innocent, eyes. She looked thoroughly satisfied. I closed my eyes in ecstasy, knowing that all these other eyes were on me and my little slut. Being watched made the excitement of the moment even better! The warmth of her mouth felt so good, and her lips felt so slick and smooth. I felt like I was going to come any second, so I guided her head up and down, urging her on.

I told her I was about to come, so she put a hand on the base of my rod and pumped as she sucked. I felt my body stiffen, and then I was squirting jism down her throat. She gulped and swallowed, sucking me dry. It seemed like I came forever!

Finally she raised her head and looked around at all of the incredulous eyes. Then Jill cracked a smile and kept on smiling. I had to smile myself. There I was, in jail, and I had just gotten the best blowjob of my life. Jill says she likes to try new things.—*J.B., Tulsa, Oklahoma*

True Confessions: The Wife Watcher

A BIG DISCOVERY

What do you do when it comes to pass that your spouse feels there is something missing in your marriage? Here's what one husband did when he finally found out, the hard way, that his wife needed a little something extra in bed—about four inches extra, to be exact.

My wife and I enjoy reading the letters written to your magazine by couples who have experienced a ménage à trois, and by husbands who enjoy watching their wives with other men, but we've never come across a letter like the one I'm about to write. It's not only about what my wife and I have done, but about how we came to honestly confront our desires and enjoy the experiences that have changed our lives.

Amy loves having sex with two men at a time. Most of all she loves to do it with well-endowed men. Like a lot of your readers, we have a hard time believing all the guys who write you about their ten- and twelve-inch cocks. Well, I've been in a lot of locker rooms and seen hundreds of other guys, but I've never seen a cock bigger than that of my wife's favorite lover, Andy. He was blessed with a huge penis that, when hard, measures just over nine inches in length and six and a half inches around. He is not the first, or only, lover we have taken into our bed, but he is by far the best, and the one with whom we have had most of our threesomes.

As great as our sex life was after we got involved with Andy, Amy and I both dreaded that someone, whether friends, neighbors or family, would find out about our little secret, and that we would be ridiculed and embarrassed to death. Oddly enough, it's that fear that led to this letter.

Several months ago I came home early one day from work. Our housekeeper Millie, who comes in once every two weeks, was there. Millie is in her fifties and divorced, with grown children and grandchildren. She has worked for us, and our next-door neighbors, for about five years. That day, as Millie was getting ready to leave, she came up to me. With a slightly embarrassed look, she said there were some "personal" items we had left out in the guest bedroom that she thought we'd want to put away ourselves. We had been with Andy in that room a few nights earlier, and I instantly knew what Millie had seen. One look into her eyes and I realized she knew our secret.

For the next couple weeks, I wondered what Millie thought of us. I imagined she thought we were swingers or wife-swappers, which is not the case at all. Aware that just a little knowledge can be dangerous, and not wanting her to think the absolute worst of us, I decided to speak with Millie about what she'd seen. I can't tell you how nervous I was when I approached her. But when I brought up the subject, Millie smiled and put me at ease. She said that what we did in bed was none of her business. She said she'd seen a lot of things in other houses over the years, and that we weren't the only couple with a secret sex life.

With great candor she informed me that, from what she'd seen in our guest room, she knew that my wife's lover has a large penis. I humbly admitted that it was true. Imagine my surprise when Millie laughed and said it was only normal for a woman to enjoy a well-endowed man. She blushed and said, "To be perfectly honest, penis size *does* make a difference in a woman's sexual pleasure. Even to me." She went on to say that she'd even heard that some men liked to watch their wives with other men. "If that's your thing, it's fine by me."

Millie laughed when I told her Amy and I considered me her main course, while Andy is dessert. Then she really stunned me by congratulating me on being open-minded about my wife's desire to enjoy a well-endowed man. She smiled and said, with no embarrassment, "If my husband had been as understanding as you are, my marriage might've turned out differently. A little variety does add spice to your sex life. You don't have to be in love with someone to enjoy good sex with them." Frankly, she even seemed a little envious, and surprised me again when she admitted that she'd often fantasized about being in a threesome.

I felt relieved after telling her our secret. It felt good to know there was someone out there who understood and accepted our feelings about sex. That's why, the next time I picked up a copy of *Penthouse Letters*, I decided to share our story with you.

First, a little about our sexual histories. My wife is thirty-nine years old and very attractive, with dark hair, green eyes and a great smile. It is not uncommon for her to be the best-looking woman at any function we attend. In addition, she has a bubbly, cheerleader personality that just draws people to her. She is a career woman, and we have no children by choice.

Her first sexual experience was with her high-school boyfriend, a big football star, and big in another way too: he was endowed with an eight-inch penis. From the start, she loved to fuck, and had orgasms the first time they had sex. When she finally broke up with him in college, she couldn't believe how small other men's penises were compared to his. When she confided in her friend Cheryl, she found out that five- and six-inch cocks were the norm, and that she'd been lucky that her first lover had been so big. Don't get me wrong—she enjoyed fucking men, and had no problem having orgasms with cocks of any size. She just felt that bigger is better.

In college she worked summers at the beach, and shared a house with her friends. She had a boyfriend back home, but had the hots for a lifeguard who went through girls as fast as they threw themselves at him. When it was her turn, she found him well-endowed, with a set of big balls she just loved. Then they had sex. He only lasted about one minute, and then went to sleep. When his performance was identical the next two times, she gave up on him. He taught her that a big cock doesn't automatically mean a good fuck.

She became involved with another lifeguard. One rainy afternoon they were in her room fucking, when one of her roommates knocked on the bedroom door to tell her that her boyfriend from back home had just arrived for a surprise visit. They hid the lifeguard in another bedroom just as her boyfriend walked into her room. Guess what he wanted to do? That's right—fuck. So she did, just a few minutes after having another man's cock in her pussy!

After college, she and Cheryl got an apartment together. That winter, they went on a Club Med vacation. One morning, after spending the night fucking a guy in his room, Amy entered her room to find Cheryl having a morning ménage à trois with two guys she'd spent the night with. They didn't hear or see her at first, and it was obvious to Amy that Cheryl was loving it. When they talked about it later, Cheryl told Amy that the sex had been fantastic. From that time on, Amy always knew in the back of her mind that she wanted to have a three-way, but never really thought she would have the opportunity. It became her main fantasy.

The next year she started grad school and met Sean. He was a big man, with big hands and feet, and his cock was huge: eight and three-quarters inches long! Amy nicknamed Sean's penis "Trigger." Sean wasn't like that lifeguard—he was well-hung *and* knew how to fuck. They dated for eighteen months, until Amy realized their relationship was built only around sex. She knew she needed more than just a big cock and great sex to build and sustain a good relationship, so she broke up with him.

By then she was working full-time and going to grad school at night, which didn't leave much time for dating. She went out to the bars and had one night stands when she got horny, but not too often. She ended up meeting Don, a married man. He was an Alec Baldwin look-alike with a nice body, and had quite a reputation as a ladies' man. When he came on to her, she decided to fuck him because he was so handsome. He was modestly hung, at six inches, but he had very big balls. Their affair didn't end until after we met.

As for myself, I have always been considered cute and have had a pretty good sex life. I lost my virginity in the backseat of my father's car, like most men of my generation. My girlfriend was wearing stockings with a garter belt that first time, and I've never forgotten that. A garter belt still excites me to this day. By the time I had my second partner, women were wearing panty hose.

The most erotic experience I ever had before meeting Amy was on a double date in college. My friend and I ended up having sex with our dates in my car. I remember looking into the backseat and being able to watch his cock slide in and out of his date's pussy. I found it incredibly exciting, and often thought about it later on when I masturbated. It's okay to see it in a porn movie, but nothing is more of a turn-on than watching two people fuck in the flesh.

I met my first wife a year out of college, and our relationship was the pits. Our sex life was one of our biggest problems. After we got married, she decided she didn't like to give head, and didn't like this or that position for fucking. I gave her a garter belt and G-string to satisfy my fantasy, and she practically threw it back in my face. She told me only whores wore those, and she wasn't going to "cheapen" herself. When I left, I swore that if I ever married again, my next wife would have a much better attitude about sex.

My best friend at work, who was a stud, got drunk one night and confided his big secret to me. One night he, a coworker and the coworker's wife all got drunk and ended up in bed together. At one point, while he was fucking the wife, the husband was sitting in a chair, looking on and masturbating. The wife told him that her husband got off watching her fuck other men. At the time, I couldn't imagine watching someone fuck my wife and enjoying it—but I had a lot to learn.

A year after I left my first wife, I met Amy at a Christmas party and noticed she didn't have a date. When I asked her friend Lorraine, who worked with me and was married to a friend of mine, about Amy, she encouraged me to ask her out. I did so, and we hit it off. We didn't have sex until about our fourth date, but when we did, it was great. She was very responsive in bed, a real vocal lover given to moaning and yelping while being fucked. Unlike my ex-wife, she loved both giving and receiving oral sex. And when she got horny and wanted to fuck, she didn't like to wait. One night, after we'd just left a party, she had me pull into a lover's lane and we fucked in the car—even though her apartment was just a few blocks away.

Several weeks after we started to have sex, I went out of town to a convention. I was gone five days, and came back a few days early because I missed her and was horny. I called her, but she begged off seeing me that night, saying she'd brought some work home. When I said I would come over and help her, she was emphatic that I not do that, and promised to make it up to me the next night.

The next night she cooked dinner, and we later ended up in bed. She was as responsive as ever, and I assumed she had been as horny as I. Wrong! After we had sex, I went into her bathroom and just happened to glance into her wastebasket. I got quite a jolt. Atop the trash were not one, not two, but three used condoms, and they weren't mine. When I told her about my discovery, she turned about sixteen shades of red. I said something about her "fucking around on me," and she quickly let me have it. She told me she was unaware that we were in an exclusive relationship, and that who she had sexual relations with was nobody's business but hers.

I was hurt, but over the next several days I realized everything she'd said was true. I had screwed an old girlfriend once after Amy and I had started to date, and didn't feel like it was any of *her* business. I swallowed my pride, called her and admitted she had been right. She apologized for any embarrassment she'd caused me, and said she cared very much for me.

From that point on, everything was fine. I gave her a garterbelt outfit for her birthday and, unlike my ex-wife, she thought it was romantic, erotic and sensuous. She had it on within minutes, and seemed to enjoy it as much as I did.

Several experiences we had during our first eight years of marriage had a bearing on our later sexual practices. One night, after we'd been married about a year, I needed some cold medicine. Amy told me to look in the drawers of her bedside table. When I opened one drawer, I got quite a surprise. I found a vibrator and a box of three dozen condoms, with only about a dozen left. When she saw what I'd found, she stammered that the condoms were from her single days, and that she'd won the vibrator as a door prize at one of those home lingerie parties. She also insisted that she never used the vibrator, which was a lie, as it smelled strongly of cunt.

That night, when we were in the 69 position, I took out the vibrator. Amy asked, "What's the big idea?" But when I started buzzing the tip against her clitoris, she didn't stop me. She enjoyed it and had a tremendous orgasm. The vibrator became a regular part of sex for us. In a way, it was the first time I ever "shared" my wife in bed. The vibrator gave her climaxes that were different, and sometimes more powerful, than those she got from my cock. I found myself very aroused by being able to maximize her pleasure in this way.

The next Christmas I bought her an immense vibrator that looked like a real penis, with veins and a large, wide head. I'd actually bought it for her as a joke, but she enjoyed it even more than the smaller one. She sucked my cock with great vigor and intensity when I used the large vibrator on her, and her orgasms seemed more intense. One night she had a very strong orgasm, and I kidded around with her that someday the vibrator might replace me. She assured me that no toy could ever replace the feel of a real penis. I suggested that if the larger vibrator felt better than the smaller one, and a real cock felt better than the larger vibrator, then it really stood to reason she would love having a huge cock fuck her while she sucked me off.

Taking the discussion further, I said, "I'd love to see you in action if we ever had another man in bed with us." She laughed and changed the subject. But from time to time after that, we joked around about someday having a threesome. I would fuck her mouth with my cock, and her pussy with the large vibrator, and watch her have orgasm after orgasm, all the while imagining that she was taking on two cocks at once. I remembered my friend's story about fucking a coworker's wife while her husband looked on, and wondered what it would be like to actually watch Amy suck another man's cock, and fuck him with her pussy. Would I be able to handle seeing her with another man? I never discussed it with her, though, because I was scared of what she'd think of my fantasy.

Shortly afterward, Amy and I spent a weekend at the beach with two other couples. One of the couples, Paul and Barb, were among our best friends. Paul is a big man and keeps himself in shape. Over the years, Barb had confessed to Amy that Paul was very well-endowed, but she never said just how big he was. One night that weekend while the six of us were drinking and playing cards, we decided to play strip poker. Paul ended up being the big loser, and after much taunting dropped his underwear. Barb wasn't kidding about him having a big dick. Even I was impressed! Completely flaccid, his cock was as big as mine is when fully erect, and much thicker. He also had the biggest set of balls I'd ever seen. Each one was about the size of a lemon. Amy got a camera and took a picture of him, and we all had a good laugh.

When we went to bed that night, Amy was really hot, screaming, "Fuck me, fuck me hard!" at the top of her lungs every time I thrust into her. I was a little surprised at her behavior, considering that there were four other people in the house who could surely hear her every utterance, but I wrote it off to her being pretty drunk. It wasn't until many years later that she confessed that Paul's gigantic cock had made her so horny, she'd needed a loud, wild fuck.

Several weeks later I came home and found Amy and Barb talking in the kitchen. Lying on the kitchen table between them was the photo of Paul that Amy had taken when he was naked. Both women blushed when they realized I'd caught them talking about his big penis. When Amy and I talked about it later, I asked if she'd ever fucked a large penis like his, and if it felt better than a small one. Of course, my wife told me size meant nothing to her—which was a big lie—and said, "It's the motion of the ocean, not the size of the wave." She told me not to worry, because I was the best sex partner she'd ever had.

The first eight years of our marriage were pretty typical. Before long our frequency of sex dropped to about a third of what it had been when we were newlyweds. The nights when she dressed up in a garter belt, and the occasions that we used the vibrator, also became less frequent. Our sex had fallen into a boring routine. And then "it" happened.

On a Saturday night a few years ago, we went to the wedding of one of Amy's grad-school friends. There were people there she hadn't seen in years, and we had a great time. One of the people there was Andy. She told me they'd dated a little in school. Andy lived about a hundred and fifty miles away, and had come without his wife, who was home with their sick kids. The party was really just starting when he said he was going to have to head home. Amy and the others urged him to stay and, after getting my permission, Amy told Andy he could crash at our place. He called his wife, and she said it was okay with her.

We got home about midnight and, after a nightcap, I went to bed to rest up for an early golf game. Amy came to bed shortly after, and Andy slept in our guest room. I got up at dawn and was at the golf course by eight o'clock. I quit after nine holes because I'd pulled a muscle in my wrist.

I got home about ten o'clock in the morning, and Andy's car was still there. The garage door was up, and the door into the house from the garage was unlocked just as I'd left it. Little did I realize, when I walked in the house, that both my marriage and my sex life were about to change forever.

As soon as I stepped into the foyer, I thought I heard Amy screaming upstairs. I stopped, heard her again and realized it wasn't a scream of trouble, but one of pleasure. I quietly walked to the bottom of the stairs and listened to what was going on. It took only a few seconds to realize I was listening to her having sex—and that the sound was coming from our guest room.

I only had to walk up about six or seven steps to see the bed, so I did—and got the shock of my life. Amy was completely nude and mounted on top of Andy's cock, riding him in a frenzy. She let out a wail of joy every time she came down on his pole, and ground her pussy hard against him. It was obvious she was in the middle of a huge orgasm, and loving every second of it. She repeatedly lifted herself completely off his cock, then drove herself down on it as hard as she could. The sight was unbelievable! I could see Andy's gigantic cock glistening with Amy's dew every time she raised herself up. Her cunt lips were spread wide like the petals of an open flower. I couldn't see Andy's face, but I saw his hands rubbing my wife's hardened nipples, and knew that he was giving her tremendous pleasure.

"Keep riding my horse, baby," he grunted. "Keep pumping on my cock! Up and down, Amy, up and down. I want you to work that pussy on my dick until you come and come and come!"

I couldn't believe what I was seeing or hearing, but I especially couldn't believe that I was getting a huge erection myself! After several more minutes of fucking, Andy came. Amy had one more orgasm and then collapsed on him. Some of his cock was buried inside her, but I could still see about six inches of his fuck-meat sticking out. It was the biggest cock I'd ever seen.

After catching her breath, Amy sat up, still attached to Andy's mammoth prick, and rubbed his chest while slowly moving back and forth. She said the words I can still hear in my mind to this day: "Oh, Andy. You can't believe how fucking good Trigger feels inside me." At that time, I still hadn't heard the "Trigger" story, but it was obvious that Amy and Andy had once known each other very intimately, and that they'd done some serious fucking in the past. "It's been a long time since I rode one like this," Amy continued. "Too long—I almost forgot how good a big cock feels."

"You're probably just horny, as always," Andy said.

She laughed and replied, "Horny for a big cock like Trigger, you mean. It's been years since I last had a big one, and I've missed it." Amy scooped up a handful of their combined juices from her cunt and rubbed it all over her face. "God, have I missed it!"

She finally rolled off him, and they lay next to each other. For the next fifteen minutes I got quite an education about my wife's sexual feelings and history—especially about her liking large cocks, and the pleasure only they could give her.

Andy asked her about the size of my penis, and she described it as "normal." When he asked about our sex life, she paid me a compliment and said I was a good lover for my size, the best she'd ever had. But she followed that up by telling him that it was big cocks like his that really got her off. "You know how it is," she explained. "There are some places that six inches just can't reach."

"Have you ever told your husband you have a thing for large cocks?" he asked.

She idly grabbed his cock, soft now but still larger than mine ever got, and said, "No way. I couldn't ever tell him that. It would really upset him, and I don't want to do that. I hope you understand that I really love my husband. We have a good relationship in and out of bed. I hate to say it, but if he only had a big cock like yours, it would be the perfect marriage."

Then he asked if she'd ever screwed around behind my back. I held my breath, wondering what her answer would be. My heart skipped a beat when she said, "No . . . not really."

Andy said, "Not really? Come on, Amy. Either you have or you haven't."

She then told him about her affair with the man whose used condoms I'd found in her bathroom years ago when we were first dating. I was relieved to hear that, because we weren't married at the time.

But then she told Andy that a few years ago, she and that man ran into each other on the street, and he took her to lunch. They talked about the good sex they'd once enjoyed, and how they were both sorry their relationship had ended so suddenly. Well, before they knew it, they'd each taken the rest of the day off from work, found a motel room and had a nostalgia fuck that lasted the entire afternoon. She laughed and told Andy it was some of the best sex she'd ever had. To emphasize her point, she held her hands wide apart to indicate the size of the man's cock. It wasn't as large as Andy's, but it was still quite a hunk of meat.

She then said that the only reason she felt guilty about that fuck was because the man was a coworker of mine! She identified him by name, and I was stunned! Gregory and I still work together. He and his wife have been to our house several times for parties, and he always asked how Amy was. I thought it was because he was a nice guy. Now I know it was because he'd been dicking my wife!

Amy admitted that sometimes when we made love, she would fantasize that she was making it with Gregory and his horse cock. Andy asked why she didn't just call him up and fuck him again, and she said it was because Gregory and I were good friends, and she wouldn't cheat on me with someone I was close to. She also admitted to doing some crotch-watching at a pool party once to see how some of my other coworkers were hung, but I thought that was pretty normal. Amy concluded the conversation by telling Andy that she missed the variety of having new and different sex partners the way she had in her single days. "That's the down side of marriage," she lamented.

I couldn't believe it. I was now hearing my own wife say the things I'd heard other married women say to me when I was single and had just fucked them—namely, that they couldn't discuss their sexual feelings and desires because their husbands probably wouldn't understand, and they didn't want to hurt their feelings. It made me sad to think that married couples had such a difficult time being open and honest with each other about sex. I realized that Amy and I had also fallen into that trap, and now I was determined to break free of it.

Andy said he had to leave, but Amy reached down and started to massage his cock and balls. "You can't leave until you fuck me one more time." With that, she slid down his body, took his cock into her mouth and started to lick and suck him noisily.

I leaned into the wall so she wouldn't see, still unable to believe what was happening. But what I really couldn't believe was that, instead of being upset with her, I was turned on like never before. I peeked around the corner and stared in mute delight as I watched her lick and suck Andy's hairy balls. She held his cock in one hand as she licked up the side of his shaft and around the head. I couldn't believe the size of this guy's prick. With one of her hands wrapped around the base of his cock, at least half of the shaft was still clearly visible above her fingers. She took the head of his cock into her mouth and sucked him in deeper and deeper. With every dip of her head, a little bit more of Andy's massive limb disappeared into her mouth. She was only able to take about five inches of his cock, but that was good enough for Andy. He started to moan, then told her, "You're one hell of a cocksucker!" Amy released him from her mouth, laughed and said, "Well, you've got one hell of a cock to suck." I couldn't believe I was hearing my very own wife talk to another man like that!

Amy asked if he was ready to give her one last fuck. "I want you to be on top this time," she insisted. As they moved around on the bed, I ducked back behind the wall where they couldn't see me.

When I peeked around the corner again, Andy was on his knees, sliding a pillow under my wife's ass. (So that's who taught her that trick! I'd always wondered.) He then spread her legs and played with her clit with his left hand while stroking his cock with his right. He then placed that massive shaft of his at the mouth of her pussy, thrust his hips forward and entered her. Amy moaned loudly, bucking her hips while Andy held both of her legs straight out and vigorously humped her.

I couldn't believe how excited I was getting from watching another man take my wife like that. As he fucked her, she grunted like a mating animal and said, "Oh, you feel so fucking good!"

Andy answered her with something like, "You sure do like having a horse cock in you."

Amy replied, "You know it." After another minute or so, she finally said, "Andy, don't tease me. Give it to me hard." And man, did he ever! He stopped for a second to put her legs up on his shoulders, then leaned forward onto his hands. By now Amy was literally screaming, "Don't stop! Don't stop! Fuck me, baby. Come on, fuck me! Fuck me!" In all the years we'd been together, I had never once heard her talk dirty like that.

Now Andy really started to pound into her. After every thrust he took his tool all the way out, then slammed it home as hard as he could. The sight of his cock and balls slamming into her was the most exciting thing I'd ever seen. It was made only better by her screaming, which was so loud, I wondered if our neighbors could hear her. She was so loud I could've been in our first-floor den with the television on and probably would've still heard her screams of pleasure.

Andy was perched on his hands and toes, fucking my wife as hard and fast as he could. The bed frame was banging against the wall, and I began to wonder if it would hold up to that kind of punishment. Andy yelled, "Come, baby! Come for me. Is this the way you like it!"

Amy replied, "Oh, God, yes . . . give me every fucking inch! Don't stop. Just . . . don't . . . stop!"

Well, I lost it. I was so turned on, all I had to do was rub my hard cock a couple of times through my pants and I came. It was one of the most powerful orgasms I've ever experienced. When I was coming, I gasped loudly. Afraid they might hear me, I quickly found my composure and sneaked back down the stairs and out of the house as quietly as I could.

I drove to an abandoned parking lot near our house and cleaned myself off with my handkerchief. But while I had my cock out, I ended up masturbating myself to a second orgasm, thinking about what I'd just seen. I could still hear Amy's lust-crazed voice urging her lover on: "Give me every fucking inch of that tool!" The come poured from my cock like milk from a pitcher. I just drove around for a couple hours before returning home, running the scene over and over again in my mind.

When I got home, Andy was gone and Amy was planting flowers in our front garden. Thinking about what she'd been doing just a couple of hours earlier with another man turned me on even more. For the first time I saw my wife in a brand-new light. Of course, I knew she had fucked other men before we married, but I had never imagined or thought of her as being as responsive in bed with them as she was with me—let alone imagining that she was still capable of fucking other men after we'd been married. She had been absolutely wild in bed with Andy. Not even in the X-rated movies I've seen did the women react as passionately as Amy did that afternoon. I never thought a woman could enjoy sex that much.

That was the important thing I discovered that day. Although I'd never realized it, my wife was truly a sexual animal. While I had lusted after many other women over the years, I'd never thought that my wife was likewise lusting after other men, let alone fucking them. I realized that while she loved me, she had a sexual desire that I couldn't satisfy: namely, her desire for sex with a man who was hung like a horse. I knew that what she'd done with Andy didn't mean she didn't love me. She was just satisfying her desire for monster cock. I also knew that if Andy had an average-size penis, I would've probably only walked in on them having coffee in the kitchen and talking about old times. But he had that big dick, and that's precisely what she'd needed all these years.

I was so turned on that, that night, I ended up fucking her for seven hours straight. Over the next several days I couldn't keep my hands off her. We fucked every night, and got up by six every morning to get in a little more humping before work. She asked me what had gotten into me, and while I didn't tell her, she definitely seemed to be enjoying the fact that my libido had shifted into overdrive. Our sleepy sex life was recharged, and so was our marriage.

COMING CLEAN

The secret is out. Now Amy knows that her husband likes to see his loving lady in action. The lady finds herself loving all the action that's coming her way. And if their vacation activities are any indication, she's going to be a pretty busy woman from now on.

The Wife Watcher revealed how his beloved Amy came to crave the delights that only a well-endowed man can offer. Fantasy and reality finally met when, from the foot of the stairs in their home, he watched and listened to her make explosive love with Andy, the big-dicked lover of her past.—*The Editors*

After several days of keeping the secret to myself, I decided to tell Amy what I'd seen. I didn't get the reaction I was hoping for. She begged me for forgiveness and said she would never cheat on me again. It just didn't seem to register with her that I was telling her I had enjoyed it and wanted her to do it again!

Every time I tried to tell her how turned on I was by watching her fuck Andy, she would clam up and say she didn't want to talk about it. This went on until we went to the beach for a week-long vacation. My frustration finally came to a head one day when she tried to shut me up again. I said, "Amy, not talking about this and trying to forget it happened is just stupid. You like big cocks, and I love the idea of you enjoying a great big dick. I know you like a little variety. Well, so do I. And part of that variety for me is watching you fuck another man. Not talking about what happened is the thing that's hurting our marriage—not the fact that it happened."

I stomped out of our bungalow and went to the beach. An hour or so later, Amy came out and said, "Maybe you're right. I just can't understand how you can get turned on by watching me fuck someone else." I said I couldn't explain it. That's just the way it is.

Amy pointed out an attractive man who was sunning himself nearby and said, "Would you like if it I took him back to our place and fucked him?"

"I'd love it," I said.

Amy took a closer took at the guy. She commented to me about his nice buns, his good tan, and the fact that large hands like his often meant a big penis as well. I discreetly rolled onto my side and pointed to my crotch. Amy's eyes grew wide when she realized I had a powerful erection. I said, "That's just from hearing you talk about him!"

"I need to fuck," Amy blurted.

"Me too!" I replied.

We ran back to the house and screwed like newlyweds for the rest of the afternoon. From then on, I knew there was a good chance that, one day, I could watch her fuck someone else.

For the next couple of months we talked openly about Amy's love of big dicks, and my desire to see her in action with one. I mentioned several men she might seduce, but nothing definite was ever decided. Still, she admitted that the idea sounded interesting, and that she would even consider having a threesome with me and another man.

In September we vacationed in the Bahamas. Our second day there, I got up early in the morning for a round of golf while Amy slept in. I was teamed up with a man named Will. He was a low handicapper like myself, and we had a great game. I couldn't tell from Will's loose golf slacks if he had the kind of large tool my wife loved, but by the eleventh hole I was imagining him having full-throttle sex with her.

Amy was waiting for me when we finished playing. We invited Will to join us for lunch. He and Amy also hit it off, and we ended up sitting together at the hotel pool that afternoon. Will was recently divorced, and vacationing alone. He met us again for dinner that night. Afterward we went to the lounge, where Amy and Will enjoyed several slow dances in each other's arms. When Amy and I went to bed that night, we talked about Will while making love. "I wonder what his cock tastes like?" she said while sucking mine. "Is it sweet and smooth like yours? Maybe it drips a lot of salty pre-come, like Andy's."

"Are you thinking what I'm thinking?" I asked.

"What's that?"

"It's the perfect setup," I told her. "We won't ever have to see him again after this week, and no one back home will find out about it. I think you should seduce him. But I want to watch."

Amy admitted that she was still a little scared, and didn't know if she could go through with it. In any case, the final decision, whenever it was made, would have to be hers.

A couple of mornings later I played golf again with Will. There was a storm brewing, and it started to rain just as we finished. Amy joined us for lunch. The restaurant had a special on exotic drinks. We each had a couple and got a strong buzz. We talked about what we should do, since it looked like it was going to rain for the rest of the day. Amy and I had Trivial Pursuit in our suite, and she invited Will to our room to play a few games.

When he showed up at our room an hour later, he had a large bottle of wine, which we finished during the first game. Amy won that round, and she started to kid Will and me about women being smarter than men. We kidded her back, and said men don't play hard until there's something on the line. When she asked what we wanted to play for, I said, "Why don't we play strip Trivial Pursuit?" Will and Amy laughed and said they were game, and I set down the rules. Whoever lost each game would have to take off a piece of clothing.

Will and I were wearing underwear, shorts and a shirt. Amy giggled and said, "I'm only wearing panties and a sundress, so you and Will should take something off to make it even before we start."

I ordered another round of drinks from room service while Amy got something out of the dresser and went to the bathroom. When she came out, Will and I took off our shirts, and then we started the game. When room service came, Will got up to answer the door. Amy rubbed my leg and mouthed the words, "I love you." That's when it hit me: She was definitely going to fuck Will!

We'd pulled the table into our bedroom. Amy was sitting on the bed, and Will and I were on the chairs on either side of her. After she'd gotten several answers right, I asked Amy a question I was sure she knew the answer to. She looked me straight in the eye, smiled and gave me the wrong answer. I guess she was in a hurry to get naked in front of Will!

I won the game, and Will dropped his shorts. Amy made a big production of standing up and taking off her sundress, and what a view Will and I got! She'd put on a pair of bikini panties that were so sheer, we could see not only her mound of pubic hair, but the distinct outline of her cunt lips.

By this time Will knew something was up. There was definitely an abundance of sexual energy in the air. Amy won the next game, and told Will to take off his underwear. When he did so, we saw he had a good, solid boner that stuck straight out. His cock was average-size, about six inches, but my wife was still very turned on by it.

Amy took Will's hand and pulled him close to her. She looked at his erection and said, "I'm sorry you don't have a girlfriend here to take care of this for you. Maybe my husband will be understanding and let me give you some relief." With that, she started to rub and pump his penis.

"What are friends for?" I said, and the next thing I knew, Amy had Will's dick in her mouth. She massaged his balls and squeezed the base of his cock as she deep-throated him, plunging down on his cock until her face was buried in his pubic hair.

With the cock still in her mouth, Amy guided him onto the bed. He lay back, and she draped herself over him to continue her repast, licking him with long, wet swipes of her fast-moving tongue. I took off my clothes and joined them on the bed. Pulling off Amy's panties, I positioned myself on my hands and knees and started to lick her pussy.

After just seconds of this, she stopped me, looked me in the eye and said, "Fuck me." I got off the bed, and she took Will back into her mouth. Standing on the side of the bed, I entered her. Her pussy was so wet, it was as though she'd already come. I worked my hard dick in and out of her. Amy moaned with Will's prick in her mouth. It was the sexiest thing I'd ever heard in my life. Within seconds I had the most powerful orgasm of my life and pumped a quart of come into her slit. Then Will came. Amy opened wide to show me that her mouth was full of his spunk, then drank it down in one big swallow.

For the next ninety minutes or so, I came a total of four times. Amy was unbelievably excited and had over a dozen orgasms. Will also came several times. When we were all too tired to go on, Will excused himself, saying he had to meet some people, and left.

That night at dinner, Amy and I were surprisingly quiet about what we'd done. We headed back to our hotel and went to bed early. I lay there thinking about the events of the afternoon. I gave my wife a good-night kiss and told her I'd had a really great day. Amy rolled into my arms, and we made intense love—a remarkable thing, considering we'd already fucked ourselves to exhaustion that afternoon. I don't know how many orgasms Amy had, but again, it was definitely in double figures.

On the last day of our vacation, we ran into Will. I asked him to meet us later that night for a farewell drink. We met him about nine o'clock and had several rounds of zombies. We left him in the bar about eleven o'clock, and started back to our room. On the elevator ride up, I asked Amy if she wanted me to ask Will to spend the night with us. She gave me a big kiss as the elevator opened on our floor, and said yes. I gave her the room key and said I'd be back shortly.

Will was still in the lounge, and when I whispered in his ear what Amy wanted, it took him less than a second to pay his bill and leave with me.

When we got to the room, Amy was completely nude, waiting for us. That night was incredible! We tried every position we could think of. Hardly a minute went by that didn't find Amy with a cock pumping into some part of her body. But the best was yet to come.

At one point I went to the bathroom. When I returned, Will was eating Amy out. I sat in a chair and watched them. Amy motioned for me to join them, but I just wanted to sit and observe. When she realized this, she put her head back, closed her eyes and really started getting into being eaten. She ran her hands madly through Will's hair and rotated her hips, thrusting hard against his mouth.

When she was very worked up, Amy pulled on his shoulders and told Will to fuck her. He kissed her and slid his cock into her, then fucked her with powerful thrusts. As she got closer to her climax, she put her hands on his ass-cheeks and drew him deeper into her. Her whole body tensed up as she worked her hips in a frenzy, biting her lip and grunting.

Her legs were bent at the knee and raised slightly in the air. I noticed something for the first time, something that I've since come to love watching while she fucks: her feet. Her toes were curled, and when she had her orgasm, they immediately uncurled. With every spasm of orgasm, the toes would curl, then straighten back out again. I'd fucked her hundreds of times, but had never seen, nor paid any attention to, her feet during her orgasms. (I guess I'd never been in a position to watch her toes while we fucked!) But finally seeing this was incredibly arousing.

Needless to say, I had become quite excited, and started to stroke my own cock. As I did so, I saw Amy looking at me. Will hadn't come yet, and was still fucking her. Amy started to say, "Come! Come! Come!" over and over again as she watched me masturbate. Will and I climaxed at about the same time. I couldn't believe how much I'd enjoyed masturbating while watching another man fuck Amy, but I most definitely did! When Will rolled off her, I immediately got on the bed and gave her a hug. I'd never felt closer to her than I did at that moment. We'd experienced sex in a way that most people only dream about!

Our lives haven't been the same since, and things just keep getting better. For the next couple of weeks we fucked incessantly. The sex was even more fantastic than what we'd experienced with Will. It's something we've come to expect: our sex is always better after we've had a threesome. As great as the sex is with a third party—especially Andy, whose huge cock belongs in a museum—it is even better after he's left. These are the times that Amy and I truly make love to each other. Our three-ways seem to recharge our desire for each other.

In the weeks following our first threesome, we had a number of open and honest discussions with each other about our sexual histories, fantasies and so on. Amy told me all the things about her past that I have already related on these pages. She told me about the vacation experience where she walked in on Cheryl fucking two guys at once, and how she'd always wanted to try it herself. She had been afraid to tell me, even after the Andy episode, because she was worried about what I would think about her wanting to fuck two guys at once. She admitted that the reason she enjoyed using a vibrator while involved in a 69 was so she could fantasize that another man was fucking her while she blew me.

We began to do things to and for each other that we'd never done before. Amy masturbated for me, using her vibrator or her fingers, and allowed me to masturbate her with any of the several dildos she owns. I also masturbated for her, and allowed her to jerk me off. I now believe that masturbating for your partner is one of the most intimate sex acts you can perform. If you think you have a good, solid relationship with your spouse or lover, try it and I guarantee you'll see at once what I mean.

It was during these honest talks that Amy told me about her experiences with all the big-dicked boyfriends of her past. I loved hearing about what she did with their large cocks. She admitted that, while she enjoyed sex with me, there was just something about sex with a really large cock that excited and sexually pleased her like nothing else could. She likened it to my fetish for garter belts, only her fetish involved large penises. I knew it took a lot of trust in me, and in our relationship, for her to admit that the ultimate sexual pleasure she could experience was also a pleasure I could never provide her with. It would always have to involve another man, and that man would have to be built like a thoroughbred.

As our cleaning lady Millie said when she first learned of our wild sexual side, Amy and I are lucky to have found each other. My wife's lust for a large penis dovetails perfectly with my desire to watch her with another man. I love her more than I can describe, and have no intention of denying her the pleasure of a large cock—as long as I can watch.

THANKS FOR SHARING

It's nothing short of a dream come true. He's seen her do it with men she used to know, and he's seen her do it with men she's just met. But how will our favorite voyeur react when he sees his wife sucking off his best friend? Why not ask him? After all, he's the one who set the whole thing up!

The Wife Watcher confessed to his beloved wife Amy that the biggest thrill of his life was spying on her pleasuring herself with the huge cock of another man. Having thus broken the ice, he and Amy quickly proceeded to threesomes, mutual masturbation, sharing each other's secret fantasies—in short, to a complete sexual rebirth for the two of them.—*The Editors*

Folks, what we're talking about here is pure, erotic, lusty sexual pleasure. Frankly, I think it takes more love and trust on my part to allow Amy to be with any man she wants than to deny her this pleasure. It's like the old saying: If you set something free and it doesn't return to you, it was never yours in the first place. I trust my wife, and have faith in her and in our relationship. I know that no matter with whom she goes to bed, or how big his cock is, she will still love me and never leave me.

As you can imagine, after our experience with Will in the Bahamas we were both hot for our next threesome. We knew we were going to do it again—it was only a matter of deciding who the lucky guy would be. I picked up a few swingers magazines at an adult bookstore Amy and I frequent. It was an eye-opener for us to see pictures of women in bed with two, and sometimes even three or four men. And some of those cocks! Amy's mouth was watering just thinking about settling down around one of those giant pillars.

We talked about other men she could fuck, although we both knew it was our friend Paul she wanted. Still, we were afraid to ask him because we didn't know how he would react. What if he refused? What if he told his wife Barb, who is Amy's closest friend? Barb often talked to Amy about Paul's enormous cock, but did that mean she wanted my wife to share some of her good thing?

We wondered how we would go about getting Paul into bed with Amy. The obvious answer was suggesting a foursome with Paul, Barb, Amy and me, but I balked at that because I'm not sexually attracted to Barb. Besides, I mostly wanted to watch Amy in action with a well-hung stud. I didn't need another woman in the picture. Seeing Amy with a huge penis in her cunt would be all the arousal I could handle.

We decided to approach Paul honestly and directly. I knew, from many of our man-to-man talks, that Paul thought Amy was a fox. He loved her fleshy C-cup tits, as his own wife's breasts were tiny. I also knew that Paul was dying for a good blowjob. It was hard to believe that his wife didn't like going down on him. Shit, if Amy were married to him, I know she'd have his enormous pole in her mouth three or four times a day!

Amy and I talked all winter long about seducing Paul, and it really added spice to our sex life. "That's Paul's dick in your pussy," I'd say when I was fucking her. "Paul's great big cock is stretching your cunt wide. He's fucking you so deep you can almost feel it in your throat!" But it wasn't until spring that we finally made our move.

One weekend Barb went out of town with her sister for a few days. Paul called us on Saturday and invited us over to spend the day with him in his Jacuzzi. Amy is a great cook, so she offered to make dinner for the three of us later on. We didn't have a plan as to how we were actually going to seduce him, but we were determined that it would be now or never.

We went to Paul's place and hung out in his Jacuzzi, making jokes and kicking back. There was a lot of flirting going on between Amy and Paul, and between me and Amy, and it kept the energy high all afternoon. Amy made a fantastic dinner, and we drank a couple of bottles of wine and got very loose by the time she put dessert, a delicious raspberry torte, on the table.

"This dessert is fantastic," Paul said to her.

"Thanks, but my husband did most of the work," she told him.

"Well, guys, just put it on my bill," he said, innocently enough. Amy started laughing uncontrollably. Paul asked why she was laughing, and she blushed, but I explained it to him. Whenever I do Amy a favor, she says, "That deserves a blowjob," and usually follows through on the offer. When there's no time, or the place isn't right for oral affection, she says, "Put it on my bill."

After that, we tossed around the phrase pretty loosely and had a good laugh every time it came up. At about nine o'clock that night, we were all in the Jacuzzi. Paul got out to freshen up everyone's drink. When he returned, Amy took her drink and said with a smile, "Just put it on my bill."

"Gladly," Paul replied.

"Are you serious?" she asked. Paul didn't say a word—I don't think he knew how to respond. "Well," Amy continued, "I think it's high time I started paying off some of these debts." And with that, she draped her hand over his swimming trunks and fondled his penis.

Paul looked at me, and I said, "I don't think she's kidding." My own cock was hardening magnificently with the prospect of watching Amy go to work on Paul's big tool—or better yet, the prospect of the three of us having a nice, intimate orgy. Amy pulled on the waistband of Paul's trunks and yanked them down. She started to stroke his turgid cock-flesh with her hand, getting him hard. His penis grew to the size of a nightstick.

"Do you still doubt that I'm serious?" she asked Paul.

He looked at her, then at me, then shrugged his shoulders, leaned back and prepared to enjoy the ride.

"You're about to get the best blowjob in the world, buddy," I said excitedly, pulling off my swim trunks and taking my fully erect cock in hand. "It's all right with me. That is, as long as you don't mind if I watch."

"I . . . don't . . . mind," Paul groaned as Amy took his shaft between her lips. He quickly got into the spirit of things, and stood up in the Jacuzzi as she started to suck him. I thought his dick was already erect, but it just kept getting bigger and bigger. By the time he was completely erect, it was longer than any cock I'd ever seen in an X-rated flick. Believe me, Paul could've been a star in that field! He worked his hips in a circular motion and fed my wife all the meat she could handle. I watched, amazed, as the knob of his prick popped down her throat again and again, and all fourteen inches of his man-rod disappeared in her mouth. Later on, Amy told me that for a few minutes even she wasn't sure if she'd be able to handle a hose that big. But she met the challenge with her usual enthusiasm and slutty vigor, slathering up and down his enormous pole, pumping it, stroking it and burying it down her throat until her nose was doing a dance in Paul's pubic hair.

After about ten minutes he stopped her momentarily, took her swimsuit off and put his hands on her tits. Amy kissed him and said she wouldn't go any further unless he promised her something. When he asked what it was, she replied, "I love sucking your cock, but I really want you to fuck me soon. Promise me you'll never tell your wife about any of this, all right?"

"It's a deal," Paul answered. "But please, do this for a little while longer." He eased Amy down into the water again so that she could resume sucking his cock.

"You want me to make you come, is that it?" she asked.

"I think you're going to make us both come," I offered, pumping my cock wildly as Amy slid her mouth back onto Paul's club. It didn't take her long to get results. Less than a minute later Paul pulled out of Amy's mouth, stood back and fired a load onto her cheeks that could've filled a coffee mug. I followed suit almost immediately, standing between them and stuffing my cock into my wife's mouth just in time for her to drink my brew.

Paul, far from being spent, was in high gear. Amy was still gulping my batter when he said to her, "Let's go into the bedroom. I've been dying to fuck your sweet little pussy for years, and I can't wait another second."

We practically tripped over each other heading for the bedroom. And the rest, as they say, is history. We fucked for several hours, went to sleep, and picked up where we left off the next morning. The sex was even better than I had hoped for. I'd watched my wife fuck other men from a distance, and I'd been there with her during our threesome with Will. But this—well, this was too good to be true. Paul had so much cock that Amy was like a kid in a candy store. She didn't know whether to sit on it, take it doggie-style, have him fuck her between the tits or just cram it down her throat some more. Thankfully she didn't have to choose. She did them all, and with gusto! Although I fucked her mouth and pussy, and ate her out much of the time, my greatest pleasure was watching her in action with Paul's big whale of a penis.

When I'd watched her fuck the big dick of her ex-boyfriend Andy, I'd heard her yelping and gasping. But with Paul, she screamed and bleated and growled. "Oh, God, yes! Fuck me, you son of a bitch! Give me that fucking monster!" I don't think my cock went soft that entire weekend. And as for Paul, well, he had a look on his face like he'd died and gone to heaven. At one point he actually got up and closed the bedroom window so that his neighbors wouldn't hear Amy's cries of pleasure.

Since then we've met with Paul about ten times for sex—always when his wife is well out of range. It gets better every time and, of course, I am continually treated to the spectacle of my wife blowing, fucking, humping and pumping a big-dicked man. What's really amazing is the way Paul has changed. He's really opened up, and has begun to reveal his own fantasies and fetishes to us.

Paul's main fetish is the same as one of mine: he loves seeing women in lingerie. He had a birthday several months after we started our threesomes with him, and we helped him celebrate. Amy dressed up in a garter belt and stockings, and showed up at his door as his birthday gift one night when his wife was working late. Paul's eyes nearly popped out of his head when he saw what she was wearing. He'd never seen a woman in a garter belt before, not in person anyway, and he went crazy over her outfit.

That night Paul let us know that one of his favorite things was for Amy to sit on his face and have him eat her out, while she rubbed both her bare skin and her nylons against his face. She did so, and the results were explosive. He ate her pussy and sucked her tits until she was going wild herself, having little orgasms and juicing profusely every time he made contact with her body. When it came time for the fucking to begin, Paul was so keyed up he literally ripped Amy's panties apart with his hands and slammed his cock into her with one fantastic thrust. Keep in mind that Paul's cock is fourteen inches long, and you'll have some idea of how wet my wife's pussy was that night.

Since then, we have made it a point to indulge Paul's lingerie fetish. Amy now wears either a garter belt, bustie, teddy or, at the very least, a sexy bra-and-panty set whenever she sees him. Paul, for his part, has bought Amy many types of "naughties," as he calls them, with the request that she wear a different item each time she shows up to enjoy his monster cock. Between what he and I have given her to wear over the past year, I'm sure that Amy now has the most extensive collection of lingerie in Florida.

As much as I love seeing Amy in sexy lingerie, I couldn't care less what she wears when she's with Paul. I just love watching the two of them fuck. There's no doubt that he can take her to a level of sexual pleasure that a man with an average-size cock, like me, simply can't do. I've seen my wife in bed with small cocks, and I've seen her with horse-hung men, and there's no comparison. She really lets herself go with a giant shank. It's great the way a big, stiff dick makes her scream out and talk dirty and beg for more. I still find the size of Paul's cock pretty unbelievable, and I love what it does to her. When Amy fucks Paul for a solid hour, which they often do, it's hard to tell whether she's having one sixty-minute orgasm, two thirty minute orgasms, twelve five-minute orgasms, or sixty one-minute orgasms. I think you get the idea.

Once Paul said to me, "I hope you don't mind me saying this, but your wife is the greatest fuck in the world!"

"Mind?" I said, beaming with pride and throbbing with arousal. "What could be better than to be married to the greatest fuck in the world?"

"All I can say," Paul replied with a grin, "is thanks for sharing."

Amy has only fucked Paul once when I wasn't around, and in a way, that led to the most unique birthday present she ever gave me. About a year after we started our relationship with him, he stayed with us one weekend when Barb was out of town. After we'd enjoyed a particularly satisfying evening of sex, Amy and I went to bed in our room, and Paul slept in the guest room. I left at six o'clock in the morning for an early golf game, so it wasn't until later on that I found out exactly what happened at the house that morning.

Amy woke up and made coffee. She was reading the newspaper when she heard Paul get up. She brought a cup of coffee upstairs for him, and found him taking a shower. She told him she was going to take a shower too, and then they could have breakfast afterward. He opened the shower curtain and said, "Get in with me. You'll save money on your water bill."

Amy decided to call his bluff, and stepped into the shower with him. He lathered up her tits, she soaped up his penis, he soaped up her ass-cheeks . . . and before long they ended up leaving the shower and going back to bed to fuck for a couple of hours.

Amy didn't tell me about their private romp for a few days, then felt guilty about it and confessed everything. I told her I would prefer if she only fucked Paul when I was there to share the experience with her, but I admitted that it still excited me to know what she'd done.

"I just wish you would've taken some pictures," I joked. Little did I know what those words would lead to!

One of Amy's best friends is a woman named Nancy. Nancy is the sort of woman who makes other women, Amy included, extremely jealous. She has a fantastic body. I'll bet she could put on a burlap sack and look good at a White House dinner. She has the best body I've ever seen on a woman in her forties. I admit that she's one of the women I've lusted after in my heart for many years. She often joked about "borrowing" me for a night. I always said I was game, but Amy wouldn't allow it.

Nancy was going through a divorce, and told Amy she wanted to treat herself to a really good vacation. She decided to go to France and take a bicycle tour of the countryside, but she didn't want to go alone, and asked Amy to go with her. Amy had always wanted to see France, and decided to join Nancy.

Nancy had confided in Amy that she hadn't had sex in almost two years. She was so horny, she told Amy, that she planned to find some French stud on the trip and fuck his brains out!

A week after they returned from their vacation, Amy and I invited Nancy over to look at the photos and videotapes they'd shot in France. That afternoon, I went to the store to pick up Nancy's photos for her. Naturally I looked them over while I was still in the store. Two of the pictures were of special interest to me. One showed Amy and Nancy on the beach in Nice with a handsome man. The other one showed the three of them walking, hand-in-hand, into the ocean. Amy and Nancy were topless, and I sensed at once that the man in the photographs had fucked them both.

When Nancy came over, there were more pictures that caught my eye. They pointed out two men from Norway they'd met. They were in their mid-twenties, with blond hair, blue eyes and good bodies. Nancy told me that instead of renting bikes, she Amy, Keil and his friend Gregor had rented a car and driven to the Riviera. One of them, Keil, was the man I'd seen in Nancy's beach shots.

"Jealous?" Nancy teased me.

"Not yet," I said, secretly disappointed that the photographs didn't show what I really wanted to see: my wife Amy with Keil's cock in her pussy, and Gregor's cock in her mouth.

That night I said to Amy, "I bet you fucked those men." She denied it, but her denial was so halfhearted that I was sure she had. I just had to find a way to get Amy to admit it to me and tell me all the details.

The next night was my birthday. As a special treat, Amy bought a new lingerie outfit with crotchless panties. We fucked and sucked for a long time, just to the point of orgasm, but decided to bring each other off with masturbation. I fucked her with her longest dildo, while she jerked me off into her mouth.

When we were drifting off to sleep that night, Amy asked, "Would you have minded if I'd fucked those guys in France?"

"No," I assured her. "Just thinking about it turns me on."

"Good," she said. She then pulled a gift-wrapped box from beneath the bed and gave it to me. "Happy birthday," she whispered in my ear.

My cock bounced to attention as I opened the box and saw a videotape inside. I immediately popped it into the VCR and scrambled back to the bed to watch it with my wife.

"You said you were sorry that I didn't take pictures of the time I fucked Paul when you weren't around, so I didn't want to make the same mistake twice. I think you're going to love this," Amy said excitedly.

A picture came on the screen. Amy was on a bed, naked, fingering her cunt. In walked Keil, also nude. His cock was erect, and it looked like a big one. Amy must have some kind of radar for big dicks. Keil's seemed to be a foot long. I'd never seen a cock as fat as his. It looked like a child's arm.

Soon they were rolling around on the bed, feeling each other up and making out. They moved into the 69 position, and I could hear Amy talking dirty, saying, "Your tongue feels so good in my pussy," and, "I'm going to suck this big dick until you're out of come!"

My cock was bobbing crazily between my legs as I watched the tape. Amy wished me happy birthday again and leaned over to take me into her mouth. What a fantastic present! I was watching a tape of my wife going to town on a stranger's cock, while she blew me with her sweet, warm mouth. I came just as Keil pumped his first load onto Amy's erect nipples.

On the tape, Keil put his come-soaked cock back into Amy's mouth, and she promptly sucked him to another erection. Watching her mouth work its way up and down and around his hard pole was like watching a squirrel running up and down the side of a big tree. But damn it if she wasn't able to deep-throat Keil's entire prong—even his massive balls! I now had another hard-on too, and Amy lapped hungrily away, coaxing some pre-come out of it with the tip of her tongue.

Suddenly Nancy and Gregor walked into the picture. They were naked, flushed and covered with sweat. I didn't need to be a detective to figure out that they'd just done some vigorous fucking. Gregor's cock wasn't nearly as long as Keil's, although his nine inches were clearly enough to get my wife's interest. She lunged after him like a jungle cat, taking his dick into her mouth with an audible growl.

It wasn't long before Amy, Gregor, Nancy and Keil were tangled up in a sex-knot that had to be seen to be believed. Every few minutes or so the scene would change. First Amy would be fucking Gregor while Nancy sucked Keil's dick. Then Keil would stick his cock in Amy's mouth while he munched on Nancy's gash. The ladies were coming so often that after a while, the only sounds on the tape were female squeals and sighs.

The videotape was of a very high quality, and showed the remarkable sex the four of them shared from a number of different angles. Amy explained that they'd stayed in a very secluded inn run by a young couple who agreed to shoot the video for them. That explained the appearance, a while into the tape, of a third man: a chubby, dark-haired man with a noticeable lack of body hair. But he had a cock you could've used for shade.

As I said earlier, my wife sure knows how to pick them. I wonder if other women who love huge dicks have as much success finding them as does my wife. She certainly seemed happy with the innkeeper's big hose. She pistoned herself up and down his shaft until she was a blur on the screen, groaning and screaming as she impaled herself on the object of her fulfillment.

The tape ended with all three men coming at the same time. Gregor pumped his milk down Nancy's throat, while the innkeeper deposited a load into my wife's mouth. A split second